"Ms. Hoffmann dishes up luscious entertainment
spiced with tangy sensuality."
—*Romantic Times*

"Kate Hoffmann traverses the minefield of
relationships...and comes up a winner."
—*Under the Covers*

"Kate Hoffmann pens an amazing story!"
—*Romantic Times*

Dear Reader,

The Mighty Quinns are back! When the very first Quinn book was published in 2001, I never imagined that they would become so popular with readers. Now that all seven Quinn siblings have found love, I've gone back to tell the story of three generations of Quinns in Ireland. That book, *The Promise*, will be released next month as a Harlequin Signature Select Saga.

For all the readers who joined the Quinn saga midway, here's a chance to read the first two stories in the series, *Conor* and *Dylan*. Will there be more Quinns? I hope so. Keep watching my Web site, www.katehoffmann.com, for news about all my upcoming releases.

Happy reading,

Kate Hoffmann

MINISERIES

Irish Charmers:
The Mighty Quinns

Kate Hoffmann

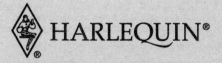

HARLEQUIN®

TORONTO • NEW YORK • LONDON
AMSTERDAM • PARIS • SYDNEY • HAMBURG
STOCKHOLM • ATHENS • TOKYO • MILAN • MADRID
PRAGUE • WARSAW • BUDAPEST • AUCKLAND

ISBN 0-373-21756-0

IRISH CHARMERS: THE MIGHTY QUINNS

Copyright © 2005 by Harlequin Books S.A.

The publisher acknowledges the copyright holder
of the individual works as follows:

CONOR
Copyright © 2001 by Peggy A. Hoffmann

DYLAN
Copyright © 2001 by Peggy A. Hoffmann

CONOR

Prologue

THE WIND HOWLED and the rain raged outside the tiny house on Kilgore Street in South Boston. The nor'easter had battered the working-class neighborhood for nearly two days, the pleasant autumn sunshine giving way to the first sting of winter.

Conor Quinn tugged the threadbare blanket around his youngest brothers, sleeping three to a bed. The twins, Sean and Brian, were already half-asleep, their eyes glazed with exhaustion. And the baby, three-year-old Liam, lay curled between them, his breathing gone soft and even, his dark lashes feathered over chubby cheeks.

But Dylan and Brendan were still wide awake, the two of them perched on the end of their bed, listening raptly as their father, Seamus Quinn, spun another tale. It was well past eleven and the boys should have been asleep. While his father was away, Conor made sure bedtime was strictly adhered to on school nights. But Seamus, a swordfisherman by profession, stayed in port only a week or two before heading out to sea for months at a time. And with winter coming, his father and the crew of *The Mighty Quinn* would be heading farther south, following the swordfish into the warmer waters of the Caribbean.

"This is a story of your long-ago ancestor, Eamon Quinn. Eamon was a clever laddie, so clever he could build a nest in your ear."

Conor listened with half an ear to Seamus's colorful tale, wondering whether he'd ever find a proper time to bring up Dylan's failures in math class, or Brendan's habit of pinching candy from the local market, or the immunizations that Brian and Sean still needed for school. But one subject *had* to be discussed, a problem his father refused to acknowledge.

Mrs. Smalley, their neighbor and regular baby-sitter, was up to a quart of vodka a day. Concerned for the safety of his three youngest brothers, Conor had been anxious to find another person to watch the little ones while he and Dylan and Brendan were at school. Social Services had already paid a surprise visit and he'd managed to hustle them off with an elaborate excuse about Mrs. Smalley's allergies. But if the social workers realized he cared for his five brothers almost entirely on his own, they'd declare neglect and send them all to an orphanage.

"One fine day, Eamon was fishing off the Isle of Shadows. As he passed by a rocky shore, he saw a beautiful lass standing near the water's edge, her long hair blowing in the breeze. His heart swelled and his face shone, for Eamon had never seen a more lovely creature."

Conor had every confidence that he could keep his family

together. Though he was only ten years old, he'd been both mother and father to the boys for over two years. As Mrs. Smalley's drinking problem escalated, he'd learned to do the laundry and shop for food and help his brothers with their schoolwork. They had a simple life, complicated only by Mrs. Smalley's binges and infrequent visits from Seamus.

Whatever time Seamus didn't spend with his sons was spent at the local pub where he frittered away his take from the catch, buying drinks for strangers and gambling against huge odds. By the end of the week, he usually handed Conor just barely enough to pay household expenses for the coming months, until he and *The Mighty Quinn* chugged back into port with another holdful of swordfish. A few days ago, they were dining on week-old bread and soup from dented cans. Tonight, they'd enjoyed bulging bags of takeout from McDonald's and Kentucky Fried Chicken.

"Eamon talked to the lass and, before long, he was enchanted. All the village said that it was time for Eamon to take a bride, but he had never found a woman to love—until now. He brought his boat ashore, but as Eamon set foot on land, the lass turned into a wild beast, as fierce as a lion with breath of fire and a thorny tail. She snatched Eamon between her great jaws, splintering his boat into a thousand pieces with her giant claws."

Though Seamus Quinn wasn't much of a parent or a fisherman, he did have one talent. Conor's father could spin a beguiling yarn—rich Irish tales filled with action and adventure. Though Seamus always substituted a Quinn ancestor in the hero's role and often combined elements of two or three stories, Conor had come to recognize the bits of Irish myths and legends from books he'd sought out at the public library.

Conor preferred the stories of the supernatural—fairies and banshees and pixies and ghosts. Eight-year-old Dylan liked tales of heroic deeds. And Brendan, a year younger than Dylan, hoped for a story of adventure in a far-off land. And the five-year-old twins, Brian and Sean, and baby Liam, really didn't care what tale Seamus spun; they only cared that their da was home and their tummies would be full for a while.

Conor sat down beside Dylan and watched his father in the feeble light from the bedside lamp. At times, listening to his father's thick brogue, he could picture Ireland in his mind—the misty sky, the emerald green fields lined with stone fences, the pony his grandfather had given him for his birthday, and the tiny white-washed cottage near the water. They'd all been born there, save Liam, in that cottage on Bantry Bay. Life had been perfect then, because they'd had their da and their ma.

"Eamon knew it would take all his brains to trick the dragon. Many fishermen had been captured by this very dragon and held prisoner in a great cave on the Isle of Shadows, but Eamon would not be one of them."

The letter from America had been the start of the bad times. Seamus's brother had emigrated to Boston as a teenager. With grit and determination, Uncle Padriac had saved enough money crewing on a longliner to buy his own swordfish boat. He'd offered Seamus a partnership in *The Mighty Quinn*, a way out of the hardscrabble life that Ireland promised. So they'd moved half a world away, Seamus, his pretty wife Fiona, pregnant with Liam, and the five boys.

From the start, Conor had hated South Boston. Though half the population was of Irish descent, he was teased mercilessly for his accent. Within a month, he'd learned to speak in the flat tones and grating vowels of his peers and the occasional teasing resulted in a black eye or cut lip for the teaser. School became tolerable, but life at home was deteriorating with every passing day.

He remembered the fights at home the most, the simmering anger, the long silences between Fiona and Seamus…and his mother's devastating loneliness at his father's endless absences. The soft sobs he heard late at night behind her bedroom door cut him to the quick and he wanted to go to her, to make everything all right. But whenever he approached, her tears magically dried and all was well.

One day she was there, smiling at him, and the next day, she was gone. Conor expected her to come home by morning, as did Seamus when he stumbled in from the pub just as the sun was rising. But his mother never returned. And from that day on, Seamus would not speak her name. Questions were met with stony silence and when they persisted, he'd told the boys she'd moved back to Ireland. A few months later, he finally told them she'd died in an auto wreck. But Conor suspected that this was only a lie to end the questions, just revenge for his mother's betrayal.

Conor had vowed never to forget her. At night, he'd imagined her soft, dark hair and her warm smile, the way she touched him when she spoke and the pride he saw in her eyes when he did well in school. The twins and Liam had just vague memories of her. And Dylan and Brendan's memories were distorted by their loss, making her seem unreal, like some fairy princess dressed in spun gold.

"So this you must remember," his father said in a warning tone, interrupting Conor's daydream. "Like the clever Eamon Quinn who drove the dragon off the cliffs and saved many fishermen from a fate worse than death, a man's strength and power is lost if he gives in to a weakness of the heart. Love for a woman is the only thing that can bring a Mighty Quinn down."

"I'm a Mighty Quinn!" Brendan cried, pounding on his chest. "And I'm never going to let a girl kiss me!"

"Shhh!" Conor hissed. "You'll wake Liam."

Seamus chuckled and patted Brendan's knee. "That's right, boyo. You listen to your da on this. Women are trouble for the likes of us Quinns."

"Da, it's time for us to get to bed," Conor said, weary of the same old cautionary tale. "We have school."

Dylan and Brendan both moaned and rolled their eyes, but Seamus wagged his finger. "Conor is right. Besides, I've got a powerful thirst that only a pint of Guinness can quench." He ruffled their hair, then pushed off the bed and headed toward the front door.

Conor hurried after him. "Da, we need to talk. Can't you stay in tonight?"

His father waved him off. "You sound like an old woman, Con. Don't be a nag. We can talk in the morning." With that, Seamus grabbed his jacket and slipped out into the storm, leaving his son with nothing more than a cold draft and an uneasy shiver. Defeated, Conor turned and walked back to the bedroom. Dylan and Brendan had already climbed into their bunk beds. Conor turned off the lights and flopped down on the mattress in the corner, drawing the blankets up to his chin to ward off the chill.

He was almost asleep when a small voice came out of the darkness. "What was she like, Con?" Brendan asked, repeating a question he'd been asking nearly every night for the past few months.

"Tell us again," Dylan pleaded. "Tell us about Ma."

Conor wasn't sure why they suddenly needed to hear. Maybe they sensed how fragile their life had become, how easily it could all fall apart. "She was a fine and beautiful woman," Conor said. "Her hair was dark, nearly black like ours. And she had eyes the color of the sea, green and blue put together."

"I remember the necklace," Dylan murmured. "She always wore a beautiful necklace that had jewels that sparkled in the light."

"Tell us about her laugh," Brendan said. "I like that story."

"Tell the story about the soda bread, when you fed it to Mrs. Smalley's wee dog and Ma caught you. I like that one."

So Conor spun his tale, lulling his brothers to sleep with visions of their mother, the beautiful Fiona Quinn. But unlike his father's stories, Conor didn't have to embellish. Every word he spoke was pure truth. And though Conor knew that love for a woman was a sign of weakness and trouble for any Quinn, he didn't heed his father's warning. For, in a secret corner of his heart, he'd always love his mother and that would make him strong.

1

THE SHOT CAME out of nowhere, shattering the plate-glass window of Ford-Farrell Antiques into thousands of pieces. At first, Olivia Farrell thought one of the display cases had fallen over, or a crystal vase had tipped off a shelf. But then a second shot rang out, the bullet whizzing by her head and embedding itself into the wall with a soft hiss and thud. Frantic, she glanced up to find shards of glass tumbling into the window display around a Federal-era breakfront.

Her first impulse was to throw herself over the breakfront, a rare piece valued at over 60,000. After all, the multipaned doors still contained all original glass! And the piece would be virtually worthless to her discerning clientele if it contained any scratches on the exquisitely preserved marquetry. But then, common sense took over and she dove for cover behind a rather overblown chaise longue in the Victorian style, a piece that might actually benefit from a few bullet holes.

"Oh, damn," she murmured, not sure what to do next. Should she run? Should she hide? She certainly couldn't shoot back since she didn't own a gun. She thought about locking the front door, but then whoever was shooting could just walk through the gaping hole in her plate-glass window. "Why didn't I listen? Why did I sneak out?"

Pushing up from the floor, she gauged the distance between her location and the back door of the gallery. But what if they were waiting for her in the alley? Since she wasn't familiar with wiseguy protocol, she had no idea whether her unseen assassins were determined to kill her at all costs or whether they'd regroup and try again later. Then again, they'd missed. Maybe they'd just meant to scare her.

"Phone," she murmured, reaching into her jacket pocket to pull out the sleek little cell phone she always carried. "Nine-one-one." She punched in the number and immediately began to pray. Perhaps she should just play dead, in case they burst into the shop, guns blazing.

Tears pressed at the corners of her eyes and her hand trembled as she waited for the emergency operator to answer. But she refused to give in to fear, pushing back the tears and summoning up her courage. She'd taught herself to control her emotions, to maintain a cool demeanor, but that was for business purposes only. Maybe a gunshot through the window was a good excuse for a little hysteria.

None of this would have happened if she'd just kept her mouth shut, if she'd just turned around and walked away that night a few months back. But she'd been scared back then, scared that everything she'd worked so hard to achieve was about to be taken from her.

The closest she'd ever come to breaking the law was fudging a few numbers on her tax return and ignoring the speed limit on the I-90. Now her business records had been impounded, her past scrutinized, her partner thrown in jail, and her reputation left nearly in tatters. She was a material witness in a murder and money-laundering trial against a very dangerous man—a man who obviously thought nothing of killing her before she had a chance to tell her story in court.

Olivia listened as the operator came on the line, then quickly gave her location and a brief description of what had happened. The operator asked her to stay on the line and she listened distractedly as the woman tried to keep her calm. Olivia had always heard that when someone came close to death, their life passed before their eyes. All she could think about was how she hated feeling so vulnerable, so dependent on someone else's help.

"Just keep talking to me, ma'am," the operator urged.

"What should I talk about?" Olivia asked, her voice edgy. The only subject that came to mind was how quickly her life had changed in such a short time. Two months ago, she'd been on top of the game, Boston's most successful antiques dealer. She travelled all over the country, searching out the finest American antiques for her shop. Her client list read like a Who's Who of East Coast society. And she'd recently been named to the board of one of Boston's most prestigious historical societies. There was even talk that she might be asked to appear on the public television show *Antiques Caravan*.

All this for a girl who'd grown up not on Beacon Hill, but in a working-class neighborhood of Boston. But she'd risen above her rather common beginnings, leaving her past far behind and creating a whole new identity for herself—a wonderful, exciting identity, filled with travel and parties and influential friends. And financial security. She had saved only one thing from her childhood—an interest in anything one hundred years old or older.

"My parents were antique fanatics," she murmured to the operator, surrendering to the memory. "They used to haul me from auction to auction as a child, eeking out a living with a tiny little secondhand shop on the North End. We never knew where the next meal was coming from, never knew if we'd scrape together enough to pay the rent. It was frightening for a child, that uncertainty."

"Don't be frightened," the operator said. "The police are on their way."

"When I got older," Olivia continued, "they turned to me for authentication and I became an expert in 18th- and 19th-century New England furniture makers. My parents never had a very good eye for fine antiques and when I was just out of high school, they decided to try the restaurant business, managing a truck stop off the interstate in Jacksonville, Florida."

"The police are just a few minutes away, Ms. Farrell."

She continued talking, the sound of her own voice soothing her fears. As long as she could talk, then she was still alive and the fear couldn't consume her. "I stayed behind to attend college. I worked three different jobs for pocket change. I lived from hand to mouth for nearly my entire freshman year at Boston College, scraping to pay tuition and rent. I hated that. And then I found my very first 'treasure,' a Sheraton chair I bought for 15.00 at a tag sale and resold for 4,000.00 at a consignment auction."

From that moment on, Olivia had paid for her college education by buying and selling antiques. She discovered she had an uncanny eye for spotting valuable pieces in the most unlikely places—garage sales, thrift shops, estate auctions. She could tell a reproduction from an original at fifty paces and was a skilled bidder.

"Even though I majored in art at Boston College, I fell naturally into a career in antiques. I rented my first showroom space the year I graduated. Six years later, I formed a partnership with one of my clients. Kevin Ford was a man with money. I thought I had it made. He bought a beautiful retail space on Charles Street at the base of Beacon Hill." Olivia sighed. "How could I have been so naive?"

"The police will be there in approximately thirty seconds, ma'am," the operator said.

Olivia could already hear the sirens in the distance over the traffic outside the gallery. But even the police couldn't get her out of the mess she'd made of her life. She blamed herself for this whole thing. When Kevin bought the building, she'd had her doubts. Though he was wealthy, he certainly didn't have the millions to buy retail space on Charles Street. But all Olivia could see was the next stage in her meteoric rise to the top of Boston society—and all the business that would come her way.

Had she trusted her instincts, she might have realized that Kevin Ford's bottomless wallet came from underworld connections. That fact had been proved when Olivia overheard a late-night conversation between Ford and one of Ford's most important clients, Red Keenan—a man she later learned was a Boston crime boss who'd ordered a handful of murders last year alone.

The sound of more glass smashing made her jump and she prepared herself for the worst. But then a familiar voice brought a rush of relief. "Ms. Farrell? Are you all right?"

Olivia poked her head up over the back of the chaise. She waved weakly at Assistant District Attorney Elliott Shulman, the man in charge of the murder case against Red Keenan. "I—I'm still alive," she said.

He hurried through the shop and helped her to her feet. "This is just unacceptable," he muttered. "Where was the police protection I ordered?"

"They're still parked outside my flat," Olivia murmured, a warm flush flooding her face.

Shulman gasped. "You went out without telling them?"

She nodded, her spine stiffening at his censorious tone. "I—I just needed to get some work done. The shop has been closed for almost two months. I have bills to pay, antiques to sell. If I don't work with my clients, they'll go someplace else."

Shulman grabbed her by the elbow and led her toward the front door, his fingers firm on her arm. "Well, you've seen what Red Keenan is capable of, Ms. Farrell. Maybe now you'll listen to us and take his threats seriously?"

Olivia yanked her arm from his grasp. "I still don't understand why he'd want me dead. Kevin can testify to the whole sordid business. I just overheard them talking. And I didn't hear that much."

"As I told you before, Ms. Farrell, your partner isn't talking. You're the only witness who can put the two of them together. After what happened tonight, we're going to have to hide you. Somewhere safe, out of town."

Olivia gasped. "I—I just can't leave. Look at this mess. Who's going to repair the window? I can't let the weather come in. These antiques are valuable. And what about my clients? This could ruin me financially!"

"We'll call someone to replace the window right away. Until then, I'll leave a patrolman outside. You're coming with me down to the station until we find a safe house for you."

Olivia grabbed her coat and purse from a circa 1830 primitive wardrobe next to her desk, then reluctantly followed Shulman to the front door. Maybe it was time to go into hiding. It was only for a couple of weeks, until the trial started. At least she'd feel safe again. When she stepped out onto the sidewalk, she gave her keys to the patrolman and murmured detailed instructions on the security code. When she finished, she closed her eyes and drew a long breath.

"Promise me I'll have my old life back soon," she said, trying to still the tremor in her voice.

"We'll do our best, Ms. Farrell."

CONOR QUINN knew the meaning of a bad day. Drugs, hookers, booze, smut—this was his life. Working vice for the Boston Police Department, he couldn't recall a day that hadn't been tainted by society's ills. He reached inside his jacket pocket for the ever-present pack of cigarettes, his own private vice, then remembered he'd quit three days ago.

With a soft oath, he slid his empty glass across the bar and motioned to the bartender. Seamus Quinn approached, wiping his scarred hands on a bar towel. His dark hair had turned white and he now walked with a stoop owing to years of back-breaking labor on his swordfish boat. Conor's father had given up fishing a few years back. *The Mighty Quinn* now bobbed silently at its moorings in Hull harbor, brother Brendan using it as a temporary home on the rare occasions he stayed in Boston. Seamus had moved on, using his meager savings and a gambling boon to purchase his favorite pub in a rough and tumble section of South Boston.

"Buy you a pint, Con?" Seamus asked in his rugged brogue.

Though Ireland was still thick in his father's voice, little of the Quinn brothers' birthplace remained in their memories. Yet, every now and then, Conor could still hear traces of the old country in his own voice, traces that he sometimes caught in Dylan and Brendan, too. But they were Americans through and through, all of the brothers had become naturalized citizens—save Liam, who'd been born in America—the day their parents took the oath.

Conor shook his head. "I'm on duty in a half hour, Da. Danny's picking me up here."

Seamus gave him a shrewd look, then set a club soda in front of Conor, before serving the next patron. Conor watched as his da expertly pulled the Guinness, tipping the glass at the perfect angle and choosing the exact moment to turn off the tap. He set the tall glass on the bar and the pale creamy foam rose to the top, leaving the nut brown brew beneath.

His father didn't bother asking. Though the rest of the patrons profited from Seamus's sage advice, over the years the Quinn boys had learned to handle their own problems without parental involvement. In truth, Conor had been the one to dispense advice and discipline to his younger brothers. He still did. Nearly his entire life, from the time he was seven, had been consumed with keeping his family intact at all costs and keeping his brothers on the straight and narrow. Making life safe had been his job, then and now. Now, he was just watching out for a city of a half million instead of five rowdy boys from Southie.

He glanced around the bar, searching for a diversion, anything to get his mind off the events of the day. Seamus Quinn's pub was known for three things—an authentic Irish atmosphere, the best Irish stew in Boston and rousing Irish music played live every night. It was also known for the six bachelor brothers who hung out at the bar.

Dylan was playing pool with some of his firefighter buddies, all dressed alike in the navy T-shirts of the Boston Fire Department. A bevy of girls had gathered to watch, sending flirtatious looks Dylan's way. Brian worked the other end of the bar this night and was occupied charming the newest barmaid. Liam had found himself a lively round of darts with a pretty redhead. And Sean stuck to the rear of the pub, dancing to the music of a fiddle and tin whistle with a striking brunette.

It was no different for Brendan when he was in town, finished with another magazine assignment or a research trip for his latest book. A soft and willing woman was the first thing he looked for. And though their father's warnings about women had been drilled into their heads from an early age, that didn't stop the six Quinn brothers from sampling what the opposite sex offered so freely—without love or commitment, of course.

But lately, Conor had tired of the shallow interaction he'd enjoyed in the past. Maybe it was his mood, the indifference he felt for life in general. Hell, the blonde at the end of the bar had been giving him come-hither looks for the past hour and he couldn't even manage a smile. Though a woman to warm his bed on this blustery fall night was tempting, he was too tired to put out the effort to charm her. Besides, he only had a half hour before he had to report to the station house—not nearly enough time.

"Good evening, sir. I've got the car outside when you're ready to leave."

Conor glanced to his right to see his partner, Danny Wright, slide onto the bar stool beside him. The rookie detective had been assigned to Conor last month, much to Conor's dismay. Although Wright was a good detective, the kid reminded him of a great big puppy, wide-eyed and always raring to go.

"You don't have to call me 'sir,'" Conor muttered, taking another sip of his soda. "I'm your partner, Wright."

Danny frowned. "But the guys in the squad room said you like to be called 'sir.'"

"The guys are pulling your leg. They like to do that to rookie detectives. Why don't you have something to drink and relax for a while."

Anxious to please, Danny ordered a root beer, then grabbed a handful of peanuts and methodically began to shell them. When he'd arranged a neat little pile in front of him, he popped a few into his mouth and slowly munched. "Lieutenant wants us down at the station house by the end of the shift. He says he's got a special assignment for us."

Conor chuckled. "Special assignment? Special punishment is more like it."

Danny sent him a sideways glance. "Lieutenant's pretty steamed at you," he murmured. "The guys say you're a good cop who just has a bit of a temper. Lieutenant says the skell is bringing brutality charges though. Already hired himself a lawyer."

Conor's jaw tensed. "That slime bilked an 84-year-old woman out of her life savings. And when she wouldn't give up her credit cards, he beat her within an inch of her life. I should have knocked his teeth through the back of his head and tied his arms and legs behind him. He got off easy with a split lip."

"The guys say—"

"What is this, Wright? Don't you ever speak for yourself?" Conor said. "Let me tell you what the guys are saying. They're saying this isn't the first time I've gone off on a suspect. They're saying Conor Quinn is getting a reputation. And that reputation doesn't help my chances of moving over to homicide. Combine the split lip with my other misadventures and the brass has got me pegged as a rogue cop."

"I—I didn't mean to—"

"You don't have to worry, Wright. It's not contagious," Conor muttered.

"I'm not worried about me. You've been waiting for an assignment in homicide for two years and there are only two slots open. You're a good detective, sir. You deserve one of those slots."

Conor shook his head. "I'm not sure I'm even interested anymore."

"Why not?"

He'd been mulling over that question for weeks now, but Conor hadn't been able to come up with an answer, at least one that made sense. "I've been trying to make this city safe for more years than I'd care to count. I honestly thought I could make a difference and I haven't even made a dent. For every hooker and bookie and scam artist I put behind bars, there's another one right behind. What makes me think I could do better with murderers?"

"Because you will," Danny reasoned in his own guileless way.

"Hell, I'm sick of playing it safe. It's time I started living my life. I want to get up in the morning and look forward to the day. Look at my brother Brendan. He chooses what he writes, when he writes, if he writes. He's living life on his own terms. And Dylan. What he does makes a difference. He saves lives. Real lives."

"So what are you going to do? You're a cop. You've always been a cop."

"Maybe that's the problem. I went from taking care of my family to taking care of this city. I was nineteen when I went into the academy, Wright. I had responsibilities at home, I needed a steady job. Maybe I would have chosen differently. I certainly would have enjoyed going to college rather that taking years of night courses to get a degree."

Danny gave him a sideways glance. "You'll feel better when the lieutenant lets you out of the doghouse," he said. "He can't stay mad forever."

"So what kind of scut work does he have for us this evening?" Conor asked. He took a long sip of his soda, then wiped his hand across his mouth.

"Actually, it's pretty interesting, sir," Danny said. "We're protecting a witness in the Red Keenan case. We've got to transport the guy out to a safe house on Cape Cod and then keep watch for a few days. Kind of an odd place for a safe house, don't you think?"

Conor shook his head. "I guess they figure they can monitor everyone coming and going this time of year. One highway, one airport. Easier to spot suspicious characters."

Conor pushed back from the bar and started toward the door, Wright dogging his heels. He gave Sean a wave, then called out a farewell to his brothers. When he reached the street, he pulled up the collar of his leather jacket and turned his face into the wind. He smelled the ocean on the stiff, damp breeze and he knew a storm was on the way. For a moment, he worried about Brendan, almost two days late on a return trip from the Grand Banks where he'd had a last run with the swordfishermen before they started to work their way south. Why he'd decided to write a book about swordfishing, Conor would never understand.

Hell, swordfishing had been the ruin of their family life, the reason their mother had walked out, the reason their father had left the parenting to Conor. He sighed and cursed softly. Brendan could handle a storm at sea—he'd spent many a summer vacation making runs with their father. And Dylan could handle a fire out of control. It was Conor who was having trouble handling his life of late, making sense of it all.

His head bent to the wind, hands shoved into his pockets, Conor strode down the rain-slicked street toward his car, Danny hard on his heels. He glanced up when he heard footsteps coming his way, his instincts automatically on alert. A slender woman with short, dark hair passed, nearly running into him in the process. Their eyes met for only a moment. He glanced over his shoulder, thinking he recognized her. Bunko artist? Hooker? Undercover cop?

He watched as she slowly stopped in front of Quinn's, then peered through the plate-glass window. A few seconds later, she started up the steps, then paused and hurried back down, disappearing into the darkness. Conor shook his head. Was he so jaded that he now saw criminal intent in a perfectly innocent stranger? Maybe a few days of solitude on Cape Cod would put everything back in perspective.

The District Four station house was buzzing with activity when Conor and Danny arrived in the unmarked sedan. Conor was used to working the day shift, but days and nights would mean nothing now that he'd been assigned to protect a witness. Just endless hours of boredom, bad takeout, and what amounted to nothing more than baby-sitting.

According to Danny, the witness had been transported earlier that evening from the downtown station house. The lieutenant had been vague on the particulars of the case, preferring to speak to Danny and Conor in person about their new assignment—no doubt to use the meeting as a lesson for an unruly detective.

But when they strode into the squad room, the lieutenant's office door was closed. Conor checked for messages, grabbed a cup of coffee, then searched the mess on his desk for his pocket pad, the leather bound notepad that each detective carried for witness interviews. He remembered that he'd had it last in the observation room while he watched an interrogation through the one-way window.

He grabbed a pen and backtracked, finding the door to the room open. But his search for the missing notepad was stopped short when he glanced through the one-way window into "the box." The featureless interrogation room contained a single table with a chair on each side, a light above, and the mirrored window on one end, through which Conor now stared.

The sole occupant of the room was a woman, a slender figure with ash-blond hair, patrician features and an expensive wardrobe. He wasn't sure how he knew, but he was certain she wasn't a call girl or a drug dealer or a con artist. He'd be willing to bet his badge that she hadn't committed any crime. She lacked the hard edge to her features that most criminals acquired after working the streets. And she looked genuinely out of her element, a butterfly in the habitat of…cockroaches.

He stepped closer to the window and watched her for a long moment, noting the tremor in her delicate hand as she sipped at the paper cup filled with muddy coffee. Suddenly, she turned to look his way and he quickly stepped back into the shadows. Even though he knew she couldn't see him, he felt as if he'd been caught looking.

God, she was beautiful, Conor mused. No woman had a right to be that beautiful. He found in her features sheer perfection—a high forehead, expressive eyes, cheekbones that wouldn't quit and a wide mouth made to be kissed. Her hair fell in soft waves around her face, tumbling just to her shoulders. Conor's hand twitched as he imagined how soft the strands might feel between his fingers, how her hair would slide over his skin like warm silk.

A soft oath slipped from his lips and he turned away from the window. Hell, what was he thinking, fantasizing over a complete stranger? For all he knew, she could just be a better class of call girl, or some drug-runner's high-living girlfriend. Just because she was beautiful, didn't automatically make her pure.

Old habits did die hard. How many times had he looked at an attractive woman only to have his father's voice nagging in his head? All those cautionary tales, hidden between the lines of Seamus's old Irish folk stories. *A Quinn must never surrender his heart to a woman. Look beyond the beauty to the danger lurking beneath.*

He turned back to the window in time to see her wrap her arms around herself. Her shoulders slumped and then she rocked forward, her body trembling. When she tipped her head back, he saw the tracks of her tears on her smooth complexion. Conor's heart twisted in his chest at the fear and regret in her expression, the raw vulnerability of her appearance. She looked small and all alone.

Had she been standing next to him, she might have crumpled into his arms, hiding her sobs against his shoulder. But the glass between them was like an impenetrable barrier and he'd become nothing more than a voyeur. He'd never seen a woman cry before, except for the hookers he'd arrested, but those tears were usually just for show.

She cried for a long time while Conor watched, memories of his mother's pain flooding his mind. He knew he should leave and allow her the privacy of her emotions, but he couldn't. He felt as if his feet were glued to the floor, his gaze caught by her beauty and her pain. The tears had opened her soul and for a moment, he could see inside. He fought the urge to pull open the door and go to her. Whoever she was, criminal or not, she deserved a shoulder to cry on.

Conor reached out to turn the doorknob so he could enter the box, but just as he was about to open the door, he saw Danny Wright stroll into the room, a grocery bag in his arms. Slowly, he drew his hand away, stunned by the unexpected change in the woman's expression. The transformation was astounding. Almost instantly, the vulnerability vanished and her expression became cool and composed, almost icy. Surreptitiously, she brushed away all traces of her tears and glanced up at his partner, her lips pressed into a tight line.

Conor flipped the switch on the intercom, then braced his hands on the table beneath the window and listened to Danny's voice, crackling through the speaker.

"Ms. Farrell, I'm Detective Wright. My partner and I have been assigned to protect you until the trial. I'm sorry you've been waiting so long, but we've been making arrangements to take you to a safe place."

Conor sucked in a sharp breath. *This* was his witness? This woman who'd drawn him into her troubles with just a few tears and a stunningly beautiful face? "Aw, damn it," he muttered, throwing his notepad onto the table. He figured he'd be baby-sitting some wimpy little accountant or slimy two-faced informant. Considering his reaction to Ms. Farrell so far, spending the next two weeks in her company would be hell on earth.

"I don't understand why I can't just disappear," she said, a sharp edge to her voice. "I can go to Europe. I have business associates there who would be happy to—"

"Ms. Farrell, we'll keep you safe. There's nothing to worry—"

She brought her palms down on the table and shot out of her chair, the action causing Danny to jump. "I don't need you to keep me safe," she cried, her voice suffused with anger and frustration. "I can keep myself safe. I don't want your help."

Danny took a step back, caught offguard by the intensity of her outburst. "But—but we won't have any assurance that you'll return to testify."

"What if I don't testify?" she demanded. "Then you'll have to let me go, right?"

"Keenan will find you eventually, Ms. Farrell. Because, if you don't testify, he'll be out on the street and he won't leave any loose ends."

She gripped the back of the chair with a white-knuckled hand. "That's what I am? A loose end?"

Danny blinked, then shook his head. "Th-that's not what I meant. I was just telling you what Keenan would think. Listen, I'm going to go find my partner and let him talk to you. He's a good cop. He won't let anything happen to you, either."

Conor snatched up his notepad and stalked out of the observation room, straight through the squad room to his lieutenant's office. He wanted a reassignment and he wanted one now. He'd even settle for desk duty if that got him out of watching over this woman. Conor rapped on the door, then closed his eyes as he waited for an answer.

"Lieutenant went downtown," Rodriguez called. "The commissioner is holding some big press conference on his Cops and Kids program. He talked to Danny a few minutes ago. I think your witness is in the box."

Conor turned on his heel and walked back through the squad room, muttering beneath his breath. He met Danny halfway down the hall.

"There you are," his partner said. "Are you ready to roll?"

"Lieutenant's gonna have to find someone else for the job," Conor muttered. "I've got too many open cases to take time off. Besides, District One should be handling this witness. It's their case."

"What? You can't bail on me now. I need you to talk to the witness. Her name's Olivia Farrell. Red Keenan's guys took a shot at her earlier this evening and she's pretty shook up. She doesn't want to testify. I don't know what to say to make her—"

"So let her take her chances on the street," Conor muttered. "If she doesn't want to testify, she doesn't have to."

Danny frowned. "What are you saying? We've got a chance here to nail Keenan. Besides murder and drug dealing, the guy's been running us ragged in vice. You should want him off the street."

Conor raked his hand through his hair and shook his head. "I do. But I'm not going to talk to her. She's your responsibility, Wright. You're the point man on this one. You get her ready to go and you drive her out to Cape Cod. I'll be in the backup car watching your ass."

"I gave her some clothes," Danny said. "Lieutenant figured we should sneak her out of here in disguise, like a suspect transfer. We'll drive past the South Boston station house on the way out of town, and if you don't see anyone on our tail, we won't stop until we get to the safe house."

"Sounds like a plan," Conor muttered. "I'll wait for you in the parking lot and follow you out."

Conor shoved his hands in his jacket pockets and started down the hall. Suddenly he needed fresh air, time to breathe. What had this woman done to him? With just one look, she'd sapped his strength and sent him running for cover. If he didn't know better, he'd have to believe his father's warnings were true. But this was just a job and he could certainly maintain a professional demeanor if he had to. Besides, as with all women in his life, the fascination would soon fade.

Consumed by his own thoughts, his gaze fixed on the floor, he didn't notice the figure who stepped out of the doorway to the box. She slammed into him and he grabbed her as she bumped against the wall. With a soft curse, Conor looked into the most incredible green eyes he'd ever seen.

She'd changed out of her designer clothes and was now dressed in a faded T-shirt, tattered chinos and a slouchy hat. An old camouflage jacket was clutched in her hands. If he didn't know her, he might mistake her for one of the vagrants who hung out down on the waterfront. Conor stepped to one side and, at the very moment, she made the same move. Twice more, they tried to get past each other, the two of them participating in some bizarre little tango right there in the hall.

Finally, he grabbed her arms and impatiently moved her against the wall. But the instant he touched her, his anger with her dissolved. Her skin was warm and so soft. A current shot up his arms, and as if he'd been burned, he snatched his hands away. "Sorry," he muttered.

"It—it's all right," she said. "It was my fault. I wasn't watching where I was going."

The sound of her voice surprised him. The intercom in the box had distorted it until she sounded like some harpy fishwife. But here, standing so near to him, her words were low and throaty, wrapping around his brain like a mind-numbing drug, immediately turning him into an addict for the sound. "No, it was my fault," he said, hoping she'd speak again.

"Can you tell me where Detective Wright is?" she asked. "He gave me these clothes to wear but I'm afraid they don't fit very well."

She glanced up at him again and he saw the vulnerability return to her eyes, the hard facade gone. "Detective Wright will be with you in a moment, miss," he said, steering her back through the door to the box. "Wait in here until he returns."

With that, he turned and strode down the hall, rubbing his tingling palms together as he walked. "See? She's nothing special," he murmured. "Just an ordinary witness. Sure, she's a beautiful woman. But sooner or later they all turn into clinging, grasping shrews." Conor repeated these words over and over as he walked to the parking lot.

By the time Danny helped a handcuffed Olivia Farrell into an unmarked sedan and roared off into the night, Conor had nearly convinced himself that his words were true. But as he followed the taillights of his partner's car, memories of the feel of her skin and the sound of her voice flooded his brain.

She wasn't like the others. He wasn't sure how he knew, but Olivia Farrell was different. Conor couldn't help but feel a small measure of regret at the revelation. He'd never really know how she was different, or why she made him feel the way she did.

The only thing he knew for sure was that he damn well didn't intend to get within fifty feet of Olivia Farrell ever again!

2

CAPE COD during an October nor'easter—Olivia Farrell couldn't think of anything worse, except maybe a root canal without anesthesia. October was supposed to be warm and sunny. But the sky remained endlessly bleak and the wind blew off the Atlantic, seeping through every crack and crevice in the beach house and rattling the single-pane windows until she was certain she'd go mad from the sound. The fireplaces throughout the cottage blazed but they did nothing to take the damp from the air. And the furnace, meant only to keep the pipes from freezing in the winter, did a pitiful job of staving off the cold.

She peered through a slit in the curtains, staring out at the restless waters of Cape Cod Bay, a sick shade of green and gray beneath the slowly rising sun. Rubbing her arms through the thick wool sweater, she fought off a shiver. How had she managed to get herself into such a predicament?

"Ms. Farrell, please stay away from the windows. We don't know who might be out there."

Olivia sighed. She'd been in protective custody for only two days, but already she'd had enough. She couldn't breathe without permission from Dudley Do-Right, the by-the-book cop that had been assigned as her shadow. Detective Danny Wright looked all of about fifteen years old, with a fresh-scrubbed face and a pudgy build. If she hadn't known he was a cop, she might have thought the gun he carried was a toy. Olivia ran her hands through her hair, then turned away from the window. "How much longer do we have to stay here? Can't we find a place with heat?"

"We're thinking of keeping you here until the trial."

"But that's twelve days away!" Olivia cried.

"We've got men posted at the airport, on the highway and even at the ferry landing in Provincetown. The only way one of Red Keenan's men can get past them is if they come over on a private boat and land on the beach. And with this weather, they'd be crazy to try. Local law enforcement knows all the year-round residents on this stretch of the Cape. This is the safest place for you."

"Then why can't I at least go out for a while? You said it. I'm perfectly safe here. We could go shopping, or go for a walk. Maybe get some breakfast in town?"

Detective Do-Right shook his head. "I'm afraid that won't be possible, miss. If there's anything more you need, I can send a man out. Books, snacks, whatever. The district attorney wants you to be comfortable."

"Fine!" Olivia snapped. "Send him out and tell him to buy me my old life back. I want my own bed and my cat and my hairdryer. My shop can't survive another two weeks of closed doors. My clients are going to go elsewhere. Will the department pay for all the lost business?"

The officer looked genuinely apologetic. "We're very sorry about that, miss, but you are doing society a great service by helping us shut down Keenan's operation."

She sighed then bit back a sharp retort and flopped down on the sofa. She knew she ought to be grateful for the protection, but she felt like a hostage, held against her will. Her incarceration would probably be much more enjoyable if she'd cut Detective Wright a little slack. "Since we're going to be spending so much time together, you might as well call me Olivia. I'm getting tired of miss."

"Actually, Ms. Farrell, it's best if we don't get friendly. Department policy says that we should keep our relationship strictly professional."

She grabbed the book she'd been reading from the end table. "I'm going to lie down. I didn't get much sleep last night." Officer Do-Right was about to issue another warning but she held up her hand to stop him. "And don't worry, I won't stand near the windows."

She closed the bedroom door behind her, then leaned back against it. The least they could do was put her up in a house with heat. It was probably warmer outside. Olivia crossed to the bed and grabbed her jacket, then tugged it on. In truth, she wasn't tired. She'd been so inactive over the course of her imprisonment she'd gained five pounds. Had she been at home, she'd be heading out for her morning walk right about now, taking her usual route, down Dartmouth to the river and then back again. She'd stop in her favorite coffee shop for a half-caf, no-fat latte, then grab copies of the morning papers, and head for her flat on St. Botolph Street.

Olivia paced the length of the bedroom, then turned on her heel and retraced her steps. She picked up the speed and before long she was jogging in place. If she closed her eyes she could almost feel the brisk morning air on her face, hear the wind rustling in the leaves and smell the river in the distance.

But when she opened her eyes, she was still stuck in what amounted to a prison. Olivia glanced at the window, then walked over and pushed aside the curtains. The drop to the ground wasn't so bad. She could easily fit through the window without making a sound. All she needed was a little time to herself, some fresh air and exercise.

She reached up and flipped the latch open. Wincing, she slowly pushed the creaky sash up, the wind buffeting her face. The sound of crashing waves filled the room and she waited to see if Officer Do-Right would burst through the door with gun drawn. When he didn't, she threw her leg over the sash and wriggled out the window. The sandy ground was damp beneath her feet, muffling the sound.

Olivia turned around and pulled the window shut, then stepped out from the shadow of the house and headed toward the beach, avoiding the sight lines from the big wall of windows across the back of the house. The wind cut through her jacket and chilled her to the bone, but the sense of freedom sent her pulse racing and she wanted to dance and sing and shout with joy.

She ran over the dunes, through the wind-whipped sea grass to the hard-packed sand at water's edge. The roar of the waves filled her head and she jogged along the beach, drawing deeply of the salt air, caught up in the fierce weather. No one had ventured out this morning. Not a footprint marred the damp sand, no human for as far as the eye could see. "There you are, Officer Do-Right, I'm perfectly safe. Not a hit man in sight."

She wasn't sure how long she ran but by the time she sat down on a small patch of damp sand, she was breathless. Olivia knew she should go back inside before her watchdog noticed she was missing, but now that she was warm, she just needed a few more minutes to—

Arms clamped around her torso and she felt herself being lifted from the ground. The shock knocked the air out of her lungs and, for a moment, Olivia couldn't scream. She struggled to catch her breath as she was spun around and tossed over the shoulder of a dark-haired man dressed in a leather jacket and jeans.

He trudged up the dunes, carrying her as if she weighed nothing more than a sack of feathers. Finally, she drew enough air to make a sound. First, she screamed, long and hard, a shriek guaranteed to carry on the wind. Then she began to kick her legs and pummel his back with her fists. "Let me go!" Olivia cried. "This place is swarming with cops. You'll never get away with this."

He stopped, then hoisted her up again, adjusting her weight until his shoulder jabbed into her belly. "I don't see any cops, do you?"

"I—I'll make you a deal," she pleaded, staring down at his backside. She'd do well to keep her head about her. Surely she could reason with the man. From the look of his behind, he was young, fit, probably attractive. "I—I won't talk. I'll refuse to testify. Your boss doesn't have to worry. He won't go to jail. Just don't kill me."

She pushed up and looked around, then noticed they were heading toward the house. Officer Do-Right was inside! With his gun! Oh, God, she was about to be caught in a hail of bullets. And the way he was carrying her she'd be shot in the butt first. "You can't go in there," she warned. "The cops are in there. See, I'm on your side. I'd never say anything to hurt your boss."

When he reached the steps to the deck, he grabbed her waist and set her down in front of him, his fingers biting into her flesh.

Olivia swallowed hard, looking up at an expression as fierce as the weather. Even through his anger, she could see he was a handsome man—for a criminal. And his features were strangely familiar. She knew this man. "You!" Olivia cried. "I saw you at the station house. You're—you're a—"

An unexpected smile touched the corners of his hard mouth. "I'm the man who just saved your life. Now get in the house."

Olivia gasped, then narrowed her eyes. "You're a cop!"

He nodded once, dismissively, and she felt her temper rise. She let out a colorful oath, then drew back and kicked him squarely in the shin. "I thought you were a bad guy!" she cried, ignoring his yelp of pain and the little one-footed dance he did as he rubbed his bruised leg.

"Damn it, what did you do that for?"

"You scared me half to death! I thought you were going to kidnap me. And—and then, put a bullet in my brain or—or fit me with cement overshoes. My life flashed before my eyes. I nearly had a stroke. I could have died."

He stared up at her, bent double with the pain. It was only then that she noticed his eyes, an odd shade of hazel mixed with gold. She'd never seen eyes quite that color. Eyes filled with cold, calculating anger—directed at her. "Yes, you could have died," he muttered. "And I want you to remember how scared you were. Because that's what it's going to be like when Keenan finally gets you. Now get in the house," he continued, emphasizing each word. "Or I'll shoot you myself."

With a sniff, she spun on her heel and flounced up the steps. Of all the nerve! What right did he have to treat her like some—some recalcitrant child? Next thing, he'd be throwing her over his knee and spanking her. Olivia risked a look back as she walked in the door. Good grief, why did that notion suddenly appeal to her?

When she got inside, she found Detective Wright nervously pacing the room. He looked up and relief flooded his expression. Olivia almost felt sorry for him and was about to apologize when the door slammed behind her. "What the hell were you thinking, Wright? You never, *ever,* let a witness out of your sight. She could be dead now and then where would we be?"

Olivia turned and sent the dark-haired cop a livid glare, one he returned in equal measure, sending a shiver down her spine. "Don't you think you're being a bit dramatic? Besides, it's not his fault. I snuck out."

He took a step toward her and she backed away. "Did I ask for your opinion?" He turned back to Detective Wright. "Why don't you watch the road and the perimeter? I'll stay with Ms. Farrell for now."

"I don't want you here," Olivia said, tipping her chin up defiantly. "I want Officer Do-Right to stay. You can leave."

"Officer *Wright* is needed outside. And since you've decided to ignore his warnings, you're stuck with me. Or more precisely, I'm stuck with you." His gaze raked the length of her body and stopped at her toes. "Give me your shoes."

"What?"

"Take them off." He turned and stalked to her bedroom, then emerged a few moments later with the boots and loafers she'd hurriedly packed after the incident at the shop. "You can have them back once I'm sure you're going to stay inside. Now, give me your shoes."

Olivia had every intention of refusing but the look in his eyes told her otherwise. She sat down on the sofa and yanked both shoes off, then threw them in the direction of his head. Then she crossed her arms and sank back into the cushions, watching him suspiciously and waiting for the next demand.

He drew Detective Wright aside and spoke softly with him, giving Olivia a chance to observe him in an objective light. He stood at least half a head taller than Wright and his dark good looks stood in sharp contrast with Dudley's clean-cut choirboy features. When his face wasn't filled with fury, the guy was actually quite handsome—high cheekbones and a strong jaw, a mouth that looked as if it had been sculpted by an artist. His hair was dark, nearly black, and his eyes were that strange shade that she couldn't quite describe in words. Fascinating. Unearthly. Riveting.

While Dudley looked conscientious and trustworthy, this new guy had a wild and unpredictable air about him. His hair was just a little too long, his clothes a bit too casual. He had a sinewy build, long legs and broad shoulders and a flat belly that showed no evidence of too many donuts. When they both turned her way, she averted her eyes and casually picked at the fringe of a throw pillow she'd pulled onto her lap.

Detective Wright approached the sofa. "Ms. Farrell, I'm going to leave you in the care of Detective Quinn. He'll be with you until the trial. I hope you won't give him any more trouble."

She forced a sweet smile and slowly rose. "That all depends upon Detective Quinn's behavior. As long as he can stifle his Neanderthal tendencies, it will be pure bliss."

Wright looked back and forth between the two of them, then nodded before hurrying out of the room. Left alone with Quinn, Olivia wondered whether she might be better off taking her chances with Keenan's hit man. It would be best to keep Quinn off guard, to refuse to give in to his bullying. Twelve days of "yes, sir" and "no, sir" would be completely intolerable. She shrugged out of her jacket and tossed it his way. "You might as well take it," she said. "Do you want my socks as well?"

A muscle in his jaw twitched and he didn't speak for a long time. "I don't want to be here any more than you do, Ms. Farrell. But it's my job to keep you safe. If you let me do my job, then we'll get along just fine."

When he wasn't yelling at her, he had a very pleasant voice, deep and rich. His accent was working-class Boston, but there was something else there, a hint of something exotically foreign. "You said that you're being punished," she ventured. "What did you do wrong?"

"Nothing you have to worry about," he muttered. "As long as I don't lose my temper again, you should be safe." He wandered around the room, checking every window and door, then disappeared into her bedroom. She imagined him rifling through her bag, plucking at the lacy scraps of underwear and smelling her perfume. She could always tell when a man was attracted to her, but Quinn was impossible to read. He was probably telling the truth when he said he'd just as soon shoot her.

When he returned, he had a pillow and comforter in his arms. He set them on the back of the sofa. "You'll sleep in here tonight," he murmured.

"I sleep on the sofa and you get my bed? That doesn't seem fair."

"No," he said, "you sleep on the sofa and I sleep on the floor. We sleep in the same room, Ms. Farrell. If that doesn't suit, we can sleep in the same bed. That's up to you. I just need to be able to get to you quickly."

Olivia scowled. "Listen, Quinn, I—"

"Conor," he interrupted. "You can call me Conor. And there's no use arguing. I'm not going to change my mind."

Olivia opened her mouth to protest, then snapped it shut. She'd never felt entirely safe with Detective Wright. But with Conor Quinn, there was no doubt in her mind that he'd do what he had to do to protect her, regardless of her feelings in the matter. When he'd grabbed her on the beach, she had to admit she'd been scared. What if he *had* been one of Keenan's men? Chances were she'd be floating facedown in the bay right about now.

"I'm going to make a fresh pot of coffee," she said grudgingly. "Would you like a cup?" He nodded, but when she got up, he followed her into the kitchen. He methodically checked the windows and doors, then sat down on a stool at the breakfast bar. "Are you going to follow me around all day?" she asked as she filled the pot with cold water.

"If I have to," he said. His shrewd gaze skimmed over her body, blatantly, as if he were trying to see right through her clothes. "Why did you climb out the window?"

Olivia sighed. "You have to understand that I'm used to my own space, my own life. I never wanted this, never wanted to get involved. I shouldn't be here."

"But you are involved," he murmured, his eyes probing, his expression curious.

"I tried to explain to the district attorney that I didn't want to testify but—"

"Ms. Farrell, you have a duty to do what's right. Red Keenan is scum, a big player in the mob. With your testimony, we can put him away. A little inconvenience on your part is nothing compared to the pain that man has caused countless innocent people." With that, he pushed away from the counter and walked out of the room. "And stay away from the windows," he called.

The rest of the day passed in excruciating boredom. She stayed away from the windows and out of Conor Quinn's way. And he stayed just close enough to make her uneasy. Whenever she looked at him, he was watching her, silently, intently. Olivia assumed he was waiting for her to make another run for freedom. But she'd already resigned herself to her fate. The trial was twelve days away—twelve long days spent in the company of the brooding Conor Quinn. She'd need to choose her fights carefully if she expected to survive.

THE SMELLS coming from the kitchen were too much to resist. Conor glanced up from an old issue of *Sports Illustrated,* then levered himself up from the overstuffed chair he'd occupied for the past hour. Furrowing his hands through his hair, he wandered into the kitchen to find pots bubbling on the stove and Olivia Farrell busily chopping vegetables.

"Smells good," he said.

She looked up at him for a brief moment, then turned her attention back to the salad she was preparing. "I asked Detective Wright for some groceries yesterday. I was getting a little tired of take-out meals and a little angry with my situation, so I made the grocery list as complicated as I could."

He slid onto the kitchen stool. "What are you making?"

"Paella," she said.

"What?"

"It's an Italian seafood stew. They probably had fits trying to hunt down fresh shrimp and scallops. But then, I could afford to wait. I've got plenty of time, which is what it takes to make paella, and it's always better the second day." She looked at him again, this time letting her gaze linger for a long moment. Olivia Farrell had very alluring eyes, Conor concluded. Wide and trusting, ringed with thick lashes. She didn't wear much makeup, allowing her natural beauty to shine through. "There's a bottle of wine in the fridge. You can open it, if you like."

"I shouldn't drink on duty," Conor said, reaching for the wine.

Olivia managed a tiny smile. "I promise I won't try to escape again. You can have a small glass, can't you?" She reached into a cabinet next to the sink and pulled out two wine goblets, then set them down in front of him.

Had this evening occurred under different circumstances, Conor could imagine them on a first date—Olivia cooking dinner for him at her apartment, Conor bringing the wine. He grabbed the bottle, then took the corkscrew and opened it. Perhaps if he thought of this as a personal rather than a professional relationship, it might be much more tolerable. "Do you like to cook?"

Olivia shrugged. "I don't cook often," she said, "at least not like this. It's kind of silly to cook for one."

"Then you don't have a…" He let his question drift off. Maybe that was getting too personal.

"A boyfriend?" She shook her head. "Not right now. How about you?"

He smiled. "No boyfriend for me, either."

She glanced up, then giggled softly. "I meant, do you have a girlfriend? Or maybe a wife?"

He poured her a generous glass of wine, then splashed a bit into a goblet for himself. He wasn't much of a wine drinker, but he had to admit that the crisp Chardonnay tasted good. "Cops don't make good husbands."

She reached for her glass, then took a sip as she studied him shrewdly. "The accent," she said. "I can't place it."

"Southside Boston, with a dash of County Cork," Conor replied. "I was born in Ireland."

She raised her eyebrow. "When did you leave?"

"Twenty-seven years ago. I was six." Conor hated talking about himself. His life had been so ordinary, of no interest to a sophisticated woman like Olivia Farrell. "Where are you from, Ms. Farrell?" he asked, deftly changing the subject.

"Olivia," she said. "I've lived in Boston all my life."

A long silence grew between them as he watched her preparing the meal. She moved with such grace, everything she did seemed like part of a dance and Conor found himself fascinated by the turn of her head or the flutter of her fingers. Even though she was casually dressed in a bulky cable-knit sweater and jeans, elegance and class seemed to radiate from her body.

"What made you become a cop?" she asked, interrupting his thoughts.

Conor pushed up from the stool and circled around the counter to peer into the pot she was stirring. "It's a long story," he said.

"Like I said, I've got plenty of time. Twelve days, in fact. Which is good, because trying to carry on a conversation with the likes of you is like talking to a—a bowl of vegetables."

Conor chuckled. "I guess I don't talk much."

"Ah, a sentence with more than five words," she said sarcastically. "We're making progress. Before the night is out, I expect scintillating repartee."

She dipped a spoon into the pot and tasted the sauce. Then she held out the spoon to him. He took her hand and steadied it as he licked the end of the spoon. The feel of her tiny wrist, her soft skin beneath his fingertips, sent a frisson of electricity up his arm.

Their eyes met and, for a long moment, neither one of them moved. Had it been a first date, Conor may have taken the spoon from her hand and swept her slender body into his arms, kissing her until he lost himself in the taste of her mouth and the feel of her soft flesh.

But this was not a first date, he reminded himself. He was a cop, charged with protecting a witness. And fantasizing about this witness, no matter how beautiful she was, would only take his mind off the real dangers that waited for her outside the beach cottage. He drew back, forcing his gaze to fix on a spot over her shoulder. "I should go check everything outside before it gets dark," he murmured, schooling his voice into indifference. "Make sure Danny hasn't fallen asleep."

He strode to the kitchen door, not bothering to fetch his jacket from the other room. The icy air would do him good, clear his head. "Don't go near the windows," he said as he stepped outside.

Conor waved at his partner, stationed in a parked car near the road. He was tempted to switch jobs again with the poor guy. To give him paella and fine wine in turn for endless hours of lukewarm coffee, stale donuts and talk radio. Conor had always taken his job seriously, but it was hard to think about work while sitting in the same room as Olivia Farrell. Why did she have to be so beautiful?

He'd flipped through the case file in the car, but hadn't really bothered to read it in detail. In truth, he didn't want to know more about Olivia Farrell. He already knew she was attractive and desirable and intriguing. But after spending the afternoon in her presence, his curiosity had been piqued. Right now, he wanted to know every detail he could about her and her involvement with Red Keenan.

Maybe, after that, he could start looking at her as just a witness and stop thinking of her as a beautiful woman.

THE LIGHT from the fire had waned and Conor rose from the floor to poke at the embers. Outside the wind howled and shrieked, waves crashing against the shore. He'd watched the weather reports earlier in the day and knew the nor'easter was blowing itself out. He thought again about Brendan, wondering if he'd put into port yet. The only solace he could find in the storm was that Keenan's men wouldn't dare to venture outside.

Inside the beach house, the remains of dinner were scattered across the coffee table, dirty bowls, half-eaten bread, and the empty bottle of wine. Conor glanced over at the sofa. Olivia Farrell lay curled up asleep beneath a soft afghan, her hands clutched beneath her chin. He recalled a picture he'd found in one of his Irish storybooks, a drawing of Derdriu, an ancient beauty, betrothed to a king yet loved by a common warrior. Olivia's hair, like Derdriu's, was a pale shade of gold. The waves and curls spread over the pillow and her perfect skin shone like porcelain in the dim light from the fire.

He tossed another log on the fire. Sparks scattered across

the hearth and the log popped and sizzled before it caught fire.
His father had often told the tale of how Derdriu's beauty had
brought only death and destruction to her people. But Conor
remembered the drawing, how sweet and vulnerable her face
had looked to his ten-year-old eyes. Even then, he'd doubted
his father's warnings about the opposite sex.

He'd been sent to protect this woman, been asked to lay
his life on the line for her like some ancient warrior. Yet what
did he really know about her? Conor crossed the room and
pulled the copy of the police file from his duffel bag. Then he
wandered back to the fire, drawing nearer to the light to read.
From what he could tell, Olivia Farrell was an ordinary citizen, caught up in extraordinary circumstances.

Her partner, Kevin Ford, had been arrested for participating in a money-laundering scheme for organized crime boss
Red Keenan, a scheme that had included murder. The mechan-
ics of the scheme were quite complex—buying expensive antiques for Keenan, reselling them to bogus clients for three or
four times the value, then handing over the freshly laundered
money to Keenan.

Olivia hadn't been aware of the scheme, but she had had
the misfortune of overhearing a conversation between her
partner and Keenan, providing the only solid evidence to link
the two. Conor looked up, wondering if she realized the true
danger she was in. He also wondered what kind of relationship she had with Kevin Ford.

He flipped past the report of Ford's criminal activity to a
photo of the guy. He wasn't bad-looking, Conor mused, in that
polished, sophisticated, Ivy League way. A woman like Olivia
probably found him endlessly charming…intelligent…sexy,
even. Perhaps they'd been lovers at one time, maybe still

were. Conor shoved the photo back into the file and grabbed the page that included a rundown on her background.

Olivia Farrell. Graduate of Boston College, lived on a nice street in the South End. No criminal record. Single. Twenty-eight years old. Co-owner of one of Boston's most success-ful antique galleries, Ford-Farrell Antiques. Well-known throughout certain social circles in Boston. Dated an invest-ment banker, a corporate attorney, and a shortstop for the Red Sox. No long-term relationships since college. Both parents living, residing in Jacksonville, Florida.

Conor closed the file and turned his gaze back to her. "Stubborn to a fault," he murmured. "Possible potential as a kick-boxer. Sharp tongue. Great cook. Incredibly beautiful."

His gaze drifted down to her mouth. Though she'd worn a grim expression for most of the day, all traces of irritation had been dissolved by the wine and good food. They'd chatted over dinner, each of them revealing just enough about them-selves to keep the conversation interesting. She'd told him about her shop, the excitement of finding valuable antiques, the wealthy clients she worked with, the elegant parties she'd attended.

He told her about the seamy underworld of the vice cop, the endless schemes criminals found to circumvent the law and the frustrations he felt when they got away with it. To his surprise, she seemed fascinated by his work and questioned him until he'd told her about the most interesting cases he'd ever worked. Conor sighed. He really shouldn't have been sur-prised. Olivia Farrell was used to sparkling conversation. She could probably make an undertaker sound like he was the most intriguing man on the planet.

She may be out of his league, but Conor still couldn't deny

he was attracted to her, even though he'd always been drawn to women with more obvious beauty. Olivia Farrell's features were subtle, plain almost, yet so perfectly proportioned that a man couldn't help but notice. She looked…fresh. Clean. Pure.

He stood up and quietly walked to her side. Without thinking, he reached out and took a strand of her hair between his fingers. Startled by the silken feel of it on his skin, he drew his hand away then knelt down to examine her face more closely.

A tiny smile curled the corners of her mouth. She slept soundly, secure in the knowledge that he was there to watch over her. But could he really protect her against the power of Red Keenan? There was no doubt in Conor's mind that Keenan would risk anything to stay out of prison. He had money and power, and those two in combination could convince unscrupulous men that a favor done for Keenan would be handsomely rewarded—even if that favor involved killing Olivia Farrell.

As he stared down at her, so unaware, so vulnerable, Conor knew he'd step in front of a bullet for her. Not because it was his duty, but because here he could make a difference. Olivia Farrell was worth saving and, for the first time in a long time, he was proud of the career he'd chosen.

He reached out and gently pulled the afghan up around her shoulders. For a moment, she stirred and Conor sat back on his heels, holding his breath. Then her eyes fluttered and before he could move away, she was looking up at him. "Is—is everything all right?" she murmured, sleep turning her voice throaty and breathless.

He nodded, then pushed to his feet and walked to the fire. He heard her sit up, a soft sigh slipping from her lips. "You're worried, aren't you," she said.

Conor turned and looked at her. Her hair was mussed and her nose was red from the cold. She rubbed her eyes, then turned her gaze to his. "Not worried," he replied. "Cautious. This place may be secluded, but that can work against us, too."

"Do you really think they'll come after me out here?"

The fear in her voice caused a stab of regret at his honesty. "No," he lied. "Your testimony is important, but I think Keenan has more to worry about from your partner. Hopefully, they'll be able to flip Ford before you actually have to take the stand."

"Flip?"

"Yeah. They offered him a deal for his testimony against Keenan. He's refused to talk so far, but as the trial draws closer, he might reconsider. If Ford talks, your testimony won't be that crucial. And Keenan won't have a reason to risk adding another murder onto the charges."

This seemed to reassure her and she pulled the afghan around her shoulders and lay back down on the sofa. "That makes me feel better," she murmured. "Thank you."

She closed her eyes and curled up beneath the afghan. For a moment he'd thought she'd fallen back asleep. He braced his hand on the mantel and stared into the fire. But then her voice came out of the silence. "I'm glad you're here," she said.

Conor smiled to himself. Strange, but right now there wasn't any place he'd rather be.

3

OLIVIA WOKE UP with a jolt. Suddenly, she couldn't breathe. Her eyes slowly came into focus and she found Conor lying across her body, his hand over her mouth, his breath warm on her face. She wriggled beneath him, but he refused to budge.

"Don't make a sound," he warned in a voice just barely above a whisper. "There's someone outside."

She swallowed back the choking fear that threatened to erupt in a scream then pried his fingers off her mouth. "What are we going to do?" she whispered.

He scrambled off the sofa, then handed her her shoes and jacket. "Put these on—quickly. I want you to go to the bedroom, open the window and wait. I'll take care of whoever's outside then I'll come and get you."

"Shouldn't we call for help?" Olivia asked.

He placed a finger over her lips. "I tried to raise the officer outside on my radio, but he didn't answer. If Keenan found you here, then we've got a leak in the department. And we need to get out of here as fast as we can. Now, crawl over to the bedroom and wait beneath the window. If you hear gunfire, I want you to get out as quickly as you can and keep running until you're safe. Understand?"

Olivia nodded and he smiled. Then he brushed a quick kiss across her mouth. His boldness didn't surprise her, merely made her feel more confident—and a little warm and tingly inside. "We'll be all right," he said. "I promise."

He moved to get up, but she grabbed his arm. "Please, don't get shot. I'm not sure I can do this on my own." She winced. "And I faint at the sight of blood."

He brushed a strand of hair from her eyes. "You'll be all right. If anyone grabs you, just give him a good knee in the crotch. That should give you a decent head start." A moment later, he was gone, disappearing silently into the shadows of the darkened room. Olivia waited a few seconds, gathering her courage, then slowly began to make her way to the bedroom. Her heart slammed in her chest, so hard that she was certain it could be heard over the howling wind.

She waited for what seemed like eternity, silently praying that the next sound would be Conor's voice and not gunfire. When she heard her name called softly from outside, Olivia nearly cried out with joy. She scrambled out the window and he caught her, carefully lowering her to the ground, his hands firm around her waist.

"What's happening?"

"I'm not sure. The cop that relieved Danny isn't there anymore. The car is gone and so is he."

Conor wrapped his arm around her shoulders, then led her

out toward the beach. Only then did she notice the gun in his other hand. She stumbled in the wet sand and Conor took her arm and pulled her along. For a while, he led her one way on the beach, then they suddenly ran closer to the water and started in the opposite direction.

She could barely see her hand in front of her face as blackness engulfed them. Icy water soaked into her shoes and she tried to draw a decent breath, but Conor's pace was unrelenting as they continued down the beach. Every now and then, they stopped and he listened, staring back into the darkness. Then they continued on.

When she didn't think she could go any farther, Conor led her along a concrete seawall, then up and over a dune to a darkened beach house. The sound of breaking glass cut through the roar of the waves and she squinted to see him reaching through a broken pane to open a door. He silently led her inside, then closed the door behind him.

Olivia felt her knees folding beneath her and he reached out and grabbed her waist, his arm supporting her weight. He drew her body against his and rubbed her back to warm her. How could she feel so safe, yet so scared, at the same time?

"It's all right," he murmured, cradling the back of her head in his hand. "We should be fine here, at least for a little while."

"But we were supposed to be safe there," Olivia cried. "What happened?"

"I don't know," he said. "The phone was out and there was someone prowling around the front door. It could have been the wind and the storm, but I don't think so."

"I don't want to do this anymore," Olivia said, tears pressing at the corners of her eyes. "I just want to go far away, where no one knows me."

But if she didn't testify and put Keenan in jail, how would she ever feel safe again? She'd spend the rest of her life looking over her shoulder, waiting for him or one of his henchmen to silence her for good. "I—I just want to forget I ever heard anything. You can't keep me here. I won't testify."

He placed his palm on her cheek, his grim expression softening. "Don't talk like that, Olivia. I'll keep you safe, I promise. From now on, it's just you and me. And people I know I can trust."

He pulled her along to the kitchen, then withdrew a cell phone from his pocket. Conor punched in a number, then waited. "Dylan? This is Con. I know it's late, but this is important. I need you to get a boat." He paused. "When did he get in?" Conor turned to her and smiled. "I want the two of you to bring *The Mighty Quinn* across the bay into Provincetown Harbor. If you leave now, you can be here before dawn. Tie up at the gas dock and make up some excuse for staying there—mechanical problems. Just wait and I'll find you. I'll explain everything then." He didn't say anything more, just hung up the phone as if his request had been understood without question.

He crossed the room to Olivia and rubbed her arms distractedly. "I need to go find us transportation into town. You're going to have to stay here by yourself. Just for a little while."

She shook her head. "No, I'm coming with you."

He considered her request for only a moment, then nodded. "This place has a garage. Let's hope the owners leave a car here during the off-season."

They moved through the dark house, eyes fully adjusted to the lack of light. The door to the garage was just off the kitchen and Conor opened it. He flipped on the overhead light and held his hand over her eyes to shield them. "Bingo," he muttered. When her eyes had adjusted, she saw a jeep parked in the center of the garage. "It doesn't have a roof or windows, but it has four wheels. The ride might be a little cold and wet, but we won't have to walk into town." He turned to Olivia. "Let's get some rest. We don't need to leave for a while."

"Shouldn't we find the keys?"

"If they aren't in the ignition, I'll just hot-wire it. Come on, my brothers will be here just before dawn. Hopefully, who-ever's looking for us will wait until after the sun rises to con-tinue the search."

"I—I don't think I can sleep."

Conor took her hand and laced his fingers through hers. "We'll get you warm and you'll feel much better."

They went back inside and he led her to the sofa. Then he sat down beside her and gathered her into his arms. How had they become so close so quickly? Olivia wondered. Was it the danger they faced, the two of them against the rest of the world? Or was this simply some police tactic to make her compliant with all his requests? Olivia closed her eyes and leaned against his shoulder.

She hadn't been touched by a man in such a long time. She'd had men in her life, but lately Olivia had found search-ing for antiques much more satisfying than looking for love. Still she'd never felt so close to another man as she did to Conor Quinn right now. How long had she been searching for this elusive feeling, the security of knowing that someone— even a virtual stranger—cared?

Olivia drew a ragged breath and tried to calm her chaotic thoughts. It would be so easy to fall for this man, she mused. But in eleven days, he'd disappear from her life and she'd be expected to put the pieces back together and go on as if nothing had happened.

She didn't want to think about the future. Right now, she could only think about the present, the next minute, the next hour. If she thought too far ahead, the fear would engulf her and she'd be too terrified to open her eyes, too afraid even to breathe. "Talk to me," she murmured. "I can sleep if I just hear your voice."

"Not a scintillating conversationalist, huh?"

She looked up at him and smiled. "I like the sound of your voice. It has magic in it."

"Then I'll tell you a magical story," he said, putting on a thick Irish accent. She listened as Conor wove a fascinating tale about a beautiful fairy named Etain. He patiently explained in a soothing tone that fairies, or the Sidh, were not tiny creatures with wings, but human size. They lived in a parallel world, a world that met the real world at times when one thing became another—dusk into night, dawn into day, summer into fall.

Etain had bewitched a king with her beauty, but when the king's brother met her, he fell in love with her as well. Conor filled the story with vivid detail, and by the time he had finished, she was captivated by the images he wove in her mind. Such a complex man, she mused. So tough and calculating on the outside, and so sensitive on the inside.

Olivia looked up at him. "How do you know that story?"

"My da used to tell us. He wasn't home much, so we'd try to memorize all the details so we could retell them after he was gone. It was like a competition between me and my brothers as to who could tell it the best."

Without thinking, she reached up and placed her palm on

his cheek. He gazed down into her eyes and, for a moment, she was certain he'd kiss her. Olivia thought about making the first move, curious as to how he'd taste, how his lips would feel on hers. Would they be hard and demanding? Or gentle and tentative?

"We shouldn't do this," Conor murmured, his gaze fixed on her mouth. "You're a witness. I'm supposed to protect you."

Hesitantly, Olivia drew her hand away. She shouldn't have assumed he'd be as attracted to her as she was to him. Such a fantasy, lusting after her protector. And how silly that she couldn't see it for what it was—a way to escape the troubles of her real life. He was just a convenient man, someone to make her feel safe and cherished. "I'm sorry," she said, drawing away.

"Don't be," Conor replied uneasily. "It—it's pretty common. You're afraid—I'm…reassuring. It happens all the time."

"Then it's happened to you before?" she asked.

"No," he murmured. "Never."

"Well, that makes me feel so much better." She pushed up from the sofa. "I'm going to go find a bed. Wake me when it's time to leave."

She wandered down a long hallway, anxious to put as much distance between Conor Quinn and herself as she could. When she finally closed the bedroom door behind her, she leaned back and sighed. Everything seemed so unreal, as if she were watching herself in a movie. What had happened to her life? Just a few months ago, she'd been consumed with work, finding no time to even think about her pitiful social life.

And now she was tossed into the company of the most intriguing and handsome man she'd ever met. She should be thrilled. But the more she got to know Detective Quinn, the more she began to believe that Red Keenan wasn't the dangerous one. Conor Quinn was.

CONOR STARED out over Provincetown Harbor, scanning the waterfront for any sign of Brendan and Dylan. The sun was just brightening the eastern horizon and the weather had begun to clear. Stars were visible through the cracks in the clouds and the wind had picked up again, blowing from onshore. The tiny village was beginning to stir and Conor was afraid that they'd be sitting ducks once the sun came up.

He'd parked the jeep in the shadows of a fishing shanty near the docks, giving them a good view of the water and anyone approaching from town. "Damn it, Bren, where are you?"

"What if he doesn't come?" Olivia asked, her voice thin and tired.

Conor glanced over at her. He was tempted to draw her into his arms, to reassure her with physical contact. But he wouldn't be touching Olivia Farrell again. Not that he couldn't exert self-control; she was the one to worry about. He didn't need her mooning around after him, messing up his concentration and putting them both at risk. "He'll come," Conor said. "I called him and he'll come."

He felt her gaze searching his face, looking for some sign of the closeness they'd shared just hours ago. When she didn't find it, she sank down and wrapped her arms around herself, trying to keep warm in the chill morning air.

"If he isn't here in ten minutes," Olivia said, "I think we should leave."

Conor felt his temper rise. No way in hell was he going to let her start calling the shots! "I'll decide if and when we leave," he said in an even voice.

"I'm just saying that—"

"I don't need your opinion!" he shot back. Maybe his frustration came from lack of sleep. Or maybe he didn't like her questioning his competence. Or maybe he didn't like the fact that she was probably right. But once the words had left his lips, he knew chastising her had been a mistake.

"You seem to forget it's *my* life. They want to kill *me,* not you. I should at least have some say in the—"

Conor turned in his seat and faced her. "And if you refuse to listen to me, I might get caught in the cross fire. So, you see, it's not just your life. It's mine, too. We're in this together." At least until he got Olivia to safety. Then he had every intention of calling his lieutenant and getting someone else to do the baby-sitting. He'd make sure the cop was trustworthy, of course, but that would be the end of it. He'd rather face a year of desk duty than risk succumbing to the temptation of Olivia Farrell's body, her sweet lips and alluring smile at every turn.

"There's a boat coming in," Olivia said, interrupting his thoughts. "See it over there?"

The low rumble of diesel engines echoed through the crisp air and Conor squinted. As if by magic, *The Mighty Quinn* appeared out of the darkness. Conor had never cared for that boat. In his mind, *The Mighty Quinn* had come between his mother and his father, it had taken his father away from home for long stretches of time, and it had forced Conor to grow up way too fast. But he felt pretty damn happy to see her now.

Unlike Conor, Brendan loved the water and always had, using the captain's quarters on the boat as his home when he was in town during the summer months. During the colder winter months, he usually slept on the sofa at Conor or Dylan's apartment—or in the bed of his current girlfriend, lost in the throes of a weeklong affair that always ended when he headed out on a research trip or another magazine assignment.

The boat maneuvered through the narrow waters, then headed for empty dock space near the gas pumps. Conor took one final look around, then nodded to Olivia. "Come on. We can go now."

He stepped out of the jeep, then circled around to take her hand. They didn't run, just walked calmly toward the water, Conor protecting her back and keeping a wary eye on their surroundings. Conor counted on the fact that Keenan would post his men at the airport and along the highway. Extra personnel would be slow in arriving on the Cape. He'd never expect them to leave on a private boat. When they reached the dock, Conor pressed his palm into the small of her back, urging her forward.

Brendan didn't ask questions. He simply reached down and took Olivia by the hands, then drew her gently onto the deck of the boat. When she was settled, Conor stepped up and they pushed away from the dock without even bothering to tie up. It took no more than a minute before they were once again swallowed up by the dark, and for the moment, safe from Red Keenan.

The running lights from *The Mighty Quinn* were barely visible through the early morning mist that hung over the bay. The prevailing wind had knocked down the waves from the storm and the water wasn't as rough as Conor had expected. He glanced at Olivia, but she stared out at the western horizon, the salty breeze whipping at her hair, her face ruddy with the cold.

He wouldn't feel safe until the two of them were back on

dry land, somewhere warm and secure. He wasn't sure where they'd go. His apartment was too obvious, and probably way too messy for guests. He might be able to commandeer Dylan's place, although his brother's housekeeping abilities weren't much better than Conor's.

He glanced up at the pilothouse, watching as his brothers carried on a quiet conversation. Whenever Conor saw Dylan and Brendan outside the confines of the pub, he was always amazed at how they'd grown into such fine men. He still thought of them as kids, the skinny, untamed lads he'd watched over. The temptation to parent them was still strong, to tell Bren he needed a haircut and a shave, to chastise Dylan for not wearing a jacket in the cold.

Though he'd never told them, he saw his ma in their faces every time he looked at them—in the striking bone structure and the thick, nearly black hair. He saw the same face in the mirror every morning as he shaved, but watching his brothers, so strong and well grown, he couldn't help but wonder what Fiona Quinn might think of them now. Whether she ever thought of them at all. Conor didn't believe for a second that his mother had died in an auto wreck.

When Dylan glanced over at Conor, he gave him a lascivious grin and low whistle, nodding his head at the spot along the rail where Olivia stood. Conor shook his head, then climbed up to the pilothouse. "Don't even think about it," he warned, stepping inside.

"Think about what?" Dylan whispered.

"What you're always thinking about when you see a beautiful woman."

"Ah, brother, a woman like that is obviously wasted on you," Dylan said.

"She is a pretty little thing, isn't she," Brendan added.

Conor growled softly. He wondered whether his younger brothers would ever grow up. Would they ever realize there was more to life than an endless string of women traipsing in and out of their bedrooms? "Just get us back to Hull," he said. "That's all I need from you two right now."

He climbed back down to the main deck and joined Olivia at the rail. She looked a bit seasick and completely exhausted. He gently took her icy hands and drew her toward the main cabin, holding her arm as she gingerly walked through the companionway. Bren had warmed up the main cabin and lights glowed softly around the spacious interior. Conor walked over to the galley and poured a mug of coffee from the huge thermos he found there, then held it out to Olivia. "Are you all right?"

She slowly sat down, bracing herself with her hands against the rocking of the boat.

"You'll get used to the motion," he said. "And once we're across the bay, it'll calm down. Have some coffee."

She took the hot brew and sipped at it as she glanced around. "It—it's warm in here. I haven't been warm in two days." She hesitated, then looked up at him with wide eyes. "How can you be so mean to me one minute and so nice the next?"

Chastened by her question, Conor turned away and fetched himself a mug. "It's my job," he said, stirring in a generous amount of sugar.

"Is that all it is?"

"What else would it be?" He faced her, leaning up against the counter and crossing his legs at the ankle.

She forced a smile. "Then I suppose I should apologize—for earlier. I didn't mean to get…carried away. It's just that my nerves have been a little frayed lately and I thought you—"

"It's all right," Conor said. He wasn't going to tell her that he'd wanted to kiss her as much as she wanted to kiss him. He wasn't going to say how much self-control it had taken for him to draw away, to resist savoring just one taste. Damn, he'd love nothing better than to forget all his responsibilities and do something reckless. To throw caution to the wind and drag her into his bed. But he'd already nearly screwed the pooch at the precinct. He wasn't going to give his boss anything more to use against him. An affair with a witness was more than enough to cost him his badge.

"Where are we going to go now?" she asked.

"Back to Boston—or Hull, to be more precise. After that, I don't know," Conor said.

She bit her bottom lip, her gaze dropping to her coffee mug. "If he found me at the beach house, then he's going to find me no matter where we go."

"I won't let that happen."

She drew a ragged breath. "As soon as we get back to Boston, I have to stop at my apartment. I don't have any clothes. We left everything at the beach house. And there's something else I need to get."

Conor shook his head. "No, we can't. It would be too dangerous. We'll buy you new clothes."

"Please," Olivia pleaded. "I've got nothing. My shop is closed, my apartment is deserted, I haven't slept in my own bed in days. I just want some things around me that are mine."

He didn't want to listen to her pleas. In truth, he was scared he'd give in. It was hard to refuse Olivia anything, especially when he saw the vulnerability in her eyes. All he wanted to do was protect her, but sometimes his instincts as a man were in direct conflict with his instincts as a cop. "I said no." With that, Conor turned and walked to the companionway. "If you need me, I'll be up on the bridge."

Conor cursed softly as he climbed the ladder back to the pilothouse. Dylan and Brendan both turned as he stepped inside, watching him with perceptive eyes. There were no secrets between the Quinn brothers. "So, what's going on with you two?" Dylan asked.

Conor shrugged. "Nothing. She's just a witness."

Brendan chuckled. "Give me a break, Con. We see the way you look at her, the way you hover. When was the last time you ever treated a woman like that?"

"Never," Dylan answered. "He treats her as if she's made of gold. Did you see that, Bren? Like gold."

"It's part of the job," Conor said. "If I don't keep her happy, she doesn't testify. Or worse yet, she runs off and gets herself killed and I get my ass booted out of the department for dereliction of duty."

"He's fallen for her," Dylan commented. "But he's deluding himself. Lying in lavender like Paddy's pig, he is!"

Conor forced a chuckle. Dylan might be quick to jump to conclusions, but he was dead wrong. The last thing he'd allow himself to do was fall for Olivia Farrell. Sure, he might be attracted to her. What man wouldn't be? She was a beautiful woman. But that was where it ended. "You forget. I was raised on the same stories that you were. I know what happens if a Quinn falls in love. Hell, I might as well just throw myself off a cliff and save everyone the trouble."

His brothers stared out at the horizon, remembering the tales of their childhood as clearly as Conor did. "I'm amazed we're not all psychologically scarred," Dylan muttered.

Brendan sighed. "Maybe we are. I don't see any of us in

real relationships. Something permanent. Something that lasts longer than a month. Six decent-looking guys, good jobs, straight teeth. What are the odds?"

In truth, Conor had wondered the very same thing. He couldn't deny that their father's attitude had something to do with his own approach to women. He remembered all the stories. He also remembered his mother and the pain he'd felt when she'd left.

Olivia Farrell could make him feel that pain again. She had that power. But he'd never let it happen. He wasn't going to fall for her, because as soon as they got to shore, he was going to call the station and get himself reassigned. Olivia Farrell wouldn't have the chance to bring this Quinn down.

OLIVIA WASN'T SURE where she was when she opened her eyes. She only knew that she was warm and that she'd slept soundly for the first time in days. Tugging the rough wool blanket up around her nose, she sighed softly. She didn't know where she was, but she somehow sensed that she was safe.

"Mornin'."

Startled by the sound of an unfamiliar voice, Olivia bolted upright. But the unfamiliar voice came with a familiar face. A strikingly handsome man, with the same dark hair and hazel eyes as Conor, sat at the small table in the galley, a newspaper spread in front of him. Her brow furrowed as she tried to recall his name.

"Brendan," he said, as if he could read her mind.

"Brendan," she repeated. Raking her hands through her tangled hair, she glanced around the cabin. "Where are we?"

"Hull," he said. "We put in about four or five hours ago."

She glanced at the brass clock above Brendan's head. It was nearly two in the afternoon. "Where's Conor?"

"He went out to find you a safe place to stay."

"And the other one, your brother?"

"Dylan? He went to pick up some groceries."

Olivia sighed. "And you were the one who drew the short straw and got to baby-sit me?" she asked, a hint of sarcasm creeping into her voice.

"As my da used to say, a wise head keeps a shut mouth." Brendan chuckled softly. "Or something to that effect."

Though the pressures of the past few days had dulled her instincts, Olivia could have sworn Brendan Quinn had just paid her a compliment. "At least someone wants to spend time with me. Your brother acts like he's been forced to take his pimply-faced cousin to the prom."

Brendan slid out from behind the table and rummaged through the galley until he found a coffee mug. "My brother takes his responsibilities seriously. Sometimes too seriously."

The offhand comment piqued Olivia's curiosity. She knew so little about the man who'd taken control of her life. Perhaps she could learn something from Brendan that might even the odds a bit. When Brendan handed her a mug of steaming coffee, she sat up, tucked her feet beneath her, and rearranged the blanket on her lap. "Tell me about him," she said. "Why is he always so grumpy?"

"Would you like some breakfast?" Brendan countered, avoiding her question altogether. "I can whip up some eggs and I think I have some bacon that hasn't gone bad. Dylan's bringing orange juice and when Conor gets here we can send him out for—"

"Conor is here."

Brendan and Olivia glanced up at the companionway to find Conor looming above them. He swung down the steps and stood in the middle of the cabin. Compared to Brendan's cheerful disposition, Conor seemed to suck every ounce of sunshine out of the room. Olivia raised her guard, ready to defend herself against Conor's bristling mood. "Brendan was just going to make us some breakfast," she said.

"I'm sure he was," Conor muttered, sending his brother a pointed look. "When it comes to the ladies, it's what he does best."

"Hey," Brendan protested, "I was just being—"

Conor held up his hand to interrupt Brendan, then turned to Olivia. "Come on. We have to go. I found a place for us to hole up for a while. Get your things and let's go."

"Things? I don't have any things."

Conor crossed the cabin in a few short steps then grabbed her arm and tugged her to her feet. "Good. Then we won't have to wait around while you put on your lipstick and curl your hair."

Brendan cursed beneath his breath. "You are a charmer, now, aren't you, Con. It's no wonder you have women fightin' over you."

This time the look Conor shot his brother was pure murder. Olivia decided it was probably best to go along with the plan, before the brothers came to blows over her need for breakfast. She smoothed her hair, then stepped up to Brendan, giving him a grateful smile. "Thank you for your hospitality, and for helping to rescue me."

Conor's brother returned her smile with a devilish one of his own. Then he gently took her hand and drew it to his mouth, placing a kiss on the tips of her fingers. "The pleasure was all mine."

Conor growled impatiently, then snatched Olivia's fingers

from Brendan's hand. "Brendan is also known for his kiss-offs. He disguises his motives so cleverly that the women actually feel good about being dumped." With that, Conor pulled Olivia along to the companionway then hurried her up the steps.

When they reached the deck she turned on him, yanking her arm from his grasp. "You can stop bullying me now," she said. "There's no need to show off to your brother."

Conor fixed his gaze on hers, his eyes penetrating, his demeanor ice-cold. "Believe me, if I hadn't come back when I did, breakfast wasn't the only thing you two would have been sharing."

Olivia gasped at the outrageous suggestion in his tone. "Well, then I guess I'm lucky to have you to protect me." She started off down the dock, determined to put some distance between them before she hauled off and slapped that smug expression off Conor Quinn's face. But, a few seconds later, he fell into step beside her, alert, his gaze taking in their surroundings as if he were calculating the angle of the next attack, ready to put himself between her and a bullet.

As they walked along the wharf, past restaurants, taverns and bait shops, Olivia tried to maintain her indignation. But, in truth, all her whining seemed petty and childish. This man had devoted himself to keeping her alive and all she could do was complain.

Dylan was waiting for them, leaning up against the side of a red Mustang. He handed the keys to Conor, then opened the passenger door for Olivia. "If I find one dent, one scratch," he warned Conor, "I'll hunt you down."

When she and Conor were both inside, she turned to him, anxious to set things straight between them, but his jaw was set and his expression so distant that the words died in her throat. And by the time they reached the motel on the highway to Cohasset, she was afraid to say anything to him at all.

Conor helped her out of the car, then reached in his pocket and withdrew a room key. When he opened the door and stepped aside, Olivia got a chance to see how low her life had sunk. The room was straight out of a bad movie, with a lumpy iron bed shoved up against the wall and faded wallpaper in putrid shades of orange and avocado green. The linoleum floor was scarred with cigarette burns and the room smelled of stale smoke and mildew. She slowly walked to the bathroom, afraid of what she might find there. But the bathroom was surprisingly clean, the old fixtures had been scrubbed white and smelled of strong disinfectant.

"It's not a palace," Conor murmured. "But we'll be safe here for now. And if we need to make a run for it, Brendan's boat is just a few miles away."

Olivia turned to him and forced a smile. "I'm sorry," she said. "I don't mean to seem ungrateful."

He stared down at his shoes, then shrugged. "And I don't mean to be so dictatorial. It's just hard when you fight me on this. I know Red Keenan and he'll stop at nothing to keep you from testifying."

"I feel like my life has been taken away from me. All I have are the clothes I'm wearing. I'm worried—about my business, about my apartment, about Tommy."

She'd worried how her cat was surviving with her landlady. Usually Mrs. Callahan cared for the cat in Olivia's apartment, but Olivia had been afraid if anyone broke in, Tommy would make his escape and be left to fend for himself on the street. A notorious cat hater, Mrs. Callahan had reluctantly agreed to take the cat in trade for an addition to her huge collection of Hummel figurines. And though Olivia didn't usually deal in Hummel pieces, she quickly agreed.

"Tommy?"

"I left him with my landlady," Olivia explained. "She lives just down the street. I just didn't want him to get mixed up in this. And she's taken care of him before. I just wish he were here with me. I'd sleep better if I knew he was safe."

Conor stared at her for a long moment, his mouth agape. "You have a kid? And you didn't tell the police about this?" He turned away from her and began to pace the room.

Olivia opened her mouth to correct his assumption, then reconsidered the impulse. "Tommy is everything to me," she said, careful with her words so she wouldn't tell an outright lie. "I'm just so worried that Red Keenan might find out about him and…" She let her voice trail off. If she couldn't have her own clothes and she couldn't sleep in her own bed, she could at least have her cat!

"I have to go get him," Conor said. "He won't be safe if he isn't with us. How old is he?"

"Nine," Olivia replied.

"What about his father?" Conor asked. "Isn't he around?"

His direct gaze told her that his question was more than just a matter of police business. He wanted to know whether she shared a passionate relationship with another man. "He's out of the picture. He was kind of a…tomcat." A flood of guilt washed over her. She really should tell him the truth! But she'd been bullied and badgered enough over the past few days. It felt good to exert a small measure of control.

Conor reached into his jacket pocket and pulled out his car keys. "I'm going to go get him." He strode over to the phone and picked it up, then held it out to her. "I want you to call your landlady and tell her I'm on the way. One phone call and keep it short. Don't answer any questions, understand? What's her address?"

Olivia told him and he wrote it down in a little notebook he kept in his jacket pocket. "She'll be happy to see you," Olivia explained. "She'll be glad to have Tommy out of her hair."

He shook his head again, as if he couldn't quite get his mind around the notion that she was a mother. "Geez, Olivia, why didn't you say something?"

Olivia managed a contrite shrug and took the phone from his hands. To her surprise, he reached up and touched her cheek with his palm. Another wave of guilt consumed her. "Conor, you don't have to—"

He pressed a finger to her lips. "I'll be all right," he said. "I can sneak in and sneak out without anyone noticing. If Keenan's men are watching your flat, they'll never see me or Tommy. You'll stay on the boat with Brendan while I'm gone."

"But I thought I was safe here. And—well, I was looking forward to a hot shower. I promise I won't budge from this room."

He considered her request for a long moment, then agreed by giving her a brief but potent kiss. Olivia stared up at him and saw that the impulse had taken him by surprise. He cleared his throat and forced a smile. "I'm still going to ask Brendan to keep an eye on things outside."

Olivia winced. This had gone entirely too far! She had to tell him that Tommy was her cat, not her son. But she'd been on the receiving end of his anger enough for one day. She'd just have to take her chances when he returned. "Are you positive you'll be all right?"

He nodded, then turned for the door. When it closed behind him, Olivia's hand came to her mouth and she touched her lips. They were still warm and damp from his kiss. "If he gets shot, you'll never be able to forgive yourself."

But then Conor wouldn't get shot. He wouldn't allow it. He was brave and strong and clever. And when he returned he'd be seething with anger. But he wouldn't desert her, no matter what she did to deserve such a fate. For though she'd known him barely a day, she already knew that there was no one else she'd rather trust with her life than Conor Quinn.

4

CONOR CIRCLED the block once just to make sure the house wasn't being watched. He didn't expect any surveillance at the landlady's place, though it never hurt to be certain. But he wanted the chance to check out Olivia's flat as well. He noticed a nondescript sedan with tinted windows nearby and made a note to call Danny and have him check it out.

He parked Dylan's Mustang a block away, then kept to the shadows of the houses. He took one last look over his shoulder before he climbed the front steps and rang the bell. Like so many other homes on St. Botolph Street, the spacious red-brick townhouse, once inhabited by a single family, was now divided into several apartments.

The lace curtain over the window fluttered and then the door flew open. He found himself face-to-face with an elderly woman, her gray hair askew and her faded housedress wrinkled. "It's about time," she muttered.

"Are you Mrs. Callahan?"

The woman nodded, her thin lips pursed.

"I'm here to pick up Tommy," Conor said.

She motioned him inside, then slammed the front door behind him. They were both crammed into a tiny little foyer and he pressed himself back against the wall as she moved around him, her ample body brushing up against his. "I'm damn glad to be rid of him," she said. "He's nothin' but trouble. Stays up all night long, sleeps all day, never stops eating. And the noise is about driving me to drink."

Olivia must have been in a desperate state to leave her son with such a harridan, Conor mused. He was glad that he'd be responsible for reuniting mother and son. And though protecting the two of them would be more work, at least there'd be a buffer between them, a reason to keep from touching her at every whim. "Where is he?" he asked, holding his arms up above his head to avoid touching the woman.

"He's on the bed in my bedroom."

"I'd appreciate it if you'd gather his things. I don't have much time."

Mrs. Callahan muttered a curse. "I should make you get him. He's got a wicked temper, that one. He'll scratch your eyes out." She sniffed disdainfully, gave Conor the once-over, then opened the inside door. "Wait here," she ordered.

As Conor waited, he peered out the lace curtains onto the street, puzzling over her words. He'd rather not give the neighbors anything to talk about, he mused. If he could get the kid to his car without being seen, then all the better.

A few moments later, he heard shouting from inside the

house, then an ungodly howl that sounded more like an animal than a human being. He reached for the doorknob, but the door swung open in front of him. Mrs. Callahan shoved a cardboard box into his arms. "Good riddance," she said and moved to shut the door in his face.

Conor jammed his foot against the bottom of the door. "Wait a second. Where's Tommy?"

"He's in the box," the landlady said.

"In the box?" Conor carefully set the box on the hardwood floor, then peered beneath one of the flaps. A low growl emanated from the interior, and before he could pull his hand away, a paw snaked out and scratched him. Conor gasped, shaking his hand with the pain. "Tommy is a cat?"

"Yeah," Mrs. Callahan said. "What'd you think he was, one of them fancy French poodles?"

Conor didn't care to illuminate the old lady on his expectations. Right now he was having enough trouble keeping his temper in check. Of all the scheming, low-down, ridiculous— He ground his teeth, reserving his anger for the confrontation he planned to have with Olivia Farrell. "Does he have things? I mean, cat toys, food, stuff like that?"

"It's all in the box." She nodded, then smiled disdainfully. "Just don't touch his tail or you'll be scraping pieces of your hand off the ceiling." With that, she shut the door, leaving Conor cramped inside the little foyer with just a thin layer of cardboard separating his manhood from a spitting and hissing hellcat. He turned and opened the door, then hefted the box up into his arms. "You're going to pay for this, Olivia Farrell," he muttered.

As he walked down the sidewalk with Tommy the cat, the animal made a valiant attempt at escape. Though Conor was tempted to open the top of the box himself, after all the trouble he'd gone through to get the cat, he sure as hell wasn't going to let him go. After all, the cat was evidence. He was proof that Olivia Farrell had deliberately lied to him, had sent him on a fool's errand, and had put his life in danger in the process.

One of Keenan's men could have recognized him and taken a shot. Or he could be followed back to the motel where Keenan would take care of Olivia as well. Conor checked the street again as he put the box on the passenger seat of the Mustang. Then he jogged around to the other side of the car and hopped in.

He continued to watch his rearview mirror for signs of a tail and made a series of illogical turns through the South End neighborhood until he was certain he wasn't being followed. Then he headed for the interstate, his mind carefully reviewing the conversation he was about to have with Olivia.

Though he wanted to rail at her, to scold her until he extracted both a confession and an apology, Conor was secretly relieved. She didn't have a child. And without a child, there'd be nothing standing between them. He hadn't been sure what to think when she first mentioned Tommy, only that he felt an unbidden flicker of envy that her heart might belong to someone else.

Why feel envy, though? He'd tried to convince himself that his feelings for her were purely professional. After all, protecting people was what he did best. From the time he was a kid, he'd taken more than his share of responsibility. Still, he couldn't ignore the attraction between them, the sudden impulses to touch her and kiss her.

Hell, he'd heard about cops falling for the women they

were assigned to protect and he'd always thought a guy had to be crazy to risk his career for a woman. But now he knew how it happened. She was just so frightened and needy, and his immediate instinct was to protect and to soothe. And sometimes nothing showed concern better than a kiss or a gentle caress.

Conor drew a sharp breath. He knew the rules, and the penalties for getting involved with a witness. If anyone found out, it could be the end of his career. He'd be back to walking a beat or, worse, be off the force altogether. And all for the pleasures of a woman! His father's warnings rang in his mind. The only thing that could bring down a Mighty Quinn was a woman. "So just keep your damn distance," he muttered.

As he drove south toward Quincy, he couldn't help but wonder if Olivia Farrell was worth the risk. The surge of desire he felt when he touched her, or the warm sensation of her lips on his, always seemed to thwart his common sense. Maybe it was because she was different from the girls he usually dated, girls he met in his father's pub, girls determined to tame a Quinn. Olivia was sophisticated and refined, elegant, the kind of woman who seemed…unattainable.

There'd been only one other woman in his life that had eluded his grasp. He'd been devastated when his mother had walked out, yet he still held her up as a paragon of womanhood. She was a lot like Olivia—beautiful, delicate, poised. Even though they'd been poor, she'd always set a proper table and taken special pains with her appearance and made sure her sons combed their hair before leaving the house.

As he had watched his parents' marriage fall apart before his eyes, Conor wondered why Fiona McClain had married Seamus Quinn in the first place. They were like caviar and sardines, from the same place yet worlds apart. His mind drifted back to memories of happier times. But laced within those images were thoughts of Olivia. This time, he didn't brush them aside. Instead, like the rain pelting against the windshield, he let them wash over him. From now on that would be all he'd allow himself when it came to Olivia—an occasional impure thought.

By the time he pulled off the highway near Quincy, all the anger and resentment had faded. He stopped at a red light just a few miles from the motel, his mind focusing on Olivia. But the soft swish of the wipers was interrupted by a sudden flurry of noise. Conor glanced in the rearview mirror in time to see a shadow pass behind him. His first instinct was to duck, waiting for the sound of gunfire. But then he realized the ruckus wasn't coming from outside the car, but from inside!

He glanced over at the box on the front seat. The top was open and it was empty. "Damn," he muttered. It was like a cyclone had been let loose. Fur swirled in the air as Tommy raced around in circles, leaping over the front seat, bouncing off the back window, tearing across the dashboard, and whizzing past Conor's head. Conor tried to grab him, but the cat was too fast and his claws too sharp. He nicked Conor's chin and cheek on one lap around the interior and got him in the hand on another.

"All right!" Conor shouted. "I've had enough of this!" He yanked the steering wheel to the right and pulled over to the curb, ready to face the devil. Either he caught the cat and resumed control of the situation—or he turned the car keys over to Tommy. "I'm not handing the pink slip to this car over to a damn cat."

On Tommy's next pass, Conor gritted his teeth and grabbed

at the blurry ball of fur. He caught hold of a leg and wrestled the cat back into the box, but not before suffering another round of injuries. "I should have just opened the window," he muttered as he threw the car back into gear, keeping an eye on the box.

By the time he pulled into the parking lot of the Happy Patriot Motor Lodge, he was bleeding from most of his wounds. But his pride had suffered the most. Hell, he'd brought down career criminals, ruthless men who wouldn't think twice before putting a bullet through his heart, and had come away without a scratch. It was embarrassing to be bested by a cat.

Conor grabbed the box from the front seat, then stalked toward the door. "She'd better be grateful," he muttered. "She'd better be damn grateful." He'd be satisfied with nothing less than a kiss—a long kiss, deep and wet. Brendan appeared out of the shadows and gave him a wave.

"Where's the kid?" he asked. He squinted in the low light. "And what happened to you?"

"There was no kid." Conor reached up to his cheek and came away with blood.

Brendan's eyes went wide. "You mean they got to him?"

Conor smiled and shook his head. "Tommy is a cat." He held out the box. "Take a peek. He's a fine little beast."

Brendan stuck a finger under the cardboard flap and was rewarded with a nasty howl and a vicious scratch. "Geez, what'd you do to the poor thing?"

"What did I do to him? Look what he did to me!"

With a slow chuckle, Brendan patted Conor on the back. "First a beautiful woman and then a cat. I knew when you finally fell, Con, you'd fall hard. Good luck to you. I expect you'll need it."

Conor stood in the rain for a long moment as he watched Brendan stride off into the darkness. Then he drew a deep breath and fished the room key out of his pocket. "Hold your temper, boyo," he muttered. "And watch your tongue. You have another ten days with this woman and you'd best make it easy on yourself."

When he entered the room, he found it empty. Fear stabbed at his gut, sapping the breath from his lungs. He tossed the box on the bed, ignoring the protests from inside. Had Keenan somehow gotten past Brendan? Or had Olivia slipped out without being noticed? He checked the window, but then heard the sound of the shower running.

With a soft oath, Conor crossed to the bathroom door and pressed his ear against the scarred paint. At first, he was tempted to open the door and make sure she was all right. But then he heard Olivia singing and he decided to bide his time until she emerged on her own.

He sat down on the bed next to the box to wait. Inside the cardboard cage he heard a low growl and then silence. Conor patted the top of the box. "Let's you and me get something straight," he murmured. "I'm the one in charge here. Either you listen to me or you'll be eating fish guts out of a Dumpster down by the waterfront." He paused. "Are we clear?" He turned and looked through a small seam in the cardboard. An orange nose appeared and he was tempted to give it a poke. But he'd learned to be wary of both Tommy the cat and his mistress.

A few minutes later, Olivia emerged from the bathroom, a towel draped over her head, covering her eyes. Another towel was wrapped around her slender body and tucked between her breasts. Conor held his breath, not sure what to do. Propriety would dictate that he announce his presence, before she accidentally tossed aside both towels. Or maybe he should just make a quick exit and come in all over again. Or he could just turn and face the wall and—

The time to make a decision passed as soon as she wrapped the second towel around her damp hair and threw her head back. When she saw him sitting on the end of the bed, her eyes went wide. He waited, wondering just how offended she'd be. After all, she was naked under the towel and their relationship didn't really stretch that far—at least not yet. He slowly stood, his gaze never wavering from hers.

But instead of the expected indignation, relief suffused her flushed face. She let out a tiny scream, then launched herself at him, wrapping her arms around his neck and hugging him fiercely. At first, Conor wasn't sure what to do. And then he did the only thing he could think of doing. He wrapped his arms around Olivia Farrell's waist and he kissed her.

[TIME BREAK—space or asterisks?]

SHE'D BEEN SO overcome by her relief, Olivia didn't bother to consider the consequences of kissing Conor Quinn. Throwing herself into his arms seemed like the most natural thing in the world. He was alive, he'd come back safe, and any guilt she had over sending him after her cat could now be forgotten.

Olivia wasn't sure who ended the kiss, although neither one of them seemed very anxious to pull away. But when she finally looked up into his eyes, she found them clouded with desire. Her gaze flitted over his handsome face and she noticed a trickle of blood on his cheek.

"You're wounded," she said, reaching up to touch him.

Conor grabbed her hand and gently drew it away. "It's nothing." He bent closer, as if to kiss her again, but Olivia wriggled out of his arms, her concern for his injuries taking precedence over her desire to feel his mouth on hers.

"Sit," she said, pushing him down on the edge of the bed. Olivia hurried to the bathroom and returned with a damp washcloth. She knelt on the bed next to him and examined his injuries. This served her right! She'd sent him off to retrieve her cat and he'd been grazed by a bullet. He could have been killed and all just to satisfy a silly whim, to give her a sense of control in this game they were playing. "I'm so sorry," she murmured. "I was selfish. I knew you thought Tommy was a child. Since you left, I've been feeling so guilty. I never meant for this to happen. Was it Keenan?"

"Not exactly," Conor said, his gazed fixed on her mouth as she tended to his wounds.

"Then one of his men?"

"No," Conor replied. "It was…your cat."

Olivia sat back on her heels. "Tommy did this to you?"

"Yes. And if you ever repeat that story, I'll fit you for a pair of cement overshoes and toss you in the Boston harbor myself."

Her eyes went wide then she saw the teasing glint in his eyes. "Do you forgive me?"

Conor shrugged. "You should have told me Tommy was your cat. I could have been better prepared. As it was, he tore up the leather upholstery in Dylan's '68 Mustang. I think he might have barfed on the floor. And I breathed in so much fur I should be coughing up a furball in an hour or two." Conor gave her a reluctant smile, then took the washcloth from her hand. "If you plan to let that cat out of the box, you'd better keep him away from me."

With a giggle, she scrambled over the bed to the box and called a soft "kitty-kitty." A "meow" sounded from inside the box and Olivia pulled back the flaps. Like a shot, a huge orange tabby leapt out of the box and onto the bed. She scooped him up in her arms and pressed her face into his fur, surprised at how happy she was to see him. "Were you a bad boy for Uncle Conor?" she cooed.

"I should charge him with assault on a police officer," he muttered.

Olivia set the cat down, then gave him a long scratch on the tummy before she turned back to Conor. A shiver skittered down her spine as she caught him staring. She didn't have to worry about his anger anymore, but there was something much more dangerous pulsing between them. She grabbed the washcloth from his hand and then she rummaged through her purse and found a small bottle of astringent she kept in her makeup bag.

"I expected you to take my head off," Olivia said as she poured a bit of the astringent on the washcloth.

"Believe me, I considered it."

He winced as she dabbed the astringent on his cheek. Olivia leaned closer and blew on his cheek to cool the sting. "There," she murmured. "That's better."

Conor slowly turned to face her. Their gazes locked and, for a long moment, Olivia couldn't breathe. She was suddenly aware that she was dressed only in a towel…a very thin towel. And that towel could be dispensed with by a mere flick of Conor's finger between her breasts. Another shiver skittered over her skin, raising goose bumps, and her eyes fell to his lips, hard and chiseled.

Her gaze was like a silent invitation and he accepted. He bent forward and touched his lips to hers. But this was the first time he'd kissed her merely to kiss her. Until now, their ac tions had been driven by impulse. This kiss was slow and measured and deliberate and Conor took his time with her, tasting and teasing until she tentatively opened for him.

As her lips parted, any attempt at resistance dissolved. Olivia knew it wasn't right, at least not by the policeman's handbook or her own set of relationship rules. He was a cop and she was a witness. They'd only known each other a few days. And although the kiss wouldn't cost her any more than breathless desire, it could cost Conor Quinn his job.

But she couldn't think of that now. Conor slowly pushed her back onto the bed, his mouth drifting down to the curve of her neck and tracing a warm path to her shoulder. Olivia closed her eyes and sighed, the sensations his mouth created sending tingles to her fingertips and toes.

It had been so long since a man had touched her that she couldn't bear to put an end to it. Nor could she deny the attraction she felt for Conor. Maybe it was a typical reaction, the vulnerable witness and the protective cop. It was almost a cliché, but then clichés always had a basis in reality—and her need was definitely real.

Conor was unlike any man she'd ever known and, in a secret corner of her soul, she wanted to know him more intimately. He was brave and volatile, funny and vulnerable, silent and strong, all qualities that had become pieces of a fascinating puzzle. What made this man tick? What piqued his desire? What was beneath that steely exterior? A man with such passion for his job must have other passions as intense. They'd spend the next ten days together and Olivia knew it would be impossible to deny her curiosity—or her desire.

"Why are you so soft?" he murmured, his lips pressed against her collarbone.

She furrowed her fingers through his hair as he moved to a spot just above her breast. "Why are you so tough?"

He glanced up at her and she saw it in his eyes, as if the sound of her voice had triggered a realization of what they were about to do. His jaw tightened and then he cursed softly and rolled off of her. Levering up, Conor swung his legs off the side of the bed. "You should probably get dressed," he muttered.

The regret was thick in his voice. But was it for what they'd already done or for what they couldn't do? Olivia readjusted the towel then sat up beside him, trying to maintain her composure. The towel suddenly seemed too small and too thin. "I guess we probably shouldn't do that again," she said, forcing a smile.

Conor shook his head. "It wouldn't be recommended. It's against almost every department rule."

"And if there weren't any rules?" she asked.

"I'm a cop and I deal with facts, not hypotheticals," he replied, the hard edge returning to his voice. He rose and then rubbed his hands together. "Why don't I go find us something to eat. You can finish…whatever it is you have to finish."

Olivia nodded, then hurried to the bathroom, anxious to escape his dark mood. She closed the door behind her, then leaned back against it. Her pulse still hadn't slowed and, though she wore only damp terry cloth, a flush had warmed her skin until it prickled with embarrassment. She turned and stared into the mirror, then sighed.

What stroke of luck—or misfortune—was responsible for all this? Why had she chosen to go into business with Kevin Ford? And why had she walked into the office at that very moment that her partner was meeting with Red Keenan? And why did the detective assigned to protect her have to be Conor Quinn?

"You used to be a lucky girl," Olivia said to her reflection. "Now you're plagued with misfortune."

She tossed aside the towel and gathered her clothes from the floor. But she was loathe to put them back on again. She'd been wearing the same clothes since they'd run out of the cottage on Cape Cod, a pair of jeans, a sweater, a camisole and silk panties. "I don't even have a change of underwear."

Olivia pulled on the jeans without underwear, then slipped into the camisole and the sweater. After the Tommy incident, she wasn't sure how much credibility she had with Conor. A sob story about clean underwear probably wouldn't go over very well.

She combed her damp hair and considered the best tactic to use, then remembered Tommy. He'd need food and litter and a litter box, maybe a few cat toys. A visit to the nearest discount store would take care of that, along with fresh clothes, underwear and a whole list of luxury items for her, like toothpaste and hand lotion and deodorant.

Olivia slowly opened the bathroom door, but the sound of Conor's voice stopped her. At first she thought he might be talking to Tommy. Then she wondered if one of his brothers had stopped by. But as she continued to listen, she realized he was on the phone with his station house.

"She's fine," he said. "What the hell happened to the officer at the cottage on the Cape? He was supposed to be watching the road and then he was gone." Conor paused. "He went for coffee and donuts? Listen, I want Carlyle or Sampson assigned to this case. In fact, send both of them. And don't go through regular channels; I still think Keenan might have someone inside the department." He paused again. "I can't. No, it won't work. It's…difficult. She's developed feelings for me. Yeah. You know how that goes. I just can't deal with her. All right. A half hour. Good."

Olivia slowly closed the door then sat down on the edge of the tub. He was leaving her to someone else? Just like that? She bit her bottom lip as a tremor of apprehension rocked her body. She trusted Conor. He was the only one who could protect her from Red Keenan. And she didn't want him to leave!

She fought the urge to walk out of the bathroom and tell him exactly what she thought of him! But then his words ran through her mind.

She's developed feelings...won't work...can't deal with her.

"He can't deal with me?" Olivia groaned softly. She'd thought that everything that happened between them had come from a mutual desire. Had she misread him? Was he only tolerating her until he could pass her off to one of his colleagues? Oh, God, how humiliating. She glanced around the bathroom, her gaze falling on a small window above the shower.

"I've got to get out of here," she murmured. "I just can't face him." But the window looked too small to crawl through. Maybe if she just locked herself in the bathroom until the other cops came, then she wouldn't have to talk to him again. But she didn't want to wait. All she could think about right now was escape!

CONOR STARED at the bathroom door, then glanced at his watch. She'd been in there for over fifteen minutes, long enough for him to run across the road to the convenience store and grab them a couple of sandwiches and a bag of cat litter. How long did it take to get dressed and fix her hair? Had he grown up with women in the house, he'd probably know the answer to that question. All he really knew now was that fifteen minutes should be enough.

He stood and crossed the room to the bathroom, then rapped his knuckles on the door. "Olivia? What's going on in there? Are you almost finished? I've got us something to eat." He listened carefully, but there were no sounds coming from inside the bathroom. Conor tried the door and found it locked. "Olivia, open the door." He knocked again, an uneasy feeling growing in his gut. "Damn it, Olivia, open the door or I'll break it down."

The threat was met with no reply. Conor cursed softly, then stepped away from the door. "If you're in there, you'd better step back." One swift kick right below the knob was all it took to splinter the cheap wood and to send the door crashing open. He hurried inside, expecting to find Olivia cowering in the bathtub. But instead he found a long pair of legs and a shapely backside hanging from a small window above the tub.

"What the hell are you doing?" he asked. "You can't get out that window—it's too small." He grabbed for her feet to pull her back inside, but she kicked at him, the heel of her shoe catching him in the nose.

"Leave me alone," she shouted, her voice muffled from the other side of the window.

Conor rubbed his nose. He'd had his share of bumps and bruises on the job, but this case was killing him! "You'll never get through there," he said. "You're stuck."

"Don't you think I know that?" she called.

"Then just keep still and I'll pull you out." This time he grabbed her legs firmly enough so he wouldn't get kicked again. "Raise your arms over your head." She did as she was told, and with one good pull, she fell back into the bathroom—and into his arms.

They both tumbled to the floor in a tangle of limbs. Then she scrambled away from him, brushing her hair out of her eyes and tugging her sweater down from where it had bunched beneath her breasts. Conor sighed and leaned back against the wall. "What were you thinking?"

"Obviously, I was thinking I was a lot smaller than I really was," she shot back. "Remind me to lay off the French fries."

"Where did you plan to go?"

"Shopping," she muttered.

"Shopping?"

"Yes! If you must know, I needed some clean underwear. We ran out of that cottage on Cape Cod so fast that I didn't have time to grab my things. I've been wearing the same underwear for two days."

"Someone is out to kill you and you're worried about clean underwear?" he asked.

Olivia nodded, refusing to meet his gaze, her jaw set stubbornly, her arms crossed beneath her breasts.

Conor groaned inwardly. This was just another thing he didn't understand about women. This obsession with underwear. All the lace and the silk and the pretty colors. Underwear was underwear. No one saw it so what was the big deal? "Why didn't you just ask?"

"Because you don't care what I want or what I need."

"I don't care? Who risked life and limb to get your damn cat?"

She turned to face him, a defiant glint in her eyes. "If you really cared, then why are you leaving me? Why did you call for another cop to come and stay with me?"

Conor paused. So she'd overheard his phone conversation, and she'd obviously overheard the lies he'd told. Suddenly her reasons for climbing out the window became much clearer.

He'd hurt her feelings, embarrassed her so completely that she couldn't stand to be in the same room with him. "I'm sorry. It's just that—"

"I know. I make it difficult for you. You can't deal with me. You made it sound like I was throwing myself at you. I thought the attraction was mutual."

He raked his hand through his hair, then slowly shook his head. "It was," he murmured. "It is. That's why I have to leave."

She turned, kneeling on the floor beside him, her expression anxious. "But what if I promise not to kiss you anymore? Would you stay then?"

"It's not you, Olivia," Conor said, reaching out to touch her cheek with his fingertips. "It's me. I can't promise that I won't kiss you again—or touch you. And if I can't promise that, then I'm not a very good choice to guard you. I need to be able to keep my head on the job or we're both at risk."

"But I trust you," Olivia said. "I don't want anyone else."

"The two guys they're sending are good guys. I know them both and I wouldn't let them stay with you if I wasn't sure they'd keep you safe. But I want you to promise me that you won't go climbing out of any windows or sending them after any more pets."

Olivia's gaze dropped to her lap. She studied her fingers for a long moment, then drew a ragged breath. "I don't want you to go," she repeated.

Conor hooked his finger beneath her chin and forced her eyes to meet his. The vulnerability had returned to her eyes and he fought the urge to kiss her again, to replace her sadness with passion. "Promise me?"

Reluctantly, she nodded. But Conor couldn't leave it at

that. He gave in to the impulse and leaned toward her to brush a soft kiss on her lips. One last kiss. What could it hurt? he mused. But if he thought it would be enough, he was sorely mistaken. The moment her lips opened beneath his, he was lost in the warmth of her mouth. A low groan rumbled in his throat as he pulled her into his arms.

The taste of her was like a drug, so addictive that he'd risk it all to experience it just once more. Women had always been a "take it or leave it" kind of thing for him. He'd never felt the kind of obsessive attraction he had for Olivia, when every thought was consumed with the question of when he might kiss her next and how far that kiss might go. His brain clouded with the fresh scent of her hair and the warm sensations of her tongue teasing his.

It took all his willpower to draw away. He stared down into her beautiful face and watched her eyes flutter open. "I want you to know that I lied on the phone. Kissing you isn't difficult. It's not kissing you that's hard."

A tremulous smile curved her lips. But her smile faded instantly as a knock sounded on the door of their room. She sent Conor a desperate look and he responded with a smile. "You'll be all right. I promise."

Conor stood, then reached out and helped Olivia to her feet. He moved to the door, Olivia's hand still tucked in his. He wanted to hang on to her for as long as he could. Later tonight when he was alone in his apartment, staring at the ceiling above his bed, he'd want to remember how delicate her fingers felt and how sweet her voice sounded. He'd want to remember every second he had spent with her.

He carefully pulled back the curtain and saw Don Carlyle standing outside. Then he led Olivia to the bed where Tommy had curled up on one of the pillows. "Wait here," he said. "I'll just be a minute." Reluctantly, she let go of his hand and watched him walk to the door.

Conor stepped outside and closed the door behind him. He nodded a greeting to Carlyle. "What's the plan?"

"We've got a place for her over in Framingham. Sampson is waiting in the car." Carlyle cocked his head toward the door. "So what's her problem? She have a thing for cops or is she just one of those women who's happy with anything that wears pants?"

The anger was so instant and so intense that Conor didn't think before he acted. In one swift movement, he brought his arm up and shoved Carlyle against the door, keeping him pinned there. Conor moved to within an inch of Carlyle's face, then spoke in a low, even tone. "You make one move toward her, even look at her sideways, and I'll reach down your throat and turn you inside out. Got it?"

Carlyle frowned. "Yeah. I got it. Geez, Quinn, what the hell is wrong with you? You're the one who wanted out."

"Just remember what I said." Conor stepped back and Carlyle rubbed his chest. "She's a lady. Treat her like one."

Conor reached out and opened the door and Carlyle followed him inside. Olivia was in the same spot that he'd left her, perched on the edge of the bed, looking sad and vulnerable, hugging Tommy tightly to her chest. He crossed the room and gently took her arm. "Detective Carlyle is going to take you somewhere safe. If you need anything—" Conor smiled and leaned closer "—including underwear, you just ask. All right?"

He grabbed her coat from the bed, then held it out as she slipped into it. Then she gave Tommy a kiss and dropped him in the cardboard box. Carlyle looked at the box, then at Conor. "A cat? We can't take a cat."

Olivia's eyes went wide. "But I—"

"I'll take him," Conor said. "He can stay with me and you can pick him up after the trial." Though he hated the cat, he knew returning Tommy to his owner would give him one more chance to see Olivia, after all this was over and she was no longer a witness and he was no longer the cop assigned to protect her. A few weeks with Tommy the Terror was a small price to pay.

"You'd do that for me?" she asked.

Conor reached down and picked up the box. "Sure. By the time you come for him, we'll be old friends."

Olivia pushed up on her toes and gave him a quick kiss on the cheek. "Thank you," she murmured. Then she grabbed her purse and walked to the door. Conor followed her, taking one last look around before stepping outside behind her and Carlyle, the box tucked under his arm.

The next thing he knew, the wood from the door splintered next to his head. He looked out into the parking lot and saw another muzzle flash and the plate-glass window of the motel room shattered. Holding tight to the box, he shoved Olivia aside, both of them falling onto the walkway in front of Dylan's Mustang. "Stay here," he said, shoving the box into her arms. "And keep your head down."

Conor pulled his gun and peered around the side of the car. Carlyle was crouched beneath a rusted Pontiac, returning fire. From another spot in the parking lot, Sampson had pulled his gun and was taking aim. Conor crawled back to Olivia, then grabbed the box. "We're going to get in the car," he said. "Take the cat out of the box and hold on to him. Tuck him inside your jacket. We've got to do this quickly. Just stay low."

Olivia did as she was told and they both crawled around to the passenger side. He opened the door and she got in, then Conor scrambled around the front of the car. But the driver's side was in the line of fire and he knew he'd be taking a chance. Drawing a deep breath, he checked the clip in his gun, then shouted to Carlyle for cover fire.

He'd almost made it into the car when he felt a searing heat in his side, like someone had shoved a red hot poker between his ribs. The pain took his breath away and brought a wave of nausea.

Don't lose it now, his brain screamed. *Just get her out of here.*

Wincing with the pain, he yanked his door shut and shoved the key in the ignition. The engine roared to life and he threw it into reverse and backed out, pushing Olivia down in the seat with his right arm. Thankfully, Carlyle and Sampson kept Keenan's men pinned down. They managed to target the tires of the black sedan parked near the entrance to the parking lot so there would be no way for the gunmen to give chase.

When they were well out of range, Conor glanced over at Olivia. Her eyes were closed and her lips moved silently, as if she were praying. Tommy stared up at him with luminous eyes, content to stay clutched in Olivia's arms.

"We're good," he said.

Olivia gradually straightened in her seat, but didn't loosen her hold on her cat. "How did they find us?" she asked.

"Someone in the department," he replied. He turned and gave her an encouraging smile. "I guess we're on our own now." Another wave of nausea rolled over him and, for a moment, Conor had to fight to stay conscious. After nearly getting killed, the last thing he wanted was to run the car off the road. He pulled over onto the next side street and parked the car, then pressed his hand to his side. In the dim light from a streetlamp near the car, he saw the blood covering his fingers.

"I think you better drive," Conor murmured, suddenly exhausted by the effort that it took to move. He was going into shock and he wasn't sure how much longer he'd be able to keep his eyes open.

"Me? But why?"

"Just slide over," he ordered, pushing open the car door and stepping outside. It took every ounce of his effort to walk around the front of the car without keeling over. His legs felt like rubber and he was suddenly shivering for no reason. When he got back inside the car, he closed his eyes and focused on getting through a spasm of pain.

"Where are we going?" she asked.

"We need to get back to Hull," Conor replied, his voice tight. "To Brendan and *The Mighty Quinn*. Can you remember how to get there?"

Olivia nodded. "I think so. Are you all right? You look like you're going to be sick."

"I'm fine," he said through gritted teeth. "Just get us there." She reached for the ignition and Conor closed his eyes, confident that she'd get them back to the boat, back to safety. He felt himself growing tired and his eyes fluttered shut. But no matter how hard he tried to open them, the effort was too much. Blackness engulfed him and he finally lost his grip on consciousness.

5

OLIVIA BIT her bottom lip as she turned the ignition, sending up a silent prayer she wouldn't do anything stupid, like hit a parked car or run a red light. But when she reached for the gearshift between the seats, she realized prayers wouldn't do any good. A driving instructor might. "There's no *pernundul*," she murmured. No *P*, no *R*, no *N* or *D*. The car had a manual transmission and she'd never driven a stick shift before.

"I can't do this," she said. She glanced over at Conor. His head was tipped back and his eyes were closed. She knew he'd been working hard, but this was no time to take a nap! Olivia reached over and shook his arm. His hand fell between the seats, wet and sticky. She swallowed hard. Blood. "Conor? Conor, are you all right?"

Panic rose in her mouth like bile as Olivia shook him. He

opened his eyes halfway and at first didn't seem to recognize her. "Are we there?"

Olivia leaned over and frantically examined his arm, then pulled his leather jacket open and found the source of the blood. All along his left rib cage, his shirt was seeped through. She felt faint and took a moment to draw a deep breath. "Oh, no, oh, no." She reached for the gearshift and studied the little diagram on the knob, then pushed in the clutch. "Oh, no, no." She knew the basics of a standard transmission, but she'd have to learn the finer points on the fly. "Hang on," she said. "Just don't die on me. Don't you dare die. I'm going to get you to a hospital."

"No," he muttered. "No hospital. Just get to Brendan. He'll know what to do."

She jammed the car into first, the gears grinding, then slowly let out the clutch. The car jerked and shuddered, but to her relief it started forward. By the time she'd circled the block, she had managed to try three of the four gears without stalling the engine. Olivia glanced both ways before pulling out on the highway, afraid to stop for fear she wouldn't get started again.

As she drove, she tried to contain a tremor that shook her body. "Stay calm," she murmured, searching the road for signs pointing to a hospital or for a pay phone to call an ambulance. She didn't want to obey his orders! He'd been shot protecting her and now it was *her* responsibility to save *his* life. "I'm going to call an ambulance," she said. "Give me your cell phone."

His hand shot out and clutched her wrist. "No," Conor insisted. "Do as I say."

"But the boat is at least ten minutes away. You could die before then."

"I'm not going to die," he replied. "I promise." He reached up and stroked her hair, the movement causing him to groan with the pain. "I'm not going anywhere."

Olivia glanced over at him, overwhelmed with concern and torn by indecision. "All right," she said. "We'll go to the boat as long as you keep talking. If you pass out, I'm stopping to call an ambulance. Deal?"

"Deal," he murmured, his hand flopping back to his side.

She drew a ragged breath. "Fine. So what should we talk about? Let's talk about you. Tell me about your family. Tell me about Brendan and Dylan."

He moaned softly as he shifted in his seat. "Why do you want to know about them?"

"Just tell me," Olivia insisted. "Or tell me about your parents. Or your childhood in Ireland. Tell me where you were born. Just talk so I know you're still alive."

"I was born in a stone cottage that overlooked Bantry Bay," Conor began. "On the south coast in County Cork. My da was a fisherman. And my ma was…well, she was beautiful."

"When did you come to America?" Olivia asked, her mind jumping ahead, thinking of questions to keep him talking yet not really listening to the answers. She recognized the turn to Hull and said another quick prayer. They were only a few miles away. Now her only worry was finding the boat.

"She died," Conor continued.

Olivia glanced over at him. "What? Who died?"

"Or my da says she died. I don't think she did, because I would have known. But if she didn't die, then why didn't she come back?"

Olivia frowned. He was talking but he wasn't making much sense. "You don't know if your mother is alive or dead?"

"She went away when I was seven. One day she was there and then she was gone. Da wouldn't talk about it. Later, he told us she died in a car wreck. But he was angry and I think he said that because he wanted us to forget her." Conor sighed and for a long moment he was silent.

Olivia thought he'd lost consciousness, but when she looked over at him his eyes were still open. "I never forgot her. The others did, but I didn't. I can still see her." He tipped his head her way. "She was pretty…like you. Only she had dark hair and yours is like spun gold."

His compliment was so simple and plainspoken that Olivia felt tears push at the corners of her eyes, tears of concern and affection and frustration. She was frightened, and usually when she felt that way, Conor made her feel safe. The thought that he might not be there to keep her safe tomorrow caused an ache to grow in her heart.

She turned back to the road and forced herself to concentrate. To her relief, she found *The Mighty Quinn* on the first pass along the waterfront. She slammed on the brakes and the car skidded to a stop on the street. Reaching a hand out, she placed her palm on Conor's cheek. "We're here," she said. "Can you walk?"

He nodded and she hopped out and ran around to Conor's side. She pulled, then dragged him to his feet, urging him to put one foot in front of the other and walk with her. Conor draped his arm around her shoulders and she bore most of his weight. He was still lucid, moving and talking, and Olivia hoped that she'd done the right thing bringing him here.

"What the—"

Olivia looked up to see Brendan coming toward them from the boat. "Help him," she said. "I think he's been shot."

Brendan grabbed Conor's other arm and wrapped it around his neck and, in a few moments, they were helping Conor into the cabin and onto a long narrow berth.

"It hurts like hell," Conor murmured, "but I don't think it hit anything vital."

Olivia stepped away as Brendan tended to his brother, the impact of what had happened suddenly hitting her full force. Her hands began to tremble and her breath came in quick gasps. Tears scalded the corners of her eyes. Brendan tugged off Conor's jacket and she moaned along with him, feeling his pain.

"God, Con, there's an awful lot of blood." Brendan turned to Olivia and pointed to the far side of the galley. "There's a first aid kit on the bulkhead. Grab that and a few clean towels."

Olivia did as she was told. Brendan flipped the kit open and rummaged around until he found a small bottle of alcohol. "Shouldn't we call an ambulance?" she asked. He doused one of the towels with it then pressed it against Conor's side.

Her question was met by a loud string of colorful curses. Startled, Olivia stepped back. Brendan chuckled and glanced over his shoulder at her. "It's the sting from the alcohol." He turned back to Conor. "It looks like a flesh wound, not too deep, just a lot of blood. I've got a buddy here in town who's a doctor. I'm going to call him."

"It's a gunshot wound. He'll have to report it and they'll know where we are," Con said. "You stitch it up, like you stitched up Da's arm that time when he got caught in the line."

"Con, we were four hundred miles out to sea and I used an old needle and some fishing line. I'll explain to my friend that you're a cop. And he'll report it tomorrow morning. By that time we'll be gone." Brendan grabbed a cell phone from the table and dialed a number, then spoke in soft, urgent tones to his friend.

At the same time, Conor looked over at Olivia and gave her a weak smile. She walked over to the berth and knelt down on the floor, then took his hand. "I was so scared," she murmured. "I still am."

"We'll be fine," he said, pulling her hand to his lips. "You did good."

She sat on the floor next to him, holding his hand, until the doctor arrived. Then Brendan drew her out of the cabin up to the deck. Olivia was glad for the fresh air. She was weak and dizzy, and if she had to watch Conor's pain for a moment longer, she was sure she'd faint.

They stood at the rail and stared out at the dark harbor, listening to the clank of rigging and the soft lap of the water against the hull. "You've had quite a night," Brendan said.

"I thought I had a pretty exciting life before this," Olivia murmured. "I travelled, I went to fancy parties, I took nice vacations. That was nothing compared to spending time with your brother."

Brendan wrapped an arm around her shoulders. "Thanks," he said.

She glanced up at him. "For what?"

"For saving his life. For caring about him."

"That's not hard to do," she said, a tiny smile quirking her lips. "He's a good man. Maybe the best man I've ever known."

"But sometimes he makes it hard to like him. He keeps his distance, and when anyone gets too close, he retreats."

"He told me about your mother," she said.

Brendan blinked in surprise. "Conor talked about Ma?"

Olivia stretched her arms out over the rail and stared at her hands. "I don't think he realized what he was talking about. He was just talking to stay awake."

"I think that's the reason Conor keeps to himself," he said. "When she left, he was the one who took the brunt of it. He was a kid raising five other kids. I don't think he ever wants to be deserted like that again, so he closes himself off to the possibilities and turns his energy into making everyone feel safe." Brendan sighed. "He still thinks Ma is alive."

"Do you think she is?"

Brendan shrugged. "I don't know. When we were little, Con said he would go to find her when he was old enough. Maybe that's why he became a cop. Or maybe it was because he needed to take care of everyone else's troubles. He's kind of codependent that way. But I don't think he's ever looked for Ma."

"Why not?"

"I think he was afraid of what he might find. He was happier believing she was alive somewhere, alive and living a good life." Brendan pushed back from the rail. "I'll go see how things are going. Can I get you anything? Coffee, tea? A shot of whiskey?"

Olivia smiled and shook her head. When she was alone, she walked along the deck to the bow of the boat. The shadows from the quay cast the bow in darkness and she sank down, her strength finally giving out and her emotions taking over. A sob tore from her throat and she hugged her knees to her chest and let the tears fall.

They fell for the life that she once had, calm and orderly, and for all her hopes for the future. They fell for her anger at her business partner and at Red Keenan. But mostly, they fell for Conor, for the boy he was and the man he'd become. A man who'd risked his life for her, a man she was fast falling in love with. And a man who might never return that love.

"Olivia?"

She raised her head and quickly wiped away the tears, then stumbled to her feet. Brendan was waiting for her at the entrance to the main cabin. "He's going to be fine. The doctor stitched him up. The bullet just grazed him."

A fresh round of tears flooded her eyes and Brendan drew her into his arms. "Come on. It's all right now. The doc and I moved him into my cabin where he'll be more comfortable. And I brought your cat in from the car." He leaned back and gave her a smile. "Why don't you go see him. I have to hide the car before someone recognizes it. Then I'll run and get you both something to eat. Do you want anything special?"

"Little Friskies in the can," she said. "Tuna flavor. And some kitty litter. For Tommy."

Brendan chuckled. "I'll get you a burger." He nodded toward the cabin. "It's the companionway that leads to the bow of the boat."

Olivia wiped her cheeks again and ran her fingers through her hair, hoping that she looked at least presentable. Why she bothered to worry about her appearance, she wasn't sure. Conor had certainly seen her looking worse. But she wanted to be strong for him and looking like she was falling apart didn't cut it.

When she reached the forward cabin, she knocked on the door, then stepped inside. The soft glow from an oil lamp washed the cabin in flickering shadows. Conor lay on the bed, bare-chested, eyes closed, a bandage taped to his rib cage. His jeans had been cast aside and the waistband of his boxers was visible where the bedsheet was twisted around his waist.

Tommy was sitting silently on the end of the bed, keeping guard over the man that had saved them both. Olivia distractedly scratched the cat's ears as she stared at Conor, her gaze transfixed by the planes and angles of his face.

Awake, he always had a hard edge to him, his gaze intense and his jaw tight. But as he slept, she saw a side of him revealed rarely, only in a fleeting glimpse when he smiled. Olivia tiptoed over to the bed and knelt down beside him. His hair fell over his forehead, just touching the dark slashes of his eyebrows.

She looked closer, surprised that she'd never noticed how long and thick his lashes were. Beautiful, she mused. Not a word one would usually associate with a man like Conor Quinn. Desire welled up inside of her, unbidden but undeniable. She'd always been so careful with men, but with Conor all her resolve seemed to crumble with just one touch.

He was arrogant yet affectionate, dangerous yet vulnerable, contrasts that she found irresistibly intriguing. She'd never felt such an instant connection with a man before. With a hesitant hand, she reached out and tenderly brushed the hair out of his eyes. Her breath stilled and she bent over him and placed a gentle kiss on his lips.

Conor's eyelids fluttered and he awoke.

FOR A MOMENT, he thought he might be dreaming. The light from the oil lamp shimmered around her head, like a halo. And then his vision cleared and he found himself looking at an angel come to earth. Conor smiled sleepily. "Hi," he murmured.

Olivia leaned forward and gazed into his eyes. "How do you feel?"

"Like hell," he said. "But the doctor says I'll be fine. A little sore for a while. And I'm going to have to give up my Olympic dreams in the javelin and shotput."

She giggled and the sound brought a small measure of re- lief. Brendan had told him that Olivia had been close to tears when they'd arrived. It was nice to see her smile again. Just looking at her exquisite beauty was the best medicine he could have.

"Brendan went to get us something to eat. Are you hungry?"

He pushed up on his elbow, pain shooting through his side. "I'm starved," he muttered through clenched teeth.

"Here," Olivia said. "Let me help you." She placed her arm around his shoulders and helped him sit. His face nuzzled into her chest as she moved him and he groaned inwardly, trying hard to ignore visions of the warm flesh beneath her sweater. When she had stacked a few pillows behind his back, Conor closed his eyes and leaned back, trying to banish the heat that had shot to his groin. At least he knew the bullet hadn't in- jured that part of his anatomy.

"What are we going to do now?" Olivia asked, sitting down on the edge of the berth.

"Bren called my little brother Liam. They're going to help Brendan take the boat up to Salem. My brothers Sean and Brian will meet us there with another car. After that, we're going to get lost until the trial."

"Don't you think you should call your boss and tell him we're okay?"

"I'm not playing by the rules anymore. I did, and it almost got us both killed. If they thought I was a rogue cop before, they haven't seen anything yet."

"All right," Olivia said. "Whatever you think is best."

A soft knock sounded at the door and Olivia walked over

and opened it. Brendan stood outside with two paper bags. He handed them to Olivia. "I've got cat food. Why don't you send Tommy out and I'll feed him." He looked over to Conor. "Liam's here. We're going to be casting off in about a half hour."

Olivia set the bags on the bed, then picked up the cat and shooed him out the door. When she and Conor were alone again, she carefully opened the Styrofoam containers. "We have a hamburger…a hamburger… and—ah, something different—a cheeseburger."

"My brother has very basic tastes when it comes to food," Conor said.

Olivia plucked a French fry from the bag and held it out in front of Conor's mouth. He grabbed it with his teeth and quickly devoured it. It was the best French fry he'd ever eaten and Conor wondered whether that had less to do with the chef and more to do with his dinner companion.

After they finished, Olivia cleaned up the wrappers and the soda cans, then took them out to the galley. When she returned, she stood in the doorway of the forward cabin, her hands clutched in front of her. "I guess I should let you get some rest. I'll just find a spot for myself in—"

"No," Conor said. "Stay here. I'll sleep better knowing you're close by."

She gave the twin-size berth a long look and Conor could tell exactly what she was thinking. In order for both of them to sleep in it, they'd have to practically wrap their bodies around each other. "I'll stay until you fall asleep," she said, moving to sit on the edge of the berth.

He nodded, then closed his eyes. "Tell me a story," he said. "When we were kids, my brothers and I always had a story before bed."

"About what?"

"Fairies and gnomes and elves."

"Well, I know the story of Thumbelina," she said.

"Is that an Irish fairy?"

"No, I think it's just a fairy tale."

"I suppose that will have to do. Tell me, then."

Olivia drew a deep breath and began to speak. Though her story seemed to be an odd amalgam of several different Disney movies, Conor really didn't care. He just wanted to listen to her voice, to reassure himself that she was still safe. As she launched into a subplot that had something to do with a cricket, he reached out and took her hand between his, distractedly toying with her fingers.

His touch caused her to hesitate for a moment, as if the warmth from his fingers had swept the words from her head. But then the story continued, through his gentle exploration of the soft skin on the inside of her wrist and inner arm, past the point where he gently pulled her down next to him on the bed, and beyond the moment when he tucked her body against his. It was only then that he could finally close his eyes and sleep, when his arms were wrapped around her waist and the sweet curve of her backside was tucked in his lap.

Conor drifted in and out of sleep, the painkillers the doctor had given him causing fitful dreams. He remembered hearing the engines start and then the gentle motion of the boat as it cut through the water. Olivia slept soundly, her body soft and warm in his arms, her breathing slow and even. Now that they were on the water, he was certain he could keep her safe. And though he'd always hated *The Mighty Quinn,* he had to appreciate the old boat for taking them out of danger.

Salem was fifteen miles across Massachusetts Bay and a

busy harbor town. The boat could get in and out without much notice. Though Conor wanted to put his plans all together in his head, his brain was too fuzzy to concentrate for long. Instead, he nuzzled his face into the curve of Olivia's neck and closed his eyes again.

He wasn't sure how long he slept, but the next thing he remembered was the boat bumping up against the dock. Olivia rolled slightly with the motion and he grabbed her tight to keep her from falling off the berth. She stiffened in his arms and he knew she had awakened. When she turned onto her back and glanced up at him, it was with uncomprehending eyes.

"We're just tying up," he whispered, her face so close to his that he could feel her breath on his skin.

She didn't say anything, just stared into his eyes. And then Conor bent closer and touched his lips to hers. He really hadn't expected her to respond, but when she did, he deepened the kiss, lost in the enticing taste of her mouth.

Everything about her was too much to resist and he didn't want to make the effort anymore. He'd been alone for so long and, for the first time in his life, he'd found someone who could make him forget all of the barriers he'd built around his heart. She touched a spot, deep inside of him, that he hadn't even known existed. And when he kissed her, he didn't have to wonder whether his kiss was making promises he didn't want to keep. For now, Olivia was his and that was all that mattered.

Her pale hair fanned out on the pillow and Conor ran his fingers through it, liquid and silken to his touch. She moaned softly and wrapped her arms around his neck, then teased at his bottom lip with her tongue. He sensed that her need for him was as acute as his was for her. And though he could spend the entire night just kissing her, the urge to explore her perfect body was just as overwhelming.

Somewhere in the recesses of his mind, a little voice—his cop voice—told him that spending the night in the same bed broke all the rules. And making love to her could end his career. "Why do you taste so damn good?" he murmured. "I want to stop but I can't."

She sighed softly, her fingers skimming over his face. "There are rules," Olivia whispered, "against this…" Her tongue teased at his nipple. She trailed lower, nipping and biting, and driving him mad with need. "And against this…" she said, her fingers splaying across his belly, causing a flood of heat to rush to his lap.

He'd already decided that when it came to this case, the rules didn't apply anymore. Someone in the department had nearly gotten them both killed. The police were supposed to be the good guys. Those were the rules. If they couldn't follow them, then he wouldn't either. "From now on, we make up our own rules," he said. "And rule number one is that there will be no more rules."

A playful smile quirked the corners of her mouth. "I like that rule."

He laughed softly, then captured her mouth with his again. He'd never have guessed that behind her cool, sophisticated facade lurked an uninhibited temptress. Conor turned to pull her nearer, but the shift in his weight caused a sharp pain in his side, deep enough to steal his breath. He cursed softly. "This is not going to work," he said. "I can barely move."

"Then don't," Olivia said, straddling his hips and bracing her hands on either side of his head. "Rule number two. You must stay perfectly still."

Her hair created a curtain around them and she dropped a kiss on his mouth and then another and another, dancing away when he tried to take more. When she straightened, Conor reached out and slipped his fingers beneath the hem of her sweater. He spanned her slender waist with his hands and reveled in the beauty and delicacy of her body.

She was made for his hands, every curve a perfect fit against his palms. Though he'd never touched her this way before, it was as if he knew her by instinct. Yet that didn't stop him from wanting to explore and memorize every inch of her skin.

With other women, it had been all about him and his needs, the undeniable rush toward satisfaction. Maybe it was the way he and Olivia had begun, his focus on protecting her. Suddenly, he wanted to make her ache for him the way he ached for her. He needed to see the desire grow in her eyes and feel it in her hands, until nothing could stop them from the inevitable.

Conor slid his hands along her rib cage until he found the soft curves beneath her breasts. The silky fabric of her camisole beneath his palms enhanced every warm inch of her flesh. As if taking a cue from him, Olivia reached for the buttons of her sweater and slowly undid them. When she was finished, he reached up and skimmed the sweater off her shoulders and down along her arms.

He'd chided her for her underwear obsession at the motel, but now he understood. The lace edging of her camisole offered a tempting view of the cleft between her breasts and the silk clung to her body like a second skin, outlining the peaks of her nipples.

With her eyes fixed on his, her gaze challenging him to make her stop, Olivia reached for the hem of her camisole and pulled it up over her head, then shook her hair until it tumbled around her shoulders. Conor's breath caught in his throat. She was the most beautiful thing he'd ever seen, her skin luminous in the soft light. He knew at that moment that he wanted her, more than anything he'd ever wanted in his life. But he schooled his need and promised himself that he'd go slow.

His reached up and cupped a breast in his palm, teasing at her nipple with his thumb. What bit of luck had brought her into his life? What had he done to deserve her? Whatever it was, Conor wasn't about to question his good fortune. He'd simply enjoy it while it lasted. Never in a million years could he hope that Olivia would want a future with him.

But he did know one thing. He was fast falling in love with Olivia Farrell, with her beautiful eyes and her incredible body, with her stubbornness and with her vulnerability. With the way she made him shiver with anticipation. He slipped his hand beneath the hair at the nape of her neck and slowly drew her back to him, covering her mouth with his. The blood rushed hot through his veins and his pain was forgotten as he rolled her over beneath him.

His mouth ached to taste her, his fingers craved the feel of her skin. Slowly, Conor explored her body with both, gently arousing her desire then letting it ebb. He wanted this to last as long as it possibly could, for Conor wasn't sure they'd have this chance again. But the more he touched her, the more irresistible she became.

Conor wasn't sure at what moment they reached the point of no return. Perhaps it was when she stood beside the berth and slipped out of her jeans. Or maybe it was when he cast aside his boxers. But by the time she'd retrieved a condom from Brendan's bedside table and slipped it over his hard shaft, he was certain he was lost.

She straddled his hips, then slowly sank down, taking all of him, to the hilt. For a long moment, Olivia didn't move, her eyes closed, her head tipped back. Conor's jaw went tight as the sight of her alone almost brought him to his peak and he realized that he'd relinquished all control. She was the seducer and he was the seduced.

As if caught in a dream, Olivia started to move above him, rocking slowly at first and then increasing her rhythm. It took all his willpower to wait, to tease and touch, to grasp her waist and slow her movement, until she was ready to join him. He waited for the signs, the soft sighs, the shallow gasps of breath that marked each thrust, the subtle tensing of her body.

And when she was ready, he touched her once more, at the spot where they were joined. She stilled, and then he felt her tighten around him in an exquisite spasm. She murmured his name, once, and then again, and then Conor let himself go, arching into her.

Waves of sensation shattered them both, leaving them breathless, a sheen of perspiration the only thing separating skin from skin. And when it was over and they'd both drifted back from the edges of passion, she curled up in his arms and closed her eyes.

He knew this time it had been different. They'd shared something that he'd never shared with a woman before, an intimacy so deep and stirring that it caused his heart to beat more strongly and his mind to sharpen. She'd broken through a barrier and touched his heart and, in that instant, he knew what it would be like to love a woman, so deeply that it defied reason.

Conor closed his eyes and tried to sleep, but he was afraid that when he woke up, she'd have slipped away in the night, like a dream. He turned his face into her hair and inhaled the scent, then ran his hand along her thigh. She was real and the pleasure they'd shared was real.

He didn't want to let her go. Not now. Not ever.

OLIVIA WOKE sometime in the early morning hours, confused at first by her surroundings. Then she heard Conor's soft, even breathing and the tiny edge of fear dissolved. She was safe, wrapped in his arms. For a long time, she watched his naked chest rising and falling, slowly, steadily. The lines of tension that had bracketed his mouth and eyes were finally gone and she gently smoothed her fingers over his face as if to erase the last traces of pain.

A wave of emotion washed over her. How had she grown so attached to this man in such a short time? They'd known each other less than seventy-two hours, yet she felt as if she'd already spent a lifetime with him. Circumstances had thrown them together, given them a common enemy and forced a trust that might have taken years to build, but in reality had taken no more than a day.

He had a beautiful body, lean and hard, smooth skin covering carved muscle. His broad shoulders and chest tapered to a flat belly and narrow hips. It had been so long since she'd been intimate with a man that Olivia had forgotten what the sight of the male form could do to her resolve.

Still, making love after such a short time wasn't really her habit with men. But Conor was different. She trusted him with her life, why not trust him with her body? Though she'd only known him for a few days, that had been enough for her to see that he was a good man, an honorable man. And no matter what the future held for them, she was sure she'd never regret her choice.

But then again, she didn't really have a choice. The first time Conor had touched her she'd been lost. What had happened between them was inevitable and so were the feelings that came with it. She tried to convince herself that she could separate sex from love—and maybe she could have with another man. But with Conor, her feelings were so intense, so undeniable, that she couldn't tell where love began and sex left off.

For the next ten days, they'd live together in a world of their own making. And when it was time to go back to the real world, she'd have to deal with the consequences. Until then, she'd cherish every touch and every kiss.

Olivia drew a deep breath, then let it out slowly. The scent of coffee drifted through the chill morning air and she squinted in the low morning light to read her watch. "Six a.m.," she murmured. Though she wanted to wake Conor with languid kisses and tempting caresses, to rediscover the passion they'd shared the night before, she knew he needed his rest.

She slowly rolled out of bed, careful not to disturb him. Piece by piece, she plucked her clothes off the floor and got dressed. She slipped out of the forward cabin and into the bathroom— or the "head" as Brendan had called it. After brushing her teeth with her fingers and raking her hands through her tangled hair, she ventured out to the main cabin, craving a hot cup of coffee.

Olivia expected to find Brendan up and about, but she walked into an entire cabinful of men. They all had gathered around the table, each of them with a steaming mug of coffee. Even Tommy was there, perched on a shelf and accepting small treats of table scraps. She paused, then smoothed her hands over her sweater. "Good morning," she murmured, wondering if the events of last night were evident in her appearance.

Brendan pushed up from the table and smiled warmly. "Hey, Olivia. How's the patient doing?"

She glanced back over her shoulder. "He's still sleeping," she replied. "I—I think he's feeling…fine." She felt a warm blush creep up her cheeks. He was better than just fine, she mused. He was incredibly gentle and intensely passionate. And after a night in bed with him, she felt exhausted and exhilarated at the same time.

"I don't think you know everyone here. You met Dylan a few nights ago." He pointed to the youngest man at the table. "This is Liam. And across from him are Sean and Brian."

Olivia frowned. All of Conor's brothers resembled each other with their dark hair and their unusual hazel eyes. But Sean and Brian looked almost identical. "Twins?" she asked.

They nodded in unison. Olivia had been an only child but had always wondered about the bonds between siblings. They must care for Conor very much to leap to his aid so quickly. Somehow, she knew she'd come to no harm as long as the Quinn brothers were standing behind her.

"Come on," Brendan said. "Have some coffee. Liam brought donuts and muffins. I hope you don't mind—I fed your cat."

Olivia found a place between the twins. Tommy watched her with wide eyes. She'd never considered her cat very sociable, but he seemed right at home among all these men. She noticed the empty tuna can on the table. Either Conor's brothers had unusual tastes in breakfast food, or they'd been spoiling her cat rotten.

Brendan set a mug of coffee in front of her and she picked it up, grateful for the warmth. The brothers all stared at her, as if she were some kind of bizarre lab specimen and she shifted uneasily, not sure what to say.

"So, what do you do?" Dylan inquired. "I mean, when you and Conor aren't dodging bullets?"

His teasing tone was so like Conor's that Olivia immediately felt a level of comfort that she shouldn't have felt among strangers. "I sell antiques. I have a small shop over on Charles Street." She took a sip of her coffee. "That's how this all started. My partner was laundering money for a mobster."

"And how is it, living twenty-four seven with our Conor?" Sean asked.

"It's nice," Olivia said.

Brian chuckled. "Nice. Con?"

"He's not bad. He takes good care of me. Sometimes he gets a little impatient, but that's only because he's concerned for my safety. And I—"

"What are you boys up to?"

They all turned to find Conor standing at the far end of the cabin. He'd managed to pull on a pair of jeans but hadn't bothered with the top button. His hair was tousled and the bandage was stark white against his rib cage.

"What are you doing out of bed?" Olivia asked. She scrambled from her place at the table and crossed the cabin. Conor winced as she draped his arm over her shoulders and walked with him back to the table. He didn't bother to sit and Olivia could see what it was costing him. It was as if he didn't want to show any sign of weakness.

"So tell me what you have for me," Conor said, glancing at each one of his brothers.

"Brian got you a car," Dylan said. "It's parked at the end

of the dock. It's wicked ugly, but it runs. I brought you some fresh clothes. They're in the trunk."

"Here," Brendan said. "You can take my cell phone. I'm not sure if they can trace the calls on your phone, but it's better to be safe for now."

"We should stay here for a little while longer," Olivia suggested. "You need to rest."

"No," Conor said, not bothering to look her way. "We'll leave in a half hour."

"But—"

Conor turned to look at her, his gaze unyielding. "This is not up for debate," he said. "We'll do it my way."

Olivia bristled at the tone of his voice, so different from that of the night before, and she felt a flush of embarrassment creep up her cheeks. He turned and started back to the forward cabin. Olivia glanced around the table. "He should rest," she murmured. "He was shot."

Brendan shrugged, then sent her a sympathetic smile. "Con does things his own way."

Olivia spun on her heel and followed after Conor. When she reached the forward cabin, she stepped inside and closed the door behind them. Conor stood beside the berth, trying to slip into his shirt.

"Why do we have to leave?" she asked, holding onto the shirt as he twisted into it. "We're safe here. And you need to rest." He refused to answer her, focused on his shoulder holster. "What is this?" she demanded. "Are you determined to kill yourself just to show your brothers what a tough guy you are?"

He glanced up at her. "Don't think because of what happened last night I'm going to stop doing my job," he murmured. "I'm paid to protect you and if that means we move, then we move."

Stunned by his indifferent tone, Olivia wasn't sure what to say. Had she imagined what they'd shared last night? Was she naive to believe that it changed things between them? With a soft curse, she grabbed her purse, her shoes and her jacket, then yanked open the cabin door. "Forgive me," she muttered. "I didn't realize that what happened last night was all part of the job."

Olivia walked out into the main cabin and didn't bother turning around when he called her name. Maybe this was all for the better. They'd had a little fun and now it was time to get back to business. She was a witness and he was a cop and she'd do well not to forget that in the future.

But Olivia knew in her heart that it would take her a very long time to forget her night with Conor Quinn—if she could forget it at all.

6

"WHAT THE HELL are you doing?"

Conor stepped out of the forward cabin only to find his two brothers blocking his way with broad shoulders and angry expressions. "What do you mean?"

"She's out there on deck and I think she's crying," Dylan said. "What did you do to her?"

"Nothing," Conor replied. "I'm just doing my job, that's all."

Dylan shook his head. "You seduced her, didn't you. You slept with a witness."

Conor cursed softly. "I did not—"

"Come on," Brendan said. "One look at that girl's face was all it took to know what went on in *my* cabin last night in *my* bed. She looked, as we say in the literary world, well bedded. And knowing your lack of preparedness when it comes to matters of the heart, I'm sure all I'd have to do is count the condoms in my bedside table to figure out how great the night really was."

Conor had never been one to open up his private life to family scrutiny. As far as his brothers were concerned, he didn't have a private life. "All right," he said. "So we…were intimate. Don't tell me you guys never lost control with a woman."

"Not me," Dylan said.

"Never," Brendan added.

"Well, someday you will," Conor warned, "and then you'll know what it feels like. I couldn't stop myself. It seemed— no, it *was* the right thing to do. I…care about her." He drew a ragged breath, then stepped around them to grab another cup of coffee. His side was beginning to ache again and perhaps the caffeine would dull the pain. "Da always warned us about women being the only thing that could bring a Quinn down. I have to tell you, last night, I didn't care. I wanted to be brought down. I wanted to forget about that stupid family curse."

"So what's your next move?" Dylan asked.

Conor was glad for the change of subject. Now that he'd admitted his weakness, he didn't want to dwell on it. But his reaction to the events of last night had carried into the morning. He wasn't sure what had happened between him and Olivia, beyond an incredible physical release. He only knew that it had changed something deep inside of him, opened a door that he'd always kept firmly locked.

"I called my partner," he said.

"I meant what's your next move with Olivia. If I were you, I'd apologize for every stupid thing I said. And then I'd thank my lucky stars that a woman like her wandered into my life."

"Well, I'm not you, Dylan," Conor murmured. He took a sip of his coffee. "Danny found us a place to stay."

"Can you trust him?" Brendan asked, concern coloring his tone.

Conor brushed him off with a shrug. "The kid transferred to the district three months ago. Even the most corrupt cop doesn't go bad that fast." He turned and leaned back against the rail. "His grandmother just moved to Florida and he's selling her condo for her. It's still furnished. He says we can stay there as long as we want."

"So you're going to play house with Olivia until the trial?" Dylan asked.

"I'm keeping her safe," Conor countered.

Brendan shook his head. "She's a nice lady, Con. I wouldn't want to see her get hurt any more than she already is—and I'm not talking about bullets here."

"Neither would I," Conor murmured as he ran his fingers through his hair. But then maybe he already had hurt her, simply by making love to her. Though their night together had been incredible, it was also a dangerous move. She'd come to depend on him, first for her safety and now for intimacy, and he wasn't sure that he could continue to give her what she needed.

Soon, they'd be free to go their separate ways. Would she be able to let go? And even more importantly, would he? "Right now everything is so unreal," he said. "Feelings are magnified because of the circumstances. She can't possibly know how she really feels. To her, I'm some big hero. Believe me, give her time. She'll figure out who I really am."

"And what if she does and she doesn't turn and run?" Dylan asked.

"Did you ever think she might be the one?" Brendan asked.

"Maybe," Conor said. "But I can't think about that now. From now on, I have to concentrate on the job and nothing else."

Brendan stepped around him to the hatch, then climbed the stairs. "Just don't be such a hard ass, Con. Give her a chance."

Conor and Dylan followed him out and they found Olivia sitting on a locker, her hands clasped on her lap. She'd pulled her hair back into a ponytail and her fresh face was barely touched with makeup. Whether in the soft glow from an oil lamp or the bright morning sunshine, Conor thought she was the most beautiful woman he'd ever seen. An image of her flashed in his mind, her hair tumbling around her face, her body flushed with passion and his blood warmed in the chill morning air.

"I'm ready," she murmured as she stood.

Given the choice, he'd rather take her by the hand and lead her back into the cabin to kiss away the tension that had sprung up between them and spend the day lost in carnal pursuits. Hell, why not stay on the boat and just jump from harbor to harbor until it was time to go back. Brendan could take them down the coast to Martha's Vineyard or Nantucket. Or they could go farther south, looking for warmer weather.

Conor considered the notion, then cursed inwardly. Already she was making him question his decisions, put aside his responsibility as a cop for a few more adventures in the bedroom. If he wasn't careful, that would put them both at risk.

"I told Olivia I'd take care of Tommy for her," Brendan explained. "He seems to like it here and I could use the company. When things have settled down, she can come back and get him."

Olivia pushed up on her toes and gave Brendan a quick kiss on the cheek. "Thank you," she murmured.

It was only a kiss of gratitude, but Conor didn't like it. He knew Brendan all too well, knew his penchant for charming the ladies. While Brendan was smooth and disarming, Conor had always been lacking in social skills. He'd never developed the ability to sweet-talk a woman, to enthrall her with just a few well-chosen phrases. Women usually found him attractive for what he didn't say, rather than what he did.

"Yeah, thanks," Conor said, holding out his hand for Olivia. She said her goodbyes to Dylan, and Conor watched as his brother grabbed her around the waist and swung her up onto the dock. He jumped off after her, then held his hand out to Conor.

Conor ignored the offered aid, clenched his teeth, and swung up onto the dock himself, ignoring the sharp ache in his side. He'd only been up for an hour, but already the nagging pain was making him edgy. Hell, he was ready to bite his brothers' heads off for touching Olivia.

Brendan and Dylan accompanied them to the end of the dock. When they reached the car, Dylan tossed him the keys, then jogged around to the opposite side to gallantly open the door for Olivia. Before he closed it, he leaned inside and whispered something to Olivia. She giggled softly then gave him a wave goodbye.

Conor started the car and then pulled away from the dock. As they drove through town, neither one of them said a word. He considered apologizing for his curt words. He even thought about bringing up the subject of their night together, laying down some new ground rules. But he knew the chances of him saying something stupid were pretty high. Maybe if he just didn't mention it, they could go on as they had before.

As they headed away from the water toward the interstate, he risked a glance over at her, curious to know what Dylan had whispered, yet too stubborn to ask. Olivia's gaze was fixed on the road ahead and she clutched her fingers in her lap, as if sitting next to him made her uncomfortable.

Conor turned his eyes back to the road, then noticed a sign for a discount store on the right. He glanced over his shoulder, then pulled into the parking lot. Olivia sent him a questioning look. "Where are we going?"

He smiled. "You'll see."

He found a spot near the entrance, then hopped out of the car to open Olivia's door. But she had already stepped out by the time he got there. Conor took her hand, glad to have an excuse to touch her again, and led her through the front doors. He glanced at the store directory, grabbed a shopping cart, then pulled her along behind him.

When they reached the lingerie department he stopped. Then he reached into his pocket, pulled out his wallet and handed her a credit card. She looked down at it. "What's this for?"

"Underwear," he said. "On the Boston P.D. Go crazy. Buy as much as you want." A slow smile curled her lips and relief flooded his senses. He could still make her happy.

"Underwear?"

He nodded, his heart warming beneath the delight on her face. Her earlier anger was quickly forgotten. "Even though you're used to wearing designer clothes, discount is all I can offer for now," Conor said. But that didn't stop him from wanting to give her more. "Buy anything else you need."

With a cry of delight, she wrapped her arms around his neck and gave him a fierce hug. "Underwear," she said in the same tone that a woman might say "diamonds" or "pearls." Olivia stared up into his eyes for a long moment. He fought the crazy urge to kiss her, trying to ignore the perfect shape of her mouth and the way her lips glistened beneath the harsh store lighting. He put aside the vivid memories of all the kisses they'd shared already. But, in the end, he couldn't pass on the chance to steal just one more.

Conor bent his head and touched her lips with his, just barely a kiss, yet enough to satisfy his craving and reassure himself that he'd repaired any damage he'd caused to their relationship. Then Olivia turned and began to pick through the displays and racks. At first, Conor stood back, observing her selections. But when she disappeared into a fitting room, he wandered over to a bin of black underthings. He picked up a pair of panties, no more than two scraps of satin and a bit of lace, and studied them for a long moment.

"Can I help you?"

Conor spun around to find an owl-eyed saleslady looking at him through horn-rimmed glasses. He cleared his throat and quickly wadded the panties and shoved them into his jacket pocket. "No," he murmured. "I—I'm just waiting for someone."

"You aren't planning to steal those panties, are you?" she asked.

Startled, Conor laughed uneasily. Then he reached into the back pocket of his jeans and produced his badge. "I'm a cop," he said.

She peered at his badge, then back at his face. Conor shifted uneasily. What? Did she think he planned to wear the panties himself? He pulled the panties from his pocket just as Olivia emerged from the fitting room.

"I'm done here," she said, piling her selections into the cart. "Can we look for a few T-shirts and sweaters?"

"Sure," Conor murmured, surreptitiously tossing the black

panties into the basket as well. Then he gave the saleslady a dry smile and turned back to Olivia. "Come on, let's go."

They wandered around the store, Olivia stopping in nearly every department to browse. When she got to the men's department, she pulled a couple of flannel shirts from a table, then tossed in three T-shirts. Though he didn't say anything before she moved on, Conor liked the idea of her choosing his clothes. It was a familiar, almost intimate, gesture that warmed him in the same way her touch did.

"Before we go, we need to get some medical supplies," Conor said after a half hour of shopping. Though he was loathe to put an end to her fun, his side was beginning to ache incessantly. "Bandages and alcohol and adhesive tape."

Olivia frowned, then moaned softly, her eyes going wide with concern. "I—I'm sorry. Oh, I forgot all about your wound. Let's go." She grabbed the cart and hurried down the aisle toward health and beauty. But as they passed the men's underwear department, Conor remembered he could use some extra boxer shorts. Maybe it was optimistic to believe Olivia might see his underwear again, but it paid to be prepared. He had no idea whether Dylan had thought to bring him clean underwear. Conor veered off and grabbed a few packages, then tossed them into the cart.

When they reached the checkout counter, Olivia picked the merchandise out of the basket and put it on the conveyor belt. But when she came to the black panties, she held them up, then glanced at Conor suspiciously. He forced a smile, then gave her a shrug. "How did those get in there?"

For a moment, he thought she might hand them to the checker to return to the shelf. But then she tossed the panties down next to the others, a tiny grin curling the corners of her mouth. Conor let out a tightly held breath, imagining how she'd look in black satin, imagining himself as he hooked a finger beneath that lace and tugged them down her legs.

As he walked out of the store carrying Olivia's bags, he considered the possibilities that their purchases held. And though he should have pushed the idea from his mind without a second thought, Conor couldn't help but wonder what their next night together might bring.

"IT'S A RETIREMENT COMPLEX," Olivia murmured, staring at the entrance to Waterbrook Manor. "'A complete residential community for active seniors'?" she read. "I don't think we're going to blend in here," she said.

"Maybe not," Conor said. "But then this is the last place Red Keenan would look. I doubt that the people here have any underworld connections. And it's rent-free. No one can track us."

But Olivia had learned to be suspicious of every situation. They were supposed to be safe at the Happy Patriot and Conor had gotten shot. They should have been safe on *The Mighty Quinn,* yet they'd stayed there only one night before running again. "Are you sure you can trust your partner? What if he tells someone where we are?"

"He won't," Conor said. "He may be green, but he's loyal." He put the car into gear and drove up the winding drive, past a group of seniors playing bocci ball and around a crowded putting green. The complex was huge, with four-unit condos set amidst tidy landscaping. They found the address, in a building set back from the road, and parked. But Conor waited before getting out.

"We need a story," he said.

"Like one with fairies and gnomes?" Olivia asked.

"No, a cover story. Something to tell people if they ask."

"We could say that we're renting the condo while Danny tries to sell it. Helping to make his grandmother a little extra pocket money."

"That's good," Conor said. "It makes us sympathetic." He paused. "And I think we should tell them we're married."

Olivia gasped. "What?"

"It only makes sense," Conor said. "There are bound to be people here who frown on premarital…well, you know…relations. An unmarried couple cohabitating. I just don't want to give them an excuse to gossip."

"All right," Olivia said, seeing the sense in his explanation. Besides, what harm could it do? Just because they said they were married didn't mean they had to continue the roles behind closed doors. "We'll tell them we're newlyweds. That we eloped last week."

"Eloped?"

She held up her hand and wiggled her fingers. "No rings."

"That's good," he said. "You're really getting the hang of this."

Olivia felt a small measure of pride at his compliment. At least she'd contributed a little something to the team. "I have a good teacher. Now how are we going to explain the lack of luggage?"

"We're having our things sent…from Seattle," he said. He reached in the back seat for their shopping bags. "That should take some time. And later we can tell them the moving van was in an accident and all our things were destroyed."

Olivia nodded. In truth, she was relieved they'd be sleeping in a decent place tonight. She imagined a long bath and a warm bed. She'd had precious little sleep over the past few days and, right now, all she wanted to do was crawl beneath a cozy blanket and drift off for a day or two. But as she contemplated the pleasures of hot water and a soft mattress, her mind spun a fantasy of both that included Conor.

Every time she thought of them alone, she thought of them together—in the shower, in the bedroom, even on the kitchen counter. She couldn't help but wonder what the night might bring. A shiver of anticipation skittered up her spine.

Neither she nor Conor had mentioned the events of the night before. It was as if avoiding the subject might just turn it into a dream. Olivia had searched his eyes every chance she got, hoping to see some trace of the raw emotion that had swept them away. But the Conor she'd made love to was gone. In his place was the Conor that had only one purpose in mind—keeping her alive to testify.

An odd sensation gripped her stomach. Was that what last night was about? She'd been upset over the shooting. Had he made love to her because he cared, or because he wanted to make sure her worries were soothed? Disturbed by her doubts, she hopped out of the car before Conor could open the door for her. The condo was located on the upper level of the building and they climbed the outside stairs, then found the key where Danny Wright had hidden it.

As the door swung open, Olivia stepped inside, curious to see where they'd be spending the next nine days. The apartment was tiny but very tidy. A small living room was sparsely furnished with a sofa, an easy chair and a television set. In the center of the living room, a pair of plastic garbage bags sat on the rug. Olivia crossed the room and looked inside the first one, then smiled. "Our things from the beach house." She made a mental note to give Danny Wright a big hug.

To the left of the front door was a small dining area and a galley kitchen, stocked with utensils and pots and pans, enough for them to cook at home. And down a short hallway were a bedroom and a tiny bath.

"It's very nice," Olivia said as she wandered into the bedroom. She bounced on the edge of the bed. It didn't squeak. "Better than the Happy Patriot."

Conor turned away from the door, as if the sight of her and the bed made him uneasy. "We'll be safe here," he mumbled, "and that's all that counts."

They walked back to the kitchen just in time to hear a knock at the open door. An elderly woman took a step inside. "Hello," she said, eyeing them both warily.

"Hello," Conor replied.

"I'm sorry to interrupt, but I just wanted to check on Lila's apartment. This is where Lila Wright lives. Are you friends of Lila's? We all like to watch out for each other and Lila moved to Florida to live with her sister and—"

"I'm a friend of Lila's grandson," he explained. "Danny Wright? He's renting us the place until he sells it—you know, to help Lila out. My name is Conor. Conor Smith and this is Olivia Far—Olivia Smith. My wife." He glanced at Olivia. "She's my wife."

"We just got married," Olivia said brightly, stepping to Conor's side and looping her arm through his.

Conor quickly put his arm around her shoulders and pulled her a little closer. "We're very happily married," he said.

He felt Olivia's elbow in his ribs and he was glad she wasn't standing on the other side of him. "I think we'll be very happy here," she said, glancing around the condo.

The elderly woman sent them both a dubious look. "You

do understand that this is a seniors' complex," she said. "There's not much excitement around here, unless you count that fist fight that broke out at last week's pinochle tournament. Bert Blevins accused Harvey Denton of cheating and Harvey punched Bert in the nose and—"

"Well," Conor interrupted. "I've always been very mature for my age and so has Olivia. Besides, we really wanted someplace quiet. No loud music, no parties. We're very private people."

The woman glanced back and forth between the two of them, then finally nodded. "I live just across the stairway. My name is Sadie Lewis." She held out her hand and Olivia quickly reached for it. "Congratulations, my dear."

"Congratulations?" Olivia asked.

"On your marriage," she said. "You two look very happy."

"Oh, we are," Conor said. "Very happy." He gave Olivia another hug. "We are newlyweds, after all," he said, this time with more meaning.

Sadie got the message, then nodded knowingly. "I think I'll just leave you two alone. If there's anything you need, don't hesitate to ask. I'm right there." She pointed to the front door of her apartment, just twelve feet away from theirs.

"We won't," Conor said as he closed the door behind her. "Bye now."

As soon as the door was closed, Olivia hauled off and punched him in the shoulder. "Gee, why beat around the bush? Why not just say, me and the missus want to have sex now so we'd appreciate it if you'd leave?"

"I thought it was the quickest way to get rid of her. She seemed nosy and nosy people will hang around as long as you let them." Conor glanced down at her. "What? Are you embarrassed? We're just pretending."

Olivia turned away from him. But they weren't just pretending. They'd made love last night, or had he forgotten so soon? "No. I just don't want her thinking—"

"Thinking we're hot for each other?" Conor chuckled, as if the notion was preposterous.

Why was he trying so hard to forget what they'd shared? She bit her bottom lip, trying to keep from blurting out her feelings. She already knew that Conor wasn't the type to reveal his innermost thoughts. It would probably take major surgery to find out what was inside his heart.

"I need to change this bandage," he finally said, grabbing one of the bags from the discount store. "Why don't you make a grocery list and I'll go out and get some things for dinner?" With that, he strode down the hall, leaving Olivia to wonder whether she really had imagined their night together.

After a quick survey of the kitchen, she sat down at the dining table and began a grocery list on a scrap of paper from her purse. But by the time she'd finished with nine days' worth of provisions, Conor still hadn't emerged from the bathroom. Hesitantly, she pushed up from the table and walked down the hall. "Conor?" she said, rapping softly on the door. "Are you all right?"

"Yeah," he snapped from the other side of the door. Olivia heard a soft string of curses. "No."

She slowly pushed the door open to find him standing in the center of the bathroom, shirtless. He'd managed to get the bandage off but his attempts to replace it had been thwarted. Adhesive tape lay tangled on the floor and gauze pads cast aside. Cotton balls saturated with alcohol made Olivia's eyes sting.

"I need help," he muttered. "I can't reach around and get the tape on straight."

Olivia stared at him for a long moment. In the harsh light of the bathroom, he looked even more magnificent than he had on the boat. She could see every muscle in his back and torso, bunching and shifting beneath his skin as he turned to tend to his wound. Olivia wanted to run, certain that touching him would transform her into a babbling fool. But common sense told her that she owed it to him to help.

The bathroom was so tiny, she was forced to close the door in order to have enough room to work. She grabbed the tape from his hand, then pulled two gauze pads from the paper package. "Put your arm up," she murmured.

He did as he was told and Olivia got her first real look at his wound. She winced at the angry red slash in his side and the line of neat stitches that kept it closed. "It looks painful," she said.

"Actually, I was thinking that it wasn't so bad after all. I doused it with alcohol and smeared on some of that antibiotic salve the doctor gave me. It only hurts when I twist or reach."

She pressed the gauze over the wound, then put his right hand on top of it. A length of tape secured it on top and Olivia tore off three more pieces and taped the bandage in place. "There," she murmured, slowly straightening.

In the cramped quarters they couldn't help but touch each other as they moved around. His body brushed against hers, her breasts pressed to his naked chest. And then, suddenly, his arms were around her waist and her fingers were splayed across his chest. Conor captured her mouth with his in a frantic kiss, his hands skimming along her hips, drawing her closer.

The kiss took her breath away, full of fierce longing and

fully realized need. He'd kissed her for no reason at all, only that he'd wanted her at that very moment. All her worries about his motives dissolved and Olivia was certain of his desire. He wasn't playing a role to keep her happy, he wanted her, now more than ever. He had been affected by the passion they'd shared.

But just as she allowed herself to revel in the taste of him, he pulled away, as if ending the kiss quickly would make it seem like it never happened at all. "We shouldn't do that," he said, his jaw tight.

Olivia wrapped her arms around his neck and smiled. He could make a feeble attempt to deny her, but in the end, he couldn't resist. "Why not?"

Conor shook his head, then grabbed his shirt from the edge of the tub and struggled into it. "We just shouldn't. It complicates things."

"It doesn't have to," Olivia said. "What we share here is between us and no one else."

She saw the battle in his eyes, between common sense and carnal pleasures. But she'd spoken the truth. If all they had was the next nine days, then she'd understand. The past three had been the most exciting days of her life and she couldn't regret a single minute, not if it brought her closer to Conor Quinn.

Conor dragged his gaze from hers. "I have to go," he said.

Olivia blinked in surprise. "Where?"

"I've got some things to do."

"I'll come with you," she said.

"You'll be safer here."

"Aren't you afraid I'm going to leave?" Olivia asked.

Conor thought about the suggestion for a moment, then shook his head. "You know the dangers out there, Olivia. If you really want to leave, I can't stop you. But I'd be damn angry if I came home and found out that I took a bullet for a woman who cared less for her life than I do."

With those words, he made it clear that to leave would be a betrayal he couldn't forgive. Olivia took a deep breath, then nodded. "I'll be here when you get back. You don't have to worry."

She stood in the bathroom and listened to his footsteps as they retreated down the hallway. For a few minutes there, she really believed she understood Conor Quinn. But then he threw up walls all around him, determined to keep her at a distance. Olivia couldn't blame him. After what she'd learned about his childhood, it was no wonder he was wary of women.

Still, she'd seen a vulnerable side of him and it gave her hope that, one day, Conor might want to love her. With a long sigh, Olivia sat down on the edge of the tub. "I should find myself a nice, normal guy," she murmured, her chin cupped in her hand.

But she didn't want normal. She wanted dangerous. And if the past few days had proved anything at all, it was that Olivia was beginning to thrive on danger.

THE OFFICER on duty recognized Conor the moment he walked in. But Conor had counted on the code between cops, a code that called for silence until questions were asked. He walked up to the desk at the Suffolk County Jail and pulled out his badge. But he didn't reach for the pen to sign in, by-passing the strict requirements called for when visiting a prisoner.

"Quinn," the officer nodded.

"Mullaney," Conor replied.

"Didn't expect you to turn up here," Mullaney murmured, leaning forward as he lowered his voice. He glanced over Quinn's shoulder. "I hear the D.A. and the brass are ready to can your ass. You kidnapped a witness."

"I'm just doing my job," Conor murmured. "I'm supposed to keep her alive until the trial. And it looks like someone in the department wants her dead."

Mullaney blinked in surprise, then nodded as if he sympathized with Conor's predicament. "I suppose I should be forgetting that I saw you tonight."

"And while you're at it, you can forget that you called Kevin Ford up to an interview room by mistake. And that I just happened to be in that interview room when he arrived."

"If they find out about this, your career will be over," Mullaney said.

"I'm still a cop and he's still one of the bad guys and, until he asks for his lawyer, we're just a couple of buddies chatting about a mutual acquaintance."

"If anyone asks, I never saw you. Just make sure no one else never saw you, too. Room seven."

He picked up the phone to call the guard on duty, then buzzed Conor in. He'd been to Suffolk hundreds of times before to interview suspects. He knew how to walk through the place without being recognized, how to avoid contact with anyone who looked like a lawyer. He stepped into the interview room and, a few moments later, a uniformed officer opened the door and let Kevin Ford enter.

Ford was dressed like all the other prisoners in a baggy jumpsuit. Yet he still seemed completely out of place. His pale face and horn-rimmed glasses gave him the look of a Harvard professor rather than the career criminals that populated the county jail. He walked into the room, hands cuffed in front of him, then sat down across from Conor.

Conor had developed the ability to read suspects, to know exactly what kind of people they were and what buttons to push to get them to talk. Kevin Ford was easy. He was a coward at heart, willing to do whatever it took to save his butt. The problem was Red Keenan was willing to do whatever it took to kill Ford's butt if he talked.

"I'm not saying anything without my lawyer. And I'm not going to testify against Keenan, so you might as well not waste my time."

"Yeah," Conor said. "I bet your social calendar is pretty full." He chuckled softly. "Nothing you say is going to leave this room. I'm officially not here and we're officially not talking."

"What do you want? Did Keenan send you?"

Conor tried to keep the surprise from his expression. "Keenan?" he asked. "I guess he's sent his cops around to talk to you already." Better to act like he knew exactly what Ford was talking about. "So did he send the guys in uniform or did he send his detectives?"

Ford didn't answer, but Conor could see it in his eyes. Someone from the department *had* talked to him, convinced him not to testify against Keenan, and that someone was a cop. "You don't have to answer that," Conor said. "If he'd sent the top guys, you'd be a lot more messed up."

That seemed to bother Ford, the look on his face shifting to one of fear. "You know what I don't get?" Conor continued. "How a guy like you, smooth, sophisticated, well-read, a guy with real manners, could hang Olivia Farrell out to dry? She didn't do anything to you except trust you. You were her friend. And now she's got Keenan's men shooting at her. She'll testify, and her testimony will probably put both you and Keenan away for a long time. But she'll spend the rest of her life looking over her shoulder."

Ford hung his head, his attention fixed on his folded hands. "I didn't mean to get her involved." He glanced up and, in that single moment, Conor saw the truth, all laid out in front of him. Kevin Ford was in love with Olivia Farrell!

"Why did you do it?" Conor asked, his jaw tight. "Off the record."

"I bought the shop on Charles Street. The mortgage was killing me, I made a few bad buys and suddenly I was on the verge of losing it all. I couldn't let her down, so when Keenan came to me, I took him up on his offer. At first it was just supposed to be a short-term deal. But then once I was in, I couldn't get out."

Conor almost felt sorry for the guy. Hell, he knew how Olivia could twist a man's heart a million different ways, and how Keenan could take advantage of any vulnerability. "You said a cop came to talk to you about Keenan?" Ford nodded. This was the break he needed, a way to extract Olivia from this mess and still send Keenan to prison. "What if I found a way for you to testify against Keenan, to put him in jail for the next twenty years?"

"I'm not going to testify," Ford insisted.

"What if you didn't have to do any time? I could make that happen," Conor said.

"My lawyer says I might not do any time anyway," Ford replied.

"Your lawyer is overly optimistic. Olivia's testimony will put you in jail. And I'd wager you're not the kind of guy who'll do well in prison. Even if it's only a few years, those years won't be kind."

Ford's shoulders slumped further. "Why do you care about me?" he asked.

"I don't care about you," Conor said. "I care about Olivia."

They exchanged a long look and Conor knew they understood each other perfectly. They'd both fallen for the same woman, both shared an instinct to protect her. "If you can guarantee that I'll stay out of jail, then I'll testify against Keenan."

Conor pushed to his feet. "Don't tell anyone about this, not even your lawyer. I'm going to send a detective to talk to you. His name is Danny Wright and he works for the good guys. He'll set this up for you. You can trust him."

Conor strode to the door, then hammered his fist on the window. The officer waiting outside unlocked the door and Conor stepped out. Anxious not to be seen, he hurried down the corridor and past the desk, not stopping to talk to anyone. When he got outside, he stood on the street, breathing deeply and running the plan through his mind.

Until that moment, staring into Ford's eyes, he hadn't recognized his feelings for Olivia, hadn't believed they could have a future together. But now he knew. He was in love with Olivia Farrell. He'd known her for three days and already he knew he wanted them to spend a lifetime together.

But it wasn't as easy as it all looked. Even if he wanted Olivia in his future, he didn't know if he even had a future to offer her. Hell, he wasn't sure how this would all turn out. Even if Ford made the deal, Conor was still facing some pretty serious accusations, so serious that they could cost him his job. And without a job, how could he possibly plan a future for them?

"Quinn!"

Conor spun around. Danny Wright was jogging down the sidewalk toward him. He waited for his partner, then pointed down the street where he'd parked his car.

"What are you doing here?" Danny asked, breathless.

"I was visiting Kevin Ford," Conor admitted.

Danny stopped short on the sidewalk and shook his head in disbelief. "You talked to Ford? Aw, man, this is bad. I don't mean to question your procedures, but everyone at the station is talking. First, you disappear with a witness—a beautiful, female witness—and now, you're sneaking around, talking to the perp."

Conor chuckled at Danny's police slang. "How'd you know I was here?"

"Mullaney called me at the station house. He told me to come down here and pick up my stuff. It took a while, but I figured that he meant you."

"Well, talk all you want," Conor said. "Because right now I'm not listening. I've got other things on my mind." Olivia. He had Olivia on his mind and all the things he had to do to make this work for them both.

Conor turned to Danny. "Keenan has a guy on the inside. That's how they keep getting to us. And Kevin Ford knows who he is. I told Ford you'd be visiting him. I want you to find out all you can, then take it to Internal Affairs. They'll offer Ford a deal in exchange for the dirty cops. And Olivia won't have to testify."

Danny frowned. "But what if—"

"Just do it," Conor said. "And watch your back."

Danny nodded, then Conor slapped him on the shoulder and smiled. "You're a damn good detective, Wright." A smile broke across his partner's face and Conor took that as his cue to leave. He grabbed the car door, pulled it open, then hopped inside. And as he drove off down the street, he let out a tightly held breath.

"This has to work," he murmured to himself. It was the only way he could be sure that Olivia stayed safe for the rest of her life. And right now the only thing in the world he cared for—the only thing that made any difference in his life at all— was Olivia Farrell.

As for their future together, he'd have to think about that later. "One step at a time," he said softly.

7

SHE'D BEEN CAUGHT in the middle of a wonderful dream. Everything was so warm and comfortable, the sun, the water, like a little Jamaican vacation in her sleep. Olivia smiled and snuggled down beneath the quilt she'd pulled from the bed. The television glowed in the darkened living room, a travel show softly playing in the background.

For a long time, she drifted in and out of the dream, spinning images in her brain of her and Conor, lying on the sand, swimming naked in the ocean, making love in a hammock. After this was all over and she was safe again, maybe she'd ask him to take a little vacation. She had some money saved and she probably wouldn't have to worry about her business since there wouldn't be much left to worry about.

It would be fun, a chance to really get to know each other. She turned the notion around and around in her mind. But before she'd imagined the most perfect vacation with the perfect man, she heard the sound of the door opening. Olivia opened her eyes, then pushed up on her elbow and watched Conor slip into the condo. He'd been gone for most of the day and into the evening and, though she really hadn't worried about him, she was curious about what had occupied his time.

In truth, she was also a bit jealous that he could go out and walk around without worrying about his safety and she was stuck inside for the entire day playing the responsible witness. So she'd made the best of the situation and spent a lazy hour in the bathtub. After that, she lounged around the condo, watching soap operas and painting her toenails.

"You're home," she murmured, running her fingers through her tangled hair.

Startled, Conor turned and peered into the dim living room. Then he shrugged out of his jacket, tossed it on a chair and slowly walked over to her. "Were you sleeping?" he asked.

Olivia smiled and stretched her arms over her head. "I've been a lazybones all day long. It felt good to finally relax. We've been kind of busy lately."

He sank down on the end of the sofa, far enough away from her that she couldn't give him the hug she wanted to. In truth, he didn't seem in a very huggable mood. He tipped his head back and stretched his legs out in front of him. "Yeah, we have. It takes a lot of energy to dodge those bullets."

Olivia scrambled to her knees, reminded again of his injury. She settled beside him. "How are you feeling? Does your side hurt?"

Conor winced as he shifted his weight. "It's not bad. Most times I don't notice it."

"Why don't you let me get you some dinner?" she said,

crawling off the couch. She picked up his feet from the floor and swung them around. "You stretch out and rest. I'll let you know when dinner is ready."

He groaned, then rubbed his eyes. "I didn't get any groceries. I'm sorry. I had to take care of some police business and then I met Danny and I talked with him. Then I stopped over at Dylan's place. I just lost track of time."

He made to get up, but she gently pushed him back down. "We don't need groceries," she said. "We have neighbors. Sadie from across the stairs brought us a tuna noodle casserole and an apple pie. Louise from downstairs, who is married to a retired Navy man, brought us a taco casserole and a fruit salad. And Geraldine, who used to be a Rockette, brought us a little honeymoon basket with candles and champagne and some chocolate. There are cookies from Doris—she's so funny—and some fresh lemonade from Ruth Ann who looks a little like my landlady. And we're invited to join the canasta club on Tuesday, the bocci ball couples' tournament on Saturday, and the potluck supper on Sunday night."

"I see you've been as busy as I was," Conor murmured.

Olivia sighed. "We've lived here one day and I already know five of my neighbors. I've lived in my flat on St. Botolph Street for six years and I know two people—the woman who rents the downstairs apartment and my landlady who lives down the street."

"Don't get too used to it," Conor muttered. "We won't be staying forever."

His tone had an edge to it that she'd never heard, not even when he was ordering her around. She tried to read his mood. So often over the past few days, he'd let his guard down. It just surprised her when those barriers suddenly appeared again, in the tone of his voice or in an impatient sigh. She didn't need to be reminded that they'd only be together a finite time. She reminded herself of that same thing every day—every time she looked into his eyes or touched him, every time she remembered their time together on the boat.

But Olivia had already decided that she wouldn't think about the future, even if that future was only a week away. She wanted to live for the moment, to enjoy Conor while she had him, for she knew once his responsibility to her was through, he'd rebuild all those walls so he could walk out of her life.

"Why don't you put your feet back up," she said. "I'll get us some dinner and then we can have a quiet evening. No bullets flying, no car chases."

That brought a tiny smile to his lips. He stretched out on the sofa, not even bothering with his shoes and, in a few minutes, he'd fallen asleep. Olivia gently covered him with the quilt then wandered into the kitchen. She grabbed the tuna casserole from the refrigerator, then popped it into the oven.

As she searched a drawer for serving utensils, her mind wandered to Conor. She found herself pretending that he'd just come home from a long day at work, that she'd met him at the door with a kiss, that they were married and living a happy life together. She'd never imagined an ordinary life for herself. When she'd imagined marriage, it was always so much more exciting and urbane.

But then the excitement didn't really come from a fancy apartment or a glittering social life. It came from moments like these, moments when she could make Conor's life more comfortable, moments when she could walk in the other room and just touch him when she wanted to. Olivia smiled, then pushed up on her toes and retrieved two wineglasses from the top shelf in the kitchen cabinet. But halfway there, she froze.

A soft sigh slipped from her lips. What was she doing? All these silly fantasies, tropical vacations, quiet evenings after work? "He's a cop, you're a witness," she murmured. She'd have to remind herself of that more often. This wasn't a fairy tale romance with a happy ending, this was a few stolen days with a handsome cop who'd been assigned to protect her.

A half hour later, the tuna casserole was bubbling in the oven and she'd set the coffee table in the living room for an impromptu meal. She retrieved the champagne from the fridge, then lit the candles that Geraldine had tucked in the basket. It all looked perfect…romantic.

Olivia frowned. Was she being too presumptuous thinking that Conor might want to share a romantic evening with her? Whether she acknowledged it or not, this whole meal was a prelude to seduction. She'd secretly hoped that the candlelight and the champagne would lead to a few fleeting kisses. That those kisses would lead to a few more. That they'd end up passing the night in a passionate interlude in her bed.

She moaned softly, doubts assailing her. This was way too obvious. She had to play harder to get! Reaching out, she grabbed one of the candles. But the sharp movement caused the wax to drip onto the back of her hand and she bit her lip to keep from crying out. She dropped the burning candle and it tipped over on the table, landing on the pile of paper napkins that she'd set out.

In an instant, the napkins ignited. Olivia grabbed the champagne bottle and with fumbling fingers, tried to remove the cork. But before she could, the smoke alarm on the ceiling went off, a shriek loud enough to pierce her eardrums.

Conor bolted upright and reached for the gun in his shoulder holster, dazed and confused. He glanced around the room, then scrambled off the sofa when he saw the small fire on the coffee table. "What the—" He snatched the champagne bottle from her hand and popped the cork, then dumped half the bottle on the burning napkins. The flames sizzled and then went out.

Finally, Conor's eyes cleared and he gaped at the mess on the table. "What the hell were you doing?"

Olivia opened her mouth to explain, then snapped it shut. With a soft cry, she spun on her heel and ran into the bedroom, then slammed the door behind her. She sat down on the bed and clutched her trembling hands in her lap. What was she thinking? Did she really believe that she could seduce him with a candlelit meal and a bottle of champagne?

"Olivia?" A soft rap sounded on the door.

"Go away," she muttered, too embarrassed to even look at him. True, she'd never been good at seduction, but even a dope could turn a frozen tuna casserole into a nice meal without setting the apartment on fire.

"Come on," he said. "I didn't mean to snap at you. The smoke detector just startled me, that's all. Come on out and eat with me. The tuna casserole is getting cold."

Olivia drew her knees up under her chin. "I'm not hungry!"

The door opened and Conor peeked inside. He slowly approached the bed, then reached down and grabbed her hand. "If you ignore the smouldering napkins, the table looks very nice. And the food looks great." He gave her arm a tug and pulled her to her feet. "Come on."

He dragged her along to the living room, then settled her

beside him on the floor. The smell of scorched paper mixed with the aroma of tuna casserole and spilled champagne. Conor picked up the candle and relit it with a soggy book of matches. "See, it looks good," he said as he scooped a spoonful of casserole onto her plate.

She ignored the food. "What are we doing here?"

Conor chuckled. "Well, a few minutes ago, you were torching our hideout. Now we're eating dinner."

"No," she murmured. "I mean, what are we doing? You're a cop and I'm a witness and all I can think about is plying you with tuna casserole and champagne so you'll kiss me again." She turned to him, meeting his eyes directly. "What's going to happen to us when this is all over?"

Conor's gaze dropped to the table and he picked up his fork and pushed the casserole around on his plate. "What do you mean?"

"You know what I mean. We have this attraction to each other. We slept together last night. Are we supposed to just stop when this is over and go on with our lives?"

Conor closed his eyes and released a tightly held breath. "I don't know, Olivia. I didn't expect this to happen. It just happened."

"And as far as you're concerned, this is all wrong," Olivia said.

"It's not right," he muttered. "And I could probably lose my job because of it. But there's no going back, so I guess we shouldn't worry about it."

"There is a way to go back," Olivia said.

"And how is that?"

"We just have to stop this right now. Pretend it never happened." She stood up and smoothed her hands over her thighs, hating what she'd been forced to say, yet knowing in her heart it was the best thing for both of them. They couldn't go on without one of them getting hurt. "We can do that. Before it gets out of control."

"I think that ship has already sailed," he said.

"No, it hasn't," she replied firmly. "From now on, we go back to the way it was supposed to be. I'm the witness and you're the cop." She clutched her hands in front of her to stop the trembling, then forced a smile. "I—I think I should probably get some sleep—in my room, alone."

She'd slept away most of the afternoon and wasn't at all tired. But Olivia knew if she didn't walk away from Conor, didn't lock herself in her bedroom, then there would be no way to keep herself from wanting him. "I—I'll just be going," she said, taking a step back.

Olivia waited, hoping that he'd try to stop her, try to explain all the reasons why her plan would never work. But he just stared up at her, a look of resignation set on his handsome face. She felt as if her heart had been torn in two. How could she want him so much, yet know how serious the consequences were for him? And how could he want her so little that he could let her walk away?

"Good night," she murmured. Drawing a deep breath and gathering her resolve, she turned and walked to the bedroom. She closed the door behind her, waited for him to call her name, waited for an invitation back into his arms. But Conor remained silent and his silence told her all she needed to know.

He didn't want her. Or if he did, he was strong enough to resist. Olivia sat on the edge of the bed and drew a long, shaky breath. Now, if only she could find the same strength, then maybe she could get through this without losing her mind.

OLIVIA STOOD in the darkened living room for a long time, watching him sleep by the moonlight that filtered through the windows. It was nearly three o'clock in the morning and she hadn't slept a wink. But Conor wasn't having the same trouble. He was draped across the sofa, his arm thrown over his head and one foot resting on the floor. His naked chest rose and fell in an even rhythm and the quilt was twisted around his long legs.

She wanted to touch him one last time, to run her hands over his broad chest and trace a finger along the soft line of hair that ran from his collarbone to his belly. She wanted to take his face in her hands and kiss him, just to lose herself in the taste of his mouth for a moment or two.

But they'd made a decision and she had to stick to it. To give in to her impulses now would be pure weakness. Besides, the prospect of being turned away by Conor was too humiliating to even consider. She'd see that look in his eyes, that vague indifference, and he'd draw away, as if her touch meant nothing, or worse, as if he found it repulsive. No, she wouldn't subject herself to that.

Olivia turned to walk away, but she didn't see the coffee table in the dark. Her shin banged up against the heavy wood and she bit her lip to keep from crying out. Tears of pain pressed at the corners of her eyes and she muttered a silent string of curse words. The pain gradually subsided and she tested her leg. Though it hurt, she managed to take a few mincing steps.

"Olivia?"

She froze, holding her breath and hoping that Conor couldn't see her in the dark. He moved, the blankets rustling, and Olivia winced, knowing that she wouldn't get away without speaking to him. She slowly turned and forced a smile.

"What's wrong?" he murmured, brushing the sleep from his eyes. "Are you all right?"

"No," Olivia said.

He sat up. "What is it?"

"I—I was thirsty. I needed some water." It sounded like a good excuse, though the water was in the kitchen and not the living room.

His pushed to his feet, casting aside the quilt, and Olivia noticed that he wore only his boxers. She groaned inwardly. Why couldn't they have sent her a cop with a big belly and bowlegs, she wondered. Why had she been cursed with a man who had an impossibly muscular chest and a perfect narrow waist and legs that were almost nicer than hers?

"There's water in the kitchen," he murmured. "Would you like me to get you a glass?"

She drew a ragged breath and shook her head. "I don't want water," Olivia said, her voice trembling. "I—I want you." The words barely registered. What if he refused? What if she had to walk back to her bedroom all alone? "I—I can't sleep and I want you to come to bed with me."

Conor rubbed his forehead. "Olivia, I—"

"I know what you're trying to do," she said, taking a step toward him. "And I understand. But I know this would just be a stolen week. And that when we went back to the real world things would change. But we're not in the real world now." She took another step, putting herself just an arm's length away. "Make love to me, Conor, just once more, and I promise I won't ask again."

Conor moaned softly as he reached out his hand and

skimmed his knuckles along her cheek. His touch sent her heart racing and, for a moment, she was certain he'd turn her away. But then he caught her in his embrace and drew her near. With trembling hands, she reached up and cupped his face in her palms. His beard was rough to her touch, but she smoothed her fingers over the planes and angles, determined to memorize every inch of the man she'd come to love.

He was capable of loving her, Olivia knew this. But with Conor it would take time. And time was in short supply for the two of them. All she could hope for was that once they were apart he'd realize the depth of his feelings for her and he'd come back. And tonight, she'd do what she could to make that happen.

Olivia stepped back, then reached for the hem of the T-shirt she wore and pulled it over her head. She stood before him, naked and unashamed. "Tell me what you want," she said.

"Why can't I stop this?" he whispered, closing his eyes and tipping his head back.

"Because you want me," she said. She grabbed his face and held him until he opened his eyes. "And I want you."

His eyes met hers and she saw the truth there. He didn't just want her, he needed her, as much as she needed him. Olivia reached up and brushed her hair from her shoulders. His gaze fell to her breasts, then raked along the length of her body. She felt wicked, wanton, her usual restraint gone.

She held out her hand. "Come to bed with me," she said.

He slipped his hands around her waist and pulled her against him. They kissed, clumsy at first, then more desperately. Her tongue grazed his bottom lip, probing, daring him to respond. And he did, his control shattering the moment their tongues touched.

But Olivia was in control and she pulled away, tracing a line of kisses across his jawline and down his neck. "Tell me you want me," she murmured, teasing at his nipple with her tongue.

He groaned softly. "I don't want you," he said. "I can't want you."

"But you do," she insisted. "And I can prove it."

Her fingers dropped to the waistband of his boxers and she slowly pushed them down, the fabric catching on the evidence of his desire. He was hard and beautiful, and as she bent to slide his boxers down to his ankles, she kissed him there. The sharp intake of his breath broke the silence and Olivia stayed where she was.

Slowly, deliberately, she tasted his sex, running her tongue along the hard ridge and taking him into her mouth. It was so intimate, this pleasure she gave him, that she was certain he'd stop her. But Conor wove his fingers through her hair and held her, watching as she made love to him with her mouth, stilling her movement when it became too much for him to bear, gently urging her forward when he wanted more.

A moan rumbled in his chest and he grabbed her hands and pulled her to her feet. Frantic with need, he kissed her, his mouth taking possession of hers, demanding and intense. His erection pressed against her stomach, hot and wet from her mouth and she knew she'd brought him so close that just one more touch would take him over the edge.

"Tell me what you want," she whispered. "Tell me you want me."

He grabbed her waist and lifted her up, then wrapped her legs around his hips. "I want you," he said as he buried his face in the curve of her neck. The tip of his erection teased at her entrance. "So help me, I want you so bad I can't stand it."

Olivia tipped her head back and smiled, running her fingers through her hair. She hadn't been wrong. And when all was said and done, when their days together were over and they'd both gone back to their lives, he'd remember this passion between them. And he'd come looking for it again.

Conor carried her to the dining room table, where he'd tossed his shirt and jeans. He set her down on the edge of the table, then fumbled to find his wallet. Olivia grabbed the condom from his fingers and tore the foil package open. But he was impatient and he grabbed it from her and quickly sheathed himself, as if her touch was more than he could take.

Then Conor stepped between her legs and gently pushed her back onto the table, his mouth coming down on one of her nipples. Olivia sighed softly as he took control, delighting in the feel of his body pressed into her. Wave after wave of delicious sensation washed over her as he made love to her in the same way she had to him.

He found every spot that made her shiver with need and when he finally tasted her damp core, ran his tongue over her swollen nub, she was already near the edge of conscious thought. This was all she ever needed in her life, he was the only lover she'd ever wanted. And these feelings coursing through her body were as close as she'd ever come to paradise. "Please," Olivia murmured, reaching out for him, bringing his mouth back to hers. "Please."

He drew her closer to the edge of the table, his hands skimming over her breasts, then clasping her hips. Gently, with exquisite tenderness, he entered her. Olivia murmured his name and arched against him, needing him to fill her with his heat, wanting him to take her the rest of the way.

Conor drove deep, burying himself completely, then slowly

withdrew, as if to tease her, to make her shiver and ache for him. With each thrust, his rhythm increased, but he still wouldn't give in to his own desire. He was in control now, and though Olivia felt she was near her own climax, it was Conor who would determine when it came.

Suddenly, he stopped, his body tense, his expression restrained. Olivia moaned softly. "Don't," she murmured, wriggling against him, trying desperately to reach him with her hands.

With a low growl, he grabbed her wrists and pinned her arms above her head, still buried deep inside her. For a moment, Olivia thought it was over, that he'd brought her this far only to leave her wanting more.

But then he dropped a kiss on her lips, lingering a long moment before drawing away. "Tell me that you want me," he said, staring down into her eyes, his gaze intense.

"I want you," she murmured, tipping her head back and moaning as he slowly withdrew.

"Tell me again," he demanded, plunging into her.

"I do," Olivia breathed. "I need you, Conor. Please." She opened her eyes to find him staring at her. This time, his gaze was like a caress, his expression soft. He let go of her wrists and touched her cheek with his fingers. Then he drew a ragged breath. "Tell me that you love me," he said, his words hesitant. "Just for tonight, tell me."

Olivia felt the emotion surge inside of her at his simple request. And though he just wanted to hear the words, she knew there was much more there, in her heart and in her soul. And that there was a reason he needed to hear the words. "I love you," she murmured, holding his handsome face in her hands and staring into his eyes. "Just for tonight, I love you."

He smiled down at her, then kissed her ever so softly. "And I love you," he replied. "Just for tonight."

And when they finally both cried out their release, Olivia came to a startling realization. This man was part of her and she was part of him. They'd touched each other in a way that made them one. And no matter what happened to pull them apart, they would always have each other and this perfect time they had spent together.

THE NOISE woke him up. Conor was continually amazed how he could tell the difference between a threatening sound and background noise, even when he was sound asleep. His instincts immediately sharpened. Olivia was asleep beside him in her bed, her naked body curled against his, oblivious to the danger. He thought about waking her, then decided to investigate first.

Conor carefully crawled out of bed, then searched the floor for his gun. He found it on the bedside table, still tucked in his holster. He thought about getting dressed, just in case the intruder was one of Lila Wright's nosy friends. He compromised by pulling on a pair of boxer shorts.

He took slow steps to the bedroom door, then peered around the corner before starting down the hall. Sunshine illuminated the living room and dining room and the noises grew louder. If this was one of Keenan's men, he wasn't trying very hard to conceal his presence.

The sounds came from the kitchen, clanking utensils and running water. Conor pressed back against the wall as he made his way down the hallway. Then he drew a steadying breath and rushed the kitchen, his gun aimed chest high.

He smelled the freshly brewed coffee at about the same

time that he shouted "Freeze!" at a pale-haired man in a leather jacket. The man's hands shot up and he ducked his head. It was only then that Conor recognized Danny Wright. He strung a few vivid curses together, then lowered his gun. "Damn it, I could have shot you!"

Danny slowly turned around, his hands still raised over his head. His gaze slowly took in Conor's disheveled appearance and his eyebrows shot up. But he didn't offer a comment. His only reaction was a slight blush of embarrassment.

"What the hell are you doing here?" Conor demanded.

"I had to talk to you," Danny said. "I knocked, but there was no answer. So I used my extra key. I figured after what you two have been up to, you were probably sleeping in." He paused. "I—I mean, all the excitement you've had. That is, the danger, not the excitement. I meant that—"

Conor raised his hand to stop the babbling that inevitably sprang from his partner's mouth right after he stuck his foot into it. He walked over to the counter and poured himself a mug of coffee, then turned around. "Why are you here?" he repeated.

"I—I just came to tell you that the D.A. cut a deal last night with Kevin Ford. He'll testify against Keenan in return for a plea bargain on his own charges. He was also interviewed by Internal Affairs and he gave them the name of the cop that tried to coerce him. Ford has papers and tapes and enough evidence to put Keenan away for a long time. Olivia won't have to testify."

"You're sure?" Conor asked.

"She was the only one to connect Ford to Keenan. With the evidence that Ford turned over, there'll be a lot of Keenan's associates who will be offering up testimony in exchange for deals. She should be safe."

"We're not sure of that," Conor said, suddenly faced with the fact that this might be their last day together. "Not until the trial."

"Word on the street is that Keenan has already cancelled the contract on her life."

Conor took a long sip of his coffee. This was it, then. He could take Olivia home this morning and they could both go on with their lives. What they shared together last night would fade into a distant memory. And he wouldn't have a chance to make her feel what he'd forced her to say last night—that she loved him.

Danny swallowed convulsively. "How's your side?"

Conor shrugged. He'd almost forgotten. Olivia had a way of making all his pain just disappear. "I'm all right."

"There is one other thing," Danny murmured. "The lieutenant wants to see you this morning."

"I suppose he wants to reprimand me for not checking in on a regular basis. Or maybe I'm going to have to pay for all those broken windows at the Happy Patriot?"

"I think it might be more serious than that." Danny paused. "Can I speak freely, sir?"

"Only if you stop calling me 'sir.' We're both detectives, Danny. We're partners. Although I may be a few years older than you, I don't outrank you."

Danny nodded, then continued. "You know the captain's not a big fan of yours. He's been looking for anything to bust you back down to a beat cop. He thinks you have no respect for authority. And after the incident with that con man, he's been gunning for you. There's talk that he's going to have you investigated, maybe brought up on charges."

"And why would he do that?"

"They found out about your visit to Kevin Ford and his lawyers claim that you might have threatened him."

"Did Ford tell them that?"

Danny shook his head, then gave Conor's appearance the once-over. "The captain also suspects that you and—" He cleared his throat. "You and the witness might have developed a…personal relationship. Is that true?"

"What do you think?" Conor muttered. Sure, it was true and it was very personal. It was more personal than he'd ever been with any other woman. And if that was a crime, then let him be guilty. "You don't have to answer that," he added.

"You're sleeping with her," Danny said. "And that's against just about every written and unwritten rule the Boston P.D. has. I want you to know that I like working with you and I'd be disappointed if something happened to put our partnership at risk."

Conor clapped Danny on the shoulder and smiled tightly. "You can talk to the lieutenant and tell him I'll be in later this morning. I'll answer whatever questions he has. And if the captain wants to investigate, he's welcome to do that. I've got nothing to hide."

"Danny!"

They both turned to find Olivia standing in the doorway to the galley kitchen. She was dressed only in Conor's flannel shirt, the tails barely reaching her thighs. Her hair was mussed and her lips slightly puffy. Conor wanted to pull her into his arms and kiss her, a perfect start to the day. But he held back. Last night was supposed to be the last time, he told himself.

"What are you doing here?" she asked. "Have you come to protect me?"

"Actually," Conor said, "Danny just stopped by to give me

a message from my boss. He was just leaving, weren't you, Danny."

"But you can stay for coffee, can't you?" Olivia asked. "We haven't had much company." She walked into the kitchen and poured herself a mug of coffee. "I wanted to thank you for bringing over my things from the cottage on Cape Cod."

Danny grinned, instantly besotted with her. What was this power she had over men? Conor wondered. All she had to do was smile at them and they went soft in the head. "No problem. I took home that seafood stuff myself."

"The paella?"

Danny nodded. "It was really good. You're a good cook, Ms. Farrell."

She smiled. "Has the district attorney contacted you, Danny?"

"The district attorney?" Danny asked.

Conor shook his head, warning him off. "Danny really has to leave, Olivia. He's late for work."

She held the coffee in her hands and breathed in the steam. "But shouldn't I talk to the D.A. before I testify? I mean, that's what they do on television, isn't it? I can't just walk in there and answer his questions, can I? Doesn't he have to prepare me?"

Danny glanced back and forth between them, then smiled wanly. "Yes. I—I mean, I don't know. I guess that would depend."

Conor turned Danny around and pushed him out of the kitchen toward the door. "Aren't you going to tell her the good news?" Danny asked.

"Go back to the station," Conor murmured. "I'll see you later today." He pulled open the door, gently shoved Danny out, closing it behind him. Then he turned and leaned back against the door. Conor's mind turned over all the possibilities, all the ways he could tell her that their time together was over. But he couldn't. He needed more time, just another day or two, time enough to see if what they shared would last in the real world, time to see if there was any truth to the words he'd made her say the night before.

He wanted to believe Olivia could love him, but the real truth was staring him right in the eyes. They were from two different worlds. He was a cop, making a cop's salary and living a cop's life. She deserved more than that. She deserved a man who could stand beside her at her society parties, who could meet her rich friends and make intelligent conversation, not some guy who'd taken night courses to finish college and who preferred police reports to good literature.

"I probably shouldn't have come out when Danny was here," Olivia murmured.

Conor turned. Olivia stood in the dining room, looking delicate and vulnerable and completely kissable. But he held his ground. "No problem."

"What if he says something?"

"Danny knows when to keep his mouth shut," Conor said. He pushed off the door and walked into the dining room, then picked up his clothes. He was afraid to look at her again, afraid that he'd want to take her into his arms and make love to her for the rest of the day.

"I can make you some breakfast," Olivia said.

Conor smiled tightly. "That's all right. I wouldn't want you to set the kitchen on fire." He glanced up at her and saw disappointment suffuse her pretty face. He'd insulted her. "I'm sorry. I have to go. My boss wants to see me this morning and I can't keep him waiting."

Olivia nodded and she watched as he got dressed. By the time he pulled on his socks and shoes, her brow was furrowed and she was worrying at her lower lip with her teeth. Conor grabbed his jacket and his holster, then stepped over to her to drop a chaste kiss on her cheek. "Don't go out," he warned. "I'll be back in a little while."

When he reached the safety of the hallway, he leaned back against the wall and took a deep breath. "You should just walk away now," he murmured to himself. "Just let her go while you still can."

It would be so easy. All he'd have to do was send an officer over to the condo to tell her the good news. She'd pack up and leave and he'd never have to see her again. But he couldn't bring himself to do that. He knew how much it would hurt Olivia.

No, he'd wait. Another day or two together was all he needed to find out for sure. And then they could leave this place and go on with their lives. And whether it was together or apart, Conor knew that he'd have given it a chance. That was all he could ask for—just a chance.

8

"WHY CAN'T WE go out?" Olivia asked. "The weather is beautiful. And no one has tried to shoot me for days. Why can't we go for a drive or just take a walk? We could go out for lunch! We'll drive way out in the country where no one could possibly recognize us. I'd even settle for drive-thru."

Conor looked up at her from behind his newspaper. He'd been strangely silent the past few days, distant, as if something weighed heavily on his mind. He'd made a few trips into the city and come back distracted, his face lined with tension, but when Olivia had asked what was wrong, he'd smiled and reassured her that everything was fine. She thought his worry might have to do with the trial and her testimony, that the danger to her wouldn't end at that. But she didn't want anything to interfere with the last few days they had together, so Olivia didn't press with her questions.

Their nights together hadn't changed. They'd both conveniently forgotten the promise they'd made and fallen into bed the very next night with as much passion as ever. Conor had been particularly uninhibited, making love to her each night until neither one of them could move, almost as if he were making love to her for the last time. After a night like that, she almost expected him to be gone in the morning. But Conor was always there when she woke, his limbs tangled with hers, his face nestled in the curve of her neck.

They hadn't mentioned the future, but Olivia knew with every day that passed they were coming closer to the time when they'd no longer have to be together. She'd expected that the district attorney would want to see her before she testified, but Conor hadn't mentioned anything about a meeting before the trial. She'd learned to trust him without question.

"Please," she begged, "put down your newspaper."

"All right," Conor said. He tossed aside the *Boston Globe* and levered up from the couch. "We'll take a drive. I'll show you my favorite spot in all of Boston."

Olivia clapped her hands, then raced to the bedroom to grab her jacket. She didn't care whether they were taking a risk. She needed to find out what life was like outside the condo. But, more importantly, she needed to find out what Conor was like when he wasn't standing guard or making love to her. They'd never really been out together and she needed a chance to gauge his feelings once they went back to the real world. Would he still touch her at every opportunity? Would he take her hand or drape an arm around her shoulders? Would he be at ease or would reality shatter the dream world they'd lived in for the past week?

She hurried out of the bedroom to find Conor waiting at

the door. He opened it gallantly, then swept out his arm. "Your carriage awaits," he teased.

In truth, Olivia was surprised that he'd agreed to take her out at all. He was normally so vigilant, but maybe even he had started to go a little stir-crazy. When she stepped into the sunshine and the fresh air, she stopped and held her hands out. Then she closed her eyes and twirled around. "I feel like I've been released from prison," she cried. "It's a glorious day."

She ran to the car and Conor opened the door for her. Then he jogged around to the driver's side. Though the car wasn't Dylan's Mustang, it did move. And it was taking them out on an adventure! Olivia didn't care whether the muffler rumbled or the car shook when it went fast. She was with Conor and they were spending time in the real world. That was as close to heaven as she could imagine.

Conor drove through Concord, heading toward downtown Boston. Olivia stared out the window, watching the scenery pass by. Although she'd seen the same sights many times, everything looked so much brighter and prettier to her eyes. She hadn't realized how sheltered she had been, locked away from the hustle and bustle of everyday life.

"Where are we going?" she asked.

"You'll see," Conor replied with a smile.

She slid over the wide front seat to sit beside him, then slipped her arm through his and rested her head on his shoulder. "I know I'm going to have a good time, no matter where we go."

They rode most of the way in silence, enjoying the drive together. Conor steered the car off the freeway and soon they were winding along Boston's waterfront near the Fort Point Channel. Conor found a parking spot and they got out of the car and began to walk toward Waterfront Park. Olivia wove her fingers through his and they strolled hand in hand to a grassy spot near the water's edge.

"I used to come here when I was a kid," Conor explained. He sat down on the grass and pulled her down next to him, then smiled crookedly. "Come to think of it, I wasn't ever really a kid."

"You weren't?"

Conor shook his head. "Not after my ma left. When my da was out chasing swordfish around the North Atlantic, I'd have to find things to keep my brothers busy during the summer. Dylan and Brendan liked to get into trouble. So we'd take the 'T' and come out here and watch the planes all day. And if we had enough money, we'd ride the ferry back and forth to Logan. Sometimes we'd even go inside the airport, although security knew to look out for us."

"All by yourself?"

"I was sixteen and my brothers were used to listening to me. It was cheap entertainment. And it was a favorite trip. If I ever wanted my brothers to do something, all I had to do was promise them a trip out here to watch the planes. Brendan used to love this spot. He'd memorize plane schedules and he'd know where every plane was going. I think that's what gave him such wanderlust."

"You did a good job with them," Olivia said softly as she squeezed his hand. "They're all wonderful men. I don't even know them well, but I know that's true."

"Problem is, I didn't do such a good job on myself," he said, his smile turning ironic.

"That's not true," Olivia said.

Conor shrugged. "I never gave myself much chance to have fun. My brothers say I have to lighten up."

"We've had fun together," she said, "when we weren't getting shot at."

"But I never had fun when I was younger. Never went out on a date until I was nineteen. Girls didn't exactly enjoy five younger brothers tagging along everywhere I went. And I couldn't trust Dylan or Brendan to take care of the twins and Liam. So I was a stay-at-home brother. I guess that's why my social skills leave something to be desired."

"Well, I think you have other skills that make up for that," she said as she lay back on the grass.

Olivia stared up at the sky, a perfect shade of blue. She'd been to Waterfront Park before, but today was different. She was seeing it through Conor's eyes. As the planes roared overhead, heading out in different directions from Logan, Olivia could almost picture those six lost boys. He'd been a good parent to them, and he'd probably be an even better parent to his own children. She had never thought much about a family of her own. But sitting here next to Conor, she could imagine them with children.

"Olivia, there's something I need to tell you."

She opened her eyes to find him leaning over her, a serious expression on his face. Reaching out, Olivia placed a finger over his lips. "No," she murmured. "This day is perfect. I don't want to spoil it. There'll be time to talk later. I just want to enjoy the fresh air and the sunshine." She flopped back on the grass and stared up at the sky. "How could I have been so terrified just a week ago and so incredibly happy today? I just want it to last."

"I'm glad," he said, sitting back.

She shaded her eyes with her hand to study his face, then rolled over on her stomach. "What's it going to be like after

I testify?" she asked. "Will I still have to worry about Keenan?"

"No," Conor said softly. "You won't have to worry about Keenan ever again."

"But what if he gets out and he decides he wants revenge?"

Conor took her hand and brought it to his lips, then placed a warm kiss on the inside of her wrist. "Then I'll protect you," he said.

His words were so simple and heartfelt that Olivia could almost believe he'd be there. "Will we see each other after the trial?" she asked.

Conor shrugged. "You'll be busy trying to get your business back on track. And you'll have your friends. You won't have any time to think about me."

"That's not true," Olivia said.

"It is," Conor replied. "Be honest, Olivia. If I'd walked up to you on the street and asked you out, you would have run in the opposite direction. You're from a different world, privileged, sophisticated, cultured. I'm just a cop and not a very good one at that."

"But that's not who I am," she said. "I didn't grow up on Beacon Hill. I grew up living above a little storefront in North End. My parents were hippies. They bought and sold what they called antiques, but what I'd probably call junk. We were poor, living hand-to-mouth. This me that you think you know is a me that I constructed from scratch. I read magazines to learn how to dress and studied books to understand my clients. I even took speech lessons so I could talk like I had money. I'm a complete fraud."

"But you belong in that world now," he said. "You've made a place for yourself with your high-society friends and your expensive antiques."

"But I like your world," she countered. "It's much more exciting. It makes me feel alive."

Conor shook his head. "I'll make you a deal. When this is over, we'll go back to our lives, and if you still feel the same way in a month, then we'll talk."

An entire month without Conor was unthinkable. She could barely pass an hour alone without craving the sound of his voice or the warmth of his touch. But Conor had wounds that went deep, wounds that made him distrust women. If he needed them to have time apart to prove her feelings, then that's what she'd give him. "Promise?" she asked. "Just a month?"

He nodded.

"I'll never regret what we shared," she said.

"Neither will I," Conor replied, dropping a quick kiss on her lips. "Neither will I."

THE LADIES had gathered around the table for morning coffee as was their habit but, today, they had invited themselves over to Olivia's apartment for the morning ritual. Olivia hadn't had the heart to refuse and, in all truth, she welcomed the company. She needed something—anything—to take her mind off Conor.

Since their field trip to the airport, things had changed, in some ways for the better, but in many ways for the worse. They'd become closer than ever emotionally, sharing stories from their pasts and spending the waking hours together in quiet conversation. They'd talked about his childhood, his parents, his early years in Ireland. She felt as if she'd been given a window into his soul and it was a rare gift. Conor wasn't one to let anyone see the real man beneath the indifferent exterior. She'd been allowed in.

But since that night when they had returned from Waterfront Park, Conor hadn't shared her bed. Like so many other topics of conversation, Olivia had been afraid to broach the subject with him. Besides, she suspected what he was doing. They only had a few more days together before the trial and he was preparing them both for the inevitable. Once the trial began, there'd be no more reason for them to be together. It was a sensible plan, Olivia thought, though it was hard to fall asleep without Conor exhausting her first with his lovemaking and then keeping her warm with his body. She'd been tempted to go to him, to ask him for one last night together. But she'd done that once and she couldn't bear to do it again.

Olivia drew a deep breath. She should have been satisfied with the new direction their relationship had taken—one where emotional intimacy had replaced physical pleasure. But over the past few days, she'd come to love Conor more than ever. And she wanted to express it in both words and actions.

Instead, Olivia found herself working out her frustrations by cooking. She made elaborate meals for them both. Conor, on the other hand, chose to exercise away his carnal feelings. Every morning, he headed out, only to return an hour later completely exhausted. And after a long shower, he'd run errands to the grocery store and the coin laundry and the gas station. Then, right before lunch, they'd leave for another field trip, an activity that had become a daily routine over the past three days.

Yesterday, they'd walked the Freedom Trail, something neither one of them had ever done, even though they'd both grown up in Boston. They wound their way through Boston, stopping at the Bunker Hill Monument and Paul Revere's house and the Old North Church. And the day before that, they'd visited the Museum of Science, then walked along the banks of the Charles until the sun had nearly set.

She'd managed to forget the upcoming trial, her worries fading into an occasional twinge of apprehension. Olivia wasn't sure how her life would change once she testified against Keenan and Kevin Ford, only that she couldn't imagine her future without Conor. She was madly in love with him and, for the first time in her life, she realized that there might be a man who could make her happy forever.

Olivia had tried to determine when her feelings had become so focused but, in truth, she couldn't remember a moment when she wasn't in love with Conor Quinn. They'd known each other just a week, yet she knew more about him than any other man she'd ever loved—or thought she'd loved.

She knew now that those other men had all been passing moments in her life, marking time until she was destined to meet Conor. Suddenly, her decision to testify made sense, as did all the other crazy things that had happened since she'd first called the police. This had all been part of a cosmic plan so that she could find the man she was supposed to love.

"My goodness, dear, you look like you're a million miles away," Sadie said.

Olivia blinked, then glanced around the table at the five elderly ladies who'd gathered for coffee and Danish. They were all staring at her. "I—I'm sorry. What were you saying?"

"Where is that gorgeous husband of yours?" Doris asked.

"He went out for a run. He likes to get some exercise in the morning. And sometimes in the evening, too. Can I get anyone else coffee?"

They all shook their heads and she noticed that all their cups were full and their Danish untouched. The five of them—

Sadie, Doris, Ruth Ann, Geraldine and Louise—stared at her expectantly. "Go ahead," Ruth Ann whispered, giving Sadie an elbow. "Ask her."

"Ask me?" Olivia murmured, picking up her glass of orange juice. "Ask me what?"

Sadie smiled brightly. "So tell us, dear, how is the sex?"

Olivia's eyes went wide at the same moment her orange juice went down the wrong pipe. She coughed, covering her mouth and looking at the ladies through watery eyes. "Sex?"

Geraldine leaned forward, staring at Olivia through her bifocals. "Yes, dear. Tell us, is there anything new out there? All of us have been out of the loop, so to speak. And we like to keep up on new…trends."

"And it's obvious you're doing something right," Ruth Ann said. "That man of yours always looks so satisfied." She reached over and patted Olivia's hand. "Don't be embarrassed, dear. Sex is a regular topic of conversation with us."

Olivia forced a smile, a warm blush rising on her cheeks. "Ladies, I really don't think—"

"Maybe if I picked up a few new tricks," Louise said, "my George wouldn't always be making eyes at that hussy, Eleanor Harrington. Ever since her husband died, she's been on the prowl."

The other ladies nodded their heads in sympathy. "With the ratio of women to men at Waterbrook, it's a dog-eat-dog world," Sadie said. "I have to keep my Harold under lock and key for fear that one of those widows might charm him away."

"So how is it you keep your man happy?" Doris asked. "Do you cook him special foods? I hear oysters are supposed to make a man very randy."

Olivia swallowed hard. "Randy?"

"Oh, Doris, I've tried oysters and Harold just got gas," Sadie said. "I think there must be some new techniques. I see the books at the bookstore, although I'd never be caught dead taking one to the checkout counter. *How to Drive Your Man Wild in Bed.* It's one thing to discuss it over coffee, but can you believe someone would write about that?"

"I wonder if they'd have that one at the library," Louise asked.

The door to the condo opened and Conor strode in, dressed in sweatpants and running shoes, his damp T-shirt tossed over his shoulder. He'd left before the ladies had arrived and Olivia hadn't bothered to tell him about her plans for entertaining, certain he'd disapprove. "Hi, darling!" she cried, jumping up from her spot at the table.

Conor glanced between her and the ladies, who were staring at him with undisguised appreciation. He gave them all a quick glance, then planted a clumsy kiss on Olivia's lips, surprising them both.

The ladies giggled amongst themselves and Conor smiled at them all. "Good morning, ladies. How are you today?" They giggled again, like a bunch of shy schoolgirls. He gave them an odd look, then turned to Olivia. "Could I speak to you in the bedroom?"

Olivia followed him down the hall, then closed the door behind her. All of his things were scattered around her bedroom, tossed inside before the ladies had arrived. "I'm sorry, I know you don't want me talking to the neighbors, but—"

"No," Conor said, staring at the piles of clothes. He spied his jeans, then picked them up and rummaged through the pockets. "Where are my keys?"

"No?"

He picked through a pile of clothes until he found yesterday's flannel shirt. Then he checked that pocket. "No," he repeated. "I don't mind. Do you know where my keys are?"

Olivia stepped over to the dresser and grabbed the keys, then held them out to him. "They were in your shoe underneath the coffee table. I—I had to clean up before the ladies arrived."

Conor glanced up distractedly. "I have to go," he said. "Are you going to be all right here alone?"

"I thought we were going to go out to—"

"No, we can't. I've got business to take care of down at the station house. I'm going to run home first and shower and change. I'll probably be gone most of the day."

"Is this about the trial?" Olivia asked.

"No. It's just some business that I have to take care of." He pulled the door open, then started off down the hall, Olivia right on his heels.

"Conor, wait."

He stopped and turned to her at the front door, then glanced over her shoulder at the ladies. With a tight smile, he bent close and placed another awkward kiss on her lips. "I'll see you in a little while, darling." He gave the ladies a wave and then walked out, leaving Olivia to wonder just what was so important that it preoccupied his thoughts so completely.

"Bye," she murmured, closing the door behind him. Olivia slowly walked back to the table and took her place.

Sadie sighed. "I suppose the honeymoon has to be over sometime, dear."

Olivia forced a smile, then reached for the pitcher of orange juice. As she poured herself a glass, she noticed the little bouquet of flowers that Geraldine had brought over to brighten the table. The daisies were placed in a faux silver tankard that had a remarkably realistic patina. Olivia reached for it and plucked a daisy out, then began to pull the petals off one by one. He loves me, he loves me not, she chanted silently.

The ladies continued to chat while Olivia listened with half an ear. She picked up the tankard and idly studied the design. For a reproduction, it really was quite remarkable. The weight was almost perfect for one of real silver. Usually she could tell real Colonial silver from reproduction without a second glance, but this piece almost left her guessing.

"Where did you get this?" Olivia asked. She held it up and stared at the bottom, looking at the mark. Her stomach did a quick flip-flop and she tried to remain calm.

"At the supermarket," Geraldine said. "I love fresh flowers and they have bouquets of daisies and carnations and mums for 3.99. They last nearly a week."

"Not the flowers," Olivia said. "The silver tankard."

Geraldine stared at it for a moment. "Oh, I don't know. I used to go to a lot of rummage sales when Louis and I were first married. We didn't have much money so I had to decorate on a budget. I must have picked it up then."

"At a rummage sale?"

"What difference does it make? It's just a cheap little thing, but I always thought it made a pretty vase."

Olivia pushed up from the table. "Would you mind if I borrowed this for a while?"

Geraldine's brow wrinkled in confusion but she nodded. "Why, certainly. In fact, if you'd like it, you can have it."

Olivia shook her head. "I—I don't think you want to give this to me," she murmured. Excitement pulsed through her, the same thrill she got whenever she found a hidden treasure. She'd wondered if she'd ever get that feeling back again, and here it was, as if it were simply part of her nature. "I have to go into Boston, but Conor has the car."

"Is there something wrong?" Sadie asked.

"No," Olivia said. "In fact, there might be something really right. I just need to check it out first. Can one of you take me to the train station?"

"What is it, dear?" Sadie asked.

"It's this," Olivia said, holding up the tankard. "Geraldine, I think this might be very valuable. I'm not sure yet, so I have to check some books."

"Valuable?" Geraldine said. "That old thing? How valuable?"

"Very," Olivia said. She turned from the table and grabbed her purse and jacket from the couch in the living room. "So who can take me?"

Sadie smiled, then clapped her hands. "Why, we'll all take you. This is very exciting. A valuable treasure right in our midst. Come on, ladies, let's go. We'll get the details in the car." With that, all five of them hurried out the door. Olivia glanced around the apartment, then wondered whether she should leave a note for Conor.

In the end, she decided not to. It would take her an hour at the most to get downtown on the train and an hour to get back. She'd only need a few minutes at the shop and she'd have her answers. No, she didn't need to leave a note. She'd be back in plenty of time.

FOR ONCE in his career, Conor wished he was back in a patrol car. At least he'd have a siren and lights to clear the way. But instead, he was stuck with the heap that his brother had procured, a car that shimmied over the speed of fifty and cornered as if the street were covered with Crisco.

He'd arrived home from his meeting with the brass to find the apartment empty. At first, he'd assumed that Olivia had gone over to one of the ladies' apartments for whatever it was they did together. But when he knocked on Sadie's door, she informed him that they had taken Olivia to the train station and that Olivia was on her way into Boston.

The first thought Conor had was that she'd somehow found out about Kevin Ford, that she wouldn't have to testify and that their past four days together had been stolen time. He knew in his heart he shouldn't have lied to her and the guilt had been killing him. He'd wanted to tell her the truth, been tempted to tell her nearly every hour of every day.

But after that wonderful night on the dining room table, he knew that he couldn't let her go. She might be able to forgive him for wanting more time, but she might never forgive him for taking advantage of that time. Conor cursed softly.

He'd always had such a strong moral compass. What had happened to it? Since he'd met Olivia, he'd done things that would have once been unthinkable, bucking department regulations, falling in love with a witness, then deceiving a woman he'd come to love. But he'd done everything for the right reasons, in the hopes that Olivia might want a future with him.

Charles Street, as always, was bustling with shoppers and workday pedestrians and even a few groups of tourists. Conor double-parked, not even caring that the cops might tow the heap he was driving. He found the front door to Olivia's shop locked. Peering through the windows, he couldn't see anything in the dark interior except the shadowy forms of huge pieces of furniture—no movement, no light, nothing.

His heart slammed in his chest, his instincts on alert, but then he remembered there was no longer any danger. He wouldn't find Olivia inside, lying in a pool of blood. Keenan had called off his dogs and she had nothing to fear. He pounded on the door and waited impatiently. Sadie had mentioned something about a silver tankard and a special mark. He'd assumed she'd come to the shop, but maybe she'd gone home—or to one of the museums or libraries.

Conor hammered on the door again with his fist and, a few moments later, he heard a voice coming from inside. "We're closed," Olivia called.

"Olivia, let me in. It's Conor."

An instant later, the door swung open and Olivia stood in the doorway. "Conor!"

Conor stepped by her and walked into the shop. He glanced around, curious as to what it was she did for a living and impressed by the assortment of antiques in her shop. Even in the dim light he could see the fine quality of the furniture, the careful craftsmanship. This was her world, a world completely unknown to him. Hell, he had a twenty-year-old sofa and a coffee table he'd found in the alley behind his house. He reached over and grabbed the price tag for a huge wardrobe. It cost more than he made in a year.

"I'm sorry I left," Olivia said softly. "I—I thought I'd be back before you returned."

Conor turned and found her staring up at him, a frightened look on her face. Good grief, she still thought Keenan was after her. And she still believed that what she'd done would bring out his temper. He never, ever wanted to see that look of fear in her eyes again.

"Please don't be angry. I was careful," she said.

"I'm not angry with you," Conor replied.

"I just had to come. I wasn't sure about the mark but I

knew I had a book here to check it out." She held up the tankard. "I thought I'd never feel this way again, Conor. Every time I remembered what I did for a living, I just got sad and depressed that it was all over. And then I saw this and I got that old feeling."

"Feeling?" he asked.

"It's like a little flutter in my stomach, a little lurch of excitement. Usually, I try to contain it, to tell myself that I might be too optimistic. But it's like digging in your garden and discovering gold."

"And this is all over a beer mug?"

Olivia sighed dramatically and rolled her eyes. "It's a silver tankard. And it's a Revere," she said, her voice full of awe and wonderment.

"A Revere? Like Paul Revere?"

"Not *like* Paul Revere," she repeated. "It *is* Paul Revere. He was a silversmith. His pieces have turned up in the oddest places, buried in peoples' backyards, hidden in walls. Do you have any idea how much this is worth? There are so few of these that have survived. When an original piece comes on the market, people take notice."

Conor stared down at her, the excitement suffusing her face making his guilt more acute. She looked so happy, so alive. She was doing something she loved, excited about the possibilities. He glanced around the shop at all the fancy furniture with the expensive price tags. This was her world. This was where she belonged and he'd kept her from this, from everything she'd loved. "Olivia, we need to talk."

"Geraldine was putting flowers in a Paul Revere silver tankard. Do you know what this means? I can put it up for auction and everyone will come to see it here in my shop before it's sold. The prestige of having this in my shop will do wonders to restore my reputation." She reached up and placed her palm on his cheek. "Please, don't be mad at me. I know I took a risk but—"

"No," Conor interrupted.

"No?" Olivia asked.

"There's no risk," he murmured. "That's what I came here to tell you."

She frowned. "What do you mean?"

"You're free," he said, the words burning in his throat. "Kevin Ford agreed to testify. Ford's got all sorts of incriminating evidence against Keenan and his whole wiseguy family. They're all scrambling over each other to see who can be the first to cut a deal. So you're off the hook."

Olivia let out a long breath, then smiled in amazement. "I don't have to testify?"

"You don't have to testify," Conor murmured.

With a squeal of delight, she threw herself at Conor and hugged him fiercely. Then she kissed him long and hard until he had no choice but to respond. When she finally pulled back, she was breathless with excitement. "I can't believe this. It's all over. I can get back to a real life."

A real life, Conor mused. Her words were like a dagger to his heart. A life without him. A life living among her expensive antiques and society friends. "So, I guess this is it," he said, schooling his voice into indifference. "I can have your things from the condo delivered to your house. And I'll make sure Tommy gets back home, safe and sound. And once—"

"You're talking like we're never going to see each other again," Olivia interrupted, her eyes wide, her mouth still damp from the kiss they shared.

Conor gently set her away from him and stared down into her wide eyes. "Remember that deal we made? The one where we go our separate ways, and then if you still feel something for me in a month, we can talk? Well, I was thinking we should do that. Only not for a month, but maybe for three or four?"

Conor saw the hurt in her eyes, and he knew he'd caused it, yet he couldn't take back the words. He hardened his heart and shored up his resolve. Once she went back to her world, she'd forget all about him.

"I don't like that deal," Olivia said stubbornly.

Conor sighed. She wasn't going to make this easy. "I've been suspended, Olivia. That's what I found out today at a meeting with my boss. There's going to be an investigation into my…improper behavior."

"You saved my life!" Olivia cried. "How can that be improper?"

"You were a witness and I exerted undue influence. I developed feelings for you when I knew it was wrong. I ignored departmental procedure. I figure my career with the Boston Police Department is probably over."

"That doesn't matter," Olivia said, reaching out to touch his arm. "I don't care if you're a cop or not."

"But I do," Conor said, evading her touch. "Just like this is who you are, a cop is who I am. If I'm not a cop, then I've got nothing."

"You have me," Olivia insisted.

"But I don't have anything to offer you. Come on, Olivia, at least you should know that much about me. I have to take care of the people I love. I can't let them take care of me."

She blinked once, her gaze fixed on his. "Then you admit it?"

"Admit what?"

"You love me," she said. "And I love you. And we can get through this."

Conor shook his head, then cupped her cheek in his hand. He wanted to believe in the truth in her words, but all this had happened so quickly between them. People didn't fall in love in a week. And those who did usually fell out of love just as quickly. "I have to get through this on my own. And I think you need time to realize that what we had didn't ever exist in the real world. You live in the real world, Olivia, where people like you don't socialize with cops."

"Please, don't leave me," she said, her eyes filling with tears.

"Give it time," he murmured, taking a step back. The very effort made his heart twist in his chest. Then he turned and walked toward the door. A muffled sob echoed through the shop and he cursed himself for hurting her. But it was better this way. She would hurt for a few days and then she'd realize that she never really loved him at all.

When he reached the street, he stopped, fighting the urge to go back in and kiss away all his doubts. "Give it time," Conor murmured as he started toward the car. "Just give it some time."

9

CONOR STOOD outside Quinn's Pub, staring at the building from across the street. Neon beer signs blazed from the plate-glass windows and Irish music drifted out every time the door opened. His brothers had insisted that he meet them for a drink and he already knew what was going on inside. The pub had played host to many celebrations. Any excuse to hoist a pint or two was welcomed at Quinn's. But this time, the celebration was meant for Conor.

Earlier that morning, Detective Conor Quinn's suspension had been lifted. The investigation into the improprieties in the Red Keenan case had been dropped and he was told to be back on the job the next morning. As far as his superiors cared, he'd been guilty of nothing more than poor judgment. Conor sighed softly, his breath clouding in the cold, damp fog that had fallen over Boston. So that was the end of it. Poor judgment.

Somehow, it seemed to be an awfully simple explanation for such a complex time in his life. Hell, a little more than three weeks ago, he'd arrived at that cottage on Cape Cod to do a job. And in the process of doing his job, he'd fallen in love with the most incredible woman he'd ever known. He'd spirited her away, safeguarding her life while violating a host of departmental policies and procedures. And even after the danger was over, he'd tricked her into believing that she still needed his protection.

Poor judgment didn't even begin to describe his actions over the past few weeks. He'd been crazy, out of his mind, wrapped up in a world that was pure fantasy. Yet here he was, standing in front of Quinn's, back to his old life and his old ways, ready to spend his evening lost in a bottomless glass of Guinness while he recounted his regrets.

He'd thought about calling Olivia. The trial had begun and was over within three days, Red Keenan choosing to plea bargain against overwhelming evidence provided by his associates. Kevin Ford had never even had to testify, yet he walked as a result of his own plea bargain. In the end, protecting Olivia had become a moot point and everything that they'd shared now existed in a strange limbo between real life and fantasy.

Chances were, Olivia had already settled back into her life. He'd once thought he could be a part of that future, but then he'd been hit with the Internal Affairs investigation. With his job in jeopardy, Conor had believed that he'd had nothing to offer her. But now that he had his job back, he'd begun to fantasize that maybe they could make it work.

She'd never really disappeared from his life. Every hour of every day, he thought about her, replaying their time together over and over again in his head, until he could recite their conversations by heart. He'd learned to conjure up an image of her face, a memory of her scent and her taste, the sound of her laughter, by just closing his eyes and allowing his mind to drift.

At night, when he lay in bed alone, his hands could still feel her silken skin and the soft contours of her naked body molded against his. The memories were so intense that he wondered if they'd ever fade. In truth, he didn't want them to. He wanted to make more memories, a lifetime full of memories with Olivia.

Yes, things had changed. But he still couldn't bring himself to contact her. Hell, she was probably better off without him. Now that she was back to her old life, she probably barely thought of him. And he'd never been the sort to settle down into domestic bliss.

Conor cursed softly. But he could be. With Olivia in his life, he could be a loving husband and a terrific father. He wasn't sure how he knew for certain, but Conor was sure he had what it took to make her happy. She'd given him that, a glimpse inside his heart, a realization that he could love—and be loved—without fear. Olivia wasn't Fiona Quinn, and if they had a life together, he'd never do anything to make her run away.

He had control, Conor mused. If he wanted to make a relationship work with Olivia, then he could make it work. Conor glanced up and down the street. Suddenly, he needed to see her, to hear her voice and to touch her face. He could make it happen if he just told her how he felt. Conor started toward his car, determined to find her and convince her that he loved her.

"Damn it!"

The sound of a voice on the empty street stopped him short. Only then did he notice a woman bent down on the pavement a few cars away. She seemed to be struggling with a tire iron. A few minutes earlier, he might have been glad for a diversion and an excuse not to go inside the pub. Now that he'd decided to find Olivia, he was anxious to leave. But his duties as a cop couldn't be put aside. If there was a citizen in distress, he was bound to render aid. He hurried over to the spot. Changing a tire. How long could that take? "Can I help?"

The woman screamed, then jumped to her feet, clutching the tire iron in her fist.

Conor held out his hands. "It's all right," he said. "I'm a cop. I can help you."

The young woman regarded him warily, raising the tire iron a few more inches. "Let me see your badge," she demanded, the tremor in her voice giving away her fear.

Conor impatiently reached into his pocket and withdrew the leather case, then flipped it open. He should have just walked away. She obviously didn't want his help. "See," he said. "Detective Conor Quinn. Boston P.D."

She blinked in surprise. "Quinn?" Her gaze darted across the street.

"Yeah," Conor said. "My da owns Quinn's Pub." He stared at her for a long moment as the light from the streetlamp caught her face. A strange sense of déjà vu flashed though his mind, so brief that he wasn't able to focus on it. "You look familiar. Have we met?"

She shook her head. "No. Never."

But Conor had an eye for faces, a skill well honed by his career as a cop. And he knew he'd seen this woman before.

Not in the smoky interior of the bar and not at the bustling squad room at the station, but on a street, in the dark, much like this. "Are you from the neighborhood?" he asked.

"Yes," she said, answering a bit too quickly for his liking.

If she lived in the neighborhood then she should have known it wasn't the best idea for her to be changing a tire—alone—on a dark street in Southie, she hadn't hesitated to threaten him with a tire iron. "Where?" he asked.

She pointed off to the west. "Over in that area. Do you think you could help me change my tire? I—I'm in a big hurry."

Conor took the tire iron from her hand and turned his attention to the stubborn lug nuts. This was exactly what he wanted to be doing right now, getting his hands dirty doing his duty as an officer of the law for a citizen who was obviously lying to him. Once he had the nuts all loosened, he quickly jacked the car up and finished removing them. But his mind really wasn't on the task at hand. Instead, he was determined to remember where he knew this woman from.

He grabbed the tire and wrestled it off the bolts, then rolled it to the rear of the car. She wasn't really a woman, but then she wasn't a girl either. She seemed to be caught in between. Her dark—almost black—hair was cropped short and her delicate features made her look much younger than she probably was. But it was the eyes that made Conor curious. Though she knew he was a cop, they still held a large measure of apprehension and indecision.

"You know, you could have just come into the bar," he suggested, "and used the phone to call a friend. You shouldn't be out on a dark street like this alone." He grabbed the spare and rolled it toward the front of the car.

"I don't have any friends," she murmured. "I—I mean, no

in the neighborhood. Not home. They're all…out. So is the bar a family business?"

Conor glanced over his shoulder. "Me and my brothers all take turns working on the weekends."

"Brothers?" she asked. "You have brothers? How many?"

Conor frowned. For a stranger who lived in the neighborhood but didn't know exactly where she lived, and didn't have any friends, she certainly was curious. As he replaced the lug nuts, a slow realization dawned. So that was it! She was probably one of Dylan's girls or maybe a friend of Brendan's. His brothers always had women hanging around, giggling and whispering over them, staring at them with cow eyes. The poor girl probably had a crush and was waiting outside, hoping to catch a glimpse of whichever Quinn she'd fallen in love with.

"I have five brothers," he said, wondering which one she was interested in hearing about. Most girls gravitated toward Dylan, swept away by the notion of being with a real live hero. But there were others who found Brendan's lust for danger too attractive to resist. And then there were Sean, Brian and Liam, each of them holding their own particular charms.

"Five brothers," she said. "I—I can't imagine having five brothers. What are their names?"

Conor stood and brushed off the knees of his jeans, then moved to release the jack. "Dylan, Brendan, Sean, Brian and Liam." Her eyes went wide and Conor couldn't help but feel sorry for the poor girl. She had it bad for a Quinn. It really didn't matter much which one, since his little brothers weren't in the market for love and Conor had already been taken.

"They're all inside waiting for me. Why don't you come in? You can wash your hands and I'll buy you a soda."

She shook her head as if the notion of going inside with him was completely improper. "No!" she cried. "I have to go. I'm late." She grabbed the tire iron from his hand then scrambled to drag the jack from beneath the bumper. She tossed them both in the back seat then ran to slam the trunk shut. A few seconds later, she roared off down the street, without the flat tire and without even giving Conor a "thank you" for his efforts.

"You're welcome!" he shouted after her car. He stood on the sidewalk, racking his brain, trying to figure out how he knew her. She looked so familiar. And then he remembered. It had been that night he'd stopped at the pub before heading out to Cape Cod. She'd been walking on the sidewalk in front of the pub and he'd nearly knocked her over. The odd thing was, he'd thought he recognized her that time, too.

Conor shook the memory from his brain, then glanced across the street at Quinn's. The only woman he wanted to think about right now was Olivia Farrell. And his only concern right now was finding her and telling her how much he cared. Everything else could wait for later.

"KEVIN!"

Olivia stood in the middle of the showroom of the Charles Street store and stared at her former partner. He was the last person she had expected to see! He looked a bit thinner and his complexion had lost its ruddy tone, but he was still the same man. Only now, he was an admitted criminal.

"Hello, Olivia," he murmured, a faint blush rising to his pale cheeks.

She crossed her arms over her chest, not sure if she ought to be afraid or angry. "What are you doing here?"

He shrugged, then glanced around the shop. "I'm out," he said. "I cut a deal to testify against Keenan and against the cops that he'd bought off. But then Keenan cut a deal and I never had to take the stand. I'm a free man."

"I suppose I should thank you," Olivia said. "If it weren't for you, I'd have had to testify."

His gaze dropped to his expensive Italian loafers. "I'm sorry about that, Olivia. I should have stood up and taken responsibility for what I'd done rather than pass off my problem to you. It was my fault, but now I'll pay the price. I'll be the one looking over my shoulder for the rest of my life, wondering if one of Keenan's associates might be following me."

"I suppose you expect to pick up where we left off," she said, a defensive edge to her voice. Olivia straightened her spine. "Well, I don't want to do that. I've gone through our inventory and separated our acquisitions. I'm going to take my stock and start over somewhere else. I'll be out by the end of the month."

"That's what I wanted to talk to you about," Kevin said. "My credibility is pretty much shot in this town. I want to turn over my client list to you and I want to give you the shop. You can take over the mortgage." He shook his head, a sardonic smile curling his mouth. "You were always better at this business, anyway. You can take my name off the sign. I'd just ask one thing."

"What's that?" she asked, her mind racing at this new development.

"That you let me sell through your shop. I'm going to be moving around a lot and I need a way to make a living. I'll send you stock from around the country and you sell it, on consignment. You'll get a cut of everything you sell."

Olivia thought about the proposal for a long moment. It was a perfect plan. She could keep the Charles Street shop, a location that she'd never be able to replace. And she wouldn't have to pack up all her stock and pay for the move. And Kevin really wasn't asking for much, just a way to make a living. Didn't she owe him at least that much?

"Why would you do this for me?"

"Because it's the right thing to do," he said. "I'm going to have my lawyer call you and make all the arrangements. And you can expect stock whenever I find something interesting." He stepped toward her as if to kiss her on the cheek, but settled for a pat on her arm. Then Kevin turned and walked toward the door.

"What made you change your mind about testifying?" she called, just as he reached for the knob.

"A visit from a cop named Quinn."

Olivia blinked in surprise. "Conor Quinn? He convinced you to testify?"

Kevin shrugged. "He came to see me about ten days or so before the trial was scheduled to start. He was concerned for your safety. I decided to cut a deal right after I talked to him."

She frowned, her mind troubled by the admission. It didn't fit. "Are you saying that Conor knew I didn't have to testify a week and a half before the trial started?"

Kevin nodded. "He and his partner worked with me to put together the deal. It only took a day for my lawyer to convince the D.A. that I had something to trade for a suspended sentence." He stared at her for a long moment. "He's in love with you, you know."

"What?" Olivia asked, her gasp echoing in the silent shop.

"That's why he was so determined to keep you from testifying. He loves you. Believe me, I know the signs." He paused, a look of regret washing over his face. "And if I don't miss my guess, you're in love with him."

The moment he said the words, Olivia realized the truth in them. She'd known in her heart how *she* felt, but gauging the depth of Conor's emotions was almost impossible. But perhaps she shouldn't have waited to hear the words. Instead, she should have known from his actions. He'd kept her close, even after the threat to her life had been eliminated. She could only hope that he'd done that because he couldn't bear to let her go.

"I—I have to talk to him," Olivia said. "I have to see him." She tossed aside the clipboard she'd been using for inventory, then grabbed her coat from a nearby Empire settee. "You have a key. Lock up before you leave."

She had no idea where Conor lived, his phone number was unlisted, and she didn't have the time to call every precinct house in Boston, if he hadn't been thrown off the force. She only knew one place to go—Quinn's, his family's pub. She got the address from the phone book, then hurried out the front door. Her breath came in quick gasps as she ran down the sidewalk and she could feel herself trembling with anticipation.

She was taking a chance going to him. They'd only been apart ten days. But Olivia had to believe he cared, that, if confronted, he'd be forced to admit his true feelings. Perhaps she should play harder to get, wait for him to come to her. But she knew Conor well enough to know that probably wouldn't happen. And now that she'd decided she wanted to spend the rest of her life with him, she wanted their life together to start right away.

Her car was parked at home, so she grabbed the first cab that she saw and directed him to South Boston. They skirted around the edge of the Public Gardens and wound their way to the Broadway Bridge, her mind going over everything she planned to say. She still wasn't sure how to begin. She could just blurt out that she was madly in love with him, then leave it to Conor to respond. Or she could list all the reasons why they belonged together. Or perhaps a better strategy would be to throw herself into his arms and kiss him and show him why he couldn't live without her.

Once she crossed into Southie, Olivia peered out the windshield of the cab, squinting to read the street numbers above the taverns that she passed. Though she'd never been to Southie in all the years she'd lived in Boston, she didn't think finding Quinn's Pub would be difficult. It was located just off Broadway, the main thoroughfare. But then a person couldn't spit in Southie without hitting an Irish pub.

The street was lined with cars, and as she stepped out of the cab and paid the cabbie, she could hear music drifting through the misty night air. The sound of an Irish band, a fiddle, a flute and a drum, drew her closer. Before she reached for the door, she smoothed her hands through her hair, then she drew a deep breath. No matter what happened, this moment would change her life forever.

She stepped inside and found herself in the middle of a party. The Irish band was playing on a small stage at the far end of the long, narrow bar and people stood shoulder to shoulder, talking and laughing. She glanced around, praying she'd find a familiar face, hoping that Conor would appear out of the crowd and sweep her off her feet.

"Olivia?"

She spun around to see Brendan standing at the end of the bar, waving in her direction. Relief washed over her. It was only then that she noticed Dylan sitting next to him and Sean and Brian, the twins, behind the bar. A moment later, Liam appeared out of the crowd.

She pushed through the crush of people to the spot where the Quinn brothers had congregated. Brendan gave her a quick kiss on the cheek and Dylan slipped off his stool to give her a place to sit.

"I'm looking for Conor," she said nervously. "Is he here?"

Brendan laughed. "Nope. We're all waiting for him. This party is in his honor."

"A party for Conor? For what?"

"A work thing. He's back on the job," Dylan explained. He paused, then winced as if he realized he'd probably spoken out of turn. "He didn't tell you about the Internal Affair investigation?"

Olivia nodded. "He did. But Conor and I haven't seen each other for a while. Since the case is done, there's no reason to…" She drew a shaky breath. "I just need to talk to him." She stood up. "Can you tell me where he lives?"

"You stay here," Dylan said. He pushed away from the bar. "We'll find him for you. Brendan, you check his apartment. I'll stop by the precinct and see if he's still working. Sean and Brian, why don't you check out his favorite cop bars? And Liam, you keep Olivia company. Get her something to eat and drink. This damn party was for him and it's about time he showed up, whether he wants to or not."

Olivia watched as they all strode to the front door, tall and dark and each one as handsome as Conor. She turned back to Liam and forced a smile, then folded her hands in front of her on the scarred wooden bar. "I guess I'll have a soda while I wait."

Liam sent her a devilish smile. "You're sittin' in Quinn's Pub, lassie. You'll have a Guinness or you'll have nothing at all."

CONOR STEPPED OUT of his car in front of Quinn's Pub for the second time that night. The street was dark and quiet, almost eerily so in the heavy fog. The bar had closed fifteen minutes ago, but Conor knew a few of his brothers would still be inside, ready to draw him a Guinness.

He'd been all over the city in search of Olivia. He'd even had his buddy at dispatch put out an APB on her car only to find it parked down the block from her house on St. Botolph Street. He'd stopped at her flat twice, checked the shop three times and had even knocked on Mrs. Callahan's door, wondering if she might know anything about Olivia's whereabouts. The landlady had regarded him suspiciously, as if he were there to return Tommy to her care. Once she was certain he didn't have the cat with him, she grudgingly told him that she hadn't heard from Olivia since she'd paid her rent a week ago.

He slowly strolled across the wet street toward the pub. Now that Red Keenan was incarcerated and awaiting sentencing at the Suffolk County Jail, Kevin Ford was free to go on with his life. Conor had wasted more than a few hours wondering if he and Olivia were relaxing on some tropical beach somewhere.

He'd seen that look in Ford's eyes when he'd talked about Olivia. He had a suspicion Ford wouldn't stop at anything to make Olivia his, in the same way Conor wouldn't. But then Ford had the advantage of proximity. Conor cursed softly. He should never have let her go. Though his job had been in jeopardy and he didn't have anything to offer her, he still should have grabbed for the gold ring while he had the chance.

He yanked open the front door and stepped inside the dimly lit pub. The air was hazy with smoke and the jukebox played softly in the far corner. A few stragglers still sat at the bar and in the booths near the back. Conor slid onto a stool, then waved at Dylan who nursed a beer just a few stools away.

"You missed your party," Dylan said.

"What party?" Conor asked with a wry smile.

Sean stepped up and placed a half pint of Guinness in front of Conor. "Where were you? We've all been out looking for you. Geez, Con, you're a hard man to find when you don't want to be found."

"I had some business to take care of," Conor said. He reached out for the Guinness and took a long drink.

Sean wiped the bar around him with a damp towel, then tossed the towel over his shoulder. "Well, you had business here, too."

Conor shook his head wearily. "I wasn't in the mood for a party," he countered. In truth, all he wanted was to find Olivia. Unfortunately, he hadn't been able to make that happen.

"He's not talking about a party," Dylan explained. "He's talking about Olivia."

Conor's head snapped up at the mention of her name. "Olivia?"

Sean cocked his head toward the back of the bar. "Brendan's keeping her company at the dartboard. She's been waiting for most of the night."

"For me?" Conor asked.

"No, idiot," Sean muttered. "For his Holiness the Pope. If

I were you, I'd get back there before Brendan has her completely charmed and she decides she came here for the wrong Quinn."

Conor sat frozen to his seat. What would he say to her? What would she say to him? He'd made so many mistakes already, an apology was probably in order. But after that, the only thing he could think to tell her was that he loved her. "It all comes down to this," he murmured. In just a few minutes, he'd know whether he'd found the woman he was meant to spend his life with or whether he'd made a mistake he'd regret for the rest of his life.

"Just tell her how you feel," Dylan suggested, as if he could read Conor's mind.

Conor had always been the one to provide sage advice to his younger brothers, but now he was on the receiving end of their advice and he wasn't sure he should trust them. Besides, what about all those family legends about the Mighty Quinns? Was he willing to trust his heart to a woman, to risk that she might someday walk out on him?

"She loves you, Con," Sean murmured. "She wouldn't have come here if that wasn't so. Don't be a jackass and mess this up. Besides, it's about time one of us tested that damn family curse. It might as well be you."

Conor pushed off the bar stool, took another long drink of his Guinness, then wiped his mouth on the back of his hand. He started toward the back of the bar, and though he'd walked that same path hundreds of times before, this time it felt like he was walking a mile, every step filled with doubt and insecurity.

He walked past Liam and Brian, who were deep into a game of eight ball. Both Brendan and Olivia had their backs to him as they aimed darts at the board mounted on the rear wall. Olivia was laughing and Brendan was teasing her. When they both went to reclaim their darts and count the score, Conor held his breath. And then she turned and faced him and their eyes met.

Everything and everyone around them suddenly faded into the background. He didn't hear what Brendan said and the music playing from the jukebox became just a jumble of sound. Instead, he heard her soft gasp, saw the light reflecting off her pale hair, smelled the scent of her perfume. It was all magnified a hundred times until his heart and soul was filled with her.

"Hi," he murmured.

"Hi," she replied.

Conor drew a shaky breath. "I've been looking for you. I went to your apartment and to the shop, but you weren't there."

"I was here," she said, glancing around nervously.

He swallowed hard, the words he wanted to say catching in his throat. "You look beautiful." It was all he could manage but it was the truth. He was stunned by the sight of her, shocked that his memories of her hadn't even come close to the reality of the woman before him. Conor silently vowed that he'd never depend on memories again.

He took a step toward her. "I wanted to find you because there are some things I need to tell you."

"There are some things I need to tell you," she countered.

"Those last few days when we were together, I—"

"I know," Olivia said. "They weren't about the job, were they?"

"How did you know?" Conor asked.

"Kevin Ford told me that he cut a deal the day after you

visited him, nine days before the trial began. You got around to telling me I was safe four days before the trial. So I had to wonder, what was going on for the rest of that time. Why didn't you just take me home?"

Conor raked his hand through his hair, then tried to calm his nerves. "Olivia, I don't know any better way to put it than to just come out and say the words. I love you. Hell, I've probably loved you since the very moment you kicked me in the shin and called me a Neanderthal. And I'm sorry it's taken me so long to realize it, but I kept trying to convince myself that it was just part of the job. That my feelings of protectiveness were all mixed up with feelings I thought I had for you." He drew a long breath. "But now I know that's not true. I know how I feel and I don't want to live another day of my life without you."

Now that the words had started to come, Conor couldn't seem to stop them. He grabbed Olivia's hands and led her over to a booth, then slipped in opposite her. When they were both seated, he wrapped his fingers around hers and stared her eyes.

"I suppose you're wondering how I know I love you," he continued.

"Not really," Olivia murmured. "I just—"

"Well, let me explain," he interrupted. "You see, when my mother left she just forgot all about us. We were her children and she just walked away. And I guess I always thought if it was so easy for our own mother to walk away, then it would be even easier for any other woman to do the same. Including you."

"I would never—"

"And when we first met," Conor said, "I tried to maintain

my distance, but you needed me. And in the end, I think I needed you just as much." He took a quick breath, then continued on, certain that if he stopped talking she'd find some gentle way of rejecting him. He had to lay out his whole case and prove the truth of his words. If he didn't, she might just walk away. He drew her hands to his lips and kissed her fingertips. "You got inside of me, Olivia, and no woman has ever done that before. And I—"

"Can I just say something, please?" she asked in an impatient tone.

Conor froze, his lips just inches from her fingertips. This was it. She was going to brush aside everything he'd said and tell him that they could never have a future together. "All right."

A smile broke across her face and her eyes glittered with unshed tears. "Would you please stop talking and just kiss me?"

Stunned, he stared at her for a long moment. In that time, he saw all the emotion, all the love that he had for her, reflected in Olivia's eyes. With a low growl, Conor leaned over the table and did exactly as she requested. And as he kissed her, Conor knew that this woman would never bring him down. With every moment they spent together, he would become a better man. She loved him and with her love he felt as if he could rule the world.

He cupped her face in his hands and deepened the kiss until the need inside him grew to a soft ache. When they finally paused to draw breath, he gazed into her eyes. "Marry me," he murmured. "Make me the happiest man in the world."

"I will," Olivia said.

Conor laughed, then sat back in the booth. He'd expected an excuse, a plea to wait before they took such a serious step.

After all, they'd known each other less than a month. But as Olivia smiled, he knew she was as anxious to begin their future together as he was, and they already knew enough to want that future to begin now. "Really? You'll marry me?"

She nodded. "I will marry you, Conor Quinn. And we'll live together and love together and I promise to give you handsome Irish sons and pretty Irish daughters." She reached out and softly touched his cheek. "And I promise that no matter what troubles come our way, I will never, ever leave you."

With that, Conor stood and slipped out of the booth, then tugged her out behind him. He couldn't resist pulling her into his arms and kissing her again, long and hard. When he was through, he glanced around to find his brothers all standing nearby. He laughed, then hugged Olivia to him. "I'm getting married."

"Oh, yeah?" Dylan shouted. "And where did you find a woman crazy enough to marry you?"

"The same place he found a woman willing to be a sister-in-law to a bunch of rowdy Irish brothers," Olivia said. "That is, if you'll have me."

The Quinn brothers gathered close, showering Olivia with their best wishes and a fair share of kisses as well. Conor stood back, watching the woman he'd come to love more than life itself, and the brothers who had been his life up until he'd met Olivia. And when all the congratulations were given, he grabbed his glass of Guinness from a nearby table and raised it above his head.

"To the Quinn family legend," he said.

His brothers grabbed their own glasses and held them up. "To the Quinn family legend."

Conor stared into Olivia's eyes, unable to believe that he'd won such a prize. "May you all find a woman as wonderful as Olivia, and may you all be laid low by your love for her. For a Mighty Quinn is nothing without a woman by his side."

They all took a drink of their Guinness and then Conor grabbed Olivia around the waist and kissed her again. Liam put a quarter in the jukebox and the strains of a lively Irish reel filled the bar. Conor swept Olivia into the dance, spinning her around and around until her face was flushed and she was breathless. And as they danced, he thought about all the dances they'd share in their future—the first dance together as man and wife, a dance on each of their anniversaries, a dance at the wedding of each of the children they would have.

He knew as long as he had Olivia at his side, in his arms, he would never regret a single moment of his life. A Mighty Quinn had found a mate and now that he'd found her, he'd wasn't about to let her go.

DYLAN

Prologue

THE WINTER'S SNOW had melted and a damp wind blew off the Atlantic, bringing the scent of the ocean into the South Boston neighborhood around Kilgore Street. Dylan Quinn climbed higher into the old tree, scrambling up branches that were just beginning to show their springtime buds, branches that could barely hold the weight of a squirrel much less an eleven-year-old boy. If he could just get a wee bit higher, maybe he could see the ocean from his perch. His da was due home today after almost three months away.

Winter was always a difficult time for the six Quinn boys. When the weather became too brutal in the North Atlantic, the swordfishing fleet drifted south, following the fish into warmer waters. And *The Mighty Quinn,* his father's boat, followed the fish wherever they went. With the coming of winter came the familiar fear that always grew in the pit of Dylan's stomach. Would Da remember to send them money for food? Would Conor be able to keep the family together? And would they all avoid the mistakes that might bring the social workers calling?

"Can ya see him?"

Dylan glanced down to find his younger brother Brendan standing beneath the leafless tree. He wore a tattered coat and his da's cast-off wool cap and his breath frosted in the air around his head. Like all the Quinns, he had nearly black hair and pale eyes that were an odd mixture of green and gold, strange enough to cause comment whenever they all appeared as one.

"Get away," Dylan yelled. Though he and Brendan were close in age, lately he'd come to resent his little brother's constant presence. After all, Dylan was eleven and Brendan was only ten. The kid didn't have to follow him everywhere he went, hanging on his every word.

"You're supposed to be watchin' Liam and the twins," Brendan said. "If Conor comes home and finds you out here, he'll eat the head off you!"

Their older brother, Con, had left the two of them in charge while he walked to a nearby market to buy food. They were down to their last dollars and if Da didn't come home today, Con would be forced to pinch whatever he could from the grocery to feed them for the weekend. They got breakfast and lunch at school, so it was easy to get through the week. But weekends were the worst—especially when the money ran out.

"Ah, shut your gob, you maggot," Dylan shouted, the

ache of hunger acute in his stomach. He hated being hungry. It was the worst feeling in the world. When the pangs got too bad, he focused on his future, on a time when he'd be grown and living on his own. He'd have power over his own life then and the first thing he'd be sure of was that his cupboards would always be filled with food.

He saw the hurt in Brendan's eyes and immediately regretted his angry words. They'd always been the best of friends, but something inside Dylan had changed. Lately, he felt the need to distance himself, to rebel against the hand he'd been dealt. Maybe it would have been different if his mother had stayed. Maybe they'd be living in a nice warm house, wearing new clothes and having food on the table every night. But any dream of that ended six years ago, when Fiona Quinn left the house on Kilgore Street never to return again.

There were still traces of her to be found, in the lace curtains that now hung limply from the kitchen window and in the pretty rag rugs that she'd brought from their home in Ireland. Dylan really didn't remember much of Ireland. He'd only been four years old when they'd left. But Ireland was still thick in his father's voice, and he held on to that—maybe because it was the only thing he had of Seamus Quinn that he could hold on to.

But his mother was a different matter. He'd lie in bed at night and close his eyes and try to conjure a picture of her in his head, of her dark hair and pretty face. But the image was always faded and blurry and just out of reach. He remembered her voice though, the lilting sound of Ireland in her every word. He wanted to feel safe again, but Dylan knew that the only thing in the world that could make him feel that way was her. And she was gone—for good and forever.

"If you fall out of that tree and break your leg, you'll bring that witch from social services back down on us," Brendan called.

Dylan cursed beneath his breath, then slowly made his way down the tree. Usually Con was the one with all the common sense and Brendan was up for a bit of trouble. About ten feet above Brendan's head, Dylan swung from a branch and then dropped lightly to muddy ground beside him. With a playful growl, Dylan grabbed his brother in a headlock and rubbed his skull with his knuckles. "Don't give me any of your guff, boyo!"

They both raced toward the house and once inside, kicked off their muddy boots and shrugged out of their coats. In comparison to the damp outside, the house almost seemed warm, but Dylan knew that within a few minutes, the chill would begin to seep into his bones and he'd wrap himself in his coat again.

He wandered into the front parlor where Con had set up a small space heater. The floor was littered with blankets and pillows. The six of them slept here, together, for most of the winter. Dylan walked over to the heater and kicked away the sweater that Sean had so carelessly tossed aside. "Keep your stuff away from the heater," he shouted. "How many times do I have to tell you that? It'll start a fire and we'll all be burned to a crisp."

Dylan sat down in the center of the room and grabbed the stuffed bear that was Liam's favorite, then made it dance on the floor in front of his little brother. Brendan brought out a deck of cards and a box of stick matches and then dealt three hands of poker between him and the twins, Sean and Brian. Though it was nearly five o'clock, no one mentioned dinner. It was better not to think about it and simply pray that Da would come soon, his pockets bulging with money.

The front door creaked and they all turned, each of them hoping to see Seamus Quinn enter. But it was Con who came in, holding a single grocery bag in his arms. Though he was only thirteen, in Dylan's eyes Conor was already a man. Tall and strong, he could best any boy his age and five years older on the neighborhood playgrounds. And no matter how bad things got, Con was always there, silent yet reassuring.

He glanced up at them then grinned against the hopeful looks sent his way. "Da will be home soon," he said. "And I've got dinner." He pulled a TV dinner from the bag. "Three for a dollar. There's spaghetti and fish sticks. Dylan, why don't you tell the boys a story, while I warm these."

"A story," Brian cried. "Tell us a Mighty Quinn story."

"Let Brendan tell," Dylan grumbled. "He's better at stories than I am."

"No," Conor said. "It's your turn. You're just as good at stories."

Grudgingly, Dylan settled himself on the floor. The twins wriggled closer and Liam crawled into his lap and looked up at him with wide eyes. Conor's stories always featured the supernatural—elves and trolls and gnomes and fairies. Brendan had a knack for stories of faraway places and magical kingdoms. Dylan's specialty was action, stories filled with deeds of derring-do—highwaymen who robbed from the rich and gave to the poor or brave knights who rescued fair maidens.

They had all played storyteller at one time to the younger boys, a trait inherited from their father. Seamus Quinn was always ready with a mythical tale of the Mighty Quinns, long-ago ancestors who followed only one rule—they never succumbed to the love of a woman. For Seamus Quinn believed that once a Mighty Quinn gave his heart away, his strength would leave him and he'd become weak and pitiful.

"This is the story of Odran Quinn and how he battled a giant to save the life of a beautiful princess," Dylan began.

Brendan flopped down on his stomach and cupped his chin in his hand, ready to listen. They'd all heard the tale many times before from their father, so Dylan knew they would correct any mistakes he made in the telling of it.

"You know the story of how Finn sent his son Odran Quinn to serve the great king of Tiranog. Odran was brave and loyal and the king wanted him to live in his kingdom and rule beside him. Tiranog was a paradise beneath the waves, where the trees were heavy with fruit and there was wine and food aplenty. The king sent his most beautiful daughter, the Princess Neve, to convince Odran to come. Of course, Odran didn't really like Neve, but he decided to go anyway, just to see what this fancy place, Tiranog, was all about."

"That's not the way it goes," Conor called from the kitchen.

"He fell in love with the Princess Neve. She was beautiful and she had a dowry of gold and silver," Brendan added.

"Well, he may have liked her a wee bit," Dylan said. "But he was careful not to love her."

"He said, 'Father, she is the most beautiful woman I have ever met,'" Brendan countered.

"All right, who's telling this story, you or me?"

"You!" Liam said.

"It was with a heavy heart that Odran left his father's home and rode away with the Princess Neve. They rode swiftly across the land and when they reached the sea, their white horses danced lightly over the waves. And then the sea parted and Odran Quinn found himself in a beautiful kingdom, full of sunshine and flowers and tall castles."

"When does the part about the giant come?" Liam asked.

Dylan gave him a playful hug. "Soon. On their long ride to the king's castle, Neve and Odran came upon a fortress. Odran asked Neve, 'Who lives in this place?' and Neve answered, 'A lady lives there. She was captured by a giant and he keeps her prisoner until she agrees to marry him.'" Dylan paused. "Odran Quinn looked up and saw the lady sitting by a window in the highest tower. A tear on her cheek glinted in the sunlight and Odran knew what he had to do. 'I must save her,' he said."

This was the part that Dylan liked the best, for when he told it, he pictured his mother as the lady sitting by the window. She was wearing a beautiful gown, all shiny and new, and her dark hair was braided and twisted elaborately around her head. And at her neck she wore a pendant, sparkling with emeralds and sapphires and rubies. His mother had a necklace like that and he remembered her rubbing it between her fingers when she looked worried.

"The giant's name was Fomor," Sean interrupted. "You forgot that part."

The image dissolved and Dylan turned back to his brothers. "And he was as tall as two houses with legs like huge oaks," he continued. "He carried a sword that was as sharp as a razor."

"Tell us about his hair," Brian pleaded.

Dylan lowered his voice and bent closer. "It was long and black and infested with spiders and weevils and his tangled beard nearly reached the ground." His brothers' eyes widened in fear. "And he had a big belly for every day he ate three little boys for lunch and three more for dinner. Bones and all." When they were properly terrified, Dylan sat back. "For days and days, they fought, the giant with his strength and mighty Odran Quinn with his cunning. And on the tenth day, when he was near death himself, Odran dealt the giant a mortal blow with his sword, and the giant came crashing down, the earth trembling all around. He was cold and dead as a stone."

Sean clapped. "And then Odran cuts his head off!"

"And then he climbs the castle wall and rescues the woman from the fortress and frees her from her prison," Brian added.

"That he does," Dylan said. "That he—"

The front door crashed open and they all turned to look. A moment later, Seamus Quinn strode in with a chilly gust of wind. "Where are my boys?" he shouted, his voice slurred. With joyous cries, Brian and Sean and Liam scrambled to their feet and went running toward their father, ending the tale of Odran and Fomor. Brendan and Dylan gave each other a long look, one laced with both relief and resignation. Though they were glad to see him, it was clear that Seamus had stopped for a pint or five before he'd come home. At least he'd come home.

"In all your stories, there's always a rescue," Brendan commented softly.

Dylan shrugged. "There's not," he replied. But he knew that wasn't true. With every story he told, he imagined himself as the Mighty Quinn, risking his life to save others, hailed as a hero by one and all. And the princess in need of rescuing always looked like his mother, or what he remembered his mother to look like. Dylan got to his feet, ready to greet his da. Someday he would be a hero. Someday, when he was all done growing and he could fend for himself, he would ride to the rescue and save those in trouble.

And maybe, against all his father's warnings, there would be a beautiful damsel who would thank him for his good deed by loving him forever.

1

THE ALARM SOUNDED at precisely 3:17 p.m. Dylan Quinn looked up from polishing the chrome fittings on Engine 22. He couldn't count the times he'd spit-shined the engine only to have the alarm sound. Most of the men of Ladder Company 14 and Engine Company 22 were upstairs relaxing after a long lunch but as they started to come down, Dylan tossed the polishing cloth aside and moved toward the alcove that held his boots, jacket and helmet.

A voice blared over the speaker system, the dispatcher repeating the address of the fire three times. The moment Dylan heard the address, he paused. Hell, it was just a few blocks from the station! As the others pulled on their gear, Dylan stepped out the wide garage doors and looked down Boylston Street.

He couldn't see any smoke. Hopefully, they'd arrive to

find a contained fire that wasn't blazing out of control. The buildings in the older areas of Boston were built one right next to the other, and though firewalls prevented the spread of a blaze, the cramped spaces made it harder to get to a fire and then fight it.

The horn of the fire engine blared and Dylan slowly turned and gave Ken Carmichael, the driver, a wave. The truck pulled out of the station and as it passed, Dylan hopped on the rear running board and held on as they swung out onto the street. His heart started to beat a little quicker and his senses sharpened, as they did every time the company headed out to a fire.

As they wove through traffic on Boylston Street, he thought back to the moment he'd decided to become a firefighter. When he was a kid, he'd wanted to be a highwayman or a knight of the Round Table. But when he graduated from high school, neither one of those jobs were available. He wasn't interested in college. His older brother, Conor, had just started at the police academy, so Dylan had decided on the fire academy, a place that felt right the moment he walked in the door.

Unlike the days of his reckless youth when school barely mattered, Dylan had worked hard to be the top recruit in his class—the fastest, the strongest, the smartest, the bravest. The Boston Fire Department had a long and respected tradition, founded over three hundred years before as the nation's first paid municipal fire department. And now, Dylan Quinn, who had had the most rootless upbringing of all, was a part of that history. As a firefighter, he was known to be cautious yet fearless, aggressive yet compassionate, the kind of man trusted by all those who worked with him.

Only two other firefighters in the history of the department had made lieutenant faster than him and he was on track to make captain in a few more years, once he finished his degree at night school. But it wasn't about the glory or the excitement or even the beautiful women who seemed to flock around firefighters. It had always been about the opportunity to save someone's life, to snatch a complete stranger from the jaws of death and give them another chance. If that made him a hero, then Dylan wasn't sure why. It was just one of the perks of the job.

The engine slowly drew to a stop in the middle of traffic and Dylan grabbed his ax and hopped off. He double-checked the address, then noticed a wisp of pale gray smoke coming from the open door of a shop. A moment later, a slender woman with a soot-smudged face hurried out the front door.

"Thank God, you're here," she cried. "Hurry."

She ran back inside and Dylan took off after her. "Lady! Stop!" The last thing he needed was a civilian deliberately putting herself in harm's way. Although at first glance the fire didn't look dangerous, he'd learned to be wary of first impressions. The interior of the shop was filled with a hazy smoke, not much thicker than the cigarette smoke that hung over his father's pub after a busy Saturday night, but he knew a flare or an explosion could be just a second away. The acrid smell made his eyes sting and Dylan recognized the odor of burning rubber.

He found her behind a long counter, frantically beating at a small fire with a charred dish towel. Grabbing her arm, he pulled her back against him. "Lady, you have to leave. Let us take care of this before you get hurt."

"No!" she cried, trying to wriggle out of his arms. "We have to put it out before it does any damage."

Dylan glanced over his shoulder to see two members of his team enter, one of them carrying a fire extinguisher. "It looks like it's contained in this machine. Crack it open and look for the source," he ordered. Then he pulled the woman along beside him toward the door.

"Crack it open?" The woman dug in her heels, yanking them both to a stop.

Even beneath the light coating of soot, Dylan could see she was beautiful. She had hair the color of rich mahogany and it tumbled in soft waves around her shoulders. Her profile was perfect, every feature balanced from her green eyes to her straight nose to the sensuous shape of her wide mouth. He had to shake himself out of a careful study of her lips before he remembered the job at hand.

"Lady, if you don't leave right now, I'm going to have to carry you out," Dylan warned. He let his gaze rake her body, from the clinging sweater to the almost-too-short leather mini to the funky boots. "And considering the length of that skirt, you don't want me tossing you over my shoulder."

She seemed insulted by both his take-charge attitude and his comment on her wardrobe. Dylan studied her from beneath the brim of his helmet. Her eyes were bright with indignation and her breath came in quick gasps, making her breasts rise and fall in a tantalizing rhythm.

"This is my shop," she snapped. "And I'm not going to let you chop it apart with your axes!"

With a soft curse, Dylan did what he'd done hundreds of times before, both in practice and in reality. He bent down, grabbed her around the legs, then hoisted her over his shoulder. "I'll be back in a second," he called to his crew.

She kicked and screamed but Dylan barely noticed. Instead, his attention was diverted by the shapely backside nestled against his ear. He probably could have spent a little more time convincing her to leave the shop, but her stubborn attitude indicated that it would probably be a long fight. Besides, she was just a slip of a girl. He'd once carried a three-hundred-pound man down three flights. She weighed maybe one-twenty, tops.

When Dylan got her outside, he gently set her down next to one of the trucks, then tugged at the hem of her miniskirt to restore her dignity. She slapped at his hand as if he'd deliberately tried to molest her. His temper flared. "Stay here," he ordered through clenched teeth.

"No!" she said, making a move toward the door.

She slipped past him and Dylan raced after her, catching up a few steps inside the door of the shop. He grabbed her around the waist and pulled her back against him, her backside nestling into his lap in a way that made him forget all about the dangers of fire and focus on the dangers of a soft, feminine body.

They both watched as Artie Winton hooked his ax behind the smoking machine and yanked it onto the floor. Then he dragged it into the middle of the shop, raised the ax and brought it down. A few moments later, Jeff Reilly covered the mess of twisted stainless steel with a coating of foam from the extinguisher.

"This is the source," Jeff called. "It looks like that's all the farther it got."

"What was it?" Dylan asked.

Reilly squatted down to take a better look. "One of those frozen yogurt machines?"

"Nah," Winton said. "It's one of those fancy coffeemakers."

"It's an Espresso Master 8000 Deluxe."

Dylan glanced down to see the woman staring at the mess of stainless steel. A tear trickled down her cheek and she gnawed on her lower lip. Dylan cursed softly. If there was one thing he hated about fighting fires, it was the tears. Though he had given bad news to victims before, he'd never really known what to do about the tears. And to his ears, his words of sympathy always sounded so hollow and forced.

He cleared his throat. "I want you two to check around," he ordered as he patted the woman's shoulder. "Make sure we don't have any electrical shorts or hot spots in the walls. We don't know what kind of wiring they've got in here. Look for a breaker panel and see if it's flipped."

He pulled off his gloves and took the woman's hand in his, then gently pulled her toward the door. He should have been thinking about what to say, but instead he was fascinated by how delicate her fingers felt in his hand. "There's nothing you can do in here," he said softly. "We'll check everything out and if it's safe, you can go back in after the smoke clears."

When they got outside, he led her toward the back of the truck and gently pushed her down until she sat on the wide back bumper. A paramedic came rushing up but Dylan waved him off. Her tears came more freely now and Dylan felt his heart twist. He fought the impulse to gather her in his arms. She really didn't have much to cry about. All she'd lost was a coffeemaker.

"It's all right," he said. "I know you were scared, but you're fine. And you barely lost a thing."

She snapped her head up and leveled an angry glare at him. "That machine was worth fifteen thousand dollars! That's the best machine on the market. It makes four shots of espresso in fifteen seconds. And you and your ax-wielding Huns chopped it to bits."

Stunned by the intensity of her outburst, Dylan took a step back as if scorched by her words. She owed him at least a small bit of gratitude! "Listen, lady, I—"

"My name's not lady!" she cried.

"Well, whatever your name is, you should be happy," he said, unable to keep the anger from edging his voice. "No, you should be thrilled. Today was a good day. No one died." Dylan sighed, then lightened his tone. "You didn't get hurt, no one got hurt, you didn't lose precious family mementos or your favorite pet. You lost a coffeemaker, and a defective one at that."

Her mouth snapped shut and she looked up at him through thick, damp lashes. Dylan watched as another tear trickled down her cheek and he fought the temptation to reach out and catch it with his thumb.

"It's not just any coffeemaker," she reminded him.

"I know. It's an Espresso Deluxe 5000 whatever," he said. "A big hunk of stainless steel with a few gauges and a lot of tubing. Lady, I have to say that—"

"My name's not lady," she insisted. She brushed the hair from her face, then wiped off a smudge of soot from the end of her nose. "It's Meggie Flanagan."

Up until that very instant, the moment she'd said her name, Dylan hadn't recognized her. She'd changed—a lot. But there were still traces of the girl he knew so long ago. "Meggie Flanagan? Mary Margaret Flanagan? Tommy Flanagan's little sister."

She sent him a dismissive look. "Maybe."

Dylan chuckled, then pulled his hat off and ran his fingers through his hair. "Little Meggie Flanagan. So how's your brother? I haven't seen him for ages."

She regarded him suspiciously at first, then her gaze flitted over to the name tape on his jacket right below his left shoulder. Her expression fell and a blush rose on her cheeks, so intense Dylan could see it beneath the soot. "Quinn," she murmured. "Oh, God." She braced her elbows on her knees, then buried her face in her hands. "I should have figured you'd show up and try to ruin my life all over again."

"Ruin your life?" Dylan asked. "I saved your life!"

She jumped to her feet. "You did not," Meggie countered. "I was perfectly capable of putting out that fire on my own."

Dylan crossed his arms over his chest. "Then why did you call the fire department?" he inquired.

"I didn't," she muttered. "The alarm company did."

He grabbed the dish towel from her hand and waved it in her face. "And is this how you were planning to put it out?" Dylan shook his head. "I'll bet you don't even have a fire extinguisher inside, do you. If you only knew how many serious fires could be stopped with a simple fire extinguisher, I—" She tipped her chin up defiantly and his words died in his throat.

Meggie Flanagan. He almost felt embarrassed by his earlier attraction. After all, she was the little sister of one of his
old buddies. There were unwritten rules between guys and
one of the biggest was you didn't hit on a friend's sister. But
Meggie wasn't that gawky kid with the braces and the goofy
glasses anymore. And he hadn't seen Tommy for years. "I
could cite you for a code violation."

"Oh, go ahead," she challenged. With a soft curse, she
neatly turned on her heel and walked back toward the shop.
"Considering our history, I wouldn't put it past you."

History? Dylan stared after her. "Meggie Flanagan," he
repeated, this time out loud. He'd always remembered her
as a shy and nervous kid, the kind of girl who stood back
and watched the world from a safe distance. This woman
could never be classified as shy. She used to be so skinny—
and flat as a board. Even from his vantage point, he could
see that she'd filled out in all the right places.

He'd spent hours after school at Tommy Flanagan's
house, listening to music or playing video games. And she'd
always been there, silently watching them through those
thick glasses, standing in the shadows so she wouldn't be
seen. He'd practically lived at the Flanagan house when he
was a senior, but it wasn't the video games that brought him
back again and again. Tommy's mother was a cheerful and
loving woman and she could always be depended on for an
invitation to dinner, which Dylan gladly accepted.

Meggie always sat across from him at the table and whenever he'd looked up, she was always staring at him, the very
same stare she fixed on him whenever they met in the hall-
ways at school. She was two years behind him, a sophomore

when he was a senior, and though they'd never shared a class, he saw her at least once or twice a day near his locker or in the lunch room. He'd seen how the kids poked fun of her and Tommy had been particularly protective, so Dylan had felt the same, considering her a surrogate little sister.

He watched now as she paced back and forth in front of her shop, rubbing her arms against the early November wind. The urge to protect was still there, but it was heavily laced with an undeniable attraction, an overwhelming need to touch her again just to see if his reaction was the same. Dylan shrugged off his jacket then walked over to her. "Here," he said. "You're going to catch a cold."

He didn't wait for her assent, merely draped the heavy waterproof jacket over her shoulders, allowing his hands to linger just a moment. The tingle that shot up his arms when he touched her did not go unnoticed. She stopped pacing and gave him a reluctant "thank you."

"What did you mean?" he asked, leaning back against the brick facade of the building to watch her pace. "When you said I'd ruined your life once before?"

She frowned. "Nothing. It doesn't make a difference."

Dylan shook his head and smiled in an attempt to lighten her mood. "I hardly recognize you, Meggie. Except for the name. We never really knew each other, did we?"

An odd expression crossed her face and he wasn't sure if he read it right, through the soot and the windblown hair. Had he hurt her by his words? Was there a reason he was supposed to remember her?

To his disappointment, their conversation ended there. The radio on the truck sounded another alarm and the firefighters gathered at the scene stopped to listen. Dispatch gave an address in an industrial area, a factory fire, already a three-alarm blaze. "I have to go," he said, reaching out and giving her hand a squeeze. "It should be safe to go back inside now. And I'm sorry about your machine."

She opened her mouth, as if she had something more to say, then snapped it shut. "Thank you," she murmured.

He walked backward toward the truck, strangely unable to take his eyes away from her. For a moment, she looked like the girl he'd remembered, standing all alone on the sidewalk, unsure of herself, hands clutched in front of her. "Say 'hi' to Tommy the next time you see him."

"I will," she called, her gaze still fixed to his.

The truck rumbled to life behind him and Ken Carmichael honked the horn impatiently. "Maybe I'll see you around," Dylan added.

"Your jacket!" she called, slipping out of it.

He waved. "We've got extras in the truck."

He hopped inside the cab and took a spot behind the driver, then pulled the door shut. As they drove away from the scene, sirens wailing and lights blazing, Dylan glanced up and found Artie and Jeff grinning at him. "Gee, Quinn, what happened to your jacket?" Artie asked. "Did you lose it in the fire?"

Dylan shrugged.

"We could be fighting a fire on the moon and you'd still manage to find a woman to charm," Jeff said. He leaned forward and shouted to the driver. "Hey, Kenny, we have to go back. Quinn left his jacket behind again."

Carmichael chuckled, then yanked on the horn as he maneuvered through afternoon traffic. "That boy has a nasty habit of losing jackets. I'll just have to tell the chief to take it out of his pay."

Dylan pulled the extra jacket off the hook beside his head and slipped into it. This time he wasn't sure he wanted it back. Meggie Flanagan wasn't like the other women for whom the ploy had worked so well. For one thing, she didn't gaze up at him with an adoring look. From what he could tell, she pretty much hated him. And she certainly wasn't the kind of girl he could just seduce, then leave. She was the kid sister of a very old friend.

He drew a long breath, then let it out slowly. No, it would be a long time before he retrieved his jacket from Meggie Flanagan.

A THIN COAT OF GRIMY soot covered every surface in the shop. The grand opening of Cuppa Joe was scheduled for the day after Thanksgiving and Meggie was overwhelmed by the task in front of her. She still had to train eight new employees and finish up with the last details of the decor. A call to the insurance company assured her of a check for both a cleaning crew and a new machine. But she didn't have time to wait for the crew to come. Tables and chairs were due to be delivered tomorrow. If they expected to open on time, she and her business partner, Lana Richards, would have to get the place in shape on their own.

The smoke hadn't been the worst of yesterday's fire. The destruction of her espresso maker had been a crushing blow. "Three months," she muttered. "Three months until they can deliver another machine. I even offered to pay them extra for a rush order, but they said they couldn't do it. Every coffee shop wants one of those machines."

"Can you please stop with the machine?" Lana struggled to her feet and tossed a dirty rag into the bucket of warm water, then brushed her blond hair out of her eyes. "We'll just buy two Espresso Master 4000s. Or four Espresso Master 2000s. Anything so we don't have to talk about the espresso maker anymore."

In truth, she'd had to force herself to think about the machine. It kept her from lapsing into daydreams about the handsome firefighter who had ordered it destroyed. How many times over the past 24 hours had she caught herself adrift in a contemplation of Dylan Quinn? And how many times had the contemplation ended in a surge of well-remembered humiliation.

"This is our business," Meggie said softly. "We didn't spend the last five years saving every penny we made, working at jobs we hated, begging the Bank of Boston for a loan, just to have some overenthusiastic firefighter end it all with one swing of his ax."

Any woman might be fascinated by Dylan Quinn. After all, it wasn't every day you met a real life hero, tall and imposing in his firefighting gear. He seemed made for his job, dauntless and determined…strong and… Meggie sighed softly. There was probably a Dylan Quinn in every woman's life, a man who was the subject of an endless string of "what ifs."

What if she hadn't been such a geek in high school and he hadn't been such a god? What if she'd gotten her braces off a year earlier? What if she'd been able to talk to him without giggling uncontrollably? A moan slipped from her lips. Though she'd come a long way since those days, the memories were still acutely embarrassing.

Over the past years, she'd thought about Dylan Quinn every now and then, wondering what had happened to her first love. On lonely nights or after disastrous dates, she'd even conjure up a fantasy of what it might be like to meet him again. After all, she was different now. The braces and thick glasses had been replaced by perfect teeth and contact lenses. Her once lackluster hair color was now enhanced by one of Boston's best hairdressers. And most importantly of all, she'd grown curves in all the proper places.

Still, there were a few things that hadn't changed. She still wasn't very good with the opposite sex. Though she'd accomplished a lot in her professional life, her personal life left a lot to be desired. It probably had more to do with the men she chose to date, but Meggie just wrote her bad luck off as a lingering effect from too many years as a geek.

Dylan, on the other hand, had been one of the most popular boys in high school. With his dark and dangerous good looks and his devastating charm, he'd been every girl's dream date. But he'd still been a boy and her memories of him had always held an image of a tall, lanky, high-school Casanova with a killer smile. That image had shattered the moment she met those strange and beautiful eyes again.

All the Quinns had those eyes, gold mixed with green, a shade too unique to be called hazel. Those eyes that held the power to turn a girl's knees weak and make her pulse race. And to send Meggie right back to the pain and humiliation of that one night, the night of the Sophomore Frolic.

"The fire wasn't all bad," Lana said. "You got to see Dylan Quinn again."

"I needed that like a sharp stick in the eye," she said.

She and Lana had been friends since their college days at the University of Massachusetts, so there was very little that Lana didn't know about the men—or lack of them—in Meggie's life, both past and present. But the picture of Dylan Quinn she'd painted for her friend hadn't been very flattering—or entirely truthful. Had Lana been asked she probably would have described him as a cross between Hannibal Lector and Bigfoot.

The bell on the front door jingled and Meggie popped up from behind the counter, hoping that her new Espresso Master 4000 Ultra had arrived from the restaurant supply house. But it wasn't Eddie, the usual driver, who walked in the door. This man was tall and good-looking and…Meggie swallowed hard. This man was Dylan Quinn!

With a tiny groan, Meggie dropped back down behind the counter, then tugged on the leg of Lana's jeans. He was the last person she wanted to see! "It's him," she said.

Lana shook her leg until Meggie let go. "Who?"

"Dylan Quinn. Tell him to leave. Tell him we're not open. Tell him there's another coffee shop over on Newbury."

"Oh, my God," Lana murmured, staring toward the front of the shop, stunned by the revelation. "*That's* Dylan Quinn? But he doesn't look—"

Her words were stopped when Meggie slammed her fist down on Lana's big toe. Lana yelped in pain. "Get rid of him. Now!"

Her partner muttered a quiet threat, then stepped out from

behind the counter. "Hello. I bet you're here looking for a good cup of coffee. Well, as you can see, we're not open yet. Our grand opening is in three weeks."

"Actually," he said. "I didn't come for coffee."

The warm rich sound of his voice seemed to seep into her bloodstream as Meggie cowered on the floor. She wondered what it might be like to listen to that voice for an hour or two. Would it become so addictive that she couldn't do without it?

"But I'm sure I could make something for one of Boston's finest," Lana continued. "We'll be one of the few places that serves Jamaican Blue Mountain. Would you like to try a cup? It's like nectar of the gods. An appropriate drink for you, I'd say."

Meggie groaned, then grabbed Lana's leg as she moved to the coffeemaker. "Don't serve him the Jamaican," she whispered. "It's the most expensive thing in the shop. Just get rid of him!"

Lana scooped some beans from a plastic container in the refrigerator, then dumped them in the grinder. "You're Dylan Quinn, aren't you?"

"Do I know you?" Dylan asked.

Just by the tone of his voice, Meggie could tell that he'd turned on the charm full force. And Lana, an accomplished flirt, was lapping it up like a sex kitten with a bowl of cream. He'd give her that boyish smile and those little crinkles at the corners of his eyes would make him look so appealing. And Lana would toss her perfect blond hair over her shoulder and laugh in that deep, throaty way she had. And before Meggie could stop them, they'd be rushing to the drugstore for a box of condoms.

"No," Lana said. "But I'm sure we can remedy that fact. I'm Lana Richards, Meggie's business partner. Meggie told me how you saved her life yesterday—and our shop. We're very grateful. Very. I hope there's a way I—I mean, we—can repay you."

Meggie cursed softly. Lana was doing this on purpose, teasing and taunting her, tweaking her jealousy until she'd be forced to stand up and show herself. Grudgingly, she stood up, then brushed her hair from her eyes. Dylan, who was now leaning over the counter, stepped back in surprise. "Meggie!"

She forced a smile. "I'm sorry, I was just…there was a thing I was…I had my head in the cooler and didn't hear you come in." She cleared her throat. "I'm afraid we're not open for business yet," she said, smoothing her hands over her jeans.

"The poor man has been fighting fires all day long. We could at least offer him something," Lana said.

Meggie crossed her arms beneath her breasts and watched Dylan warily. He'd changed out of his firefighting gear and now wore faded jeans, a T-shirt and a leather jacket, but he looked as rakish as ever. His hair, thick and dark, was still damp at the nape of his neck and she couldn't help but wonder how long ago he'd stepped out of the shower…wet…and naked.

She swallowed hard, then grabbed a rag and began to polish the copper-clad counter. "Gee, I would have thought you'd still be out pillaging," Meggie murmured.

Lana walked behind her and Meggie felt a sharp pain on the back of her arm as her partner pinched her. She cursed softly and rubbed her skin, then spun around and sent Lana a withering glare.

"Be nice," Lana whispered. "I'm going to do some book-work in the office."

"I don't have to be nice," Meggie muttered. "I detest the man."

"Then you go do the bookwork and let me be nice. He's gorgeous. And you know what they say about firefighters."

"What's that," Meggie murmured.

Lana leaned closer and whispered in her ear. "It's not the size of the hose, but where they point it that counts."

An unbidden giggle burst from Meggie's throat and she gave Lana a gentle shove toward the office. When they were finally alone, Meggie sent Dylan a sideways glance, then pulled a paper cup from beneath the counter and set it in front of him. He'd be getting this cup of coffee "to go."

He observed her intently as she waited for the coffee to dribble down into the tall carafe. A smile quirked the corners of his mouth, so easy and confident in his power over her. God, he was even more gorgeous than she remembered. All her friends in school had crushes on the New Kids On The Block, but Meggie had held out for the real thing—Dylan Quinn. Though he was two years older and a high school senior, she'd somehow deluded herself into believing that the feeling was mutual, that Dylan was in love with her. After all, every time he saw her, he'd smiled. And once or twice, he'd even called her by name.

And then it happened. Her brother, Tommy, had mentioned that Dylan was interested in taking her to her Sopho-more Folic. It was the first big dance of her high school career and she'd just assumed she'd be staying home like most of the other wallflowers in her class. But then, Dylan, the most handsome boy in all of South Boston High School, had agreed to escort her to the dance.

She could barely contain herself and she had told all her friends and they told all their friends until the entire sophomore class at Southie knew that Meggie Flanagan had a date with *the* Dylan Quinn. She'd bought a new dress and had shoes dyed to match. And when a corsage arrived earlier in the afternoon, she'd been so excited she'd nearly burst into tears. Then Dylan arrived, dressed in jeans and dragging his little brother, Brian, behind him. Brian, who was dressed in the tux and wearing a goofy grin.

At first, she hadn't understood, but then it became clear—Brian was her date, not Dylan. Though Brian was a Quinn, he hadn't really reached his full Adonis-like potential yet. He was still at least six inches shorter than she was and his idea of charm was staring at her dreamily while he tugged at his bowtie. She would have been better off going with her cousin or even her brother Tommy.

"I suppose you've come to apologize," she said, her back still to him.

He chuckled. "Actually, I came for my jacket. Remember?"

"Oh, right," she murmured. Of course, he wouldn't have come to see her. He was simply retrieving his gear. She slowly turned, then walked to the end of the counter. "I'll go get it. It's in the office."

"No hurry," he said. "You can give it back to me later. After I take you to dinner."

Meggie's heart stopped about the same time her feet did, and for a moment she couldn't breathe. Had she heard him right? Or was her mind playing tricks on her the same way it had all those years ago, when she'd convinced herself that Dylan Quinn harbored secret passions for her. "What?"

"Dinner," he said. "You look like you could use a break and it would give us a chance to catch up on old times."

Meggie swallowed hard. This wasn't happening, this couldn't be real. "I—I really can't," she murmured, turning away to busy herself wiping the back counter. "Not tonight."

"Then tomorrow night? I get off at eight. We could get a bite to eat, then maybe catch a movie."

She shook her head. She'd made a fool of herself once before, falling for him then having her heart stomped on. It wasn't going to happen again. She wouldn't allow it. "No," she said firmly. "I have too much work to do." Meggie grabbed his cup from the counter, then hurried over to fill it from the carafe.

When she'd finished, she spun around to hand it to him. But the hot coffee sloshed over the edge of the cup, scalding the top of her hand. She cried out in pain and dropped the cup, the hot liquid spattering over her shoes. In an instant, he was beside her, taking her hand gently in his and leading her to the small sink tucked beneath the counter.

Dylan flipped on the cold water, then held her hand beneath it. "Do you have ice?" he asked.

Meggie winced, then nodded at the icemaker nearby. He grabbed a towel then wrapped it around a handful of ice before returning to her side. "How does it feel," he asked.

"It hurts," Meggie replied. But in truth, she barely noticed the pain. It had vanished the moment he'd touched her, the flood of adrenaline simply washing it away. He touched her again, this time pulling her hand from beneath the water. He pressed her palm against his chest, then laid the ice over it. Beneath her fingers, she could feel his heart beating, strong and even.

She was thankful their roles weren't reversed for if he felt her heart racing, he'd know exactly how his touch had affected her. "That feels good."

He smiled down at her. "You should be more careful," he murmured, his gaze drifting lazily over her features. He stopped at her lips and she held her breath. For a moment, she was sure that if she closed her eyes and tipped her head up, he'd kiss her.

But then he chuckled softly, and pulled the ice from her hand. "Let see here," he said, carefully examining the skin just below her wrist. "It's a little red but no blistering. I think you'll be all right." He drew her hand up to his lips and pressed a cool kiss on her flaming skin.

Stunned, Meggie yanked her hand away as if she'd been burned all over again. He was teasing her, taking advantage of her nervousness when he was near. Dylan Quinn knew exactly how he made her feel and he was using it against her. "Please, don't do that," she murmured. She snatched the ice from his hands and drew a ragged breath. "I'll just go get your jacket and then you can be on your way."

Dylan stared at her for a long moment, then shrugged indifferently. "I'll get it another time," he said, stepping around the end of the counter. He looked back once. "I'll see you around, Meggie Flanagan." With that, he strode toward the door.

She fought the urge to run after him, to order him to stay away from her coffee shop and out of her life. But instead, all she could manage to do was admire the wide shoulders hidden beneath his leather jacket and the narrow hips accented by his jeans. He stepped through the door and a soft sigh slipped from her lips.

"I am such a coward," she murmured. She'd wanted to accept his invitation to dinner and she'd wanted his kiss to drift from her wrist, up her arm, to her mouth. She wasn't that same clumsy girl that she'd been thirteen years ago. She was a woman, now, almost thirty years old, and only occasionally clumsy. And most men even considered her pretty. She was smart and well-read and always felt that given the right man, she could be a sparkling conversationalist.

Yet the prospect of getting to know Dylan Quinn frightened her. Whenever he was near she reverted to that insecure and anxious teenager. Meggie groaned then pressed her forehead against the cool copper counter. If she'd only been able to think straight, maybe she could have done something once and for all, to even the score between them.

She imagined a wonderfully romantic dinner with witty repartee. He'd fall madly in love with her in just one night and then she'd oh-so casually tell him that she wasn't really interested in a relationship. Or maybe she'd allow him to kiss her and he would experience an instant passion for her before she walked away.

Another groan slipped from her lips. This whole incident only proved one point. She was not the kind of woman who could handle a man like Dylan Quinn. So she had only one choice—she needed to stay as far away from him as possible.

2

DYLAN PARKED JUST down the block from Quinn's Pub. He let the Mustang idle, not sure he wanted to go inside. Saturday night was always a rollicking good time at Seamus Quinn's South Boston watering hole, with an Irish band and free corned-beef sandwiches. And there were sure to be plenty of beautiful women waiting inside, ready and willing to be charmed by one of the Quinn brothers.

How long had he gotten by on just charm alone? Since he was a kid, he'd used his winning personality and good looks to make a place for himself in the world, with his teachers, with his friends, with the opposite sex. Everyone loved Dylan Quinn. But no one ever got to know the real Dylan, the kid whose home life was in such chaos. They could never see how scared he was behind the smiles and the clever quips.

He wasn't scared anymore, yet he hadn't given up trying to charm every woman he met. But since Conor had fallen in love, Dylan realized that he wanted something more from life than just an endless string of beautiful women. He wanted something real and honest. Why couldn't *he* find a woman to love? And why couldn't a woman care enough about *him* to return that love?

"I probably should see a shrink," he muttered as he reached over to flip off the ignition. A weaker man would make an appointment immediately, but he was a Quinn. Quinns just sucked it up and got on with their lives. If they had a problem, they didn't discuss it, they just fixed it. He shoved the car door open and stepped out into the chilly November night. Now, if he could only fix this strange attraction he had to Meggie Flanagan, he'd have all the answers he needed.

Dylan glanced both ways, then jogged across the street, following the sounds of a tin whistle and a fiddle and an Irish drum. After their first encounter, he'd written off any chance of a date with Meggie. Besides the fact that she held some grudge against him, she was still Tommy Flanagan's little sister. But after their second encounter, all the rules had been cast aside. The moment he'd touched her, something inside of him had changed. Though he'd tried, he couldn't think of her as anything but a sexy, desirable woman—who didn't want anything to do with him.

Maybe he was going through a phase. He'd had his fill of women who wanted him. Now, to avoid boredom, he'd become fascinated with the only woman in Boston who had ever rejected him, a woman completely immune to his charms. He shook his head. "You don't need a shrink, boyo, you just need a few pints of Guinness. That'll straighten you out."

He yanked the pub door open and immediately stepped into an atmosphere custom-designed to make him forget his problems with women. He took his time weaving through the crush of patrons and made a slow perusal of the room, searching for a pretty diversion, determined to forget Meggie Flanagan. Dylan started toward an empty stool at the middle of the bar, right next to a cute little brunette who was nursing a beer.

Sliding onto the stool, he waved at Sean and Brian who were taking their turns behind the bar. Seamus was shouting his way through a round of darts and Brendan stood nearby, chatting with one of their father's old friends. He glanced over his shoulder to find Liam at a booth with his current girlfriend. To round out the impromptu family reunion, Dylan was surprised to see Conor and Olivia sitting at the far end of the bar, deep in conversation, their heads close.

His big brother looked completely besotted and every now and then, Conor would pull Olivia near and kiss her without regard to the crowd around him. Had someone told him that Conor would be the first Quinn to fall prey to the love of a woman, Dylan would have laughed. Brendan or Liam were the more logical choices, the more tender-hearted of the bunch. But then, when it came to love, a guy never knew when it might lay him low.

Dylan looked across the room and watched his father engaged in a rousing argument over the exact position of a dart. They'd all heard the tales, the yarns Seamus Quinn spun about the Mighty Quinns and the dangers of love. Dylan had always wondered if he'd become the man he was in an effort to please his father—a guy who had never seemed to approve of anything Dylan did.

He hadn't been Conor, the son who kept the family together. And he hadn't been Brendan, the son who loved to work the lines on his father's swordfishing boat, *The Mighty Quinn*. And he certainly hadn't been Brian or Sean or Liam, the sons who adored their father without questioning his flaws. He'd been Dylan, the guy who could charm any woman, then walk away without a second thought.

But deep inside lived a person he'd rarely showed anyone—Dylan, the rebel, the kid who really didn't have a role in the family, the kid who blamed his father for the empty bellies and the endless insecurity. When his mother had been around, he'd felt safe. And after she'd left, he'd experienced the loss as deeply as if she'd ripped his heart from his chest and taken it with her. The man he'd become was all tied up in the past. He just hadn't been ready to untangle it yet.

Sean sauntered over with a pint of Guinness and Dylan cocked his head to the left. "Baby brother, why don't you buy this lovely lady a drink while you're at it." Though a free drink was always a good icebreaker, he really wasn't interested in conversation. The woman just looked a little lonely—a little vulnerable. The least he could do was to offer her a fresh beer while she waited for whatever or whomever she was waiting for.

The woman turned suddenly, as if surprised that he'd noticed her at all. For a moment, he was taken aback. A current of recognition shot through him and he tried to place her, to recall her name. But Dylan was certain that he'd never met her. He would have remembered because though she was pretty, she was also young, with a face that could only be described as…innocent. And those eyes, such an unusual shade. He would have remembered her eyes.

"What are you drinking?" Dylan asked sending her a warm smile.

She forced a smile in return, then stumbled off her stool. "I—I have to go," she murmured. "Thanks anyway." She grabbed her purse and her jacket, then hurried to the door, slipping out quietly.

Dylan turned back to Sean. "That makes me two for two today. I'm actually beginning to enjoy rejection."

"Don't beat yourself up," Sean said. "I've been trying to talk to her all night long but she'd have nothing of it. She just wanted to sit there, alone, sipping her beer and staring at me and Brian. You know, she looked familiar at first, but I'm pretty sure I don't know her."

"You, too? I thought I recognized her." Dylan shrugged, then grabbed his Guinness. He pushed off his stool. "If I'm going to spend the night crying in my beer, then I might as well do it with people who'll feel sorry for me." He wandered over to an empty spot next to Olivia, then sat down.

"Hey, Dylan," she said, her smile bright and affectionate. She leaned over and gave him a kiss on the cheek. "What have you been up to?"

In just a few short weeks, Olivia had become part of the family. Even though she and Conor weren't married yet, she was like a sister to him. Dylan liked having her around. After all, it was nice to get a woman's point of view every now and then. Growing up in a household of boys had its disadvantages.

"You look like you've had a rough day," Olivia said, draping her arm around his shoulders. "You want to talk?"

The offer was made facetiously for Olivia knew full well that the Quinns didn't talk about their problems. But maybe she'd be able to explain why he was attracted to the maddening and mercurial Meggie Flanagan, a woman who stumbled all over herself to stay away from him, a woman who hurled insults at him like fastballs in Fenway Park.

Had he suddenly developed a streak of masochism that only Meggie Flanagan could feed? Or was the notion of a woman playing hard to get so foreign to him that he found it irresistible? All he knew was that he couldn't stop thinking about her, recalling how soft her skin felt and how perfect her mouth was and how tempting her body looked.

"Well?" Olivia asked, interrupting his thoughts.

"Today?" Dylan asked. "Just the usual. Rescued a few kittens from trees, put out a few raging infernos, saved a few dozen lives. No big deal."

"And whose life have you saved lately?" Brendan slipped into the spot on the other side of Dylan and sent Olivia a warm smile.

"Mary Margaret Flanagan," Dylan said. Just the sound of her name on his lips brought back a flood of images. The sight of her face, covered in soot and marked with the tracks of her tears, then the fresh and natural beauty he discovered just an hour ago. Why couldn't he put her out of his head? There was just something so fascinating about her—the contrast between the girl she'd been and the woman she'd become.

Conor frowned. "Mary Margaret who?"

Sean leaned over the bar and chuckled. "Meggie Flanagan? Meggie Flanagan with the horn-rimmed glasses and the mouth full of metal?" He glanced over his shoulder toward the far end of the bar. "Hey, Brian, come here. Guess who Dylan saved."

"I didn't save her," Dylan insisted. "It was just a little fire. She's opening a coffee shop over on Boylston, not too far from the station. It looks like it'll be a real nice place. Anyway, yesterday afternoon her coffee machine shorted out and started a small fire. I had to carry her out when she refused to leave."

"You carried her out of her shop?" Conor asked.

Dylan took another long sip of his Guinness, then licked the foam from his upper lip and nodded. "Yeah, like a sack of potatoes. Although she wasn't nearly as lumpy."

"Oh-oh," Olivia warned. "That's how it starts."

Dylan's eyebrow rose. "What?"

Conor chuckled softly. "That's how Olivia and I met. I picked her up, tossed her over my shoulder and hauled her back inside the safehouse. Then she kicked me in the shin and called me a Neanderthal. After that, it was true love. That must be how it starts for us Quinns. We carry a woman away and that's the beginning of the end." He shrugged. "I guess I should have warned you."

"I'm not going to fall in love with Meggie Flanagan," Dylan insisted. "Carrying her out was part of the job, I had no choice. Besides, she hates me. She was downright hostile. She called me a Hun."

"Why?" Brendan asked. "You barely know her."

"But she knows you," Brian said. "At least by reputation. You cut a wide swath through the girls at South Boston High School. Was she one of the girls you left weeping in your wake?"

Why was that the quality that seemed to define Dylan Quinn? He wasn't remembered as a great athlete, which he was. He wasn't remembered as a loyal friend or a nice guy. It always came back to the women. "She was the kid sister of my best friend," Dylan muttered. "Even I have scruples. In fact, I was the one who got her a date to that sophomore dance. Didn't Sean take her?"

Brian shook his head. "No, that was me. And that was my very first date and probably the most traumatic experience with the opposite sex I've ever had."

"Oh, do tell," Olivia said, bracing her arms on the bar and leaning forward.

There was nothing a Quinn brother could refuse Olivia. Each one of them would jump into Boston Harbor in the dead of winter if that's what she asked. Recounting an embarrassing memory, complete with mythical Quinn embellishments, was nothing as long as it pleased her. "I was a foot shorter than Meggie and I had a pimple the size of Mount Vesuvius on my nose that night. I was so nervous I almost puked on her shoes. After that night, I didn't ask a girl out for two years."

"Do you think she's still mad about the pimple?" Dylan asked. "Or did you do something stupid? Did you try to feel her—" He stopped, then gave Olivia an apologetic smile. "Did you try to get to first base with her?"

"Second base," Sean said. He pointed to his chest. "That's second base."

"I didn't touch her," Brian insisted.

"Why don't you just ask her why she doesn't like you?" Olivia suggested.

All the brothers looked at each other, then shook their heads. "That would involve a discussion of feelings," Brendan said. "It's part of Quinn family genetics that we avoid discussions like that. Haven't you read the manual?" He turned to Conor. "You have to give her the manual."

"Hell, it doesn't make a difference," Dylan said. "I'm not going to see her again, anyway."

But even as he said it, Dylan knew it was a lie. He had to see her again, had to figure out this strange and undeniable attraction he had to her. Maybe if he figured that out, he'd be able to unravel the rest of his feelings.

"I guess you're just going to have to wonder, then," Olivia said, giving his arm a squeeze. "But she must have a good reason. After all, how could any woman resist the charms of a Mighty Quinn?"

"YOU LOOK LIKE A girl who just found out her dress was caught in the back of her panty hose during the Grand March," Lana commented as she looked over Meggie's shoulder.

Meggie stared down at the photo from the Sophomore Frolic. She was dressed in a pouffy formal that looked like it was already out of style when she'd chosen it. But it was pink and shiny and at the time, it was the most beautiful gown she'd ever seen. She and her date stood beneath a flower-draped arbor. "At that moment, I would have rather walked the length of the gym with my dress up over my head," she murmured to Lana. "It was tragic. Humiliating. I thought I'd never be able to love another boy in my entire life."

"Your evening couldn't have been that bad. He's cute. A little short, but cute." She squinted at the photo, then reached over and scratched her nail on the surface. "What's that on his nose?"

"He wasn't Dylan," Meggie continued. "When they played our song that night, I thought I'd cry. 'Endless Love.'"

"See there," Lana said. "You two had a song. It couldn't have been that bad."

"It was *our* song—Dylan's and mine."

A frown wrinkled Lana's brow. "How could you and Dylan Quinn have a song? He barely knew you existed."

Meggie shoved the photo back into her purse and tossed her purse behind the counter. Then she grabbed a handful of pour spouts and began to shove them into the bottles of flavoring syrup. "Believe me, we had a whole relationship— in my poor deluded sophomore mind."

Lana slid onto a stool on the opposite side of the counter, then sipped at the latte she'd just prepared. "Sounds like you had it bad. No wonder you want revenge."

"Not revenge," Meggie said. "Just a little payback. Maybe then I wouldn't always wince when I think about high school. That whole thing followed me around until I graduated. I was defined by that night. I was the girl who carried the huge torch for Dylan Quinn, then got it dropped on her head. The geek and the god." She paused. "I've come a long way since then, but all it takes is one look at Dylan Quinn and I'm right back there, standing in the gymnasium with everyone staring at me."

It sounded like a good explanation for her attraction to Dylan—just a few residual feelings left over from that night so long ago. She was attracted to him because she hated him. After all, there was a thin line between love and hate, isn't that what people said? Or maybe seeing him again just threw her off.

She led such a well-ordered existence, focusing all her energies on the shop. Everything else, including her personal life, had its place and he was an anomaly. Even she knew a crazy attraction to Dylan Quinn didn't have any place in her life!

Lana shrugged. "Too bad you can't get him to fall in love with you. Then you could dump him and everything would be cool."

"*You* could do that," Meggie said. "You can wrap a man around your little finger and make him love every minute of it. And considering your strategical abilities, you'd go in with a battle plan that was sure to succeed." She grabbed a bottle of hazelnut syrup and turned the notion over and over in her brain as she twisted off the cap. If only she were more like Lana. More brazen with men, more uninhibited, more—

"We could do it," Lana murmured. "Why not? I mean, we put together a business plan for this place then convinced the bankers to finance it. If we use the same approach, we could make Dylan Quinn fall for you. We'll just use the same basic business and marketing principles we learned in b-school."

"How will that work?"

"We're selling a product—you. And we have to make the

consumer—Dylan Quinn—want that product. Once he does, we'll just discontinue production and close the factory doors." Lana slipped off her stool, hurried around to the other side of the counter and rummaged around in a small drawer. She pulled out a battered old notebook where they kept a list of supplies they needed to order. She grabbed a pencil and drew a square at the top of an empty page. "This is our end goal. R-E-V-E-N-G-E."

"Not revenge," Meggie said, her interest piqued. She stepped to Lana's side. "That sounds so nasty. I'd rather call it…the careful restoration of the balance in my love life."

"We'll just call it revenge for short," Lana countered. "Now our intermediate goal is to get him to fall in love with you." She drew another box, then an arrow between the two. "Once that's accomplished, you can dump him and all will be right with the world."

"And just how do I make that happen?" Meggie asked. "You know what a disaster I am when it comes to men. As soon as I say something stupid or do something weird I get all flustered and they think I'm mentally unstable."

"You're exaggerating," Lana said. "You've just had bad luck with men."

"Do you have any little boxes and arrows to change my personality?"

"We won't need to change your personality," Lana said with a sly grin. "With my vast and detailed knowledge of the male ego, I could make Dylan fall in love with a parking meter if I wanted. Dylan Quinn is an unrepentant ladies' man. As such, he'll be quite easy to manipulate. All you have to do is play hard to get."

Meggie laughed. "I can barely get a date when I'm working at it. Why would he ask me out if I act uninterested?"

"Because you'll be a challenge and men like Dylan want what they can't have." She quickly wrote numbers down the side of the page. "Now, we'll have to develop guidelines. And you'll have to trust that I know what I'm talking about."

"I do," Meggie said. When it came to men, Lana definitely knew what she was doing. What Meggie didn't trust was her own feelings. Could she actually maintain her resolve and her objectivity around Dylan Quinn? She cursed silently. If she didn't do something, she was doomed to spend the next thirteen years as she had the last, reliving her mortification at the hands of Dylan Quinn, caught in the humiliation of a certified wallflower. "And I'll do whatever you say."

"There are few unbreakable rules regarding scheduling. First, there has to be at least four days between the time you accept a date and the time you go out on a date. If you accept a date for the same day, you'll appear too eager."

"All right," Meggie said. "What else?"

"When he calls, you have to wait at least a full day to call him back. And you can only call him once. If he's busy or he's not home, you don't call again."

Meggie nodded. This didn't seem difficult. It was all about what she couldn't do, not what she had to do. "Rule number three?" Meggie asked.

"On your first three dates, he can't pick you up at the house. You have to keep it casual. You'll meet him there, you'll be polite and gracious, and you'll call an end to the date at least an hour before you really want to."

She stepped back from the counter and frowned. "And this is supposed to make him fall in love with me? If I were him I'd slap me silly and leave with the next woman who walked out of the ladies' room."

"Think about it," Lana said. "This is the sex that invented the lost cause. Every man wants to be either a professional baseball player, a photographer for *Playboy* or the next lotto winner. Even if they can't hit a ball, operate a camera or don't bother to buy lottery tickets. It's part of their nature to want things they can't have."

"Is that it?"

"Then there are the kissing rules," Lana said. "No good-night kiss on the first date, a kiss on the cheek for the second date, and lips, no tongue, on the third."

"He'll think I'm prissy," Meggie said.

"This is all basic economics, Meggie, supply and demand. The less you supply, the more he'll demand. You have to give him just enough to keep him coming back for more. He'll think you're mysterious and unattainable and he'll try even harder."

"This seems a little manipulative."

"Of course it's manipulative," Lana said. "The great thing is that men are so easy to manipulate."

"I'm not sure I can do that," Meggie murmured.

Lana scoffed then glanced around the shop. "Look around you. What we do at Cuppa Joe's is manipulative. We sell the best-smelling product on earth, we tempt people with special blends and fancy recipes. But basically we're selling them legal stimulants made with almost one-hundred-percent water at a seven-hundred-percent markup.

When you have a good marketing plan, you can't go wrong."

Meggie considered the notion. It was a good plan and with any other woman, it might just work. But she'd never been a smooth operator with men. If she had to remember charts and diagrams and rules and regulations, she might just pass out from the effort. "It's too complicated," she said.

"We'll use my planning software to make a flowchart," Lana said. "Then you'll just have to remember one step at a time."

Meggie considered her options for a long moment. If she could pull this off, then she'd never have to think about Dylan Quinn again. And maybe she'd learn something. She hadn't had much luck with men up to this point. And the men in Lana's life seemed to multiply like rabbits. If anything, this was good practice. Why not just brush aside her reservations and go for it? "All right," she said.

Lana smiled and wrapped her arm around Meggie's shoulders, giving her a reassuring hug. "This will be fun. I'm bored with my own love life. It'll be interesting to run yours for a while. Now the only thing we have to do is pray that he stops in again. You're Catholic. Maybe you can go light a few candles."

"That's not what candles are for," Meggie said. "I can just call him and—"

"Nope," Lana said, shaking her head.

"I could walk past the firehouse and just casually—"

"Nope," Lana repeated.

"How is this going to work if he doesn't call me again?"

Lana sighed. "It won't work if he doesn't call you again.

And it definitely won't work if you contact him first. So we just have to wait."

Just then, the phone rang and as Meggie studied the list of rules, Lana reached for the cordless. "Cuppa Joe's," she said. "The best beans in Boston."

Meggie listened distractedly until she heard her own name come up in Lana's conversation. Then she looked up and watched her partner chat amiably.

"Meggie isn't here," Lana said. She grinned and waved her hand, then pointed to the phone and mouthed something Meggie couldn't decipher. "Oh, I'm not sure when she'll be back. Should I have her call you?"

"Is that about the Espresso Master 8000 Deluxe?" Meggie whispered. "If that's Eddie, tell him I'm still willing to pay extra for a rush shipment."

Lana frowned and shook her head, pressing her finger over her lips to silence Meggie. "All right. I'll be sure to give her the message. Right. She'll get back to you as soon as she can." She hung up the phone, then took a deep breath.

"So?" Meggie asked. "Are they going to get us the 8000 or not?"

"Forget about that damn espresso machine! That was Dylan Quinn on the phone."

Stunned, Meggie pressed her hand to her chest. Her heart had already started to beat faster and for a moment she couldn't catch her breath. She cursed softly and tried to gain control over her cardiopulmonary system. "He called me?" First his visit last night and now a phone call. "What did he want?"

"He wanted to talk to you," Lana replied.

"But—but why didn't you—I was here!" Meggie cried. "Why did you take a message?"

Lana grabbed the notebook and waved it under her nose. "It's all part of the plan," she said.

Meggie crossed her arms beneath her breasts then stared at her partner for a long moment. Though the reasons seemed perfectly obvious to Lana, Meggie didn't have a clue. "If the goal is to get a date and I can't get that date unless Dylan Quinn calls, then why wouldn't you let me talk to him?"

"It's too soon," Lana said.

"So, I'll call him back in twenty-four hours, right?"

Lana considered that for a second, then shook her head. "No, I think we're going to play this a little differently. You'll wait for him to call two more times, then you'll call him back. That'll make him squirm a little."

Meggie couldn't imagine Dylan Quinn squirming under any circumstances. He just wasn't the squirming type. But if this plan had any chance of working, she'd have to trust Lana's instincts. And bury her own. Because Meggie knew that the moment Dylan showed any interest in her at all, she'd be lost to his charms. She pressed her palms down on the counter and drew a steadying breath.

She could make this happen—or she could make a complete fool out of herself by trying. Either way, her social life was about to become a lot more exciting than it had been in recent memory.

THE DAMP NOVEMBER chill that had hung over Boston for the past week had fled with the arrival of the sun. Dylan strolled along Boylston Street, staring into a bookshop window as he passed. He knew exactly where he was headed, but he wasn't ready to admit it to himself quite yet, so he slowed his pace and tried to focus on his window shopping.

All he was willing to admit was that he was in the area on his day off, picking up his paycheck from the station, and the day was so beautiful, he decided to take a walk.

Leaves skittered over the streets, pushed along by the warm breeze that blew from the south. It would have been a perfect day to head out on *The Mighty Quinn*. Brendan had called early that morning and wanted Dylan to help him ferry the boat up to Gloucester, but Dylan had other things on his mind.

He'd called Meggie three times in the past three days, but she hadn't returned a single call. Though he knew he ought to take the hint and forget her, he was starting to wonder if Olivia's advice might be right. Maybe he should just ask Meggie why she hated him so much. At least he'd have an answer and he'd be able to get on with his life. But pride had kept him from calling her a fourth time. Instead, he'd decided to pay her a visit.

When he reached the block of Boylston where Cuppa Joe was located, Dylan crossed the street, determined to observe the shop from a distance before venturing inside. And he was lucky he did, for he saw Meggie standing out in front of the shop in the sidewalk.

Two workmen stood on ladders, holding a sign between them as they struggled to hang it above the door. This would be the perfect time to talk to her, he mused. Her mind would be occupied with other things and he could just say his piece and get it over with. But Dylan hesitated, unable to step off the curb and cross the street.

"You're a right *eejit,*" he muttered to himself, invoking one of his father's favorite put-downs in a thick Irish accent. "And you'll never learn when to leave well enough alone."

But in the end, he couldn't resist just one more chance to talk to her, one more opportunity to figure out why he couldn't get her out of his mind. Why all he could think about was touching her and breathing in the scent of her hair and gazing down into her pretty green eyes. He glanced both ways, then jogged across the street.

She didn't notice his approach, her back to him as she shouted directions at the workmen. He stood beside her and watched them work. "Nice sign," he finally said.

For a moment, he didn't think she heard him. But then Meggie slowly turned. From the look on her face, she wasn't very happy to see him. Her expression was one of thinly veiled apprehension. "Hi," she said, forcing a smile. "What are you doing here?"

Dylan shrugged, trying to appear nonchalant. "Nothing much. I had to stop by the station and I thought I'd do a little shopping."

"Here?"

"Yeah," he said, scrambling to make up a decent story. "Yeah, my brother Conor and his fiancée, Olivia Farrell, are getting married at the end of November and I thought I'd look for a wedding present." He glanced around. "Any suggestions?"

"There's a cooking store over on Newbury," she suggested. "You could get them a…blender. Or maybe some pots and pans." She shrugged. "Knives are always a nice present."

"Right," Dylan replied. "Knives."

The silence between them grew strained and he wondered whether he ought to just walk away and leave it at that. But he'd come this far. He reached out and grabbed her arm and turned her toward him. "Meggie, I—"

His words were interrupted by loud shouts and they both turned to see the workmen struggling with the heavy wooden sign. The breeze had caught it and they balanced precariously on the ladders, the sign swinging between them. But it was too heavy and an instant later, they were forced to let go.

Dylan barely had time to think. He grabbed Meggie around the waist, picked her up and shoved her toward the curb. But he wasn't quick enough to save himself. The sign crashed down, the corner grazing his forehead as it hit the ground and landed with a "whoof" between his feet and the shop.

He slowly shook his head, then turned to check on Meggie. She stood unharmed, her back pressed against a car parked at the curb, her eyes wide with shock. She blinked once, as if to bring herself back to reality. "You saved my life," she murmured.

He moved to stand in front of her, then skimmed his hands lightly over her face and her shoulders. "Are you all right? You're not hurt?"

She shook her head, gazing up at him. Relief washed over him and he took her face in his hands. "You're sure?" She nodded. And then, as if it were the most natural reaction in the world, Dylan leaned forward and pressed a kiss to her lips.

She moaned softly, but rather than draw away, he was caught by the feel of her mouth beneath his, soft, pliant, tempting. Hell, talking hadn't gotten him anywhere, so he had to resort to more blatant tactics. Dylan deepened the kiss, tracing a line between her lips with his tongue. She opened and he tasted, the blood rushing through his veins until he could hear his own heartbeat in his head. He'd never experienced such need from a simple, spontaneous kiss. The desire to continue kissing her was almost overwhelming, and if they hadn't been standing on Boylston Street with two workmen looking on, he might have kept on kissing her until neither one of them could stand.

Dylan hesitantly drew away, then stared down into her eyes, which were wider than they were when the sign had fallen. He drew his thumb along her lower lip, still damp from his kiss. "I'm sorry I pushed you, but I'm afraid if I hadn't you'd be underneath that sign right now."

"I know," she murmured. "Thank you. I guess I was lucky you were passing by."

"Actually, I wasn't just passing by. I wanted to talk to you and I was hoping you'd be here. I wanted to know why you hadn't returned my calls." Dylan prepared himself to accept all the standard answers. She was too busy, she was already involved, she was in the midst of moving and she didn't have a phone, she had to care for a sick aunt.

"I meant to call you back," Meggie said.

"You did?"

She nodded. "But, you see, if I had called you, you never

would have walked by. And you never would have saved my life. So I guess it was a lucky thing."

Meggie rubbed her arms as if she were cold, but Dylan suspected it was a just a nervous reaction, as was her convoluted logic. The knowledge that he made her nervous gave him some hope. At least he wasn't making her angry. He reached out and placed his hands over hers. "The reason I called was that I wanted to ask, again, if you'd have dinner with me. I know we didn't get off to the best start, but I—"

"Yes," she blurted out, a blush staining her cheeks. "Yes, I'd love to have dinner with you. That would be great… wonderful. When?"

"How about tonight?" Dylan suggested.

Her smile faded slightly and she considered his suggestion for a long moment. "Could—could you just wait here a moment? I'll be right back."

Dylan watched her hurry up the steps to the front door of the shop. She disappeared inside and he wondered if she intended to come out again. She sure was an odd girl, that Meggie Flanagan, all nervous and fidgety, as if she were about to fall apart right in front of him.

He turned his attention to the two workmen who were now grinning at him in admiration. "Smooth," one of them said.

Putting on a stern expression, Dylan pointed to the sign still lying on the ground at his feet. "That's more than I can say for you two. You nearly killed her. Now, if you don't want me to call your boss, I'd get that sign up there and I'd make sure that it won't be coming down any time soon."

The pair did as they were told and by the time Meggie

came back outside, they'd managed to attach the sign to the brackets. It was the perfect size and Dylan could see it would be visible up and down the street.

Meggie stood beside him and gazed up at the sign. "It looks good. I wasn't sure about the lettering and the colors, but I think everyone will be able to see it from a distance. And the coffee cup kind of says 'coffee shop,' so that helps."

"Yeah, it does," Dylan said. He turned to her. "So, is everything all right?"

"All right?"

"Yeah. Inside."

She smiled apologetically. "Oh, I just had to talk to Lana for a second. About the date—I mean, I didn't talk to her about our date. I just meant, regarding your invitation, tonight wouldn't be good."

"Then tomorrow night?" he asked.

"No, that wouldn't be good either."

Dylan reached down and caught her chin with his finger, then slowly tipped her gaze up until she met his. "Are you sure you want to go out with me at all?"

"Sunday would be perfect," she suggested, her eyes wide and unblinking.

"You want to go out on Sunday? Not Thursday, not Friday, not Saturday, but Sunday?"

"Yes," she said, nodding. "Sunday."

"All right, Sunday, then. How about I pick you up at seven? We'll have dinner at Boodle's."

"I'll meet you there," she said. "And six would probably be better." She hesitated. "And I'm really not a steak person. How about Café Atlantis instead?" With that, she put on a bright expression, then pointed toward the shop. "I should go back inside. Lana needs my help."

Dylan nodded, then leaned forward to brush a quick kiss on her cheek, but whatever had possessed her to return his first kiss in full measure had disappeared. She deftly avoided him, skipping away and hurrying up the steps. Before she opened the door, she turned around and gave him a hesitant wave. "Café Atlantis, six, Sunday night," she called.

Dylan watched the door close behind her, then raked his fingers through his hair and cursed softly. He'd made a lot of dates in his life with a lot of different women. And they'd all expressed different levels of delight at the prospect. But this was the first time he'd asked a woman out and gotten the distinct feeling that this wasn't really a date at all. Sunday night? Six? At a place that specialized in sprouts and tofu?

Dylan sighed. Well, at least they had a date. That was a first step. And if he had to choke down textured vegetable protein instead of the best steak in Boston, then that's what he'd do. He figured as long as he was sitting across the table from the beautiful Meggie Flanagan, he'd be willing to eat cardboard and act like he enjoyed it.

3

MEGGIE JAMMED THE key into the door of her flat on the South End, then hurried inside. Lana trailed in after her, grumbling and complaining as she had all the way over.

"I still don't know why you need me here," she said. "We've got loads to do at the shop before we open. I have to proofread the take-out menus and the workmen want to put up the chalkboard menu tomorrow. And that second cash register still isn't working right."

Meggie kicked off her shoes, tossed her purse aside, and tugged her sweater over her head. "This was your plan," she said. "I just need to make sure I get everything right. I'm supposed to meet Dylan in an hour and it's going to take me fifteen minutes to get to the restaurant. I don't understand why

I couldn't leave earlier. We were just sitting there drinking coffee for the past three hours."

Lana wandered into Meggie's kitchen and grabbed a bottle of juice from the refrigerator. "I kept you at the shop because I didn't want you to get crazy thinking about this date. And I'm glad I did. Look at yourself. You're a mess." She flopped down on the sofa. "Have you learned nothing?"

"It's not the date that's making me crazy," Meggie replied, brushing her hair out of her eyes. "I've had enough caffeine to keep me awake until next Tuesday." She unbuttoned her jeans and skimmed them down over her hips to her feet, then kicked them aside. She paused, staring down at her legs, her mouth agape. "Oh, no. I can't believe this."

"What?"

Meggie stuck her leg out in front of her. "I haven't shaved my legs in a month!"

"So what," Lana said with a shrug.

"I can't go out on a date with hairy legs."

Lana bent closer and studied the proffered leg. "Yes, you can. Hairy legs are the modern-day equivalent of a chastity belt. With those legs, you won't be hopping into bed with a man any time soon. Consider it a blessing."

"And what about my eyebrows? If I don't pluck, I'm going to look like Ernie. Or Bert. Or whichever Muppet it is that has that big eyebrow across his forehead." She moaned, then threw herself down beside Lana on the sofa. "This is no way to get ready for a date. I'm going to call and cancel."

Lana grabbed her hand and pulled her up, then dragged her to the bathroom. They stopped in front of the mirror above the sink. "Your eyebrows look fine. You're having a good hair day. Throw on a little blush and some lipstick, maybe some perfume and you'll be ready to go. Remember, don't take this too seriously. You're just having dinner and then you're going home. You don't even have to act like you're having fun."

Meggie grabbed her mascara, while Lana turned her attention to the closet, searching for an appropriate outfit for the evening ahead. As Meggie finished her left eye, she decided that Lana was probably right. A little mascara and some blush was enough for a date with—her hand shook and the mascara wand jabbed her eye. With a soft curse, she pressed her fingers against her eyelid to quell the burning. Both eyes began to water and by the time she was able to see again, her mascara was smudged to her cheekbones.

Lana tossed a dress into the bathroom. "That one is nice. Very flattering but not too sexy. And taupe is a neutral color. Red would be too obvious and black is too severe and any kind of pattern will distract from your natural beauty."

Meggie snatched the hanger from Lana, still rubbing her eye. "Maybe you should go on this date with me. You can hide under the table and do all the talking while I just move my lips."

Lana rolled her eyes in exasperation. "Just get dressed while I review everything you need to remember."

Meggie hurried out of the bathroom to grab fresh underwear from her dresser drawer. She decided if she couldn't shave her legs, then at least she'd wear decent underwear—and new panty hose. "We've reviewed this ten times already. I know it by heart. Maintain an air of mystery. Don't reveal too much. Avoid eye contact that lasts more than five sec-

onds. Keep conversational topic light and irrelevant. And…"
She knew there was one other point she was supposed to
remember. She hurried back into the bathroom. "Don't drink
any more coffee!"

Lana leaned into the bathroom, puckered her lips and
made a loud smacking sound.

"Right," Meggie responded. "No kissing." She hadn't
bothered to tell Lana about the kiss she and Dylan had already shared in front of the shop. It was a delicious memory she'd replayed over and over in her head.

At first, the feel of his mouth on hers had been a bit
shocking. And then, after the initial surprise wore off, Meggie couldn't help but enjoy it, the warmth of his tongue, the
taste of him. She'd never been kissed like that before. In ret-
rospect, she really ought to put the whole thing out of her
mind. It wouldn't do to get all caught up in the passion of
that moment. But she couldn't help but relive it a few more
times.

A faint buzzing sound filtered through the bathroom door
and Meggie poked her head out. "Did you put something in
the oven?"

Lana stumbled off the bed. "That's the front door. Probably one of your other admirers?" she asked in a teasing tone.

A withering glare was all she got in return from Meggie.
"I'll just go get it."

Meggie was glad to have a few moments to herself. She
pulled the knit dress up over her hips, then slipped her arms
into the sleeves. Then she closed the bathroom door and
stared at herself in the full-length mirror. Lana was right. The
color was perfect for a casual date. And the dress was flat-

tering, clingy enough to show off her figure but not so tight as to make her look trashy.

"Maybe this won't be too bad," she said, snatching up the package of panty hose. "After all, it's only dinner. I can handle that."

Meggie bunched up the panty hose in her fists, then tugged them over her feet. But the hose wouldn't stretch and she wrestled to get it up over her knees. Sitting down on the toilet to tug didn't help, so she waddled back into the bedroom and grabbed the bedpost. But a moment later, she felt herself losing her balance.

She tried to take a step but the tangled panty hose restricted her movement. With a cry of alarm, Meggie crashed into the dresser, then tumbled to the floor, her dress hiked up over her hips, her panty hose tangled around her ankles and a knot growing on her forehead.

Glancing up, she found Lana staring at her, her hands on her hips. "What are you doing?"

Meggie grunted as she kicked the panty hose off. "I'm trying to get dressed for my date." She cursed softly, rubbing her head. "Who was at the door?"

"Not was. Is," Lana said. "Dylan."

Meggie scrambled to her feet. "Dylan?"

"He decided to come and pick you up for your date, rather than meet you there." Lana reached out and tugged Meggie's skirt down. "Isn't that sweet? He's a real gentleman. Very considerate."

Meggie stumbled over to the door. Silently, she opened it, caught sight of the back of Dylan's head, then quickly shut the door. Even the back of his head was enough to set her pulse racing. "He's not supposed to come here! It's against the rules. You said I'm supposed to meet him there. What am I going to do now? The whole plan is messed up and we haven't even started yet."

"I don't think you have any choice. You can't very well tell him to leave. You'll just have to be gracious and acknowledge his thoughtfulness."

"That's easy for you to say. Your mascara isn't smudged so bad you look like a raccoon. You don't have that unibrow look going for you. And you don't have furry legs!" Meggie moaned, then leaned back against the door. "And I can't get my panty hose on straight."

Lana crossed the room, grabbed the wad of nylon, then readjusted the hose before Meggie stepped into them once again. "How does he look?" Meggie murmured as Lana tugged the panty hose up to her waist. "Is he gorgeous? Or just moderately hunky? If he's gorgeous I'm not going to be able to talk to him."

"Well, he doesn't have his panty hose in a twist if that's what you're asking." Lana grinned and sat back on her heels. "He looks great. He's obviously taking this date very seriously. He has on wool trousers and a really sexy sweater and a sport coat. Fashionable but still very masculine. If he weren't your guy, I'd be hanging all over him."

"He's not my guy," Meggie murmured as she glanced down at her dress. "Maybe I should change."

"You can do whatever you want," Lana said. She rose, then smoothed her hands over her thighs. "I'm leaving."

"Wait!" Meggie cried. "You can't go. We haven't reviewed everything."

"Good grief," Lana said. "You've been on a date before, Meggie. Just try to remember what we talked about and have fun—but not too much fun. Dazzle him." With that, Lana yanked open the bedroom door and stepped into the living room. Dylan turned as she walked past. "Meggie will be out in a second," she said.

Meggie slammed the bedroom door behind her, then scrambled to finish dressing. She wiped the mascara from beneath her eyes, dashed on a bit of lipstick, and tucked her flyaway hair behind her ears. As she held on to the doorknob, shoes in her other hand, she drew a deep breath, pasted a smile onto her face. "Be pleasant, easy on the eye contact and don't drool all over him the first time he smiles. I think I can remember that."

Never in her life had she been so nervous before a date. Maybe it was because she really didn't know how to handle herself since this wasn't really a date. It was more like a finely tuned military operation. But the moment she stepped into the living room, her heart began slamming in her chest and she felt as though all the oxygen had just been sucked out of the room.

Slowly, he stood and as she watched him, it was like one of those dreamy sequences in a bad movie. Everything went in slow motion. He turned and she was nearly blinded by the intensity of his smile and somewhere in the background she heard "Endless Love" playing. Meggie cursed inwardly, fighting the urge to retreat and regroup. How, in heaven's name, was she supposed maintain an air of mystery around this man? The moment he looked at her, she felt as if he could see straight through her, straight to the quivering mass of nerves and tangled panty hose she really was.

"Hi," she said, able to only manage one syllable at a time.

"Hi," he replied. His gaze raked the length of her body, then returned to her face. "You look beautiful."

Compliments. He made them with such sincerity that she almost believed what he said was true. Her mind raced for a reply. How would a woman of mystery respond? Meggie cursed inwardly. Forget the mystery, how was any woman supposed to respond with Dylan Quinn looking at her like that, like he wanted to undress her with his teeth? "Thanks," she said.

"I'm sorry to show up unannounced, but I live about a mile away. I figured it would be silly for us both to drive back downtown. The parking in Back Bay is always tricky."

Mystery, her mind screamed. "Is it? Oh, I hadn't noticed."

Dylan frowned. "But your shop is in Back Bay."

Meggie swallowed. So much for mystery. If it made her sound like a complete idiot, she'd have to abandon that plan. "I usually take the T." She hurried to the closet to get her coat, then shoved her arm into the sleeve. He was at her side in a mere second, taking it from her hands and holding it behind her. "Thank you," she murmured.

He smoothed his hands over her shoulders, his fingers warm through the soft cashmere. Manners were not a quality that she would have attached to the Quinn boys. When they were younger, they pretty much ran wild. But somewhere along the line, the rough edges had been smoothed. Meggie wondered whether the person responsible was one of the many women Dylan had known in his life, or if he'd grown into it himself.

"I'm glad we're doing this," he said, giving her shoulders a squeeze. "It will be nice to catch up."

Catch up on what? They'd never really spoken to each other in the past, beyond a quick hellö at the Flanagan family dinner table. Perhaps he wanted to talk about how she used to hang around near his locker hoping to see him, or how she bought seven different lipsticks at the drugstore before she settled on the perfect shade of pink to match her Sophomore Frolic frock. Or maybe he wanted to discuss the seven thousand times she'd written out "Mrs. Dylan Quinn" and "Mary Margaret Quinn" and "Mrs. Meggie Quinn" on scraps of loose-leaf paper.

They could always discuss what she'd been doing with herself for the past three days, since he'd stopped by the shop and asked her on a date and kissed her right in the middle of the sidewalk. But then, that would take all of about one sentence. She'd spent her time thinking about Dylan Quinn—and wondering when she'd get to kiss him again.

"I'm looking forward to our dinner," she murmured. Meggie didn't realize what she said until after the words were out of her mouth. That wasn't right. She wasn't supposed to say that! "I mean, I'm hungry. Really famished."

Dylan grabbed the door and placed his palm in the small of her back as she stepped out. "Good. So am I."

As they walked down the stairs to the first floor, Meggie was glad he was behind her. He couldn't see the blush warming her cheeks or the way she chewed on her lower lip to steady her nerves. For all he knew, she was calm and composed and ready to enjoy a pleasant evening with an old friend.

Meggie drew a ragged breath. Now if she could only make herself feel that way, maybe she could get through the dinner with Dylan without making herself look like a certified lunatic.

"HERE, TRY THIS," Meggie said. "It's marinated bean curd. It has a very unusual taste."

Dylan wrinkled his nose and drew away, holding up his hand at the offered bite. "No thanks. I had my quota of curd for the day. I eat it for breakfast. Over my Wheaties. All the guys at the station do."

Meggie giggled then dropped the forkful of vegetarian stir-fry onto her plate. Dylan reached out for his wineglass and took a slow sip, studying her over the rim. All through dinner he couldn't keep his eyes off of her. There was something about her, a light that seemed to radiate from her shy smiles and her coy gazes. He'd been accustomed to women who were a bit more obvious about their desires. By now they'd have their foot in his lap beneath the table.

But Meggie was sweet and unassuming and sexy and alluring, a confusing jumble of contrasts. Dylan took a deep breath. She was real and so was the desire that raced through him every time he looked in her eyes. "This was good," he said, glancing down at his plate.

"You're just saying that," Meggie replied. "I know vegetarian probably isn't a favorite cuisine of yours. Not many men would have been adventurous enough to try it."

"It's not the food that's important," Dylan said. "It's the company." As soon as the words left his mouth, he wished he could take them back. He'd made a promise not to heap on the charm. But he always fell back on that when he wasn't sure what to do. She deserved better from him. "Would you like dessert?" he asked.

"I think there's a dessert menu." Meggie looked around for their waitress, but Dylan reached out and grabbed her hand.

"I had something different in mind than tofu cheesecake."

Her fingers were warm beneath his and he tried to remember how many times he'd touched her over the course of the evening. So many it had become almost an instinct, a quiet desire to feel her skin against his. He couldn't seem to stop himself and he wondered, after leaving her at her front door tonight, how long it would be before he wanted to touch her again.

But he wanted to do more than just touch her. She made it almost impossible to keep from thinking of other, more passionate alternatives. He'd stopped thinking of Meggie as a vulnerable little girl the moment he'd kissed her outside her coffee shop. She didn't kiss like a teenager, she responded to him like woman aching to taste more, a woman who was slowly wrapping him around her little finger.

Dylan turned and motioned to the waitress, and when she brought the check, he paid it and tossed a generous tip onto the table. Then he stood up and grabbed Meggie's hand, suddenly anxious to get out of the crowded restaurant. "Come on."

He helped her into her coat in the restaurant lobby, then rested his palm on the small of her back as he opened the door for her. The night was chilly and as they walked down the street she looped her arm through his. She started in the direction of the car, but he pulled her along in the opposite direction, until they reached an ice-cream shop about a block away.

"I wonder if they have meat ice cream," he teased. "Or hot steak sundaes with bacon sprinkles."

"All right, all right," Meggie said with a smile. "Next time, we'll go to Boodle's and you can have a steak."

"Deal," he murmured before he pulled open the door to the ice-cream shop. He was glad to know there would be a next time. Though he'd always been the one in control of the future of his relationships with women, he didn't feel that way with Meggie. With her, he couldn't assume anything.

They walked up to the counter and Meggie ordered a single-dip chocolate cone. Dylan chose a turtle sundae with all the trimmings. When their ice cream was ready, they took a seat at a small table near the window. As Meggie licked at the cone, she watched the pedestrians pass on the sidewalk. He watched her instead.

Meggie made eating an ice-cream cone the sexiest thing he'd ever seen—sexy because she didn't even realize what she was doing to him. Her tongue slid over the creamy chocolate and then she slowly licked her lips until they were damp and cool. A shiver skittered through him and he imagined what kissing her might taste like at this very moment. Or what her lips might feel like on his neck, or his chest, or his... Dylan fought the urge to brush aside everything on the table, grab her and taste her right then and there, the way he had that day in front of her shop.

He turned his attention back to his ice-cream sundae,

pushing a cherry around the bowl with his spoon as he tried to stifle his thoughts.

"So tell me," she said, catching a drip of ice cream with her tongue. "Why did you become a fireman?"

Dylan shrugged. "When I was kid I wanted to be a highwayman. Or a knight of the Round Table." He glanced up. "But there's not much call for either in the Boston area."

"I guess not," Meggie said. "But why a fireman?"

"I always give the standard answer," he began. "I wanted to be a fireman because I could help people. But that's not really it. I think I just wanted to be worth something, to be known as someone who could be trusted when it really counted." His explanation stopped him short. He'd never said the words out loud, not even to himself. But with Meggie, he felt safe. She wasn't judging him. She'd known the boy he was and now she knew the man. "Plus, I knew I couldn't charm my way through the training. If I made it, it would be real."

"Are you ever afraid?" she asked, her gaze wide and direct.

"I don't think about being afraid, I just do my job. Besides, I think I was afraid enough when I was a kid that I've kind of developed an immunity to fear." He scooped up a spoonful of his ice cream and held it out to her. "Here, try some of mine. The caramel sauce is really good."

She leaned forward and ate the ice cream off his spoon then smiled. He was wrong. He was afraid of one thing. He was afraid he might make some stupid mistake with Meggie and she wouldn't want to see him again. He was afraid she'd see right through him and realize he wasn't the kind of man she wanted. "Why are we talking about me? Let's talk about something much more interesting."

"What?" Meggie asked.

"You," he suggested, a smile quirking the corners of his mouth.

"My life isn't very interesting. I went to college. UMass. I got a business degree and became an accountant."

"An accountant?" Dylan shook his head. He'd known she was smart in school, but the staid world of accounting didn't seem to fit Meggie—at least not the Meggie he was getting to know. Though she was quiet, he sensed there was a passionate woman beneath her calm facade, a woman who came out when he kissed her.

Meggie nodded. "It was a bad choice, but it was practical at the time. And it was good money and Lana and I were saving to open the coffee shop. We'd always talked about owning our own business, even back in college."

"Why a coffee shop?" Dylan asked.

"We wanted a place where people could come and relax. Where they could talk and read the paper and listen to music. Where they didn't have to watch the clock. Most of the coffee shops aren't really like that. They're more like fast-food restaurants. We wanted an atmosphere like the coffee shops of the fifties and sixties. We're going to have folk music and poetry readings in the evenings and on weekends. People won't just come for coffee, you'll see. It will have a real retro feel."

The excitement in her eyes was enough to make even Dylan interested in folk music and poetry. She knew what she wanted and she was going after it. And her determination to make it succeed intrigued him. No, this wasn't the Meggie Flanagan he knew as a kid. This was a passionate, determined woman.

Dylan pushed the remains of his sundae to the center of the table. He wanted to kiss Meggie more than he'd ever wanted to do anything in his life and he wanted to be alone with her when he did it. "All done?"

Meggie nodded and he took her hand as she got up from the table. He tucked her fingers in the crook of his arm and they walked out on the street. When they paused to look into a shop window, she caught him staring at her.

"What?" she murmured.

"You have ice cream on your face."

Meggie reached up, groaning softly, but Dylan caught her hand and pulled her into the shadows of a shop doorway. "Let me," he said. He bent close and rubbed his thumb over her lower lip. The contact was like a jolt of electricity, shocking but incredibly delicious. And when he licked the ice cream off his thumb, it was as intimate as if he'd kissed her. A sigh slipped from her throat and he didn't even think before he bent closer and did just that.

The instant their lips touched, he gently pulled her against him. She felt so small and delicate in his arms, soft and willing. At first her response was hesitant, but then she returned his kiss. A soft groan rumbled in his chest and he brought his hands to her face, molding her mouth to his. Dylan had kissed a lot of women in his life, but it had never felt like this, so intense.

Though desire raced through his blood, he knew that he wasn't kissing her to seduce her. He was simply kissing her to enjoy the sensation of her mouth beneath his, to savor the sweet taste of her. And when he finally drew back, he was satisfied that the kiss would be enough for now.

"I should get you home," he murmured, running his fingers along her cheek. "You've probably got a busy day tomorrow."

She blinked as if his suggestion took her by surprise. Perhaps she wanted to go on kissing him. But then, Dylan couldn't promise that after another he'd be able to stop. That was the thing about Meggie. When it came to her, he wasn't quite sure what to expect from himself. "Yes," she said. "I should be getting home."

He slipped his arm around her waist and they strolled silently down the sidewalk toward his car. Overall, he was pretty pleased with the way the night had gone. He'd convinced Meggie that he wasn't such a bad guy, he'd done enough to dispel her earlier low opinion of him and, considering her response to his kiss, there would be more dates in the future.

Dylan smiled to himself. Yep, this had been a good date as far as first dates went.

"IT WAS HORRIBLE," Meggie said. "It couldn't have been worse. With all that coffee we'd had, I had to go to the bathroom starting with the appetizers. But I couldn't remember if that fit into the flowchart or not. I was finally forced to excuse myself before they served the main course only to find out that I had a huge hunk of romaine caught between my teeth."

But in truth, it hadn't been horrible at all. It had been the best date she'd ever had. After her initial nervousness had abated, she and Dylan had thoroughly enjoyed themselves, talking and laughing and teasing as if they'd known each other for years—which they had. He'd seemed genuinely fascinated by everything she'd said and more than once during the night she caught him staring at her when he thought she wasn't looking.

Lana stared at her from across the counter at Cuppa Joe's. Meggie waited for the obligatory questions, expecting something resembling the Spanish Inquisition, complete with harsh lighting and torture devices. But surprisingly, Lana didn't press for more details.

"This plan will never work," Meggie murmured.

In truth, Meggie wasn't sure she wanted the plan to work. Dylan wasn't the man she thought he was. He was sweet and attentive and funny. He wasn't fickle and hurtful and thoughtless, like the boy she'd known in high school. No matter how hard she tried, she couldn't imagine that he'd do anything to deliberately hurt her—not now. Not after last night.

"Don't go all goofy on me," Lana said. "Just tell me, did he seem interested?"

Interested? If he wasn't interested, then that kiss they'd shared outside the ice-cream shop was an aberration. Or the kiss they'd shared in his car as he parked in front of her house. Or the kiss he'd given her at her front door. "I think he's interested."

"That's good. Did he try to kiss you?"

"No," Meggie murmured. Technically, she wasn't lying. He didn't try, he'd succeeded. And she'd been crazy enough to enjoy every moment of every kiss, from the tingling on her lips to the curling of her toes. She ran her fingers over her bottom lip, imagining that she could still feel the warmth he'd left there.

"He's nothing like the boy I remember," she said. The man he'd become was completely unexpected to her. There were many layers to Dylan Quinn and she'd just begun to discover them.

She'd known about his tough childhood. Though her parents had never talked about Tommy's best friend in her presence, she'd overheard their conversations many times. How Seamus Quinn drank too much and gambled too much, how the boys were left alone for weeks on end with a baby-sitter who was a bit too fond of vodka. But she'd always believed that they were only repeating rumors.

Now, as an adult, she could believe what her parents had said. There was something in his eyes, a wariness, that hinted he was hiding something, a vulnerability that he cloaked with a charming smile or a witty comment. The Dylan he showed the public and the man he really was were two very different people.

"Did he ask you out again?"

"Yes," Meggie murmured. "For Wednesday."

"And you accepted?"

She frowned. "Yes. Was I supposed to say no? That wasn't on the flowchart."

"That's only three days away, not four," Lana reminded her.

"Well, I didn't have a calculator along," Meggie countered. "I was trying to add it all in my head, twenty-four hours times four days. But then I wasn't sure if you meant four days on the calendar or 96 hours on the clock. I was confused, so I just said yes. Besides, he has Wednesday off. I had to take that into account."

"And did you end the date early?"

"I didn't have to," Meggie said. "After we had dessert, he suggested that he take me home. He thought I'd probably have a busy day today."

Lana scowled. "Hmm. That's not good. He didn't ask to come in?"

"No," Meggie said. A sliver of worry shot through her. "What's wrong?"

"We may have to readjust the plan. I might have to replot this on the flowchart. This isn't ordinary behavior. Are you sure he enjoyed himself? Or did he have that anxious look that guys get when they wish they were someplace else?"

A sick feeling grew in Meggie's stomach. How was she supposed to know these things? Lana was the one with all the experience. The front door to the shop opened and they both turned to see a floral delivery man stride inside. Flowers and plants had been arriving in anticipation of the grand opening. A split leaf philodendron from her parents, an azalea in full bloom from her grandmother, a potted palm from the Boylston Street Business Association.

Lana pushed away from the counter, signed for the flowers, then grabbed the huge bouquet of Old English roses. "Who are they from?" Meggie asked as Lana set the vase on the counter.

Lana plucked the card out from amidst the pastel-colored blooms. Her partner read the card, then held it out under

Meggie's nose. Meggie glanced down at the inscription and her heart skipped a beat.

> I saw these flowers in the florist's window and they reminded me of you.
>
> Dylan.

"They're from Dylan," Meggie said, a smile touching her lips. She leaned over and inhaled the scent, so much more intense than the traditional long-stemmed variety. The pastel colors of pink and peach and yellow immediately brightened her mood.

"They're beautiful," Lana commented. She sighed. "All right, I'll admit it. I really don't get this guy. He drops you off early without even an attempt at a good-night kiss, then he sends you flowers the next morning as if he just spent the most incredible night of his life. It doesn't make sense."

"What do you mean?" Meggie asked.

"Schizophrenia doesn't run in his family, does it?"

"Maybe we should just forget the plan," Meggie suggested. "It was all based on the fact that you knew the kind of guy Dylan was."

"No," Lana insisted. "We can make this work. I've just got to think about this. I want you to tell me everything that happened on your date. Spare no detail. This man is a challenge, but there's not a man on this planet that I can't figure out."

The fact that Lana wasn't really getting the whole picture was probably clouding her judgment, but Meggie wasn't about to tell her that she'd abandoned her carefully laid-out plan after just one look into Dylan's eyes. So she started at the beginning, leaving out the kisses. And as she relived every moment of her date with Dylan, she could understand why Lana found him such a puzzle.

One moment, she could swear that he was attracted to her and the next, she was certain he was just wielding his charm without even thinking. What made her believe she could possibly catch a man like Dylan Quinn? And even more crazy, what made her think she could let him go if and when she caught him?

"Can we talk about this later?" Meggie asked after recounting their dinner for the third time. "I've got other things to do. And you're supposed to drop off the proof for the take-out menus at the printers. We've got three days to decide how I'm supposed to act on our next date."

"All right," Lana said as she pushed away from the counter. "But I don't want you to give up on this. You need to even the score. You need to stand firm. It will all work out in the end."

Meggie nodded then headed back toward the office. But she couldn't stand firm. Every time Dylan Quinn looked at her she went from firm to mush in a matter of seconds. A look, a caress, a kiss, it didn't matter what. She just couldn't resist him. And if she couldn't resist him, then she'd get hurt in the end.

She found his jacket hanging on the back of the office door. Meggie picked it up and slipped it on, then wrapped her arms around herself. With her eyes closed, wearing the coat almost felt like his embrace. Memories of his mouth on hers drifted through her mind and her heart quickened.

Meggie opened her eyes and cursed softly. "I knew this would happen. One date and you're already mooning over him like some lovesick teenager!"

She slipped out of his jacket and into her own. If she waited until Dylan Quinn loved her before she dumped him, she wouldn't be able to dump him at all. Or maybe he'd dump her first. Meggie took a deep breath. He hadn't broken her heart yet. She could still get out with some measure of her pride.

Dylan Quinn had hurt her once. It was time to dump him and dump him fast—before he hurt her again.

4

DYLAN GRABBED THE hose and rinsed the rear bumper of the ladder truck. It was only then that he realized that he'd already washed that very same spot just a few minutes before. He sighed then shook his head. Luckily they hadn't been called out to any fires during his shift. His thoughts had been completely occupied with Meggie Flanagan from the moment he'd opened his eyes that morning.

He still hadn't figured out what it was that drew him to her. It had been ten days since he'd pulled her out of her shop kicking and screaming and as Conor had predicted, that one moment had caused a ripple through his life. Had she been any other woman, they would have rushed headlong into intimacy and already been on the downward slide of their short relationship by now. But with Meggie, the best was yet to come.

Dylan frowned, then snatched up a towel and began to wipe the water off the bumper. He wished he had known her better when she was younger. But maybe that wouldn't have helped. She wasn't the same girl he'd remembered. Somewhere along the line, she'd grown into a beautiful woman and the transformation was remarkable. But just as he carried the scars of his own childhood, she still held traces of the shy teenager she'd been, the girl who stood on the sidelines and watched, silent and unmoving.

"Quinn!"

Dylan peered around the back of the ladder truck. Artie Winton stood in the doorway, his arms hitched on his waist, a cagey grin on his face. "What?" Dylan asked.

"You have a visitor."

He stepped aside and an instant later, Meggie came around the corner of the truck. She was wrapped in a pretty cream-colored jacket that brought out her mahogany hair and green eyes, and her cheeks were pink from the chill in the air. And she clutched his own jacket in her hands. Dylan straightened and wiped his damp hands on his pants. "Meggie. What are you doing here?"

She glanced over her shoulder at Artie as she approached. "Is there some place we can talk?"

Dylan held out his hand and she placed her fingers into his palm. He led her toward the back of the firehouse, to a long bench. "Sit," he said. She did as she was told and he took a place beside her, refusing to let go of her hand.

"Thank you for the flowers," she said. "They're beautiful. And they smell heavenly."

He chuckled. "You're welcome. I enjoyed picking them out."

"You chose them yourself?" she asked as if the notion somehow surprised her.

"I did," he replied. Dylan groaned inwardly. If he thought they'd made any progress last night, he'd been wrong. Meggie was back to acting like a rabbit cornered by a wolf. She was skittish and wary and she could barely look him in the eye.

"I really shouldn't have come," she said. "I know it's against the rules but I had to talk to you."

"Rules?" Dylan asked.

She glanced up, her eyes wide. "I mean, the fire department rules."

Dylan grabbed his coat from her arms, then rose and pulled her up along with him. "Actually, we try very hard to maintain good relationships with the public so it's really not a problem if you visit. A lot of our time is just spent waiting anyway." He searched for an excuse to keep her there because she looked like she was about to bolt. "Why don't I show you around?"

"I just came to tell you something," she insisted. "And to return your—"

"Have you ever been in a firehouse?" Dylan asked.

She gave him a weak smile, then shrugged. "Not really. It's just that I—"

"Well, this is the pump truck," he interrupted, buying himself some time, "and that's the ladder truck. This one pumps water, the other has a ladder that we can use for access to taller buildings." He took her hand. "Would you like to sit inside?"

He helped her into the cab and then pulled himself up on the running board. Her fingers skimmed over the steering wheel and he remembered what her touch had done to him the night before, how soft and fleeting and addictive it had been. "This must be hell to parallel park," she murmured.

Dylan chuckled as he stepped down. "I don't have to drive, I just get to ride. And we pretty much get to park wherever we want." He reached up and grabbed her around the waist and then slowly lowered her to the floor. Her body slid along his, their hips making contact and sending a frisson of desire racing through his body. When she finally stood in front of him, he was tempted to kiss her right there, but he wagered a few of his co-workers were watching from the windows above.

"Maybe we should put my jacket away," he said. She followed him to the large alcove where the firefighters stowed their gear, and the moment they were out of sight of the windows, Dylan pulled her to him. He spun her around and she sank back into the jackets. With hands braced on either side of her head, he leaned forward and brushed a soft kiss on her lips, teasing then retreating, doing his best to lighten her somber mood.

How much longer could he go on like this, craving her kisses yet wanting so much more? He kept trying to think of her as that sweet vulnerable girl, hoping that might quell his desire, but that didn't work anymore. She was soft and she smelled nice and without a second thought, he could lose himself in a slow exploration of her body. "There," he murmured, smiling down at her. "That's much better."

"This has to be against the rules," she said, her eyes fixed on his mouth.

With a low groan, he captured her lips again, only this time with more intensity. The taste of her went right to his head, obliterating any thought of proper firefighter behavior. His tongue teased at hers, soft, persuasive, drawing her into the heat of the moment. And when her arms wrapped around his neck, he leaned into her, his hips pinning hers against the wall.

She was offering him more and he wasn't about to refuse. The passion they shared was unexpected and uncontrolled, a simple kiss the one thing that triggered it in full force. And though he knew he should resist, take things slow, nothing in her response gave him cause to.

His hands skimmed over her face then drifted down to her body. He pushed aside her coat and wrapped his arms around her waist. She went soft and pliant beneath his touch. The sweater she wore beneath her coat clung to her curves and he smoothed his palms over the soft cashmere as if he were touching bare skin.

And then he slipped his hands beneath the sweater and did touch bare skin, smooth, silken skin that felt like heaven against his callused palms. The blood roared in his head as desire threatened to overtake common sense. The ringing in his head was almost loud enough to drown out… Dylan froze, then slowly drew back. He stared down at Meggie, at her lips still damp from his kiss and at her face, flushed with desire and upturned to his.

"Meggie, I have to go."

"Go?" she asked, breathless.

The speaker overhead crackled and then dispatch came

on with the address of an apartment fire. "We have go. There's a fire."

There was more than one fire to put out, he mused as he grabbed her hand. Dylan slipped into his jacket in an effort to hide the evidence of his own desire, then pulled her out of the alcove before the rest of the men reached the first floor. He casually leaned his arm against the panel of gauges on the pumper truck and pasted a smile on his face. "And that's how we get the incredible water pressure to fight fires here in Boston."

Meggie glanced around, her eyes going wide with the increasing activity, the men rushing around her, jostling her as they passed. Firefighters converged on their gear, grabbing jackets and slipping into boots. Dylan stole one more quick kiss. "What did you want to tell me?" he asked. "Tell me quick."

Meggie shook her head. "It's nothing. It can wait."

"Then I'll pick you up around lunchtime on Wednesday. Wear something warm," he called before hurrying to the alcove to grab his helmet and boots. Meggie stood in the middle of all the action as the crew made preparations to leave, a distraught expression on her face.

Then the trucks slowly pulled out of the station and Dylan hopped into the cab with the rest of his crew. "Thanks for bringing my jacket," he shouted over the sounds of the sirens.

She waved then slowly wandered through the open doors to the sidewalk. Dylan hung out the window and watched her as long as he could, until the engine was far down Boylston Street and she was just a figure in the distance. His mouth was still wet from her kiss and the scent of her perfume still swam in his head. He drew back inside, then smiled to himself.

"Hey, Quinn," Artie called from the seat beside him. "I see you got your old jacket back. You gonna leave it behind at this fire?"

Dylan shook his head and chuckled, smoothing his hands over the waterproof fabric. "Naw, that's a bad habit I'm going to break. I won't be leaving any more jackets behind from now on."

"WE'RE GOING ON a boat?" Meggie asked.

She stared at the huge boat that bumped gently against the dock. Though *The Mighty Quinn* looked like a perfectly seaworthy vessel, Meggie wasn't as certain of her own seaworthiness. "I've never been on a boat before," she murmured. "I mean, not on the ocean. I went rowing once on the Charles, but the boat tipped over and I fell in. We're not going on the ocean, are we?"

Dylan chuckled. "I suppose we could drag the boat up the interstate behind Liam's car, but I don't think that would be as easy as going on the ocean," he teased, giving a her a playful kiss on the cheek. "Besides, it's not technically the ocean, it's Massachusetts Bay."

"Why Gloucester?"

"Brendan's pulling the boat out for repairs during the winter and he knows a guy up there who has a boatyard, so he'll live up there for a while. He's working on a book about the North Atlantic swordfishing fleet and he wants to soak up the surroundings while he's writing it."

"I don't know anything about boats," Meggie murmured.

She glanced nervously between the car Dylan's brother had lent them and the boat. Meggie had fully intended to break off her relationship with Dylan today. She hadn't had the chance at the firehouse, but after another two days of careful contemplation, she'd convinced herself that putting Dylan Quinn out of her life would be for the best.

But she couldn't do it on a boat! What if he got angry? There was no place to run on a boat. Or what if he tried to convince her she was wrong? She couldn't avoid him on a boat. All he'd need to do is touch her the way he had at the fire station, his warm palms sliding over her skin, and she'd forget all her resolve.

She drew a ragged breath. A decision had to be made. Either she went back to Boston right now and put Dylan out of her life, or she spent the day bobbing around on the ocean with a man who had the capacity to erase all her doubts about him with just one kiss. Meggie winced inwardly. "Oh, what the hell," she murmured. What use was it resisting him? Why not just roll with the punches, let the chips fall where they may, and any other cliché that fit her situation. She could always break up with him tomorrow, or the next day, whenever she tired of the taste of his mouth on hers or the warmth of his hands on her body.

"My brother Brendan will do most of the work," Dylan explained. "Conor and I just have to help at the dock. And Conor's fiancée, Olivia, is coming along. We'll do the navigating so you have nothing to worry about. You'll have fun, I promise."

"You promise you won't get upset if I get sick?" Meggie asked.

"You won't," Dylan assured her, wrapping his arm around her shoulder. "The boat is pretty big and the water is calm today. And we won't be heading very far from shore." He turned to her. "We don't have to go if you don't want."

In truth, now that she'd decided to relax and take things as they came, she was looking forward to the day. Dylan had invited her to meet his brothers and he seemed so intent on having her along. And she couldn't ignore her own curiosity. She'd known *of* the Quinn boys in high school. Now she'd get a chance to know some of them personally—and maybe get to know Dylan a little better in the process. What harm could there be in that?

"Hey, Brendan! There's some bum loitering on your dock. You want me to throw him to the fishes?"

Meggie looked up and watched as a tall, dark-haired man hung over the side of the boat. He was as handsome as Dylan with those golden green eyes and that devilish grin. His gaze shifted to Meggie and she couldn't help but see the surprise register.

"And who's this?" he asked.

Dylan grabbed Meggie's hand and pulled her over toward the crate that served as a step into the boat. "Meggie, this is my older brother, Conor. I don't know if you remember him. Con, this is Meggie Flanagan." He paused and Meggie knew he was scrambling for a word to describe what they were to each other. Girlfriend, acquaintance. "Tommy Flanagan's little sister," he finished.

Conor smiled warmly then reached out and helped her up on deck. "Glad to have you along," he said with a smile as disarming as Dylan's.

Dylan pointed up to the pilothouse where another Quinn stood in the doorway, as handsome and dangerous looking as the other two. "And that's Brendan."

Brendan gave Meggie a wave. He looked at her for a long moment, his eyebrow cocked up, then turned back to the business at hand. As if on cue, Conor jumped down onto the dock and a few seconds later, the engines rumbled to life. Like a finely tuned team, Dylan grabbed the bowlines and Conor the stern. At the last moment, they both jumped on board and the boat headed out of Hull harbor.

A pretty blonde came through the doorway to the main cabin and joined Conor, who introduced her as his fiancée, Olivia Farrell. Meggie had never been very good around strangers, but Olivia made her feel comfortable right away, taking her hand and leading her back through the doorway. The interior of the cabin was cozy and warm and clean, almost like a real house and nothing at all like she expected. "This is nice," Meggie commented.

"The bathroom is right down there," Olivia said. "The boys call it the head, but I think that's such an awful word for it." She opened a picnic basket on the table. "I'm so glad you came along. I was wondering when we were going to meet you."

"Meet me?" Meggie said. She nervously clutched her hands in front of her, her fingers icy cold. The boat had already begun to sway and she had trouble keeping her balance. She quickly sat down at the table and gripped the edge with white-knuckled hands.

"The way Dylan talked about you at the pub the other night, it sounded like you two would be seeing each other again." Olivia began to pull deli containers out of the basket, potato salad, coleslaw, baked beans—each new selection making Meggie's stomach roil. Olivia handed her a chocolate chip cookie, then fetched a cup of coffee for them both. "He's such a great guy. I'm glad he's found someone."

Meggie took a sip of the coffee and it immediately calmed her stomach and warmed her hands. "He hasn't found me," she said, shaking her head. "I mean, we're not serious. We've only been out on one date. He's not really the type who gets serious."

Olivia glanced up, then smiled knowingly. "He's never brought a girl along on one of these trips. At least, that's what Conor claims. That must mean something, right?"

Meggie shrugged. "Maybe. But guys like Dylan don't fall in love. At least not forever."

"It sounds like you've been listening to too many of Seamus Quinn's Mighty Quinn stories."

"What are those?" Meggie asked, nibbling on the cookie.

Olivia sat down beside her and wrapped her hands around her steaming mug of coffee. "After their mother left, Seamus used to tell them these bedtime stories about their Mighty Quinn ancestors. The stories always contained the moral that to give in to a woman's love was a weakness. And the boys used to tell them over and over again when Seamus was out at sea. Brendan is the best storyteller, but I've heard Dylan spin a few tales, too." She sighed softly. "I can only imagine what their childhood was like without a single female influence in their lives."

Though Olivia was a virtual stranger, Meggie immediately felt at ease talking to her. "Dylan's never mentioned his mother. Do they see her?"

Olivia shook her head. "Never. Seamus told them she died in a car wreck a year after she walked out. Conor doesn't believe it. I'm not sure what Dylan thinks. He keeps his feelings pretty well hidden under all that charm. But sometimes I think he was the one most affected. Conor took over raising the family and Brendan helped his father on the boat. Dylan was kind of caught in the middle with nothing to do but become irresistible and irresponsible."

"He can be so charming," Meggie said with a soft laugh. "Sometimes I get caught up in it and I actually believe he has feelings for me."

Olivia met her gaze. "And what if he did? How do you feel about him?"

A smile broke across Meggie's face. "I've been in love with Dylan Quinn since I was thirteen, since the first day he walked into our house with my brother, Tommy. He was so tall and so handsome, even back then, and I thought I'd die if he didn't love me back." She stopped suddenly, a blush warming her cheeks. "I shouldn't tell you this."

Olivia sat down next to her. "No. It's all right. The first time I saw Conor, I felt the same way, all fluttery and breathless, like a schoolgirl. There's something about the Quinn boys. They're so tough on the outside, yet so…vulnerable."

"Sometimes, I can't think straight when he looks at me. And when he kisses me I just—" Meggie stopped, certain she'd said too much. But when she glanced up at Olivia she found her smiling, as if they shared a wonderful secret.

"I know. I tried to resist, but it never worked. Maybe Seamus's tales have some truth to them. Maybe the Quinns have mystical powers."

Meggie nodded, then sighed. These were things she'd usually tell Lana, but that was impossible as long as Lana was focused on her plan. Besides, Olivia was in love with a Quinn. She knew what Meggie was going through. "Sometimes I believe I'm still in love with Dylan. And then I stop myself and try to keep from thinking about him like that. I know how he is."

"People change," Olivia said. "Sometimes the risks are worth the rewards." She rose, then pulled Meggie up with her. "It's a gorgeous day. Let's go up on deck."

They found Dylan and Conor up in the pilothouse with Brendan. The view from above the deck was spectacular. Meggie looked out at the bay, then back to the shore, the skyline of Boston visible through a thin haze. But they were up so high, the motion of the boat was even more pronounced and she grabbed Dylan's arm to steady herself. She closed her eyes and drew a deep breath, praying that she wouldn't make a fool of herself and throw up the cookie she'd just eaten.

When she opened them, she saw Dylan staring at her. "Why don't we go down on deck," he said. "You'll feel better down there." He took her hand and helped her down the ladder. They walked around to the bow, then sat down on a gear locker. "How's that?" he asked.

"Better," Meggie replied, tipping her face up into the warm sun and breathing deeply until the nausea passed.

He slipped his arm around her shoulders and pulled her close. "Good."

They sat in silence for a long time, the both of them staring out at the water, breathing in the crisp air. Gulls hovered overhead, squawking loudly and diving for scraps that they thought all fishing boats offered. If only it could be like this all the time, Meggie mused. No doubts, no demands, just the two of them and the wind and the salt air.

She turned to Dylan, hesitated, then spoke. "I like your family. Your brothers are nice. And Olivia is wonderful."

"She is, isn't she. Conor is a lucky man. I'm kind of glad he was the one who proved the family legends wrong. A Mighty Quinn can be happy with a woman—the right woman."

Another silence grew between them and Meggie's mind raced. Was she the right woman? Or was she just another in a long line of "almosts"? There was so much she wanted to know, so many questions she needed answers for. "Dylan, why did you bring me along?" she blurted out.

He considered his reply for a long time, staring out at the horizon as if the answer was there. "I'm not sure," he finally said. "I just knew that once I got out on the water, I'd want you to be here with me. I wanted you to see this." He sent her a sideways glance. "It's part of who I am. If it weren't for this boat, I'd probably still be living in Ireland, a world away from who and what I am now. A world away from you." He glanced around, as if he'd said too much. "I hated this boat when I was a kid."

The vehemence in his words startled her and his cheerful expression had turned remote. "Why?"

He stood up and walked to the bow, then faced her. Meggie's breath stopped in her throat. Standing there, the wind in his hair, the sea at his back, he was about the most gorgeous thing she'd ever laid eyes on, like some ancient god risen up from the sea. He was wrong about the boat. He belonged here amidst the wide outdoors and the dark blue sea. Meggie pressed a hand to her chest, trying to keep her heart from racing out of control.

"This boat is why we came to America. It's what took my father away for weeks on end," Dylan explained. "This boat is what drove my mother to run out on us. This boat caused all the bad things that happened to me when I was a kid. Sometimes, I just wished it would sink to the bottom of the ocean so that we could have a normal family." He laughed bitterly. "But as I got older, I realized it wasn't the boat, it was what it represented. Loneliness, deprivation, fear."

His sudden honesty stunned her. Dylan must trust her very much to be so open about his childhood in her presence. What would Lana say about this? She'd have to revise her plan again. "What happened to your mother?" she asked, hoping that he'd keep talking.

Dylan shrugged. "I'm not sure. Conor used to believe that she was still alive, but I think we're all a little afraid to find out for sure. Afraid that this perfect image we have of her might not hold up in real life. All I know is that once she left, everything went bad." He smiled wanly. "My da and all his tales of the Mighty Quinns. All he had to do was look at his sons and see how much we needed her. That's why I used to hang out at your house. Your mom was always so nice to me. And she was a much better cook than Con."

"What if she showed up one day?" Meggie asked. "What would you do?"

He considered the question for a long time, his gaze fixed on her, the wind whipping at his hair. Meggie saw the pain in his eyes and suddenly, she was able to understand the boy he'd been, the boy who had used his charm to make a place for himself in the world, to protect himself from the terrors of real life.

Dylan slowly walked over to her and sat down. "I'd take her hand," he said, as he grabbed Meggie's fingers and curled them around his. "And I'd never let go again."

Her heart twisted. For a moment she wanted to believe that he was talking about her. She leaned over and brushed a soft kiss across his lips. It was the first time she'd ever initiated a kiss. His eyes flickered and he looked surprised. Then he gave her a crooked smile and pressed his forehead against hers.

Suddenly, the barriers she'd built to protect herself from his charms completely dissolved. She didn't want to put this man out of her life, she wanted him to become a part of it. Yet everything between them was a tangle of secret motives and unresolved conflicts. She couldn't allow herself to love him, yet she couldn't seem to stop the feelings that surged inside of her.

Meggie drew a deep breath of the sea air and then kissed Dylan again, brushing aside her worries and doubts to simply enjoy the sensations that warmed her blood. She'd decide what to do later. For now, she wanted to believe that she could live in this fantasy world for just a little while longer.

"SO THAT'S Meggie Flanagan," Brendan murmured, staring down at the bow of the boat.

Dylan peered through the window of the pilothouse. Meggie and Olivia were sitting near the bow sipping at cups of hot cocoa and chatting amiably. He'd had his doubts about bringing her along. Meggie wasn't the type you just tossed into an unfamiliar setting. When she was nervous, she'd often retreat behind a wall of uneasy silence. But Olivia had made her feel welcome and Brendan had done his best to make the trip up to Gloucester smooth and uneventful. They'd docked late in the afternoon and Conor was out getting dinner for them all from a nearby tavern.

"That's certainly not the Meggie Flanagan I remember from high school," Brendan added. "She was only a year behind me, but I don't remember her having the potential to be quite so beautiful."

"She is beautiful, isn't she," Dylan said. "I mean not in that obvious, overblown way. She's real. Sometimes I think I could look at her for hours and never get bored."

Brendan clapped his hand on his brother's shoulder. "Conor said it. The minute you carried her out of that fire, you were lost."

"Maybe," Dylan said. "Maybe not. It's been almost two weeks since I carried her out of her shop. We've seen each other a handful of times. Just one official date though. And I still can't tell if she's interested."

"You can't blame her for being a little leery," Brendan said. "You are known to be quite the ladies' man, even among the six Quinn brothers."

Dylan winced. Why did that always have to come up? Why did his reputation seem to define who he was and how he'd behave? "I'm hoping to live that down sometime in the next decade. Meggie is the first woman I've really cared about. I don't want her to think I'm just marking time until another woman comes along."

"I suppose this doesn't bode well for me," Brendan said. "First Conor, then you. Da had a hard enough time accepting Conor's engagement. He'll have a stroke when he hears about you. All those cautionary tales gone to waste."

"There's nothing to hear about," Dylan said. He gaze was still fixed on Meggie. She'd turned around and spotted him up in the pilothouse, then waved cheerfully.

"I see how you look at her," Brendan countered. "I'll tell you what I told Conor. Just don't screw this up. You may only get one chance to make it work."

Dylan nodded. He squinted against the slant of sunlight washing the deck. "I wonder what they're talking about?"

"You know women," Brendan said with a shrug. "They're probably comparing notes on the sexual prowess of the Quinn men."

"Really?" Dylan asked. "That's what they talk about? But they barely know each other."

"How the hell do I know? I know they don't talk about sports. And you can only talk about lipstick and nail polish for just so long. Sooner or later, I'd guess the topic might turn to men."

"I better get down there," Dylan said. "I don't want Olivia scaring her off."

Until now, he'd never really cared whether his family met one of his girlfriends. But Meggie wasn't a conquest and he wanted them to know her the way he did, to see how pretty she was and to understand why she made him laugh. And he wanted to prove to them that not all his relationships were shallow and short-term, that maybe, like Conor, he was capable of falling in love, too.

Not so long ago, the notion of love would have been unthinkable. But Dylan had seen what Olivia's love had given Conor. In just a few short weeks, Conor had left childhood wounds behind. He was complete, content, a man assured of a happy future. Olivia had given that to him and the more time Dylan spent with Meggie, the more he wanted to believe that she could make him happy in the same way.

After all the tales his father had told about the dangers of love, Dylan had never expected the emotion to touch him. But every moment he spent with Meggie brought him closer to the realization that it was possible to find the one perfect person to spend a lifetime with. Maybe she was the one.

He climbed down the ladder and as he came around to the bow, he ran into Olivia. She smiled at him then gave him a spontaneous hug. "Meggie is wonderful," she said. "Just don't do anything to mess it up, okay."

"Why does everyone think I'll mess it up?" he asked.

He found Meggie standing at the rail staring out at the harbor. He came up behind her and wrapped his arms around her, pulling her back against his body. "Aren't you cold?" he asked.

She nodded. "I was just about to come in and—" A fish flopped below her in the water and she jumped, then looked overboard. "What was that?"

Dylan rested his chin on her shoulder and saw the ripples. "I suppose it could have been a mermaid," he teased.

Meggie smiled. "There is no such thing. Except in Disney movies."

"Ah, but you're wrong," Dylan said. "Because my long-ago ancestor, Lorcan Quinn, he met a mermaid. And her name was Muriel."

"Then your ancestor Lorcan was as crazy as you," Meggie murmured, her gaze still fixed on the water, a tiny smile curling her lips.

Dylan had never been good at telling the stories, but he couldn't refuse the challenge of convincing Meggie. Besides, standing with her in his arms and the lights of the harbor twinkling off the twilight water, it was like magic. And it deserved a magical story. "Lorcan was a wild child," he began. "A very bold boy who was irresponsible to a fault. One day, he was *foostering* about and his da told him that he must make himself useful. So Lorcan offered to take the boat out and do some fishing. Well, he had no intention of catching fish. Lorcan lay down in the bottom of the boat for a wee nap. But he didn't sleep long. He opened his eyes to hear a lovely song filling the air. When he sat up, he found himself far from shore and drifting with a strong current."

"I can hear Ireland in your voice," Meggie said.

Dylan hadn't realized that he'd been telling the tale in the lilting accents of his homeland. But that's how the tales were supposed to sound, like music. That's the way they'd always told them when they were younger, in their father's voice. "Well, he looked over the side of the boat and he found a mermaid swimming about. Her name was Muriel and she lived in a kingdom at the bottom of the sea. She told Lorcan of the beauty of this kingdom and the riches that it held and she urged him to come with her. But Lorcan didn't trust her for he'd heard tales of how mermaids had lured fishermen to their deaths, so he grabbed his oars and rowed back to shore."

"So was she a bad mermaid or a good mermaid?" Meggie asked, turning her head to look up into his eyes.

"You'll see," Dylan replied, kissing her on the nose. "But Lorcan couldn't forget this mermaid. He heard her song every day as he drifted about in his boat. As he watched her swim around, he realized that he was in love with her, with her beauty and with the sound of her voice. But she was of the sea and he was of the land and there was no way they could be together. Still, this didn't stop him from coming out to see her, no matter what the weather.

"One day there was a great storm and Lorcan's little boat was caught by a tremendous wave. Muriel was there to save him but the storm was too powerful and it hurled them both against the rocks. As Muriel lay in Lorcan's arms, dying, she begged him to take her back to the sea, for only the sea could save her. Lorcan's love was strong, and though he knew it might mean his death, he jumped back into the raging ocean with Muriel in his arms."

"And did he die?" Meggie asked.

"Well, in the story that I always told, he met a cold and icy death in blackest depths of the sea and all because he was stupid enough to believe a mermaid."

"That's terrible," Meggie cried, giving him an elbow in the ribs.

"But in Brendan's version, Lorcan returns Muriel to her kingdom. Her father, who rules the ocean, is so happy to see his daughter again that he gives Lorcan a gift in return. He gives him the power to live underwater. So by sacrificing his own life for love, he's given a new life with Muriel and they lived happily beneath the sea—mermaid and merman—for the rest of their days."

"That's much better."

"When Da was away, Brendan always used to change the endings of the stories, until every story had six or seven different endings and we'd never know which one he'd tell. It kept them interesting." He paused. "I always thought Brendan's versions were a little sappy. But I like this one. You know, love conquers all."

He gently turned Meggie in his arms until she faced him. And then he bent closer and kissed her, slowly and deliberately, until his blood began to warm. How many times had he wondered what drew him to her? He'd spent countless hours trying to figure it out. Was it her beauty? Or her vulnerability? Or was it the past they'd shared?

As Dylan pulled her slender body against his and lost himself in the taste of her, he realized that it really didn't matter. They'd found each other. And for now, they were together. There would be plenty of time to sort out his feelings later—once he knew what they really were.

5

MEGGIE NESTLED INTO the curve of Dylan's arm then sighed. She'd been dozing since they'd left Gloucester, exhausted from the fresh air and the sea spray. She would have been content to stay exactly where she was, her head resting on Dylan's shoulder, snuggled beneath his jacket. But the lights passing by on the freeway told her they were nearing Boston.

It had been a near perfect day, warm for November with a blindingly blue sky. But it could have been pouring rain with ten-foot waves and she still wouldn't have believed it could get better. At first, she'd been a bit nervous about meeting Dylan's brothers. But they'd been as charming and attentive as he was and it wasn't long before she felt the last traces of her anxiety dissolve.

Part of that was due to Olivia Farrell. Meggie didn't have

a sister, but when she imagined one for herself, she imagined someone just like Olivia. She was beautiful and sophisticated and funny and yet, she made Meggie feel as if they were the oldest and dearest of friends. With three Quinn brothers heaping on the charm, Meggie was lucky to have Olivia there to put them all back in their places. Both together and apart, the brothers had the uncanny knack of making a girl feel like she was the only woman in the world.

They'd parted with Olivia's promise to stop by the coffee shop on the day of the grand opening. And Meggie returned the promise with plans to visit Farrell Antiques as soon as she had a chance. But when Meggie waved goodbye from the dock, she knew there was every chance that she may never see Olivia Farrell again. The only connection between them was as fragile as her connection to Dylan Quinn.

Though she couldn't be sure what the future held, she was sure of one thing—making a place for Dylan Quinn in her future would be foolhardy at best. No matter how studiously she followed Lana's plan, one fact was still unavoidable. Men like Dylan didn't fall in love for keeps—maybe in romantic movies and dime-store novels, but not in real life.

But that didn't mean she couldn't enjoy what they had right here and now—just as she had today. Dwelling on the future only made the present more troubling. And she'd never really lived for the moment, tossing aside all her notions of propriety and leading with her heart instead of her head. For as long as she could remember, her life had been all planned out, studying hard in high school to get a scholarship, studying hard in college to get a good job, working hard at her job to save for the coffee shop.

Now all her professional dreams were about to come true, why couldn't she make a few of her personal fantasies happen at the same time, before the opportunity slipped through her fingers? Her thirtieth birthday was right around the corner. She'd at least like to experience mind-bending, toe-curling passion before she passed that milestone, the kind of passion that usually came with a brief and completely inappropriate affair with an unattainable man. And if that's what she wanted, then Dylan Quinn fit the bill.

"Are we home yet?" she murmured, straightening to look at him.

His face was illuminated by the lights from the dashboard and the passing streetlights and for a moment her breath caught in her throat. There were moments when she wished she could stop time so she could look at him, so she could memorize every plane and angle of his face and examine the strong line of his jaw and the sculpted shape of his mouth.

"I have to stop by the pub," Dylan said. "I promised Brian and Sean I'd take the deposit to the bank on my way home." He wove his hand through the hair at her nape and a delicious shiver skittered down her spine. "I know you're tired, but it will just be a few minutes."

She wrapped his jacket around herself, suddenly wide awake. "I had a nice time today," she said.

"Me, too."

They pulled up in front of the pub a few moments later. Dylan glanced at his watch then at the darkened exterior of Quinn's Pub. "I see Sean and Brian didn't bother to stick around. Closing time is at 2:00 a.m. and it's 2:05 right now." He turned off the ignition, then bent closer to Meggie and brushed a soft kiss across her lips. "I just have to run inside. And you have to come with me. I don't want you waiting out here alone."

Meggie straightened in her seat then stretched sinuously. "All right," she said, handing him his jacket.

Dylan hopped out of the Mustang and jogged around to her side, then helped her out of the car. They crossed the street, hand in hand, and he unlocked the front door of the pub and let her step inside first. Reaching around her, he flipped on the lights. Neon sputtered to life and bright light bounced off the wide mirror behind the bar. The smell of spilled beer and stale cigarette smoke was an assault to the senses after a day on the water, but Meggie ignored it in favor of her curiosity. So this was where Dylan spent his free time. And this is where he'd obviously met his share of beautiful women.

"I've never really been to a bar before," Meggie murmured.

"What?" Dylan asked as he tossed his jacket over the bar.

Meggie knew he'd heard her. He just couldn't believe her. "I know what they look like. I've seen *Cheers*. But in college I spent my Friday and Saturday nights studying. And after I started working, I just didn't have the time. Besides, they're always so crowded. Too many strangers."

"So where do you meet men?" Dylan asked.

A blush warmed her cheeks. So much for honesty. "That must be my problem. They all hang out at bars, don't they. And here I've been spending my free time at pottery class hoping to meet the man of my dreams."

Dylan chuckled and Meggie forced a smile, relieved that

she'd deflected his question so adeptly. She stared down at the floor and pushed a scrap of paper around with her shoe. "There really haven't been that many men in my life," she murmured. "I suppose I shouldn't admit that, but it's the truth."

Dylan hooked a finger beneath her chin and tipped her gaze back up to his. "I can tell you right now," he said. "If you walked into this bar on a Friday night, you'd have men lined up on either side of you in just a few minutes."

She couldn't help but warm beneath his compliment. He always made her feel so special. But then that was all part of his charm, wasn't it. "The next time I want to meet a nice guy, I'll just set my house on fire."

He laughed, then grabbed her hand and pulled her toward the bar. When he settled her on a stool, he helped her out of her jacket. "Meeting a man in a bar isn't so tough. It's worse for the guy. He risks rejection in front of all his buddies. That's enough to scare any man off. All a woman has to do is look pretty."

"That can't be all it takes."

"Here, I'll show you." He stepped around the end of the bar and grabbed a bottle of rum. One after another, he added liquor and fruit juice to a glass of ice, then finished it with a drizzle of red syrup and dropped in a cherry and a chunk of pineapple. He set it in front of her.

"What's this?" she asked.

"That's a rum punch. They're popular in the tropics of Ireland. And I'm the guy who just sent it over." He drew himself a Guinness from the tap, then strolled down to the last stool on the end of the bar and gave her a little wave.

Meggie waved back as she took a sip of the rum punch. It was sweet and potent and the perfect fortification for this wicked little game he was intent on playing. She drew a deep breath and steadied her resolve. If she really wanted to begin living a more exciting life, she could start here. "Now what do I do?" she asked, her inhibitions fading with the second sip of the rum punch.

"Well, if you like the drink and you want to get to know me, then I'd suggest you wander over to the jukebox and drop a few quarters in."

"Why?" Meggie asked, looking at him over the rim of her glass.

"Because that will give me a chance to see what a beautiful body you have. And it'll give me a chance to see how you move."

"What if I don't have a beautiful body?" she asked, reality intruding into the little fantasy he'd created.

Dylan groaned, then slid off his stool and strode over to the cash register. He pulled out a handful of quarters, then dropped them on the bar in front of her, leaning over the bar as he spoke. "Sweetheart, if you walked over to the jukebox in a crowded bar, I wouldn't be the only one watching. Now go play some music and quit asking questions."

Meggie grabbed her drink, then walked across to the jukebox. She felt Dylan's eyes on her and she slowed her pace and let her hips sway just a little more than normal. Though she wore a heavy wool sweater and faded jeans, right now she felt positively sexy—and a little bit naughty. She found a Clannad CD and punched in the numbers, then waited for the music to start, her racing heart providing the percussion until it did.

"Hi there."

His breath was warm against her ear and Meggie jumped, surprised that he'd snuck up on her. She spun around. But as she did, she forgot she was still clutching her rum punch. The glass hit his chest and the contents sloshed over the side and soaked the front of his sweater. She cursed softly, then risked a glance up at him. "I'm sorry. I—I didn't realize you were standing so close."

"No problem," he said. He grabbed the hem of his sweater and yanked it up over his head, then tossed it on a nearby table. But the punch had soaked through.

This was what happened when she decided to let loose! With any other man, she might have been able to play the game. But Dylan had a way of rattling her composure and setting her nerves on edge. Just the thought of him touching her…or kissing her…Meggie swallowed convulsively, knowing she was ill-prepared to continue. But desire overwhelmed common sense.

With a hesitant hand, she reached out and touched the wet, sticky spot on his T-shirt. Then she drew a shaky breath and said something that shocked even her. "Maybe you should take your T-shirt off, too," she suggested. "I mean, so I can rinse out the punch."

Dylan eyed her for a long moment, then reached down to tug it off. But she stopped him, emboldened by an uncharacteristic surge of courage. Gathering the soft fabric between her fingers, she slowly pushed it up along his torso, then pulled it over his head. "There," she murmured, her gaze falling on his smooth, muscular chest. "That's better."

He slipped his arm around her waist and pulled her closer,

all thoughts of laundry fleeing her head. Meggie pressed her palms against his naked skin, the dusting of hair on his chest soft beneath her fingers. "Now what do we do?" she murmured.

He bent closer, his lips nearly touching her cheek, then whispered in her ear. "I'd ask you if you wanted to play a game of pool or darts."

"Why is that?"

"Because you probably wouldn't know how to play," he explained. "So I would show you and that would give me a chance to touch you."

Meggie rested her head on his shoulder, turning her face up until their lips were just inches apart. "I'd love to play darts or pool," she murmured. The rest of the invitation was silent, yet understood.

She wanted him to touch her—whenever and wherever he wanted to.

"NOW YOU LINE the ball up with the pocket. Find the spot on the ball where you need to hit it with the cue ball and then just…gently…stroke the stick."

"All right," Meggie murmured. She leaned over the pool table, her backside brushing his lap. He groaned inwardly, then wrapped his arms around her as he showed her how to hold the cue. He'd already showed her how to throw darts and just when he thought he couldn't bear it anymore, when he couldn't keep his desire under control, he'd suggested they try a game of pool. But pool hadn't been any easier on the libido than darts.

Dylan wasn't sure how much longer he could play out this

little fantasy they'd begun. What started as a silly game had resulted in a very obvious physical reaction—a reaction that was getting harder to ignore by the second.

Had she been any other woman, Dylan might have thrown caution to the wind and seduced her. But this was Meggie. And Meggie was different. He wasn't sure why, but in his mind he held her apart from all the other conquests in his life. Maybe it began as a need to protect her—or at least protect the memory of the vulnerable, introverted girl she'd been. But that had changed long ago, around the time he realized that nothing he did could stop him from wanting her.

He needed her like he'd never needed a woman before. But Dylan suspected that when they did make love, there would be more to it than just a physical release. To say he wasn't a little bit scared would be lie. Meggie was the only woman he'd ever known who had the capacity to touch his heart—and she could break it just as easily.

"It went in!" Meggie cried. She spun around, but Dylan was still bent over with his hands braced on either side of her. She caught his nose with the cue stick and for a moment he saw stars. He slowly straightened, blinking to clear his head.

"Oh," she cried. "Oh, I'm sorry. I didn't realize you were so…I mean, when I turned, the cue stick just…" She reached up and gently touched his nose. "Does it hurt?"

"I suppose I should be happy I managed to escape darts without serious injury."

"I've never been very good at sports," Meggie admitted. "I get nervous and then I get clumsy." She pushed up on her toes and kissed his nose. "Is that better?"

He smiled grudgingly. "A little better."

Meggie stared at him for a long moment, her expression turning serious. Then she kissed him again, slowly, deliberately, this time on his right cheek. "How about now?" she murmured, her voice low and throaty.

"One more would probably make it feel just fine."

She leaned forward to kiss his other cheek but at the last second, he turned and her lips met his. This time, Dylan didn't take the lead. He let the kiss spin out at Meggie's pace, at first slow and hesitant. But then, she ran her tongue along the crease of his mouth, teasing, tempting him to deepen the kiss. When it came to Meggie, he couldn't resist.

Dylan spanned her waist with his hands and lifted her up to sit on the edge of the pool table, their mouths still caught in a delicate exploration. Then he stepped between her legs and pulled her nearer, molding her body against his naked chest, pulling her thighs around his hips. She was so warm and soft and touchable and no matter where he put his hands, he couldn't get enough of her.

He wanted to stop, but the urge to continue was so much greater. His need for Meggie had become almost a constant in his life. And each time he touched her or kissed her, Dylan knew there would come a time when he couldn't stop himself. His effort at control was weakening and the feel of her palms smoothing over his chest wasn't helping.

Gazing down at her hands, he watched her trace patterns with her fingers, leaving a warm brand on his skin wherever she touched. He wanted her to possess him, to treat his body as if it belonged to her. To take pleasure in making him ache for the sensations of her hands on his skin.

He reached down and tangled his fingers in hers, then drew her hand to his mouth. In the past, seduction had been a game, a means to an end, the ultimate release. But with Meggie, it was just the beginning, like a door opening into her soul. He wanted to know her, both physically and emotionally. He needed to learn what made her happy and sad, what made her shudder with desire and cry out with need.

Dylan started with the soft skin beneath her ear. He pressed his lips to the spot, then gently sucked and nipped. Meggie drew in a sharp breath and he knew he'd had the right effect. Her shoulder was next and Dylan slipped his hand beneath her sweater and tugged it until he found another spot. Slowly, he tested her reaction and before long, she moaned softly, her head tipped back, her eyes closed.

But the heavy wool sweater was becoming a hindrance. Impatient to continue, Dylan reached down and grabbed the hem, then slowly tugged it up. Meggie met his gaze and the desire burning there startled him. She'd been caught by it, too, and it was just as undeniable. With an impatient sigh, she brushed his hands away and in one quick motion, pulled both her sweater and T-shirt off at once. Then she tossed them both aside and shook her head, her hair tumbling around her face and shoulders.

Dylan could barely breathe. She was the most beautiful thing he'd ever seen. Her skin, even under the unflattering lights of the poolroom, was so luminous, so flawless that instinct drove him to spread his hands over her bare shoulders. He pushed one bra strap aside and then the other.

Meggie's teeth chattered and he caught her gaze with his. "Are you cold?" he murmured, rubbing her arms.

She shook her head. Dylan could see a flicker of indecision in her eyes and he was about to call an end to this intimate game. But then she reached out and slipped her fingers beneath the waistband of his jeans. Scooting back onto the pool table she pulled him with her, until he was nearly lying on top of her.

"I'm not very good at this," she murmured.

"Just touch me," Dylan said, dropping a kiss into the curve of her neck. "And I'll touch you. The rest will take care of itself."

Though she'd had experience with men, Dylan suspected she'd never really been well seduced, the kind of seduction where the mind loses touch with the body, where raw instinct takes over and inhibition disappears. He knew he could take her there. It would just take time. Meggie began at the notch in his collarbone, tracing a line with her fingers, then following with her mouth.

When her tongue reached his nipple, he sucked in a sharp breath and moaned softly. She froze, then looked up. "Did I hurt you?"

Dylan smiled, raking his fingers through her hair. "No. That felt incredible."

The notion that she had the power to make him moan seemed to please her and when she went back to kissing his chest, it was with a new purpose. Her hair created a curtain around her face and tickled his belly as she moved lower and lower. And then, she reached out and touched him through the faded fabric of his jeans and Dylan thought he'd go out of his mind.

Nothing had prepared him for this reaction, for the instant

need to discard every last bit of clothing, to pull her naked body against his and bury himself deep inside of her. He reached down and grabbed her wrist, then drew her back up until her eyes met his. "Is this what you want?" he murmured.

Meggie nodded.

"Say it," Dylan demanded.

She took a ragged breath. "I do," Meggie said, in voice as clear and determined as he'd ever heard. "I want you." She hesitated, and Dylan was sure she was about to change her mind. "I mean, if you want me, I want you."

He chuckled softly. "Oh, I want you, Meggie. I don't think you realize how much." Dylan grabbed her around the waist and rolled her over until he was on top. He braced his hands on either side of her head and dropped a kiss on her mouth.

"Tell me what you like," Meggie said.

"Just take it slow," Dylan said, dropping another kiss onto her shoulder. "That's what I like."

"Slow," she murmured, as she ran her hand down his chest and dipped her fingers beneath the waistband of his jeans.

"Slow," he repeated, skimming his knuckles over the soft flesh of her breast until they caught the lacy edge of her bra.

And so began a new game designed to rid themselves of their clothes. There were no rules, so they made them up as they went along. Meggie unbuttoned his jeans and he unclasped her bra. She dispensed with the zipper and he tossed aside the scrap of satin and lace.

Her body was so beautiful, so perfect, and with every inch

of skin revealed, he found himself needing more. Clothes became a barrier, unneeded and unwanted, and any hint of reticence dissolved beneath his hands and his mouth. He slid her jeans over her hips, then twisted out of his own and pulled her back into his arms.

The feel of her against his body electrified every nerve. Sensations became intensified until the mere thought of her beneath him was enough to push him toward the edge. Dylan tried to control his thoughts, fearful that he'd be done before they'd even started. He'd once considered himself accomplished in the art of seduction, but with Meggie, it was a whole new experience. He felt untried and unschooled, existing from one sensation to the next.

And Meggie wasn't making control easy. Whoever had told her she wasn't good at sex had been sadly mistaken. She combined an insatiable desire with a streak of sweet vulnerability, the contrast so intriguing that he seemed caught in her spell. Yet every now and then, reality hit him full force, in his potent reaction when she wrapped her fingers around him, in the unbidden groan that slipped from his lips and the flood of heat that coursed through his bloodstream.

Their surroundings faded into a blur. They weren't making love on the pool table of Quinn's pub. Nothing existed beyond two naked bodies taking pleasure in each other. And when he could stand it no longer, he drew her up to straddle his hips. Slowly, Dylan ran his hands over her breasts, taking the time to touch every curve, every sweet inch of flesh.

But Meggie wouldn't have any off it. Her skin was flushed and her breath came in short gasps. Dylan reached for his jeans and found the foil packet in his wallet. He tore it open with his teeth and Meggie took the condom from him. Her hands trembled as she sheathed him.

And then she was above him, pausing, waiting. Dylan thought she might stop right there, but then, as he entered her, he realized that she merely wanted to slow their pace, to savor the exquisite feel of their bodies joined in such an intimate way. For a long moment, he was afraid to move, but then he couldn't help himself.

He began slowly, but that plan was quickly forgotten the minute he got a taste of the delicious heat that raced through his body. Every thought centered on the point where they were joined, every nerve alive. He quickened his pace and Meggie matched him stroke for stroke, her gaze fixed on his.

Dylan saw the changes in her, the arch of her neck, the quickened breathing, the passion-glazed eyes, as their rhythm increased. And when he felt she was near, he touched her. An instant later, she tensed and tightened around him. Her eyes went wide, as if the orgasm was taking her by surprise. And then she shattered, crying out his name.

The sound of her voice snapped the last thread of his control and he tightened his grip on her waist and drove into her one last time. And then, pleasure, more intense and exquisite than he'd ever felt washed over him like a wave, so fierce that he felt as if he were drowning in it.

She collapsed on top of him, naked, sated, her body covered with a sheen of perspiration. Dylan curled his arm around her neck and idly ran his fingers through her hair. Then he rolled her over to lie beside him, nuzzling the soft spot of skin beneath her ear. "I don't ever want to move from this spot," he murmured.

Meggie gave him a drowsy smile. "It's going to be a little hard to put the nine ball in the corner pocket with us lying here. There'll probably be a lot of complaints from the customers."

"They can play around us," he said.

"All right." She sighed softly and wrapped her arm around his waist. And within a few minutes, she was asleep. Dylan closed his eyes. He knew he ought to wake her and take her home. Or at least find something to cover them to keep them warm. But he wanted to let the moment sink in.

He'd made love to Meggie and he knew, without a doubt in his mind, that he'd never make love to another woman in his life. There would be no reason. From now on, there was only Meggie.

MEGGIE SLOWLY OPENED her eyes. An odd blur of lights and shadows teased at her gaze. She squinted, then wondered when she'd installed neon lights in her bedroom. A moment later, she realized she wasn't in her nice soft bed. No, she was lying naked on the pool table in the middle of Quinn's Pub, curled up beneath Dylan's flannel-lined jacket.

She moved slightly, then felt Dylan stir behind her. His arms were wrapped around her, one beneath her head and the other at her waist, and his legs were tangled with hers. He hadn't bothered with clothes, instead keeping warm by tucking his body against hers.

Meggie wasn't sure what to do. She slowly moved her arm until she could see her watch. "Oh, God," she murmured. "That can't be right. Eight fifty-five?" She rolled over then poked Dylan in the shoulder. "Wake up," she pleaded. "Dylan, it's morning and we fell asleep on the pool table."

He groaned softly, then nuzzled his face into the curve of her neck. "What time is it?"

"Almost nine," she said.

"Then go back to sleep. Quinn's doesn't open until eleven."

Meggie sat up, holding the jacket around her as if it might be some antidote for the embarrassment she felt. "I don't intend to be here when your father and brothers arrive. And I was supposed to meet Lana at the shop at eight. She's going to wonder where I am."

She'd always imagined the morning after such a passion-filled night would be just as passionate—waking up to his touch, making love while still half asleep. But then, she'd never expected the most passionate night of her life would occur on a pool table in an Irish pub! "We have to go. I have to go."

Dylan reluctantly sat up then scrubbed the sleep from his eyes with his fists. He raked his hands through his hair and turned to her. "You look beautiful," he said with a drowsy smile.

"Don't you try that smile on me, Dr. Charm. Now get dressed. We have to leave." Meggie wriggled to the edge of the table, then swung her leg over the side. But Dylan caught her before she could jump to the floor.

"I've never been a very good pool player," he teased, "but I have to say, I'm learning to enjoy the game."

"I can't believe I did this," Meggie murmured. "I've never done anything like this in my life." She must have been overly tired. Or maybe it had been the rum punch. But though she should have been mortified by her behavior, Meggie almost felt proud of herself. She'd made a decision to start living for the moment and this certainly was a moment she'd never forget. In truth, she and Dylan had had a couple hundred moments that would be worth reliving over and over again.

She grabbed her clothes from where they'd been tossed on the floor and began to yank them on. But Dylan was still lying on the pool table, watching her, a satisfied smile curling the corners of his mouth. She brushed aside the urge to crawl back on the table and make love to him again, to follow those instincts that had led them to this point. Instead, she crawled underneath the pool table to retrieve her socks and shoes.

When she stood up again, he was still smiling. "Stop it," she said.

"Stop what?"

"Stop looking like the cat who just slept with the canary."

"I'm happy," Dylan said. "So sue me."

He rolled over on his stomach and braced himself with his elbows. He was stark naked, yet he seemed completely at ease with his body. And it was an incredible body, Meggie mused. Like it had been carved by a master sculptor, every muscle and angle filled with pure masculinity.

"You know, I've never done anything like this either," Dylan said.

"Don't lie to me," Meggie said.

His expression turned serious. "Meggie, I'd never lie to you, I swear. And last night was a first, in a lot of ways."

Meggie stared at him for a long moment, gauging the truth in his eyes, afraid to ask him just what he meant. Was this the first time he'd slept with such an inexperienced woman? Or maybe the first time he'd ever seduced a woman so quickly? She wanted to believe that last night had been just as exciting for him as it had been for her. But common sense overtook wishful thinking.

She tossed aside his jacket and tugged her sweater and T-shirt over her head. "We really should go," she murmured from beneath the twisted sweater. When she finally poked her head through, she searched the floor for her missing sock and found it in the corner pocket, along with her bra. "I'm just going to go to the bathroom and splash some water on my face."

But he caught her arm as she passed and pulled her to him. With the gentlest touch, he cupped her face in his hands and looked deeply into her eyes. "I don't regret a single moment of last night," he murmured, his gaze open and intense. "And I don't want you to either."

Meggie nodded, then hurried off to the bathroom, the last of her clothes clutched in her hands. She flipped on the light and stepped inside, then leaned back against the door. Maybe he hadn't lied to her, but that didn't stop her from feeling like she'd been deceiving him. This whole plan to catch him then dump him had become a weight around her neck. She wasn't sure of her motives anymore.

Did she really expect this to be a one-night stand, an experiment in pleasure meant to end once the sun came up? "I am so dumb," Meggie muttered. Now that it was all over, all she could think about was when it was going to happen again. And again and again.

"Idiot," she said. She quickly tugged on her jeans, then shoved her underwear into her back pocket. She could finish dressing in the office at the shop. With a wet finger, she did a passable job of brushing her teeth. She'd left her purse in the car, so there was no way to brush her hair.

When she emerged from the bathroom, Dylan was only half dressed. His jeans were unbuttoned and he was shirtless. He braced a hip against the pool table, then smiled.

"What?" she murmured.

"Meggie, I meant what I said. Last night was special. I know you probably don't believe that. I guess I wouldn't either, considering my record with women, but I just wanted you to know that—"

Meggie stepped forward and threw her arms around his neck. Her kiss put an end to his explanations and to her nagging need to take just a little bit of last night with her to work. "We have to go. Now."

She handed him his T-shirt and his sweater, still stained with a red splotch from the rum punch. Then she dragged him toward the door. But before he opened it, Dylan caught her up in his arms and kissed her once more, long and hard, as if reminding her of exactly what had happened the night before.

But Meggie didn't need any reminders. As they walked to the car, she recalled the way he responded to her touch. And as they pulled away from the curb, she remembered the sensation of his hips nestled between her thighs. There'd been that moment, when she'd straddled his hips and he slowly entered her—that one heart-stopping instant, that very first sensation, when they became one. No matter what happened between them, she'd always have that memory. It would never fade.

Dylan wove expertly through traffic. Every now and then, Meggie would risk a glance over at him. He seemed so happy, satisfied, a smile curving the corners of his mouth. They didn't talk much in the car and Meggie suspected that he was as occupied with thoughts of their night together as she was. Though she tried to focus on the day ahead, on all things she had to do at the shop, tantalizing images kept creeping back into her mind—naked skin, tangled limbs and the sheer pleasure of touching a perfect male body.

The next time she looked out at the street, they were parked in front of the shop. Suddenly, Meggie wished they'd stayed at the pub just a little longer.

Dylan draped his arm over the back of her seat. "Can I see you tonight?" he murmured.

"I have to go to a party. For my grandmother. It's her eightieth birthday."

"I could take you," he murmured as he toyed with her hair.

His offer surprised her. First an afternoon with his brothers, then mad, passionate love on the pool table of his father's pub. And now, a Flanagan family gathering? "Are you offering because you want to see me or do you want to spend time with my family?"

"Both," Dylan said. "I haven't seen your parents for ages. And I'd like to see Tommy again. But mostly, I'm not sure I can go twenty-four hours without seeing you."

"All right," she said.

He wove his fingers through the hair at her nape then gently pulled her closer. His kiss was incredibly sweet and gentle and given the choice, Meggie would have spent the whole day in his car doing nothing but kissing him. But Lana was waiting. When Dylan finally drew back, she gave him a shaky smile. "I better go. I'll see you tonight."

Meggie hopped out of the car and ran toward the shop. She felt like skipping and shouting and spinning around until she was dizzy. She'd just spent the most incredible night of her life. But as she spied Lana through the window of the shop, reality began to set it. Nothing this perfect ever lasted. Sooner or later Dylan would move on to someone else and she'd be left with only memories. Olivia's words came back to her, risks versus rewards. "I knew the risks," she murmured as she yanked open the door. "And I enjoyed the rewards. I have no right to complain about the consequences."

Lana was sitting at the counter when Meggie walked in, perched on a stool, the morning paper spread out in front of her. She glanced up, observing her shrewdly. "You're late," she said.

"I decided to sleep in. After the grand opening, we're both going to have early mornings and late nights. I thought I'd take advantage of the time while I still had it."

"How was your date?"

Meggie gave her a nonchalant shrug. "It was fine. We helped take his brother Brendan's boat up to Gloucester. His older brother, Conor, and his fiancée, Olivia came with. It was a beautiful day."

"You spent the day with his brothers?" Lana asked.

Meggie nodded.

A slow smile broke across her face. "This is it," she said, her voice filled with excitement. "It's actually working. And so much faster then I thought it would."

"What are you talking about?"

"A guy like Dylan Quinn doesn't introduce just any old girlfriend to his brothers. This is a big moment and you didn't even realize it."

Though Meggie wanted to believe her words, she'd learned to be cautious with Lana's proclamations. "Olivia did say that I was the first girl he'd ever brought along on *The Mighty Quinn.*"

"That's good, that's very good. And what about your third date? Did you make plans?"

Meggie knew she was about to get a scolding for breaking the rules. But she didn't care. After all the rules she broke last night, there wasn't much point. "We're going out tonight. I know, I broke the four-day rule, but I have to go to my grandmother's birthday party and I thought it might be nice to take a date along. My mother is always wondering why I don't have a social life. Maybe this will satisfy her for the next few years."

"I'm surprised he agreed to go."

"He offered," Meggie said.

Lana hopped off her stool and circled the counter, then pulled out the most recent revision of her flowchart. She smoothed it out and stared at it for a long time. "I think I might have to make another revision. This guy is moving really fast. That must be because you've been playing hard to get." She smiled. "A guy like him only does the family thing if he's falling in love."

Meggie's heart stopped as Lana said the words. Love? Could she really believe that Dylan was falling in love with her after only two dates? She held her breath and waited for her heart to start again. When it did, she gulped back a surge of panic. "That can't be right. He couldn't be falling in love with me. It's too soon." Besides, even she knew that sex didn't always mean love to a man, especially a man like Dylan Quinn.

"Why not? You've been following the plan, haven't you?"

"Yes," Meggie lied. Lana's plan had barely even entered her mind during the past twenty-four hours. The only thing she'd been following was her instincts…her hormones…her overwhelming desires.

"I think it's time to put him to the test."

"I'm not sure I like the sound of that."

"It's simple. We introduce another element to the flow-chart. We'll call him…David."

"I don't know any David," Meggie said.

Lana gave her a sly smile. "Neither do I. But Dylan Quinn won't know that."

Meggie sat down onto a stool and watched as Lana began to scribble on a scrap of paper. But she couldn't think about the plan. The plan wasn't working. It wasn't in the plan for her to enjoy his touch and crave his kisses. It wasn't in the plan to make love to him on their second date or to lie about it all to her best friend.

And it certainly wasn't in the plan for her to fall head-over-heels in love with him for the second time in her life.

6

"I'LL BE READY in a minute," Meggie said, racing from the front door to her bedroom.

Dylan glanced around her apartment. She'd greeted him, flushed and breathless, and still dressed in jeans and the sweater she'd worn last night. On the drive over he'd thought about how it would be seeing her for the first time after what had happened on the pool table at the pub. Would the desire be instant and intense? Would they tumble into her bed within the first few moments together and relive the passion they'd shared the night before?

In the seconds after she opened the door, he'd looked into her eyes for a hint of regret or embarrassment. But she'd turned away so quickly that he hadn't had time to kiss her much less gauge her mood. All he knew was that she wasn't thinking about ripping her clothes off and seducing him.

"Just make yourself at home," she shouted. "There's juice in the fridge. Or wine. I don't think I have beer." She peeked out of the door. "I'm sorry I'm late. I got hung up at the shop and I didn't realize the time. If I'm late for Nonna May's party my mother will kill me."

She slammed the bedroom door and Dylan stood in the middle of the living room, frowning. This was not the way it was supposed to go. There was supposed to be at least an acknowledgement of what had happened, maybe a sexy smile or a provocative comment. Or at least a lingering, tantalizing kiss. He strode across the room and knocked on the door.

Meggie opened it a crack. "What?"

He firmly pushed against the door until it gave way, then stepped into Meggie's bedroom. She was dressed in just her jeans and the lacy scrap of a bra that he'd removed once before. Without giving her time to protest, he wrapped an arm around her waist and pulled her against him, then kissed her long and hard.

His hands skimmed over her body in an unspoken possession, reminding himself of the feel of her, the way her curves fit his touch. Reminding her of what that touch could do to her body. When he finally released her from his embrace, Dylan was satisfied that her desire for him hadn't abated since they'd last been together. If anything it had grown more acute.

He stared down at her face. Her eyes were still closed and her lips were damp and slightly swollen. She waited for him to take her again, a tiny, but satisfied smile on her lips. But Dylan wanted to leave her aching for more. "There," he said. "Now that we've taken care of the important stuff, you can get dressed."

She opened her eyes, then gasped softly as he walked back to the door and closed it behind him. A low chuckle rumbled in his chest. He'd thought he'd experienced it all. He was thirty-one years old, a grown man by almost every standard—except maybe his own—a man with his share of experience with women. Yet a few seconds with Meggie was all it took to make him realize he hadn't experienced anything yet.

Until he met Meggie, his life had been set. He had his job, a nice place to live, brothers who cared about him and women who didn't care too much. Life had been good and he hadn't imagined it could get any better. But then Meggie had come along and she turned everything upside down. Suddenly, he found himself wanting much more from every hour of every day. It wasn't enough just to live. There was something he was searching for, something vague and elusive, something he could only find with Meggie in his arms.

But even though he'd spent a fair amount of time with her, he still felt she was holding back, keeping her emotions in check. She didn't completely trust him and he hadn't been able to change that. It was as if she, like his brothers, expected him to screw up, expected him to revert to the old Dylan Quinn behavior. Maybe he just needed a little more time to prove himself.

Dylan wandered around the living room, idly picking up photos and knickknacks, trying to get handle on the woman he'd made love to last night, the woman who could turn from demure to passionate in the blink of an eye. On her desk, he found a picture of Meggie with her family. It was an old picture, taken when she still had braces and wore glasses.

This was the girl he remembered. But as he stared at it closely, Dylan saw beyond first impressions, past the silly haircut and the horn-rimmed glasses and the mouthful of metal. Why hadn't he noticed before? She'd been beautiful even back then. She just hadn't grown into her features. Her sensual mouth and high cheekbones, her wide eyes, looked odd on a girl her age. But they were perfect on a woman.

Dylan smiled. Maybe it was lucky it had taken her awhile to attain her true beauty. Had anyone noticed her in high school, she might already have been happily married with three kids, a dog and a house in the suburbs. And by the time he'd pulled her out of her shop, it would have been too late.

He'd never been one to believe in fate or karma. Everything happened for a reason. But maybe it was fate that had put that defective espresso machine in her shop. And it could have been fate that made the machine go haywire during his shift. Whatever it was, he'd met Meggie at the right time and for that he considered himself lucky.

After all, she could have easily had a boyfriend or a fiancé and then where would he... Dylan stopped short just as he was about to continue his tour with a stroll around her kitchen. Tucked away on the counter next to the stove he noticed a huge bouquet of flowers, long-stemmed roses. The kind that cost a week's salary for a couple dozen. He took a quick look over his shoulder, then snatched the card from amongst the elegant flowers.

Suddenly, his little bouquet of roses didn't seem nearly impressive enough. This bouquet stood almost three feet tall. And whoever had sent it, had meant to make a statement. He pulled the card from the envelope. *"Until I see you again,"* he murmured. *"David."*

Dylan scowled as he carefully placed the card back into the flowers. "Who the hell is David?" he muttered. And more importantly, what was he doing sending Meggie—his Meggie—flowers? Dylan made a mental note of the florist's name. Maybe Conor could use his influence to find out a little more about… He groaned softly, then turned away from the counter. Was he crazy? How could he expect Meggie to trust him if he didn't trust her?

If she did have another man in hot pursuit, then he had only one option. He'd do his best to convince Meggie that he was the only man in her life. "Nice flowers," he shouted as he walked back into the living room.

Meggie peeked out the bedroom door again, her hair twisted into a towel. "They are nice," she said before closing the door again.

"Yeah, right," Dylan muttered. "Real nice." He walked over to the sofa and sat down, his mind spinning with all the possibilities. David couldn't be a real serious threat. After all, Meggie had made love to *him* last night, and she wasn't the type to take something like that lightly.

Dylan leaned back into the cushions, then heard a crunch beneath him. He reached around and grabbed a crumbled wad of paper from behind a pillow. Smoothing the sheet over his thigh, Dylan tried to read the printing. It was a flowchart. At first he assumed it had something to do with Meggie's business. But as he looked at it in greater detail he realized it was a very unusual plan. From what he could tell, it was plan to catch a man—and that man was him!

He quickly crumpled it back up and hid it behind the pillow, certain that it was never meant for his eyes. But his curiosity got the better of him and Dylan retrieved it. There was a red circle around one box that said "Send Self Flowers." But it was the box at the top that caused the most confusion, the box with "revenge" in big capital letters.

"So, are you really ready to spend a night with my crazy relatives?" Meggie asked as she walked back into the room.

Dylan shoved the paper into his jacket pocket then rose to his feet. She looked incredible, dressed in a figure-skimming black dress that hugged every curve. The neckline dipped just low enough to reveal an expanse of soft skin. Her hair was swept up, allowing a tempting view of her neck. And the skirt was short enough to show off her beautiful legs. He instantly forgot the paper stuffed in his pocket and wrapped an arm around her waist. "We could always stay here and call in our birthday greetings," he said. "They'd never notice we weren't there."

Her smile faded slightly. "If you'd rather not go along, I can understand. Doing the family thing probably isn't your—"

He put a finger to her lips. "I was teasing. I want to go. Really."

She nodded, then turned and grabbed her coat from the back of the sofa. "My Aunt Doris will probably be at the party," Meggie said as she walked to the door. "Avoid her at all costs. If you don't, you'll get a recap of her recent gall bladder surgery and the resulting gastrointestinal problems.

And Uncle Roscoe is a compulsive gambler, so if he tries to talk you into a bet, make sure it's only for a few dollars. And my cousin Randy, has a—"

"Meggie."

"—really obnoxious habit of eating off of—"

"Meggie!"

She turned and looked at him, her eyes wide. "What?"

"I'll be fine. I think I can hold my own with your family. It's not like I've never met them."

"Of course you can. I didn't mean to imply—"

"Of course, you didn't," he teased.

"It's just that they'll probably think that you're my boy-friend and—"

This time, Dylan didn't bother to interrupt. He grabbed her arm and pulled her back into his arms, then stared down into her eyes. "All right. I think we need to get something straight here." His jaw went tight and his temper was just barely in check. "Have you forgotten what happened last night? Or did I imagine the whole thing?"

A blush crept up her cheeks and she fixed her gaze on his chest. "No," she said in a tiny voice.

"If any of your relatives want to think I'm your boyfriend or your sweetheart or even your lover, I'm not going to ob-ject. Because as far as I'm concerned I'm all three. Got that?"

She blinked, then opened her mouth to speak. But Meg-gie seemed so taken aback by his statement that she wasn't sure what to say. Rather than wait for a comment, he hooked his finger under her chin and closed her mouth, then brushed a quick kiss across her lips. "Good. Then it's settled," he said. "And by the way, you can throw those flowers away. If David has any questions about why you don't want to see him anymore, you can just tell him to call me."

MEGGIE STARED OUT the windshield of Dylan's Mustang, watching the familiar sights go by as they drove to her parents' house in South Boston. She glanced over at Dylan, only to find his attention focused on the street. With a soft sigh, Meggie leaned back into the seat. Though Dylan had already met her parents and her brother, she still couldn't help but be a little nervous.

She'd never brought a man to any family function. And considering her parents' desire to see her happily married and raising their grandchildren, she knew they'd jump to conclusions. Knowing her mother, she'd be ready to start the wedding plans. But Meggie intended to remind Maura Flanagan of the pain Dylan Quinn had caused her all those years ago.

Her mother had been there that night after the Frolic when she'd cried herself to sleep. Even now, Meggie could remember her mother's words—how someday she'd look back on the night and laugh about it. How it was all part of growing up. And how love wasn't always a smooth ride. Meggie groaned inwardly. If only she had been able to laugh about it. Then maybe she wouldn't be caught in the middle of this mess.

She really should jump out of the car and find a pay phone. Lana would be so happy to hear that the flowers she'd sent to Meggie's apartment did exactly what they were supposed to do, even though Meggie had done her best to hide them. Dylan was now officially her boyfriend, a big leap up the flowchart to the ultimate goal. But though Meggie should have been happy, all she could muster was a severe case of guilt.

This plan had gotten completely out of control! She'd manipulated him and he'd fallen for it. She'd never expected the plan to work and now that it had, she wasn't quite sure what to do. He'd fallen for her under false pretenses and though she hadn't really broken any laws, she still felt regret. How could she ever know if his feelings were true or just a result of her manipulation?

Dylan pulled the car over to the curb in front of her house and turned off the ignition. "We're here," Meggie murmured, staring out at the little frame house painted a cheery shade of yellow.

"Don't worry," he said. "If I do anything wrong, you just tug on your ear and we'll head straight to the door." With that, he twisted around and grabbed something out of the back seat—an elaborately wrapped gift with a beautiful fabric bow and expensive wrapping paper.

"What's that?" she asked.

"It's a present for your grandmother," he said. "You told me it was her birthday, right?"

"Oh," Meggie murmured. "Right. That was nice of you. Very thoughtful."

Dylan toyed with the bow. "Olivia helped me pick it out. It's an antique silver picture frame from the Victorian era. I don't really know what that means but it's really pretty. Olivia assured me that your grandmother would like it and Olivia knows things like that."

Meggie glanced down at the gift on her lap. How was it that a complete stranger knew the perfect gift to get her Nonna May and all she'd managed was a package of embroidered handkerchiefs? Maybe it was because Dylan Quinn had charm down to a science. "She'll love it."

She stared out the window as Dylan hopped out of the car, suddenly filled with regret over inviting him. She wanted to believe that he really cared, that he wasn't just turning on the charisma for her grandmother's sake. But if he really cared, then she'd have to face the fact that she cared, too. More than she'd ever intended to.

Dylan reached out to help her from the car and as they walked up to the house, he held her hand. But a moment before her mother answered the doorbell, Meggie tugged her hand from his and fiddled with the bow on her present.

The door swung open. "Meggie!" Maura Flanagan gathered her daughter into a welcoming hug, crushing the present between them. "It seems like ages since we've seen you." Then she glanced at Meggie's "date" and raised an eyebrow. "Who is this? I think I know this boy."

"It's Dylan, Mom. Dylan Quinn. Tommy's old friend."

"Dylan Quinn?" Without a second thought, Meggie's mother grabbed him and gave him a hug as fierce as Meggie's had been. "My, look how you've grown! Such a handsome man. What are you doing here? Did Tommy invite you?"

"When Meggie told me about the party, I just had to come. I was hoping I'd get some of that wonderful cooking of yours. I wasn't wrong, was I?"

Maura looped her arm through Dylan's and walked with

him into the house, leaving Meggie alone on the porch to stare after them. The man could charm the white off rice. Her mother knew exactly the pain he'd caused her. She'd been the one to reassure Meggie that all her friends in high school would never remember that Dylan was supposed to take her to the dance.

"Traitor," she muttered as she stepped inside. "Dr. Charm strikes again."

By the time she got her coat off, Dylan had already joined the party. He'd been greeted warmly by her brother Tommy and her father. Then he moved on to Nonna May, squatting down beside her chair to offer birthday greetings. Meggie watched him from across the room, watched the easy way he interacted with her family. It was as if he belonged here and she was the outsider.

For a moment, she almost wished he was her boyfriend. She'd never had a man in her life who she felt was important enough to introduce to her family. But everyone loved Dylan. He was funny and handsome and completely at ease. And who could resist that smile? When he turned it on, anyone would feel like the most special person in the world.

"I didn't know you were dating Dylan Quinn."

Meggie glanced over her shoulder to find her mother standing behind her. "We're not dating," she murmured. "We're just friends." And lovers, she added silently. "He's a firefighter and he put out that fire at the shop. That's how we met again."

"Just friends? If you're just friends, why did you ask him to Nonna May's party?"

"I didn't really ask. He offered to bring me," Meggie said.

Maura's eyes went wide. "He offered?" A slow smile brightened her dubious expression. "He must really like you, Mary Margaret. And it's obvious from that look on your face that the feelings are mutual." Maura nodded knowingly. "He's a good man, he has a good job. You could do much worse."

"Have you forgotten what he did to me in high school?" Meggie asked, lowering her voice and leaning closer to her mother. "How he dumped me and sent his little brother to take me to the Sophomore Frolic. I was completely humiliated. I cried for two days."

Maura scoffed, then waved her hand. "Such old news. You were both kids." She gave Meggie's elbow a squeeze. "I have to fill the punch bowl. Tell your brother he needs to get ice from the fridge in the basement."

Meggie wandered through the living room to the dining room where Tommy was chatting with Dylan. When she stepped up to them, Dylan casually slipped his arm around her waist and smiled at her. Tommy gave her a sly look then grinned. "Well, little sister, you're just full of surprises. I didn't expect you to show up, much less bring along my old buddy, Dylan."

"This is a nice party," Dylan said, his gaze still fixed on her. "I'm glad you invited me."

Meggie forced a smile. "Can I borrow my brother for a while? We need to get some ice." Dylan nodded and Meggie grabbed Tommy's arm and dragged him to the kitchen. When they were out of earshot of Dylan, she scowled up at him. "How could you be so nice to him?"

"What are you talking about? That's Dylan. He's an old

friend. And it looks like you two are getting pretty cozy. I never would have thought that—"

"Of course you wouldn't have!" she snapped. "That's because you know exactly what he did to me in high school!"

"What?"

"The Sophomore Frolic?" Meggie reminded him. "He was supposed to take me and at the last minute he sent his brother instead. I told all my friends I had a date with Dylan Quinn and then he stood me up. I was completely humiliated."

"Dylan was never supposed to take you," Tommy said, giving her a look that said she'd just lost her mind. "Why would he take you? You were a sophomore and he was senior, never mind that you were a geek. Let's face it, Megs, guys like Dylan didn't date girls like you."

"But you told me he wanted to take me," Meggie insisted.

"No, I didn't. You were going on and on about that stupid dance, so I asked Dylan if he'd set up a date for you with one of his brothers. I thought he'd send Brendan, but then he sent one of the twins. What's your complaint? You had a date, didn't you?"

Meggie's eyes went wide and she gasped. "What are you saying?"

"What are *you* saying? Are you mad at him because he didn't take you instead of his little brother?"

"No!" Meggie cried. When he said it like that it sounded so…petty and immature. It wasn't a grudge, just a few hurt feelings and a lot of bad memories and scars that ran deeper than she wanted to admit. "No, I...I just thought he was supposed to take me, that's all." She swallowed hard, unable to think straight. "Mom needs ice. She wants you to get it for her."

Once Tommy had left the kitchen, she glanced around, then hurried toward her bedroom. She needed time to think! Had she been wrong all along about Dylan Quinn? Had she somehow convinced herself that he was the one who was supposed to take her to the dance? Meggie groaned softly, then pressed her fingers to her lips, biting back a quiet curse. But just as she reached for the door to her bedroom, the sound of Dylan's voice stopped her.

"Meggie?"

She spun around and pasted a smile on her face. The urge to apologize to him was the first thing that came to mind. But then, he wasn't aware of how she'd been feeling since the day she and Lana had put their silly plan together—a plan that suddenly didn't have any purpose. "Hi," she murmured. Her face felt hot and she knew she was blushing.

"Is everything all right?"

She tried to keep calm, maintaining a tenuous hold on her composure. How could she have been so wrong? He wasn't at fault, she was! "I'm fine," she said. "I was just going to get something from my purse. It's in my room."

"Show me your room," Dylan said. "I'm curious."

The room was exactly the way she'd left it when she'd graduated from college. It was filled with all the mementos of a girl whose life revolved around her studies. There wasn't a single picture of a boyfriend or a dried-up corsage or a love letter. Her crush on Dylan had been such a secret, she allowed no evidence of it in her surroundings. Meggie opened the door. Sadly, she had nothing to hide.

"So how many boys have you invited into this room?" Dylan teased as he strolled around.

His question brought a soft laugh. "Are you kidding?"

"No," Dylan said.

"You're the first boy—or man—except my father or my brother who has ever set foot in here."

He grabbed her around the waist and pulled her up against his body, kissing the curve of her neck. "I'm like Neil Armstrong on the moon or Christopher Columbus in the New World. I guess I should be honored." He pulled her along to a bulletin board that she'd put up to hold all her memories. "Look at this," he said, pointing to a certificate. "Perfect attendance."

She wasn't going to tell him that the reason she'd never missed a day during her sophomore year was because she couldn't give up a chance to see him at school. She'd even gone to school with the flu and a raging fever just hoping to catch sight of him in the hall, praying that he'd smile or say hello. "I know. It's silly."

"No," he protested. "It's nice. I've always wanted to go with a smart girl."

"Is that what we're doing?" she asked. "Are we going together?"

He turned her around and stared down into her eyes. "I guess I always figured that went along with being boyfriend and girlfriend…and lovers. Was I wrong?"

Meggie drew a ragged breath, fixing her gaze on the front of his shirt. Her fingers toyed with a button and she searched for the words to keep the conversation lighthearted. "That's a pretty serious move for a guy like you," she said.

"I feel pretty serious about you."

She glanced up at him, then sighed. "I don't know whether to believe you or not. For all I know, you're just turning on the charm again. You do have a reputation, you know. And don't think I didn't notice how you completely charmed my mother."

His smile faded and his embrace wasn't quite so close. Meggie held her breath. Had she said something to hurt him? A knock sounded at the door and Dylan turned away to look as Tommy popped his head inside. "Hey, Quinn. Me and the cousins are going to play a game of touch football on the street. We need you to even the teams."

His hands slipped from her waist and he sent her a questioning glance. "Go ahead," she said. "I have to help my mom with the food anyway."

He strode out of the room with Tommy and Meggie let out a long breath. Then she turned and flopped facedown on her bed. A groan slipped from her lips. She was going to have to have a serious discussion with Lana tomorrow morning. There had to be a way to reverse the flow of the flowchart and extricate herself from the mess she'd made of her relationship with Dylan Quinn.

"We'll just make another plan and set another goal," she said, her voice muffled in her pillow. Meggie pushed up on her elbows and considered the notion for a long moment. But formulating a new plan would require telling Lana that she'd been lying since the start of their first plan.

She could always carry on by herself, relying on her own

instincts. But those were the very same instincts that told her to make love to Dylan Quinn on a pool table! And those were the instincts that had convinced her that what she and Dylan shared might just be something worth preserving.

"So either you make him love you forever or you break up with him," Meggie said. But somehow, she suspected that either option was much easier said than done.

DYLAN STARED AT the morning paper, reading the same column over and over again. Though he was trying hard to concentrate, he wasn't comprehending a single word. In truth, nothing he did to occupy his thoughts had any effect on what was running through his mind.

He hadn't believed Tommy at first. It began as an offhand comment during the touch football game. But then, when they were sharing a beer on the porch, Tommy had mentioned it again. He'd said he was surprised that Meggie and Dylan were friends, much less involved.

Dylan had assumed the comment was based on his reputation with women. But when Tommy went on to explain the grudge that Meggie still harbored, Dylan pressed for more details. Suddenly, everything made sense—Meggie's early hostility, her sudden change of heart. And especially the big capital letters across the paper he'd found in her apartment. REVENGE. That's what all this had been about! Getting back at him for some imagined slight that happened so long ago he could barely remember.

The rest of the party had passed at a grinding pace and he'd found himself looking for other clues, in her expression, in her behavior, in the way she spoke to him. And when it came time to leave, Dylan drove her home and left her at her front door, so preoccupied with his thoughts that anything else, including a good-night kiss or plans for the next night, had fled from his mind.

Even now Dylan couldn't believe it. Meggie had been under the impression that *he* was supposed to take her to that silly dance her sophomore year. Instead, he'd showed up with his little brother in tow, a favor he'd done for Tommy and for Meggie—or so he'd thought.

He recalled her words that very first day, when he'd pulled her from her smoky coffee shop, about how he'd come to ruin her life all over again. Was that really what he'd done? Dylan raked his hand through his hair and stared down at the newspaper. Why couldn't he make sense of this? He hadn't imagined her reactions that night in the pub. It would have taken an incredibly coldhearted woman to fake something like that. But then, what did he really know about Meggie and her true feelings? She kept everything bottled up inside of her.

He cursed softly, then pushed back his chair. "I need some fresh air," he murmured to the group gathered around the table.

But as he was descending the stairs, he saw a familiar figure coming toward him through the garage doors. He stopped on the stairs and called out. "Hey, Con! What are you doing here?"

"I had to interview a witness downtown and I thought I'd drop by."

Dylan frowned as he descended the rest of the way. "You never just drop by. You always have a reason."

"Well, I'm on an official errand for Olivia," he said with a sheepish grin. "She's planning her first dinner party since we've been engaged and she's all excited about it. I told her we could send out for pizza, but she wants to do it right."

"What does this have to do with me?" Dylan asked.

"I'm here to extend an invitation to you and Meggie."

Dylan drew a long breath, then let it out slowly. This was what he got for bringing Meggie along that day on *The Mighty Quinn*. Now everyone assumed that they were a couple. "That's really nice, but I'm not sure Meggie and I are going to be able to make it."

"Well, we're flexible on the date," Conor said. "And it's nothing real fancy, so—"

"That's not what I meant," Dylan interrupted. "I'm not sure that Meggie and I are going to make it work."

Conor stared at him for a long time. Dylan could see the disappointment in his eyes, the silent accusation that this was just the same old behavior all over again. "You want to tell me what's going on?"

Dylan reached in his shirt pocket and pulled out the paper he'd found at Meggie's apartment, determined to provide a decent excuse. He sat down on one of the bottom steps and watched as Conor looked it over. Dylan had looked at it so many times that he had it memorized. In all honesty, it was an ingenious plan. It capitalized on every male weakness, employing subtle manipulation and carefully timed retreat, the old "why buy the cow" theory. For a woman who claimed to have little experience with men, Meggie knew precisely what made them tick.

"What is this?" Conor asked, flipping it over to examine the back.

"It's a battle plan. To make me fall in love with Meggie Flanagan so that she can dump me and pay me back for something that happened thirteen years ago. It's all there." He punched at the paper with his finger. "And what's even more amazing is that it worked."

"It worked?"

"Yeah," Dylan muttered. "I think I'm in love with Meggie Flanagan."

Conor chuckled. "You say that the same way a guy might say, 'I think I have a social disease.' Or 'I think I just ran over your cat.' You're not very enthusiastic."

"The minute I admit I love her, she's going to dump me," Dylan said, throwing up his hands. "And if I don't say the words, then we'll just go on playing this game. Sooner or later, she'll get bored or impatient or frustrated and she'll dump me anyway. It's a lose-lose situation."

"A woman dump you? Now there's an original concept. Have you ever been dumped before?"

"That's not the point," Dylan said. "The point is that I don't *want* to be dumped. Not this time." He sighed. "I thought what we had was real. I thought I was done with all the games. And now I find the games never ended."

"So what are you going to do?" Conor asked.

"What can I do?" Dylan countered.

"We could always go get a cup of coffee," Conor teased. "I hear there's a new place just down the street."

"Very funny," Dylan said. "Do you have any other witty comments before I kick your butt around the block?"

"Well, I'll just tell you this, little brother. If you really love Meggie Flanagan, then don't let anything keep you apart. Fix the problem. It's not always supposed to be easy, you know. In fact, sometimes it's downright difficult. But at the end of the day, it's what's in your heart, not your head, that really matters."

"Do you ever have any doubts?" Dylan asked, looking up at his big brother. "I mean, about you and Olivia. Do you ever wonder if maybe she's not the one and you're just fooling yourself?"

"Never," Conor said with unwavering conviction. "Do you have doubts about Meggie?"

"No," Dylan said. "And that's what scares me. Am I just deluding myself here?"

"I don't think so."

"So what do I do? I've never been in this position before."

"Maybe you ought to get a plan of your own. Look at this," he said, waving the paper under Dylan's nose. "She's just waiting for you to admit how you feel. So do it. Tell her you love her. And then pray like hell that somewhere along the line, she fell in love with you."

"But what if she didn't," Dylan asked. "Then that would be the end of it."

"Then do everything in direct opposition of her plan. If you don't admit you love her, you could probably keep seeing her indefinitely. And, hell, Dylan, you're a lovable guy. She can't resist you forever."

Dylan stood up and slapped Conor on the shoulder. "Thanks for stopping by. And for the advice."

"What about the dinner party?" Conor asked.

"Can I wait to give you an answer on that? Just tell Olivia I have to check my calendar."

Dylan watched as his brother walked to the door, then gave him a wave before he stepped outside. He raked his fingers through his hair and tried to put his mind to the task at hand. There had to be a way to make this work with Meggie, to turn her plan back against her and make her see that they belonged together. He reached for the pencil in his pocket, then grabbed the clipboard that they used to write down addresses of fires.

"I'll just make a plan of my own," he murmured, sitting down on a nearby bench. "And I'll make it work."

MEGGIE STARED AT the stream of coffee as it dribbled into the carafe, counting the minutes, then the seconds before she'd be able to pour a cup and take a sip. After another sleepless night spent tossing and turning, the only antidote for her exhaustion was a cup of Hawaiian Kona, extra strong, in all its caffeinated glory. When the carafe was half full, she flipped off the coffeemaker and filled her cup, then added a generous dose of cream and sugar.

The first sip was like heaven, the caffeine brushing the cobwebs from her brain. But no matter how much she drank, Meggie knew she wouldn't be able to block out the worries that nagged at her mind.

It was over. She'd seen the clues three nights ago, after her grandmother's birthday party. And though she'd always expected the time would come sooner or later, now that it was here, she couldn't believe it had all happened so fast. Dylan was starting to draw away and it began at Nonna's birthday party.

How many times had she rewound the night in her head, trying to figure out the exact moment when the tide had turned, when, instead of taking a step closer to her, Dylan took a step back? And then another and another, until by the time he said good-night to her at her front door he'd been distant and cool.

She should have never allowed him to accompany her. She knew that attending a family gathering was a big step, too much pressure, too many expectations, especially so early in their relationship. But he'd been the one to press her forward, the one who insisted that she consider him her boyfriend.

All along, she had told herself she was no match for Dylan and now she'd proved it. She'd made a mistake and though she wasn't sure what it had been, she knew it had to be her fault. Meggie took another sip of her coffee, then rubbed her forehead, trying to quell the headache that had begun the moment she got out of bed at dawn that morning.

The bell above the door jingled and Meggie turned to watch Lana walk in. All the lies she'd told her best friend had come back to haunt her and now, when she needed a friend the most, she couldn't bring herself to tell Lana what had happened.

"Morning!" Lana called, her eyes bright and her pale skin rosy from the cold.

"Morning," Meggie replied in a feeble attempt to match her good mood.

Lana stopped short, a few feet away from the counter. A

tiny frown wrinkled her brow and she stared at Meggie intently. "What's wrong?"

Meggie felt the tears press at the corners of her eyes but she refused to give into them. Tears would only be proof that Dylan Quinn had broken her heart all over again. The first time, she thought she'd never recover. But in hindsight, that had been nothing, merely a twinge, compared to the ache that tightened like a fist around her heart.

"Did something happen with Dylan?" Lana asked, quietly taking the stool beside Meggie's.

Meggie nodded and drew in a shaky breath. "Yeah, something. Actually, a lot of things. I just wish I knew what they were."

"Do you want to talk about it?" Lana asked.

Meggie shifted uneasily on the stool then turned to her friend. "If I tell you, I don't think you're going to be very happy with me." She drew another breath and pressed on. "But we're best friends and we're business partners and I think you need to keep an open mind and understand how much this has been worrying me."

Lana nodded her head. "You're in love with Dylan Quinn," she said.

Meggie gasped. She'd never said the words out loud, only imagined them. "What?"

"You heard me. You're in love with Dylan Quinn." Lana grabbed Meggie's coffee mug and took a sip, watching her over the rim.

When she put down the coffee, Lana was smiling. Meggie buried her face in her hands. Her cheeks were hot against her palms. "How did you know?" she muttered.

"Because I'm the one who made it happen," Lana proclaimed.

"What?" Meggie asked as her head snapped up.

Lana slipped out of her jacket. "My plan. Don't you see? You never would have gone near him without my plan. And I knew once you went out a few times, you'd fall in love. It was all so simple." Lana wiggled her fingers. "And I was pulling all the strings. So, when did you two finally…you know. And don't lie to me. I would have jumped into bed with him after the first date and I've had great sex in the last decade."

Meggie groaned. "I'm so naive. I can't believe I fell for this. You totally manipulated me! This was all supposed to be about revenge and you made it all about…love." The last word came out on a strangled groan.

"No," Lana protested, "it was supposed to be about restoring the balance in your love live. And I did that. You're in love, aren't you?"

"Yes! But that was never part of the plan. At least not the plan I was operating under."

Lana wrapped her arm around Meggie's shoulders and put on a playful pout. "You forgive me, don't you? Because you can't be mad at me for too long. After all, because of me you probably had the best sex you've ever had in your life. And more importantly, I have to be the maid of honor at your wedding so you can't hate me."

"There isn't going to be a wedding," Meggie said.

"Of course there will be a wedding," Lana insisted. "That's the whole reason I did this. So I can wear a silly bridesmaid's dress and spend the entire evening flirting with the best man." She paused. "Why do you think there won't be a wedding?"

"There's something wrong. It happened the night of my grandmother's birthday party. All of a sudden he turned cool and remote. I think he's going to break up with me. He hasn't called me in two days."

"Oh, honey, this is normal," she said with a careless shrug. "Every man in love goes through it. It's what I call the seven-week itch. Only since you and Dylan were on the accelerated plan, it's more like the seventeen-day itch. That's the time when his bachelor friends are starting to plant subversive messages in his brain. They use words like 'hooked' and 'whipped' and make jokes about the ring in his nose. And they tell him that his life will never be the same."

"They do?"

"They do. But he'll get over it. And once he does, he won't be able to stay away from you. Especially if the sex was good. The sex was good, wasn't it?"

"It was incredible," Meggie admitted. "Are you sure he'll come back?"

"Do I know men?" Lana asked.

"Yes." Meggie replied, not really certain of her answer any more. "So what do I do?"

"Just be patient. And whatever you do, don't call him. Let him come to you."

"What if he never calls?"

"Oh, he'll call," Lana reassured her. "Just like he called that first time." She patted Meggie's shoulder. "You're a wonderful person. You're bright and funny and beautiful. And if Dylan Quinn can't see that, then he doesn't deserve you. And if things don't work out, we can always use the plan again on some other guy. With the revisions I've made, it should work even better than before."

Meggie turned back to her coffee. The prospect of going through this whole thing with another man was daunting at best. Besides, she'd already found the man she wanted, he just didn't want her.

The bell above the door jingled and Meggie watched glumly as the mailman walked in, his battered leather bag thrown over his shoulder, a transistor radio plugged into his ear. Lana hopped off her stool and hurried around to fetch him a cup of coffee as was her custom every day when he arrived. "So," she said. "What's new on Boylston Street, Roger? Any hot gossip?"

"I hear they're going to raise the rates on the parking meters," he said as he placed the stack of mail in front of Meggie. "And Berkley School of Music just put up new banners."

Meggie idly flipped through the envelopes, listening distractedly to Lana's conversation while she opened bills and notices. But her attention was diverted from the mail when she heard the word "firefighter." At first, she thought Lana was telling Roger the mailman about all her troubles. That's all Meggie needed was an opinion on her love life from a postal employee. But when she looked up, the stunned expression on Lana's face caused her heart to skip a beat.

"What?" she murmured.

"Roger just said the men from the Boylston Street station were called to a fire at about five this morning. They said on the radio that some firefighters from that station were injured."

Meggie blinked, the impact of Lana's words not hitting her right away. "It can't be him," she said. "He doesn't work nights."

"They were taken to Boston General," Roger said. "You can probably call the emergency room and find out who the guys were." He grabbed his coffee and gave them both a wave goodbye, leaving Meggie to worry about more than the bills he'd just delivered.

Injured? She'd never really thought about Dylan's job in terms of the danger he encountered. He always seemed so sure of himself, so confident in his abilities as a firefighter. But even Meggie knew that there were some situations where even the best firefighters met their match. "What should I do?" she murmured. She pushed off her stool. "I should call him at home. Or—or maybe I should call the hospital. But they probably won't give me any information over the phone."

Lana pushed her back down, then circled the counter to grab the phone. She paged through the phone book, then punched in a number. Meggie listened as she spoke but didn't really hear the words through the haze of worry. Dylan didn't work nights, he wouldn't have been at this fire. She glanced up as Lana put the phone back beneath the bar.

"I called the station house and asked for Dylan Quinn."

"If Dylan is hurt, I want to know." Meggie didn't want to wait by the phone for someone to call her and give her the bad news. Besides, who would think to call her? It wasn't as if she was his wife or a relative or even his girlfriend.

"All they said was that he's at the hospital. But that doesn't mean he was hurt."

"I'm going to go down there. To the hospital."

Meggie expected Lana to protest, but instead her partner quickly agreed. "Do you want me to drive you?"

"I have my car. I'll be fine" She took a ragged breath and tried to slow the pace of her heart. "He can't be hurt. He just can't be. I mean, I know his job is dangerous, but he always seemed so…invincible."

"Go," Lana urged. "And call me as soon as you find out anything."

Meggie ran out the front door to her car, parked at a meter in front of the shop. She hopped inside, then paused before she turned the ignition. She wasn't sure what kind of reception she'd get at the hospital, but it didn't make any difference. Once she was certain Dylan hadn't been hurt, then she could go home.

"I guess this is what it's like to be in love," she murmured, stunned by the revelation. She'd always dreamed of falling in love, finding a man who would turn her life upside down. But she'd never expected love to be a mixture of confusion and fear and dread. If Dylan was hurt, or even…Meggie swallowed hard. She didn't want to consider that possibility! He wasn't dead. He wasn't even hurt.

But one thought kept rolling around in her mind, one thought she couldn't abide. She might never get a chance to tell him how she really felt, never get a chance to say those three special words and really mean them. And that would be the greatest tragedy of all.

DYLAN GLANCED UP at the clock on the wall in the waiting room, watching the seconds tick by. Then he leaned back in his chair and closed his eyes. He and the rest of the firefighters from the Boylston Street station had come directly to the hospital from the fire. Two of their own had been injured, two men under Dylan's command—Artie Winton and Jeff Reilly. They'd been working on the second story of a burning warehouse when the floor gave way and they both fell through to the story below.

The strange thing was, they weren't even supposed to be there. One of the guys on the night shift had gotten married yesterday and Dylan's crew had offered to cover their shift so that some of the firefighters could attend the wedding and reception. They'd done a favor that had gone sour and now he was left to figure out why it had happened in the first place.

Getting information on their condition from the doctors had been nearly impossible, but that didn't keep Dylan from waiting, watching the clock and wondering why it wasn't him in that hospital bed instead of his two friends. *He'd* been the one to take them into that building. *He'd* thought it was safe. But it had been so dark and smoky and hard to see. If he'd known it was going to go down as it had, he would have—

Dylan cursed softly. Guilt had been plaguing him from the moment the accident had happened and he'd run it over and over in his head. What should he have done differently? The floor hadn't burned through. When they fell, they fell into smoke, not fire. But if fire hadn't weakened the floor, what had?

He opened his eyes and stared at the clock again, imagining the worst. When they'd pulled Artie out of the building, he'd had at least a broken leg and possibly a punctured lung. And Jeff had been unconscious with a head wound and cuts and scrapes on his face. Dylan kept telling himself that no news was good news, but after hours of waiting, even that didn't ring true anymore.

"Dylan?"

He opened his eyes, certain that he'd slipped into a dream for just a moment. But then, he slowly turned and found Meggie standing a few feet away. Her eyes glistened with tears and she bit her lower lip to keep it from trembling. "I…I heard about the fire," she said. "The news was on the radio. Lana called the fire station and they said you were here. I just wanted to make sure you were all right."

Dylan rose and stared at her for a long moment, trying to figure out why she'd come. He was exhausted and edgy and his first thought was to question whether this visit was part of her plan. He closed his eyes and took a deep breath, refusing to give voice to the accusation. She couldn't have predicted the fire and only a first-class manipulator would use it to her advantage. There were a lot of things about Meggie Flanagan that he didn't understand, but he knew she could never sink that low.

"I'm fine," he muttered. "I can't say the same about Artie and Jeff though." She came closer, then reached out and took his hand. Her touch sent a wave of warmth though his body and he felt the frustrations of the day ebb, the worry drain out of him. He wanted to pull her into his arms and bury his face in her silken hair, to breathe in her scent. "They won't tell us anything."

"How long have you been here?"

"A couple hours." He glanced around impatiently. "Damn it, why won't they tell us anything?"

Meggie gave his hand a squeeze. "I'll go see what I can find out. Why don't you sit back down? You look exhausted."

Dylan watched her as she walked over to the nurse's station. Even after everything he'd learned and everything he suspected, he was still glad to see her. She radiated a calm that he was in desperate need of right now.

She returned a few moments later and he didn't wait for her to offer her hand. Instead, he grabbed it and pressed his lips to her fingers. "The doctor is coming right out." Meggie hesitated. "Would you like me to stay?"

Dylan nodded. She sat down next to him, leaning back in her chair and staring up at the clock as she did. They didn't speak. Dylan didn't feel the need for words. Just having her near was enough.

He closed his eyes again and as soon as he did, an image of the accident flashed in his brain. But he didn't try to brush it aside. Instead, he calmly watched it, over and over, hoping for a clue to what had gone wrong. Doubts and confusion seemed to drag him down and he knew he wouldn't figure anything out until he got some rest. Right now, all he wanted was to curl up in a clean, soft bed with Meggie tucked in beside him and sleep until he couldn't sleep anymore.

Dylan felt her grip tighten on his hand and he opened his eyes to see a doctor moving toward the waiting room. He tried to read the doctor's expression and when he thought it was positive, Dylan told himself that he was only seeing what he wanted to see.

"Your buddies are going to be fine," the doctor announced, as the firefighters gathered around him. "Mr. Winton has a broken leg. We'll be taking him to surgery later this evening and we'll set it with a few screws. He also has a few broken ribs which were causing his breathing problems, but he should make a full recovery and be back on his feet in a few months. Mr. Reilly has a concussion but the CAT scan shows no swelling. He should be able to go home tomorrow evening. They're both resting and will be able to see visitors in the morning. I suggest the rest of you go home and get some sleep." With that, the doctor turned briskly and headed back down the hall.

The men from the Boylston Street station breathed a collective sigh of relief before breaking into smiles and slaps on the back. Dylan glanced down at Meggie and smiled. "Thanks," he murmured.

She reached up and clutched the sleeve of his jacket. "Why don't you let me take you home? I've got my car outside and you probably don't need to go back to the station. It sounds like you've had a long night."

Dylan nodded, then grabbed his helmet and followed her to the elevator. Suddenly, he felt as if the weight of the world had been lifted off his shoulders. Artie and Jeff were all right. And Meggie was here and he could talk to her. There had been a time when he'd kept his problems locked tightly inside where they could gnaw away at him. But he knew he could tell her everything and she'd understand—everything except how he really felt about her.

He'd looked into her eyes and had seen the concern there. The notion that she cared gave him hope—hope that those feelings went deeper than just worry over an acquaintance. The Meggie Flanagan who had come looking for him at the hospital wasn't the same Meggie Flanagan who'd neatly written "REVENGE" on the top of her plan. And he still couldn't convince himself that the Meggie he knew possessed an ounce of vindictiveness.

They reached her car and Dylan shrugged out of his bulky jacket and kicked off his boots before he got inside. He tossed them both in the rear seat with his helmet, then crawled in and laid his head back against the seat.

"Everything is going to be all right," she murmured when she'd settled on the driver's side.

He turned and looked over at her, smiling weakly. "I know."

Her fingers gripped the wheel but she didn't make a move to start the car. "Remember when you pulled me out of my shop and you yelled at me for worrying about my espresso maker? You said, 'Today is a good day. No one died.'" She turned to him and met his gaze squarely. "Today is a good day. Your friend's leg will mend and he'll be back to work in no time. And the doctor said that Jeff will be fine."

"I just wish I knew what happened," Dylan said. "There's no reason they should have been hurt."

"You will. Tomorrow you'll figure it all out and it will make sense. But for today, you just have to let it go."

Dylan reached over and wove his fingers through her hair, then drew her closer. His gaze fell on her lips and at first, he hesitated, not sure of how to approach her. But then, there was nothing left to do but kiss her. She sighed softly as his lips met hers and the taste of her washed away the bitter taste of smoke and confusion.

This was what it was supposed to be like. This was love, solid and true and unshakable. As the kiss grew more intense, all his suspicions and concerns dissolved and Dylan knew that nothing made any difference at all except this feeling…this kiss…this incredible warmth he felt in his heart.

For now, that was all he needed. As along as he had Meggie's love, even if it was only for a day, or a week, then everything would be all right.

THE KITCHEN IN Dylan's apartment was typical for a bachelor. He had an entire cupboard full of cereal, nearly every brand that contained more sugar than nutrients. The refrigerator held little more than milk, beer, a jar of mustard and some cheese that had gone fuzzy. When Meggie found bread and a can of soup, she decided to make Dylan her favorite comfort food—grilled cheese and tomato soup.

After she cut the mold from the cheese, there was just enough for a single sandwich. She mixed milk with the soup and stood at the stove, carefully tending both. A glance at her watch told her Dylan had been in the shower for nearly a half hour.

The temptation to join him there had teased at her brain. But though she'd done something as audacious as make love to him on a pool table, Meggie wasn't certain how he'd react if she stepped into the shower with him. She turned the notion over and over in her mind, thinking of all the delicious possibilities.

A frisson of desire shot through her as an image flashed in her mind—Dylan, naked and wet and hard with need. The water would wash over them and he'd press her back against the wall and draw her legs up around his waist and…Meggie swallowed hard. It was a long leap between tomato soup and uninhibited sex in a man's shower, she mused.

Yet the urge to repeat what they'd shared just a few nights ago was stronger than ever. Meggie had never considered herself a very sensual person yet all she could think about was the reality of smoothing her hands over Dylan's chest or pressing a kiss against his flat belly or running her fingers along his rigid desire. She could even recall his scent, the smell of soap and aftershave and hard work that was unmistakably male. And then there was his voice, whispering her name as he reached his climax.

Meggie cursed softly, then flipped off the burners to the stove. She found a clean plate for the sandwich and set the mug of soup next to the grilled cheese. Then she grabbed a cold beer from the refrigerator and wandered toward Dylan's bedroom.

She knocked softly, but when he didn't answer, Meggie pushed the door open. Steam from the shower hung heavy in the air and for a moment, she expected him to walk out of the bathroom, damp and naked. But then she looked over to the bed and found Dylan there, stretched out on top of the covers, wearing only his boxer shorts, sound asleep.

A smile curled her lips and she softly approached. She set the soup and sandwich and beer down on the bedside table, but she couldn't bring herself to wake him. He looked so relaxed, the tension that she'd seen in his expression now gone. With a hesitant hand, she reached out to brush a damp lock of hair from his forehead.

He didn't stir, so Meggie knelt down beside the bed and

studied him for a long time. She'd never noticed the small scar on his upper lip or how perfectly straight his nose was. And his jaw, such a determined angle to it. A man didn't have any right to be so beautiful.

She leaned closer, then gave into impulse and brushed a soft kiss across his lips. When she pulled back and opened her eyes, she found him staring at her, his gaze fixed on hers. Meggie forced a smile. "I brought you some soup," she murmured. "And a sandwich."

But instead of thanking her, he reached out and slipped his hand through the hair at her nape and pulled her forward. His mouth met hers and almost immediately she tasted the need in his kiss. It was as if he were frantic to possess her, demanding that she respond.

Meggie moaned softly and tried to stand, but instead, she tumbled down on top of him, then rolled across the bed until she was beneath him. Desire raced through her, her reaction to his touch swift and stirring. Dylan tugged at her clothes, as anxious to feel skin against skin as she suddenly was.

This was no gentle seduction. It was raw and powerful and the need surged inside of Meggie until she thought she'd go out of her mind if she didn't feel him moving inside of her. He took her face between his hands and kissed her roughly, then drew her up until she knelt in front of him on the bed. Her sweater was the first to go and he yanked it over her head and carelessly tossed it aside. Then he reached for the bottom hem of her cotton camisole and pulled that over her head as well.

Dylan paused for a moment, smoothing his hands over her bare breasts, cupping them in his palms. But it wasn't enough and he fumbled with the button on her jeans. Meggie knew that he wanted her as much as she wanted him. His erection pressed against the front of his boxers. But rather than touch him, she pushed off the bed and stood next to it.

He watched her through half-hooded eyes as she slid her jeans down over her hips and kicked off her shoes and socks along with them. Then, she slipped out of her panties. When she stood naked in front of him, his gaze raked over her body. A tiny shiver skittered down her spine as she anticipated the next move, the move that would send her senses spinning out of control.

It came quickly. Dylan reached out and wrapped his arm around her waist, then pulled her back onto his bed and back beneath his body. Meggie stretched out along the length of him, his desire pressing between her legs, probing at her entrance. She ached for the sensation of him entering her without any barriers between them. But though he'd lost all contact with common sense, Meggie knew better.

She furrowed her hands through his hair and gently drew his damp mouth away from hers. Dylan groaned softly and stole one more kiss before opening his eyes. It was as if he could see right to her soul. He reached over to the bedside table and grabbed a box in the top drawer, then placed it in her hand without saying a word.

As she slipped the condom over him, he watched her, as if the act was more a caress than a matter of practicality. And when she was finished, she tossed the box and wrapper aside.

A moment later, he was above her and then inside her. Their joining was primitive, raw with need and almost violent in its intensity. He couldn't seem to get close enough, couldn't seem to fill her completely, his need insatiable, his mood driven. Meggie arched beneath him until she felt him deep in her core and he sighed raggedly.

She wanted this as much as he did, this mindless coupling. It drove away all her doubt and guilt, leaving pure emotion in its wake. She loved Dylan Quinn, that was all that she knew. She loved him with her heart and her mind and yes, her body. And nothing could change that. But this is what she needed right now, this exquisite pleasure she took in his body and he took in hers.

As she rose toward her climax, sensation pulsing through her, Meggie heard him murmur her name. It was like a cry for help and a plea for release, and a promise that he would be with her when she fell. And then Meggie felt herself swell around him and a tremor raced through her. The first spasm came as a shock, but then they rolled over her like waves on a beach, warm and delicious. An instant later, he joined her, tensing at first, then exploding inside her with a low groan.

When they both came back to earth, Dylan rolled to her side and curled her body against his. His breath slowed and for a moment, Meggie thought he might be asleep. But then he spoke, his breath soft against her ear. "Don't ever leave me," he murmured. "Promise me."

"I won't," Meggie said. But the promise cost dearly. Though she never wanted to leave him, that didn't mean that he wouldn't someday send her away. Or that she would choose to leave on her own. Nothing assured them of a future together. Great sex didn't magically turn into a lifelong commitment.

Meggie rolled over in his arms and stared at his face in the soft light. He slept soundly, peacefully, their joining driving away the demons that had nagged at him since the fire. She reached out and smoothed her hand over his cheek. "I love you," she murmured, the words coming out on a soft breath. "I can't help myself. I've always loved you and I always will."

But her feelings, however deep, wouldn't change the fact that she'd somehow tricked him into wanting her. All men want what they can't have, Lana had told her. How long would Dylan want her once he knew she could refuse him nothing? She'd already seen that faraway look in his eyes, felt the sting of indifference in his words. The first signs were there.

Meggie slowly wriggled out of his arms, then knelt next to him on the bed. The prospect of seeing that look again, especially after their passionate time together would be enough to break her heart into a million pieces. So rather than spend the night and dread the morning, she'd retreat and leave him to sleep alone.

And when he woke up, maybe he'd wonder whether he'd possessed her at all. Maybe he'd believe it was just a dream. And then maybe he'd come back just once more.

Meggie brushed an errant tear from her cheek then crawled out of the bed and began to gather her clothes. She dressed slowly, all the while watching him. When she was finally through, Meggie couldn't bear to make herself leave without touching him just once more. She walked to the bed and gently placed her palm on his heart. It beat slow and strong beneath her fingers.

Then, with a ragged sigh, she turned and walked out of the room. And when she reached her car parked on the street in front of his building she paused. Though she fought the urge to return to his arms and his bed, Meggie knew this was for the best. She needed time to figure out her next move, time to find a way to make him love her for real. And she couldn't concentrate when he looked into her eyes or touched her.

Meggie unlocked her car, then took one last look up at Dylan's bedroom window. She imagined him still curled up, his limbs tangled in the sheets. Someday, maybe she'd be able to stay. Someday, maybe his bed would be hers as well.

But today wasn't that day.

8

SHE WAS GONE when he woke up at dusk. Dylan rolled over in his empty bed, then moaned softly. He wasn't surprised. Hell, nothing Meggie did surprised him anymore. Not her stalwart support at the hospital, not her gentle concern when they got back to his apartment. And not even her uninhibited passion in his arms as they made love.

Now that he understood her motives, everything fell perfectly into place. Making love to him hadn't been about the two of them, it had been about her little plan for revenge, about reeling him in and turning his need for her against him.

Dylan closed his eyes and threw his arm over his face, wishing that he could block it all out of his brain. She must have a heart of ice to use him so completely, then cast him aside. But no matter how he tried to reconcile the two Meggies he knew, Dylan still came up short. He'd looked into her eyes at the very moment he'd entered her and he'd seen emotion there, passion and ecstasy, and yes, love. If she was faking it, then she was a better actress than any Academy Award winner.

He rolled over and grabbed his shirt from where he'd tossed it earlier that day. It still smelled faintly of smoke. The paper was still there, tucked in his breast pocket, a reminder of everything that was wrong between him and Meggie Flanagan. Dylan pulled it out and scanned the diagram. Over and over again, he'd tried to attach an alternate meaning to what he saw. After all, how could she possibly harbor such ill feelings over something as stupid as a high-school dance.

He raked his hand through his hair. Unless, of course, she was a psycho. A bitter laugh burst from his lips. He could attribute many qualities to Meggie, but deranged wasn't one of them. "So what the hell is this all about?" Dylan murmured, staring down at her plan.

With a soft curse, he glanced around the room, his gaze falling on the tangled sheets of his bed. An image flashed in his mind, Meggie naked, her skin flushed with desire, her mouth damp from his kisses. She was everything he'd ever wanted in a woman. But he didn't want this—the doubt, the confusion, the anger. He'd had enough.

Dylan tossed the paper on the bed, then quickly rummaged through his closet, looking for a clean pair of jeans and a shirt that wasn't too wrinkled. This had gone on long enough and it was time to put an end to it. If Meggie really loved him, then he'd force her to admit it. And if she didn't, then he'd walk away.

He shoved the paper into his pocket and shrugged into his jacket on the way out. Dylan wasn't sure what he planned to say to her, but it wasn't going to be pretty. For the first time in his life, he'd risked everything and fallen in love. And this is where it had got him. "Maybe I should have listened more closely to all those tales of the Mighty Quinns," he muttered as he tossed his helmet, jacket and boots into the trunk of his car.

What had ever made him think he could find a relationship like Conor and Olivia's? He wasn't cut out for happily-ever-after and he shouldn't have deluded himself into believing otherwise.

Dylan reached for the radio and flipped it on. The blaring sounds of Aerosmith and the play-by-play of a Patriots game didn't drown out the constant questions, the unrelenting regret. He wondered if someday, a young Quinn ancestor would hear how the mighty Dylan Quinn had fallen under the spell of the beautiful Meggie Flanagan and how she'd stomped on his heart and left him weak and powerless.

A frown creased his brow. For that to happen, there would have to be ancestors. And if the Quinn brothers never found love, then that wasn't going to happen. And if they did, they wouldn't have any reason to pass on those ridiculous tales! "You're not thinking straight," he muttered. "Just keep your eye on the ball and don't let her draw you in again."

He parked at the station and returned his gear to the alcove. Then, as he walked the distance to Meggie's shop, he went over what he wanted to say. He'd just lay it all on the line, admit his feelings for her and demand complete honesty in return. If she wanted him, so be it. And if she didn't, then he was willing to walk away. But all his resolve wavered the moment he walked into Cuppa Joe's.

Meggie was standing at the cash register, her expression intense. She looked like she'd just crawled out of his bed, her hair mussed and her lips still swollen from his kisses. She punched at the buttons, then cursed, then punched them again before she looked up. Dylan held his breath, ready to read her reaction. Would she pretend to be happy to see him? Or would she offer some lame apology for sneaking out without a word?

He didn't bother to wait. Instead, he strode up to the counter and slammed the piece of paper onto the copper surface with the flat of his hand. "Just get it over with," he demanded, his jaw tight, his temper barely under control.

Meggie gasped, taken aback by his sudden appearance and by the tone in his voice. "What?"

Dylan shook his head. "Don't play coy with me, Meggie. I know what you're up to. It's all here, in your little plan."

She stared down at the paper in disbelief. Hesitantly, she reached out and took it. Stunned recognition dawned on her face. "Where did you find this?" she asked.

"Never mind where I found it."

"I—I don't know what to say." She pushed it back toward him. "You weren't supposed to see that. It doesn't mean anything."

"Just tell me it's over," Dylan demanded, his heart pounding so hard he could hear it in his head. "Or maybe it can't be over until I admit that I love you." He drew a deep breath, his angry gaze fixed on her. "All right, here it is. I love you. I love you more than I've ever loved a woman before. Hell,

I don't think I *have* loved a woman before you. You're the first. Does that make you feel good? Because, for a while there it made me feel real good." He cursed softly. "But now it makes me feel kind of stupid."

Meggie reached out to touch his hand, but he pulled it away. "I'm sorry," she said. "But you don't understand. This was never meant to—"

"Hurt me?" Dylan interrupted. "Well, it did. And I think in the end, it hurt you, too. Because we could have had something really great. Only you can't see that."

"We do have something great," she said.

"We have something weird and kind of sick."

"No! It's not like that," Meggie protested. "Lana and I put that plan together that first night you came in here. It was silly and I didn't take it seriously. But, then when you called me up for a date, I didn't know what to do. I don't have a lot of experience with men, Dylan, at least not a lot of experience that prepared me for you. So I decided to follow the plan."

"Do you really expect me to believe this? Everything that happened between us was right there on this paper. From your four-day waiting period until accepting a date to the invitation to your grandmother's birthday party. Even those flowers from David were a lie."

"Lana sent the flowers. And I didn't invite you to that party, you invited yourself."

"And it's a good thing I did, because if I hadn't, I never would have figured out what you were up to. Your brother was the one who gave me the heads-up. He told me about the Sophomore Frolic and how you expected me to take you instead of Brian."

She stared at him for a long while and he could see the pain and regret in her eyes. Dylan wanted to take the words back, to simply pull her into his arms and erase all the anger with a flurry of kisses. But he couldn't touch her. Once he did, he knew he'd be lost.

"I was wrong," Meggie said. "I misunderstood. And by the time I found out, that stupid plan was already history."

"I thought what we had was real. And now I find out that it was all just a game to you."

"It started as a game, but it didn't end that way," Meggie insisted. "I never expected you to ask me out again after that first date and when you did, I wasn't sure what to do. I just figured, why not use the plan? I knew, sooner or later, you'd move on to someone else, so it didn't make a difference."

Dylan wasn't sure how to respond. He'd wanted to believe that Meggie was different, that what they shared was real. And maybe there were real emotions at work here, but they'd been tainted by her deceit and manipulation.

"I know you, Dylan. I've watched you since I was thirteen. I'm not the kind of girl you want. And you may think you love me, but that's just because the plan worked. It'll wear off after a while."

Her words cut right to the quick and though he knew she didn't mean to be cruel, he couldn't help his own reaction. There it was. It all came back to the same thing—his reputation, his charm and the long list of ladies he'd bedded. His feelings for Meggie didn't make a bit of difference as long as he was carrying around all that old baggage.

But hadn't he proved himself to her? What did she want that he hadn't given her? He certainly couldn't change the past. If he could, he would have. But this was who he was. A surge of anger raced through him. He'd accepted her past and hadn't let it affect their future, why couldn't she accept him, warts and all?

"Maybe you're right," Dylan murmured. Maybe he had been caught up in a fantasy that could never become reality. He'd wanted to believe that he could find a woman to love, just like Conor had. But he wasn't Conor and he never could be. "I have to go," he said. He stared at her long and hard, unable to believe that this was the end of it. He'd admitted he loved her and now he had to walk away.

"I never meant to hurt you," Meggie said, her voice soft and tremulous. "And I'm sorry if I did."

Though her apologies made a fitting end to their conversation, they didn't make Dylan feel any better. He turned and strode toward the door. He was tempted to look back, but his pride wouldn't allow it. Meggie had wandered in and out of his life once before and he'd forgotten her.

He could do it again. Only this time, Dylan suspected it would take a lot longer for the memories to fade.

"YA LOOK LIKE yer in a desperate state," Seamus Quinn muttered. "Here, drink yer Guinness and buck up, boyo. Life can't be that bad, can it?"

Dylan pushed aside his empty beer bottle, then grabbed the Guinness and took a hearty gulp. If he drank enough it might dull his senses. And if he managed that, then he might be able to forget about Meggie Flanagan and their brief, but passionate, affair.

"So, tell me," Seamus asked. "Are you acting the *gom* over a woman? Or is it something else?"

The last person Dylan wanted to discuss his love life with was Seamus Quinn. He didn't need *I-told-you-so*s on top of everything else he was feeling. Hell, he'd heaped enough of that on himself. "Nah, there's nothing wrong, Da. Just worried over my buddies at work."

"Those lads who got themselves injured in that fire? So how are they, then?"

"They're good," Dylan said. "Winton will get out of the hospital in a few days and Reilly goes home tomorrow. They should be back on the job before too long." He picked up his Guinness then slid back from the bar. "I'm going to see what Brendan is up to," he murmured.

His brother was sitting in a booth near the pool table, papers spread all over the table, and a half-eaten bowl of Irish stew next to his laptop computer. "Can I sit down?" Dylan asked.

Brendan glanced up, then shoved his papers aside. "Sure. I didn't realize you were here. When did you come in?"

"A few minutes ago."

"I heard about the fire," Brendan said, eyeing him shrewdly. "Some of your crew stopped in here on their way home. They said you left the hospital with Meggie. So what are you doing here?"

"Well, I needed a beer. A few beers. In fact, I think I'll drink so many beers that I won't be able to see straight. So," Dylan said, nodding toward the stacks of papers. "What are you working on?"

"An article for *Adventure* magazine. It's about that trip I took on the Amazon last spring. And some of this is for my book." Brendan reached out and tried to straighten the mess. "I need an assistant," he said. "I've got so much stuff to put together and it's all on little scraps of paper. Interview notes on cocktail napkins, phone numbers on matchbooks. I have to get organized or I'll never get this book—" Brendan stopped. "Are you even listening to me?"

Dylan glanced up, then nodded. "Yeah. Little scraps of paper. That's a problem."

Brendan chuckled softly. "So, you had a fight with Meggie?"

Dylan hadn't really wanted to talk about his problems, but now that Brendan brought it up, he realized that it might be good to get a second viewpoint on what went on. "Naw, not a fight. It's just over." He shook his head, then took another sip of beer. "I don't know what made me think it would ever work. I've never had a committed relationship in my life. Why should I start now?"

"Because you're in love with her, you stupid *gobdaw.* Anyone can see that."

"Is it that obvious?" Dylan asked.

"Only to your brothers. The rest of the world probably just thinks that look on your face is from a bad case of constipation. That or your underwear is creeping."

"She made up this plan to get me to fall in love with her just so she could dump me. All for something she thinks I did way back in high school."

"I know. Con told me all about it."

Dylan gasped. "What? Is my love life the hot topic of conversation at Quinn's Pub?"

"Yeah, maybe. There's not much else to talk about except for Con's wedding and I've had about enough of that. I never thought I'd see the day when he got so excited over table linens and china patterns. The poor guy has gone completely 'round the bend. I'm thinking we should stage one of those interventions."

"He hasn't gone 'round the bend," Dylan said. "In fact, I know how he feels. It's easy to be excited about those things when the woman you love is excited about them. When Meggie talked about her coffee shop, I could listen all night while she chattered on about French roast and Italian roast and how it's important to get the steamed milk to precisely the right temperature. When she talked about things like that, her whole face lit up and she looked more beautiful than she'd ever looked before."

"God, you are in love, aren't you," Brendan said, leaning back to stare at him in disbelief.

"Yeah, that's the real corker. I don't know whether to be angry or hurt or whether I should do a little happy jig on the bar. She wanted me to fall in love with her and I did. I'm in love and there's not a thing I can do about it. I said the words, but she doesn't believe me, because, of course, I'm Dylan Quinn and I can't possibly fall in love. I'm simply not capable of feeling that emotion."

"Well, you've made a mess of it, I can see," Brendan said. "I suppose you and Con are going to be lording this over the rest of us."

"Don't look so disgusted. You'll have your day and it's probably coming a lot sooner than you think," Dylan warned. "Conor started something in this family, maybe not intentionally. But he showed us all the possibilities. He proved that all those silly Mighty Quinn stories don't have to be true. And sooner or later, you're going to want what he has. And what I almost had."

"Past tense?"

"Very past tense," Dylan murmured.

"You don't sound convinced."

Dylan took another sip of his Guinness. "I'm not. It used to be so easy to forget a woman. I just moved on to someone else. But how the hell am I supposed to forget Meggie? It's like she burrowed her way into my heart and she's not leaving any time soon. I should be mad as hell that she manipulated me, yet I have to believe that what went on between us was real. I wasn't wrong about that."

"So, let's lay it on the line," Brendan said. "You told her you loved her and she didn't believe you. She didn't return the sentiment, but chances are she feels the same way. The way I look at it, all you have to do is convince her that you can't live without her and that she can't live without you. That shouldn't be too hard."

"I don't know. I don't think I can go back there."

"Are you really angry about what Meggie said and did or are you just using this as an excuse?"

Dylan had to admit that the idea had crossed his mind more than once. What Meggie did really wasn't that bad. She'd wanted him to fall in love with her and he had. And she'd made no move to dump him, to exact her revenge. He'd been the one to dump her.

"You should get out while you still can. Avoid the inevitable—a lifetime of happiness with the woman you love."

Dylan sighed, then shook his head. "I don't want to get out, but I just don't know how to fix this. Usually, whenever I had a problem with a woman, that signalled the end of the relationship. I've never really had to work at it. And don't know if Meggie feels the same way about me as I do about her. I think she does, but then I haven't been the best judge of the truth in this relationship. I just wish we could start all over again. You know, a fresh start, from the beginning. That way I'd be certain it was real." Dylan stared morosely into his glass.

"I know what will help you," Brendan said. "A nice round of darts."

"I don't feel like playing."

"Aw, now don't be givin' me that sad puss," Brendan said in a thick Irish brogue. He leaned forward, bracing his elbows on the table. "You want my advice?"

"Isn't that what you've been giving me for the past ten minutes?"

"No, that was just conversation. Listen carefully, brother, because this is advice."

Dylan held up his hand. "To be honest, I'd rather get Olivia's advice. She'd know what I should do. She knows a lot about how women think, more than you do."

"You insult me, lad," Brendan said. "I know exactly what you should do and I'll tell you."

"So tell me."

"If you want to go back to the beginning and start again, then do it. There's nothing to stop you."

"My time machine is in the shop," Dylan muttered.

"Be creative. Think outside the box. Do something unexpected." Brendan slid out of the booth, then gave Dylan a slap on the back. "Come on, I'll let you win at darts. That should make you feel better."

"Let me win?" Dylan said. "You haven't beaten me at darts in five years."

Dylan grudgingly slid out of the booth and walked toward the back of the bar. Maybe a rousing round of darts would take his mind off his troubles with Meggie. But he knew as soon as he was alone again, they'd all come flooding back.

As he plucked the darts from the dartboard, Dylan's thoughts wandered back to Brendan's advice. An idea began to form in his mind, a way to turn back the clock. He put his toe on the line painted on the floor and tossed a dart at the board. It stuck just a few inches short of the bull's-eye.

Maybe the idea would work, he mused. But something like this would take a plan. A very detailed plan.

"IT'S OVER," Meggie said, staring into her cup of coffee as if it might offer some answers. But she knew there were no answers to her problems. Nothing she said or did could repair the damage that had been done and now she was left to live with the consequences. "I should never have agreed to that plan. I should have thrown it out the minute you put pen to paper."

"I'm sorry," Lana said. "This is all my fault. Maybe I should go over to the firehouse and explain it all to Dylan. It's been three days and he's probably had a chance to cool off. Besides, he can't hold you responsible for something that I did, can he? I mean, the handwriting on that paper isn't even yours."

"That's not the point," Meggie said. "The plan worked. But in the end, it didn't work."

"I don't understand."

"He told me he loved me." Meggie's voice wavered slightly as she said the words, remembering the moment she heard them. Though he'd declared his love in anger, it still didn't erase the joy she felt. Dylan Quinn had fallen in love with her. And she'd fallen in love with him. And that, in itself, was a miracle.

"I thought when a man finally said that to me, my life would change forever. I thought I'd be picking out a wedding dress and deciding what to name my first child. But my life hasn't changed at all. I'm back to where I was the day Dylan carried me out of the shop."

"If you truly love him, Meggie, and he truly loves you, then things will work out."

"That only happens in fairy tales. I think he realizes that I never meant to reach the revenge part of the plan. He's just using that as an excuse. The little alarm bell went off in his head and now it's time for him to move on. Maybe it's time for me to move on, too."

"Don't say that," Lana cried. "You're in love and you shouldn't give up so easily."

"But everything is so messed up! How am I going to straighten this out?"

Lana thought about the question for a long moment, then smiled. "Where is the plan?" she asked.

Meggie slipped off her stool and circled the counter to retrieve the crumpled paper that Dylan had tossed in her face. She also grabbed the notebook where they'd scribbled their early strategies and the computer printout of Lana's latest revision. She handed them all to Lana. "Take them. I don't ever want to look at them again."

"I think we should get rid of it all, right now," Lana said.

"Good idea," Meggie cried.

Lana hopped off her stool, scooped up the papers and notebook and headed toward the office. "Well, are you coming?"

Meggie frowned, then hurried after her. "Where are you going?" By the time Meggie reached the office, Lana had brought out the metal trash can from beneath the desk and dumped its contents in the corner of the office. She then placed the trash can in the center of the tiny room.

With a grand flourish, she handed Meggie the notebook. "Go ahead," she said. "Tear it to bits and throw it away."

When Meggie had shredded the notebook, Lana leaned over the can and spit. "That's for all those men who don't know a good woman when they find one."

"Damn straight," Meggie added as she spit into the trash can.

Lana held up the computer report and Meggie snatched it from her fingers and tore into it. When she'd finished, she dumped it on top of the scraps from the notebook. "That felt really good," she murmured. "Give me something else." The computer disk was next and Meggie did her best to dismantle it before adding it to the pile.

Then, the only thing left was the crumpled paper that Dylan had found. But as Lana handed it to her, she smiled slyly. "Don't throw that away yet. Since he touched it, since he put his eyes on this very private piece of paper, I have something special planned." She reached into her pocket and withdrew a lighter and before Meggie could protest, Lana lit the corner of the paper on fire.

Meggie cried out as it flamed, then dropped it into the trash can on top of the other papers. "Are you crazy?"

"It's a metal trash can," Lana said. "It'll burn out in a few seconds."

But it didn't burn out. In fact, the contents began to smoke, the plastic from the computer disk causing an acrid smell. Meggie frantically searched for something to put out the fire. She grabbed Lana's jacket from behind the door, but Lana yanked it out of her arms. "That's cashmere," her partner cried. "Six hundred dollars."

"Well, we need to find something to put this out before the alarm goes off!"

Just as she said the words, a piercing sound split the air. She grabbed the phone, determined to catch it before the system automatically called the fire department, but it was too late. With a soft curse, she hurried to the counter and grabbed the fire extinguisher they'd purchased after the last fire. But by the time she reached the office, the fire had burned itself out. All that was left was smoke and some charred paper. She dropped the extinguisher on the floor.

Her partner leaned on the edge of her desk, the same sly smile curling her lips that was there when she suggested this little ritual. Realization suddenly dawned. "You did this on purpose!" Meggie cried. "You knew the plastic from that computer disk would start smoldering and set off the alarm."

Lana looked at her watch. "Dylan should be rolling up any minute now. I called the firehouse just to make sure he was on duty. If I were you I'd comb my hair and dab on a little lipstick. You look a little frazzled."

Meggie cursed out loud, then spun around to look at her reflection in the mirror on the wall. Though she hadn't spent much time getting ready that morning, she wasn't having such a bad day. She pinched her cheeks and ran her fingers through her hair, then pressed her hand to her heart.

She wasn't sure whether she really wanted to see him or not. When he'd left the shop a few days ago, he'd been so angry. She had to prepare herself for the worst, the prospect that he might walk in and not even speak to her.

Meggie and Lana stood in the middle of the shop and waited, the unused fire extinguisher at their feet. A few minutes later, a trio of firemen strode through the door. Meggie's heart fell when she saw that Dylan was one of them. But he stood back, near the door and sent the other two ahead.

"The fire is out," Lana said. "It was in the office. I'll show you the way." Lana gave her a wide-eyed smile as she tagged after Dylan's two handsome co-workers. When they'd disappeared into the rear of the shop, Meggie had no choice but to acknowledge Dylan's presence.

"Hi," she murmured. He looked so handsome in his firefighter gear, so strong and resolute. Her knees went weak as his gaze met hers.

He nodded curtly, then glanced down at the floor. "I see you got a fire extinguisher."

"It was just a little fire," Meggie said. "It went out almost as quickly as it began. Besides, I couldn't figure out how to work it."

He sighed softly. "Set it in front of you on the floor," he

instructed, "like this." He took her hand and wrapped her fingers around the handle, then covered her hand with his. "Pull the pin, squeeze and the foam will come out."

"Thanks." She swallowed hard in a feeble attempt to control the tremor in her voice. Her mind wandered back to the time they'd spent in his bed, the passion they'd shared, her shattering response to his touch. Even now, she could still recall the feel of his hands against her skin.

"How did it start?" Dylan asked, his voice cool and efficient, the perfect firefighter.

Though she could barely maintain her composure around him, he wasn't having the same trouble around her. "Lana," Meggie said. "She dropped a match into the trash can by mistake and the trash caught on fire."

Dylan glanced over her shoulder and she turned to watch the two firemen emerge from the office, one of them carrying the trash can. He brought it to Dylan. Reaching in, Dylan picked out the charred remains of the notebook. Then he pulled out a half-burned flowchart. He raised his eyebrow as he held the paper out to Meggie. "This looks familiar."

She opened her mouth to speak, but then at the last minute, changed her mind. Nothing she could say would help. He believed he'd been manipulated and he had the proof in his hands. He probably even thought that she'd set the fire herself, just to lure him back.

"Do you have a few minutes?" she asked. "I'd like to talk to you. Privately."

Dylan grabbed the trash can from his co-worker's arms. "Why don't you guys wait outside. Let Carmichael know I'll be done in here in a few minutes."

The pair walked outside. Meggie wondered how long Lana was planning to stay in the office and whether she'd have time to say what she needed to say. She took a deep breath, then hardened her resolve. She'd only have one chance and she planned on making sure he didn't walk out of Cuppa Joe's with any doubts about her feelings.

"What did you want to talk about?" Dylan murmured.

"Don't rush me," she murmured. "I have to say this right." She looked up at him, meeting his gaze squarely. "I love you." The words came out as if they were all one word. Meggie took another breath. "I—love—you. There. Now you know how I feel. I don't expect that it will change anything, but I just wanted you to know that you weren't the only one with feelings here."

Dylan stared at her, a slight frown wrinkling his brow. His mouth dropped open slightly and for a moment, she thought she saw surprise in his expression.

"I know you probably don't believe me, but I don't care. Making that plan was stupid and I know there's no way I can change the past. But I thought you deserved to hear the truth and that's it."

She took a shaky breath and waited for him to speak. But the bell on the door snapped him back to reality. Meggie turned to see one of the firefighters at the entrance to the shop. "We just got a call. Auto accident a couple blocks away. There's fuel on the street."

Dylan nodded, then turned his attention back to Meggie. His gaze probed hers, as if searching for the truth of her words. "I have to go."

"Yes," she said.

"I don't know what to say."

"You don't have to say anything. I understand."

He turned to walk toward the door, then stopped and looked back at her. For a moment, she thought he might stride right back to her, yank her into his arms and kiss her. But then, he glanced over his shoulder at his buddies waiting outside. "I'll see you."

"I'll see you," Meggie said.

Meggie stared numbly at the door as it swung shut. She had wanted to put the Frolic fiasco behind her, to banish it from her memory along with Dylan Quinn. And instead, she just made new memories to replace the old, new regrets and new heartaches. She'd poured out her heart to him, said all the words she thought he wanted to hear and he'd simply turned and walked away.

A few seconds later, Lana emerged from the office. She stood next to Meggie and draped her arm around her shoulder. "So it didn't go well?"

"I told him I loved him. And then he walked out. No, I'd have to say that wasn't the reaction I was hoping for." She paused. "Although, he didn't say goodbye. He said he'd see me. That's kind of hopeful, isn't it?"

Meggie wandered back to the counter and sat down on a stool. She loved Dylan Quinn. Not in the silly schoolgirl way she'd loved him in high school. This love was soul-deep and part of who she was. And now that she had said the words, she felt better, as if she'd been released from all the deceit and manipulation.

"You told him," Lana said. "And that's good. You gave him something to think about. And once he does, he'll be back."

"How do you know?"

Lana sighed. "I know men. What can I say? It's a gift."

Meggie wanted to believe her. And she wanted to believe that Dylan meant what he'd said just a few days ago. For if he really loved her and she really loved him, then, in the end, nothing should keep them apart.

9

"Smile. 'Say major profit potential'!"

Lana slipped her arm around Meggie's waist and smiled at the camera. Meggie held up a Cuppa Joe's coffee mug and Kristine snapped a picture.

"Just one more," she said. "Meggie, you need to smile! This is an exciting day!"

This was the day they'd been waiting for since she and Lana had graduated from business school, the day they'd talked about over take-out pizza and dirty laundry and stock market investment strategies. And now that it was here, Meggie couldn't seem to work up a good case of enthusiasm. Something was missing and she suspected it was Dylan.

This was the biggest event in her professional life and she wanted Dylan to share it with her. Since he'd responded to the ceremonial fire in her office, she hadn't heard from him. Meggie had thought about calling, but this time, she believed in Lana's admonitions. The ball was in his court; he had to make the next move.

Lana had tried her best to cheer Meggie up over the past few days. She brought her special treats, doughnuts in the morning and a sinful cheeseburger for lunch. One night, she'd even treated Meggie to a manicure. In turn, Meggie had vowed that the day of the grand opening would be the last day Dylan Quinn would invade her thoughts. There were so many other things to occupy her mind than regrets. Yet she knew, in those secret hours while she waited for sleep to come, unbidden images of Dylan would swim in her head and she'd be transported back to the night on the pool table or that morning in his bed.

"Hold the mug out a little further," Kristine directed as she snapped another photo.

They'd hired eight employees, Kristine being the most experienced. She'd been named assistant manager and would lessen the workload for Meggie and Lana. And her boyfriend was active in the local music scene and had promised to help book singers as soon as business took off.

Danielle, a college student from Boston University, was also working the counter. She'd come to them from Starbucks and knew the ins and outs of the espresso maker better than Eddie from the restaurant supply house. She could steam milk to the perfect temperature without using a thermometer and she could mix four different coffee drinks at once, keeping all the flavors and options straight in her head. Two more workers were scheduled to come on at 4:00 and since they'd decided to open at 9:00 instead of the usual 7:00 a.m., today would be a short day.

"Now, I think I need to get a photo of you two bringing out the sign," Kristine suggested.

Meggie and Lana hurried back inside the shop and dragged out the heavy sandwich sign that would sit at the edge of the sidewalk, proclaiming the shop open. They posed once more, then Lana glanced at her watch. "I think it's time," she said.

Her excitement was infectious and Meggie returned her smile. "This is it," she said. "This is what we've been saving for all this time." A tiny shiver coursed through her body. "I'm a little scared."

They walked back inside, arm in arm and flipped on the neon coffee cups that adorned the front windows. Then they stood behind the counter and waited…and waited…and waited.

They were open nearly an hour before the first customer walked inside, a delivery man carrying a huge box under his arm. Meggie stepped up to the register and smiled. The rest of the staff waited expectantly, Kristine with the camera, ready to catch the first money that crossed the counter. "Welcome to Cuppa Joe's," Meggie said. "What can I get for you?"

"Just a signature," he said, holding out a clipboard. "I've got a delivery here for Meggie Flanagan. Is that you?"

Congratulatory gifts had been arriving all week. There were more beautiful plants scattered throughout the shop and gleaming plaques from the local business associations declaring them members of the Greater Boston Chamber of

Commerce and the Back Bay Retailers and the Boylston Street Neighborhood Cooperative. Meggie took the box and set it on the counter. It didn't have a return address, it was simply wrapped in brown paper and tied with a string. She tore the paper off and pulled the lid from the box, then pushed back a layer of tissue paper.

On top was an envelope, but it was what lay beneath that caused the most curiosity. The gift was made of fabric, some type of satiny material in a shade of Pepto-Bismol pink. Meggie dropped the card on the counter and pulled the fabric out only to realize that she'd been sent a dress—a floor-length, formal dress.

"What the hell is that?" Lana asked.

"I'm not sure," Meggie said. "But it looks like—" She paused. "Oh my God, it can't be."

"What?"

"It's the formal I wore to the Sophomore Frolic." She turned it around and looked at the back. The big bow was there right where it had been all those years ago. "It's the exact same dress. Where did this come from? I had this packed away in my closet at my parents' house." Meggie pushed aside the tissue paper to find a pair of shoes dyed to match the awful pink color. "I can't believe I actually wore this. I thought it looked so cool, like the dress Madonna wore in that 'Material Girl' video. Never mind that it was already four or five years out of date."

"Why would your mother send you an old formal?"

"I don't know," Meggie said. She reached for the card, but as she opened the vellum envelope, she realized it wasn't a card at all but a hand-lettered invitation. "The Sophomore

Class of South Boston High cordially invites you to attend the Sophomore Frolic, held tonight in the gymnasium of South Boston High School. A limousine will pick you up promptly at 8:00 p.m."

Lana grabbed the invitation from Meggie's fingers and read it aloud all over again. Then she grinned. "It's from him," she said excitedly.

"Dylan?" Meggie asked. "Why would he do this? Is this some kind of joke?"

"No! It's a grand romantic gesture," Lana explained. "He's planning to sweep you off your feet."

"Dressed in this formal?" Meggie asked.

"Don't you see? He wants to take you back to that night and make it up to you. He's going to give you your Sophomore Frolic only this time, he's going to be your date."

"But why would he do that?"

"Because he probably loves you," Kristine said in a matter-of-fact tone. "Guys only do things like that when they're in love."

Lana and Meggie both looked at their assistant manager. Meggie had heard the same thing a hundred times from Lana, she'd even heard it direct from Dylan's lips, but coming from an objective observer, she couldn't help but wonder if it was true. "But how can I go? It's the grand opening of our shop. I can't just leave."

"Of course you can," Lana said. "Business is going to be slow for the first few days. Besides, this is more important than coffee. This is about a man."

Meggie stared at the dress, fingering the fabric. Dylan had to have gone to a lot of trouble to plan this evening. He couldn't have found her dress without her mother's complicity. And renting out the South Boston High School gymnasium probably didn't come cheap. And a limousine? She sighed softly. Though she didn't want to believe it, she had to agree with Lana. This looked suspiciously like a grand romantic gesture. "I guess I'll have to go out and find the perfect shade of pink nail polish before eight this evening," she murmured.

"Try it on," Lana said. "I want to see how it looks."

"It probably won't fit. I was really skinny back then. And flat as a board."

"Try it on," her partner insisted. She turned Meggie around and pushed her through the shop to the office. "If it doesn't fit we'll have to get it altered. I know a seamstress who could probably do that for you."

Reluctantly, she took the dress back to the office and closed the door. She slipped out of her Cuppa Joe's apron and shimmied out of the standard black pants and white polo shirt that made up the rest of the daytime uniform. The dress looked like it had just been cleaned and pressed and the crinolines scratched her legs as she pulled it up over her hips.

The strapless bodice made a bra unnecessary and Meggie twisted around to pull up the zipper. To her surprise, the dress fit. She smoothed her hands over her hips then turned and stared at the big bow sitting on her butt. "That's got to go," she murmured. "I'll wear the dress but there's no way I'm drawing that much attention to my nearly thirty-year-old backside." She grabbed scissors from the top desk drawer, then hurried back out into the shop.

When Lana and Kristine and Danielle saw her, they all stopped talking and stared. Meggie glanced down at herself. Except for the color and the big bow, she didn't think it looked that bad. "I know, I look like a big blob of cotton candy," Meggie said.

"You do not," Lana countered. "Actually, that dress looks better on you today than it did when you were a teenager. You fill it out rather nicely."

Meggie glanced down and noticed the considerable amount of cleavage showing. She tugged at the bodice of the dress, but it refused to rise any higher.

"I have the tackiest set of rhinestone earrings and choker at home," Kristine said. "I can run back to my apartment at lunchtime and get them."

"And you need gloves," Lana added. "Those long sexy gloves."

"And why not get me a tiara while you're at it," Meggie said. "So I can look really stupid."

"Meggie?"

The voice echoed through the empty shop and they all turned to see a customer standing near the end of the counter. Meggie stepped closer, then realized it wasn't just any customer, it was Olivia Farrell. "Olivia!" she cried. She hurried toward her, then tripped clumsily on the hem of her dress. Meggie caught herself by grabbing the edge of the counter. She straightened and smoothed the skirt of her gown, then yanked at the bodice again. She knew she must look like an absolute fool, but she was so happy to see Olivia again, it didn't matter.

"I'm so glad you came. So, what do you think?"

"It's wonderful!" Olivia said. "Very retro. You should

have told me you were going for this look. I'll bet I could find you lots of really great deals on kitschy accessories. Really cool fifties and sixties stuff." She stopped and stared at Meggie, then shook her head. "I just have to ask."

"The dress?" Meggie said.

"It just doesn't go with the whole theme you've got going here."

Meggie giggled. "It's not supposed to. I was just trying it on." Olivia raised her eyebrow and Meggie quickly shook her head. "No, I'm not wearing this out in public."

"Then why are you wearing it at all?"

She hurried to the counter and grabbed the invitation then showed it to Olivia. "I think this is all Dylan's doing," Meggie said. "I think he plans to recreate that high school dance he was supposed to take me to."

A slow smile broke over Olivia's face. "So that's what he's been up to lately."

"What?"

"He's been asking me the most bizarre questions. And he was at the shop yesterday looking for—" Olivia stopped. "No, I'm not going to tell you. It should be a surprise."

"Why is he doing this?" Meggie asked.

"I'm sure he has a very good reason. But I wouldn't ask questions. I'd just have fun with it."

Meggie nodded. But her mind still whirled with the possibilities. Did this mean that he'd forgiven her? And where would they go from here? Or maybe this was just his way of putting things right before he moved on, she mused.

Whatever his motives, Meggie was certain that after tonight, her life would change forever.

DYLAN STOOD ON the sidewalk outside Cuppa Joe's. He glanced at his watch. "Seven fifty-five," he murmured.

Now that he was here, he wondered if he'd made a mistake. Perhaps he should have included an RSVP with the invitation. At least then, he'd know whether he'd gotten all dressed up for a reason. Dylan knew he looked stupid, but that was the whole point. He'd once heard Olivia say to Conor that she realized he she loved him when he'd rescued her cat, hissing and spitting, from her landlady, then drove miles with it tearing apart the interior of Dylan's Mustang. There was something about a man making a fool of himself that women found endearing.

To that end, he'd picked out the tackiest tuxedo he could find. It was an awful shade of burgundy with velvet ribbon trim on the lapels. The shirt was straight out of a seventies Vegas lounge act, all full of ruffles. He even found patent leather shoes in the same shade of burgundy, though he'd had to pay the formal wear shop extra to dig them out of the back of the storage room.

He leaned over and spoke to the chauffeur who was standing next to the limo. "I'll be back in just a minute."

Dylan straightened his velvet bow tie then stepped up to the door of the coffee shop, the small corsage box clutched in his left hand. The interior was dimly lit and he was grateful for that. But as he slowly walked to the counter, he realized that there were more than just a few customers watching him. Though he was happy for Meggie that her first day of business was successful, he couldn't help but be a little embarrassed for himself.

Lana stood at the end of the counter, a smug grin on her face. "You look…so silly," she said with a low giggle. She stepped up to him and gave him a hug. "I hope Meggie appreciates this."

"You like the suit?" Dylan asked. "I picked it out myself."

"Either you have really bad taste or you're willing to do just about anything to make Meggie happy."

"It's the latter, believe me."

"I'll go get her," Lana said. "She's hiding in the office."

"No," he said. "Let me."

He strode to the rear of the shop, then knocked softly on the door.

Meggie's voice came from within, muffled by the door. "Is the limo here?"

Dylan didn't answer. Instead, he knocked again. The office door swung open and Meggie stood in front of him, dressed in the pink gown he'd begged her mother to find. "Hi," he murmured. Dylan couldn't think of anything else to say. He knew the moment he saw her, every clever thing he'd planned would fly right out of his brain. He hadn't seen her in days and all he really wanted to do was stare at her. "You look beautiful."

Meggie smiled. "You look very handsome," she said.

"Are you ready to go?" he asked.

Meggie nodded and Dylan offered her his arm. They slowly strolled through the shop, their exit observed as closely as Dylan's entrance. When they reached the door a smattering of applause broke out and Meggie turned back and gave the customers a playful curtsy.

They settled themselves in the back seat of the limo and

Meggie turned to him. "I was surprised when I got the invitation. After what happened the last time we—"

He reached out and pressed a finger to her lips, resisting the urge to pull her into his arms and kiss her. "That hasn't happened yet. Nothing that went on between us has happened. And some of it never will. We're starting over, going back to the beginning. We're going to do this the way it should have been done thirteen years ago." He handed her the corsage box. "These are for you."

A tiny smiled curled Meggie's lips. "You thought of everything, didn't you."

He helped her open the box then pulled out the flowers and slipped the elastic band around her gloved hand. The scent of gardenias wafted through the air. "Actually, this is a new experience for me," he said. "I never used to take dates to the high school dances. You're my first."

"I am?" Meggie asked.

Dylan nodded. "I could never afford it. But I've got a pretty good job now." He reached for the bottle of champagne that sat in an ice bucket on the opposite seat, then poured them both a glass. As they sipped at the bubbly, Dylan relaxed a bit. He'd been as nervous as a teenager getting ready for this date, wondering if he could make it work, if he could take them back to the very beginning.

He glanced over at Meggie. She sat silently, her champagne flute clutched in her fingers. Dylan had the whole evening planned for them, a perfectly timed agenda to make it the most romantic night of her life. But now that she was here, all he could think about was pulling her into his arms and kissing her. And that wasn't supposed to come until after...

He reached into his jacket pocket. "I was going to wait

to do this," Dylan said. "But I can't wait. I want you to have this." He held out the huge ring emblazoned with the crest of South Boston High School.

Meggie stared at it for a long moment, stunned speechless by his sudden declaration. "It—it's your class ring," she murmured.

"Yeah," Dylan said, nodding. "Another first. I've never given it to a girl before, but I decided we should go steady."

Meggie giggled. "Steady?"

"Yeah. And you better say yes, because you have no idea what I went through to find that thing. I tore my father's house apart. I finally found it in the last box I opened in the attic."

"Steady," Meggie murmured. "What does that mean?"

"I means that we don't date anyone else. And it means that we spend all our free time together. And it means that you're my girl."

Her eyes shimmered with unshed tears and she put the ring on her finger. "That sounds good." A tiny giggle slipped from her throat. "It's a little big," she said.

Dylan held her hand up and examined the ring closely. "So it is."

"I suppose I could wrap yarn around it or wear it on a chain, like the other girls do."

"Or I could give you a ring that fits." He reached into his pocket and pulled out another ring, then held it out to her. Meggie's eyes went wide and she gasped softly. She tried to speak but her only reaction was a tear that trickled down her cheek. Dylan reached out and caught it with his thumb, then held her face in his palm and stared deeply into her eyes. "I know it's a little early. After all, we've only been going steady for a minute or two. But this ring will fit much better."

"Is this—" She paused. "Are you—" A sigh came with her next breath. "But we've only known each other—well, we've known each other for sixteen years. But we've really only known each other for a few weeks."

He took the ring and pressed it into her palm, then gently wrapped her fingers around it. "Whenever you're ready, Meggie, you just let me know and I'll put that ring on your finger."

Meggie nodded, then pressed her fist to her chest. They gazed at each other for a long time, Dylan taking in the details of her face, the way the dim light shone off her hair and the way her lips looked so perfectly kissable. "I love you, Meggie. I said it once, but I didn't say it right. I think I've been waiting my whole life for you and you were there the whole time, waiting for me. I just didn't see it. But I promise that for the rest of our lives, I'll never take my eyes off you."

Meggie took a ragged breath, then blinked back more tears. "I used to dream about a moment like this," she said. "I had this whole fantasy worked out in my mind of how it would be. But I never imagined it this way…this perfect." She reached up and smoothed her palm over his cheek. "I love you, Dylan. Not a silly schoolgirl love, but a real love that I know will last forever. I loved the boy you were and now I love the man you became."

Dylan leaned forward and brushed his lips against hers. But it had been so long since he'd kissed her that he couldn't stop there. He pulled her into his arms and lost himself in the taste of her. This was the woman he wanted to spend his life loving and he felt like the luckiest man in the world to have found her. He drew back and gazed down into her eyes. "So I guess my plan worked."

Meggie smiled. "You had a plan?"

"I even wrote it down. And there's much more to it," he said as the limo pulled to a stop in front of the school. "Just wait. You're going to love this."

The chauffeur opened the door and Dylan stepped out, then held his hand out for Meggie. They walked to the front entrance of the school where a janitor waited to open the door for them. Meggie stopped the moment they were inside then looked around at the dimly lit hallway. "I haven't been back here since I graduated. But there's something about the smell of high school that you never forget."

Dylan pulled her along toward the gym. The double doors were open wide and a single light from above illuminated a small table set with a catered dinner. Soft music drifted from a boom box nearby. He reached over and flipped a light switch and the entire ceiling came alive with tiny twinkling lights.

Meggie gasped at the sight, then turned to him. "How did you do this?"

"It's a secret," Dylan said. In truth, it hadn't been as hard as he thought it would be. The school was closed for the Thanksgiving weekend. A deal was struck and the boys from the Boylston Street fire station put their ladder skills to work. Tomorrow morning, they'd be back to take the lights down.

"So, can I have this dance, Meggie Flanagan?" Dylan asked.

Meggie turned to him, then threw her arms around his neck and pressed a kiss to his lips. "You can have this dance and all the other dances for the rest of my life." With that, she pulled him along to the middle of the floor, her skirts rustling against his legs. And when they stepped into each other's arms, Dylan knew it was perfect.

This was what love was supposed to be. And as he gazed down at her, the twinkling lights from above glittering in her eyes, her lips still damp from his kisses, he made a vow to thank his lucky stars every day for the rest of his life. He'd cast aside the tales of the Mighty Quinns and believed that love was possible. And then he'd found Meggie.

There would be a new Mighty Quinn tale to tell his children. About the way Dylan Quinn wooed Meggie Flanagan, with a pretty pink gown and an awful burgundy tuxedo and a diamond ring that he'd someday slip onto her finger. And as time passed, the story would become a favorite that he'd tell over and over, about how true love had made a Mighty Quinn the happiest man in the world.

THE TINY STONE church was lit by hundreds of candles, casting a magical light over the evening ceremony. Meggie sat next to Dylan in one of the old wooden pews, holding his hand and listening as the minister spoke about the eternal power of love, the words as meaningful to her as they were to Conor and Olivia.

Only family and close friends had been invited to attend the Friday evening ceremony held in a small village on the coast of Maine. The church was still decorated from Thanksgiving service with beautiful cornucopias on the old altar. And Olivia had chosen to fill the rest of the space with flowers in deep jewel tones that complemented the harvest colors.

They'd all driven up that morning, Meggie and Dylan, along with Brendan, Sean, Brian and Liam. Even Seamus had grudgingly agreed to attend although he was still trying to convince Conor of the danger of his actions right up until the start of the ceremony. The family had taken over a small inn on a bluff overlooking the Atlantic.

Though Meggie had only known Olivia a short time, the ceremony was exactly what she would have expected from her future sister-in-law—sophisticated, low-key, elegant. She wore a stunning dress, a strapless sheath that showed off her perfect figure and a simple fingertip veil. And Conor looked like all the other Quinn brothers, stunningly handsome in their tuxedos. Meggie couldn't help but remember the tux that Dylan had worn the night of the "Sophomore Frolic." In truth, she thought he'd looked even more handsome that night, so determined to right the past and give them a new future. But then, her opinion of that tux had been swayed by the man who wore it so convincingly—the man who'd asked her to marry him.

She'd been carrying the ring around since the night he'd given it to her, waiting for the right time to accept his proposal. She'd thought that time would come later, after they'd celebrated Conor and Olivia's wedding, when they'd retired to their huge room at the inn and snuggled up in front of a roaring fire. But now, as Conor and Olivia were pledging their love to each other, she glanced up at Dylan to find him looking down at her.

His eyes told her everything she needed to know. He loved her and that love was deep and lasting. And someday, they would stand in front of friends and family and pledge their lives to each other. Suddenly, Meggie wanted that life together to begin now.

As the sound of the minister's voice echoed through the tiny church, it was as if his words were meant not for Conor and Olivia, but for Dylan and Meggie. Dylan pulled her hand up to his lips and pressed a kiss to her wrist. And at that instant, Meggie knew the time was right. She pulled her hand away and then reached into her purse and withdrew the ring. She held it out to him.

They both stared at the twinkling diamond for a long moment. Then with a steady hand, Dylan took it from her. There was no need for words. They knew the pledge they were making was from their hearts. Dylan held the ring on the end of Meggie's finger and then looked into her eyes. She nodded, tears blurring her vision. Yes, she would marry him and yes, she would promise to love him forever.

As the ring slid down her finger and found its place, the minister pronounced Conor and Olivia husband and wife. But as they kissed, there were two people that didn't bother to watch. For Dylan and Meggie were caught up in their own private world, where nothing else mattered but the love they shared and the love they'd pledged to keep—a love that would someday become the stuff of old Irish legends.

* * * * *

*Everything you love about romance...**and more!***
Please turn the page for
Signature Select™ Bonus Features.

Bonus Features:

BONUS FEATURES

Irish Charmers: The Mighty Quinns

EXCLUSIVE BONUS FEATURES INSIDE

A conversation with
Kate Hoffmann

Kate attributes Kathleen Woodiwiss's Ashes in the Wind as one of the reasons for her picking up the pen. Like many other writers, Kate never intended to write romance novels but we certainly are happy that she decided to turn in her music sheets to create such great romances as The Mighty Quinn series. We caught up with Kate to ask her a few questions about inspiration, vacations and the one book she'd wished she'd written.

Tell us a bit about how you began your writing career.
Oddly, I was never very interested in writing as a child. I loved to read, but I didn't have much confidence in my abilities as a writer. I was always involved in very creative activities throughout my youth and teen years—music, theater, art. I majored in music in college and ended up teaching music in an elementary school for six years. Summers off gave me a chance to devour the latest in romance novels. I shifted my career focus to the business world and landed in a small ad agency, where I wrote advertising copy. Gradu-

ally I realized that the discipline of writing ad copy eight hours a day could be translated to writing a novel. I started buying books about novel writing, joined some writers' organizations, found a critique group and I was on my way. The very first short contemporary that I completed became my first book published with Harlequin, *Indecent Exposure*.

Was there a particular person, place or thing that inspired this story?
My editors at Harlequin first suggested writing a family series. They wanted me to focus on a Scottish family, but I suggested Irish, since I'd recently returned from a trip to Ireland. My memories of Ireland, the beautiful land and the lively people, greatly inspired *THE PROMISE*.

Do you have any Irish ancestors?
I'm often asked that, since I have red hair. But the red hair comes from my German grandfather. I've done considerable work on my genealogy and have found just one Irish ancestor. My fifth great-grandfather was Patrick Doolin and I suspect he was born in Ireland in about 1744. He served in the Revolutionary War, fought at the Battle of Quebec and died in Washington, D.C., in 1826. Someday I hope to learn more about him and his ancestors, but for now I'm proud to have a tiny bit of Irish blood in my veins.

What can you tell us about *THE PROMISE*?
THE PROMISE is a prequel to the first seven Mighty Quinn books and any Quinn books in the future. Set in

Ireland, it follows the stories of three generations of Quinns and McLains, ending with the story of Seamus and Fiona (parents of Conor, Dylan, Brendan, Brian, Sean, Liam and Keely).

What's your writing routine?

I don't really have a routine. I'm a very undisciplined writer as I usually wait until inspiration strikes before I sit down and put anything on paper. But when it does strike, it usually comes in a rush and I'm forced to put in very long days and nights getting it from my brain onto the computer. I love the freedom that writing allows me. I have time to enjoy the other things in my life and still indulge in the excitement of telling a good story.

How do you research your stories?

My readers know that I'm not an author who cares to stick to one familiar setting. I like to move around a lot, from north to south, east to west, urban to country. Often, I've visited the settings for my books. But sometimes, I rely on friends who live in those areas. As for the details of the story, the Internet is the biggest help. There's always an answer to every question somewhere out there in cyberspace.

Could you tell us about your family?

My father is a former schoolteacher and my mother was a housewife. I grew up on a hobby farm in rural Wisconsin. I'm the oldest of four children, with two younger sisters and a younger brother. I'm single, so there's no husband or children to speak of, although I do have three cats to keep me company—Tansing, Tibriz and Tallassee.

When you're not writing what are your favorite activities?

I love to garden. I regularly lose myself in some kind of home improvement or remodeling project. I golf, ride my bike, take walks. I also teach guitar to some of the kids in the neighborhood and have recently started playing the flute again.

What are your favorite kinds of vacations? Where do you like to travel?

I love to see history when I'm on vacation. I can't sit on a beach or be trapped on a cruise ship. I love to walk through historic districts, tour homes, visit museums, see how people live. I enjoy trying new types of food, searching out places that the locals love to go to. I've traveled in Europe several times and throughout the U.S. Favorite places include Paris, Bruges (Belguim), New Orleans and New York City. But I think Ireland will always be on the top of my list.

What book do you wish you had written?

I could probably say something like *Gone with the Wind,* but that would be too easy. I think the book I wish I'd written is the book that's always rattling around in my head while I'm trying to write it. It has the same basic plot as the one I'm writing, only this book is perfect in every way. Every bit of dialogue, every description, every plot point is intricately planned and executed. Unfortunately, in the real world, a book like that would take me years and years to finish. But now that I think about it, I wish I could have written *Gone with the Wind.*

Marsha Zinberg, Executive Editor for Signature Select spoke with Kate Hoffmann in the Spring of 2004.

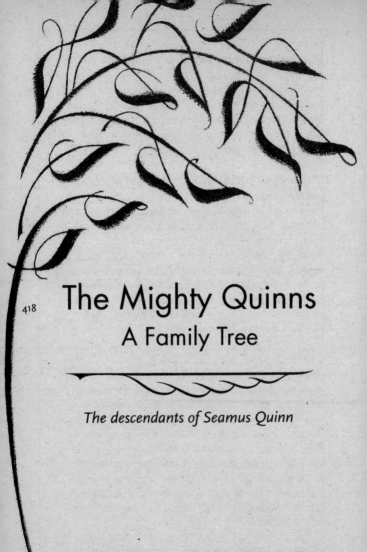

The Mighty Quinns
A Family Tree

The descendants of Seamus Quinn

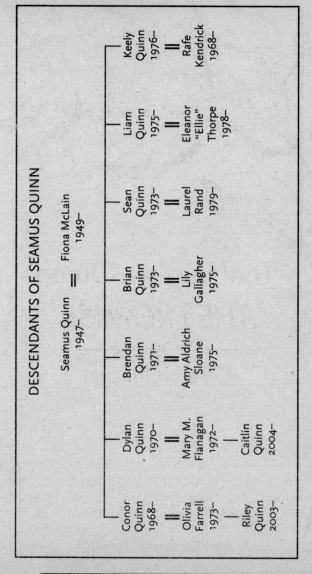

DESCENDANTS OF SEAMUS QUINN

Seamus Quinn
1947–
=
Fiona McLain
1949–

Conor
Quinn
1968–
=
Olivia
Farrell
1973–

Riley Quinn
2003–

Dylan
Quinn
1970–
=
Mary M.
Flanagan
1972–

Caitlin
Quinn
2004–

Brendan
Quinn
1971–
=
Amy Aldrich
Sloane
1975–

Brian
Quinn
1973–
=
Lily
Gallagher
1975–

Sean
Quinn
1973–
=
Laurel
Rand
1979–

Liam
Quinn
1975–
=
Eleanor
"Ellie"
Thorpe
1978–

Keely
Quinn
1976–
=
Rafe
Kendrick
1968–

THE MIGHTY QUINNS FAMILY TREE BONUS FEATURE

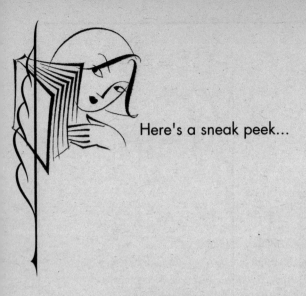

Here's a sneak peek...

THE PROMISE
by
Kate Hoffmann

Enjoy this exclusive preview!

PROLOGUE

County Cork, Present Day

FLUFFY WHITE CLOUDS hung in the sky, the sun's rays slanting through them to cast the green hills in a divine light. A slender woman looked down on Ballykirk harbor, the brisk wind buffeting her gray hair and snatching strands from the tidy knot at the nape of her neck. She drew a deep breath of the salt-tinged air, then closed her eyes and let memories of her childhood wash over her like the gentle evening tide.

Fiona McLain Quinn hadn't stood on Irish soil in many years, not since the day she'd left with her husband and family for the promise of a new life in America. She could barely remember the woman she'd been that day, dressed in her Sunday best, just twenty-six years old and already the mother of five boys.

She tried to imagine herself as a young woman, her hair long and dark, her skin smooth and her body unbent by age. Life had been so simple then, an endless horizon stretching out in front of her, all her dreams just waiting to be realized. Images whirled in Fiona's mind, flashes of the past interwoven with the hopes she'd kept hidden deep in her heart.

Fiona had been born to do great things, to make a difference in the world—at least, that's what her mother had always told her. It hadn't happened in Ireland, so she'd set off for America, sure that her destiny awaited her there.

A tiny smile touched her lips, the optimism of her youth now merely an amusing recollection. She glanced over her shoulder and watched as her eldest son, Conor, a man of thirty-seven, perched on a boulder with his own son, two-year-old Riley, tucked between his legs.

Her eyes met Conor's and held for a long moment. He nodded, as if he could read her thoughts and sense her melancholy. "It's a beautiful spot," he called.

422

"Yes, it is," Fiona murmured, her words swept away by the wind. She turned back to the sea, back to her memories. When her daughter, Keely, had first suggested this trip, Fiona had been reluctant to agree. But the more she'd thought about it, the more she'd realized that Ireland could be both an ending and a new beginning. She and her husband, Seamus, were grandparents now and all the years they'd spent together—and then the years they'd spent apart—had passed in the blink of an eye. Would this last part of her life fly by just as quickly?

She'd navigated through the previous thirty years searching the shifting currents for something to cling to, some part of herself that had been lost in her impetuous youth and had drifted just beyond her fingertips. Who was Fiona McLain Quinn? At her age, she ought to know. But standing here, in the spot where her fortunes had taken such an unlikely turn, Fiona was forced to wonder if she'd lived the wrong life, a life meant for some other woman. If she'd turned down Seamus Quinn's proposal of marriage all those years ago, where might her life have taken her?

Fiona turned away from the setting sun and walked back to Conor. "It's greener than I remembered," he said as she approached.

"It's the light," Fiona explained. "It filters through the clouds to make all the colors seem more brilliant. Especially the green." She leaned back against the rock. "We came here the day we left. Your cousin, Maeve, took a picture of us standing right at this spot."

"Odd. I remember the green, but I don't remember that day," Conor said.

"You were barely six years old. And the twins weren't even a year. But your father insisted we come here just once more before we left Ireland forever. He wanted this sight—the sea, Ballykirk below us, the hills behind us and the sun shimmering off the water—as his last memory, to hold close to his heart."

Conor's expression brightened. "This is Oisin's Rock, isn't it?"

"You do remember," Fiona said, laughing softly. "Your father used to tell the tale over and over again, and you boys never seemed to get enough of it." She bent and pointed to a chipped area near the base. "When you were little, you came up here and tried to crack the rock to let Oisin out. You were certain your Mighty Quinn ancestor was still in there somewhere."

Conor rested his chin on the top of Riley's head, the boy's nearly black hair brushing against his father's cheek. "I don't remember," he said. "It's been a long time since I've heard one of Da's tales. Tell me. I'd like to pass them along to Riley one day."

"Well, most of your da's stories were well embellished, but people around this part of Ireland believe the tale of Oisin Quinn is true." She drew a long breath and tried to recall the story as Seamus had first told it to her all those years ago. "Oisin Quinn was a strapping lad, strong and stubborn, with thick arms and raven-black hair. He was good of heart and pure of mind and loved by all who knew him. Many years ago, this part of Ireland was ruled by a kind and benevolent king, King Tadhg, who cared deeply for his subjects. Life was good. The forests were filled with game, the seas teeming with fish and the land so rich a man could grow food for ten families. But armies from the neighboring kingdoms often invaded, their leaders coveting this land and all it promised. Tadhg's soldiers fought them back, simple farmers and fishermen often joining in the fight, for they had just as much to lose."

Riley's eyes were wide and curious, his gaze fixed on her face as she spoke. "As time passed and Tadhg grew older and more feeble, the people of his kingdom began to worry. He had no son to succeed him and a kingdom without a king would quickly lapse into chaos and despair. Oisin and some of the men from other villages asked for an audience with King Tadhg and they told him of their concerns. The king, in his wisdom, told them that when he died, they would rule themselves."

Fiona reached out to brush a strand of hair from Riley's eyes, her fingertips sliding over his rosy cheek. "Freedom in Ireland had always been a fleeting dream,

Riley, even back then. But Oisin knew freedom meant a better future for everyone and he promised King Tadhg that he would fight with his very last breath to keep it."

The breeze off the sea freshened and Fiona wrapped her coat more tightly around her, slipping her hands into her pockets. "It wasn't long before King Tadhg died and the first armies gathered at the borders of his kingdom. His people were ready and they fought them back, but not without considerable loss of life. Again and again the armies invaded and Oisin fought, with a spear and a cudgel, wielding both with superhuman strength. Soon the enemy began to fear him, his feats of courage becoming legend throughout the land. They thought he might not be a man, but a god, sent by King Tadhg's spirit to protect his people. Years passed and many battles were fought and won, but gradually the people began to tire of the wars and talked about surrender. Oisin stood firm, remembering the king's words. One day an enemy army gathered in the hills above Ballykirk. Oisin tried to rouse the men of the village to battle, but no one wanted to fight. So Oisin took his spear and his cudgel and came out to this very spot, determined to protect his friends and neighbors. The soldiers came and he fought, one man against a vast army. Again and again he drove them back, killing many soldiers and striking fear into the hearts of those who retreated. He never slept or ate, standing guard day after day, year after year, fighting all who challenged him. He grew old, and people tried to convince him to surrender, but he'd made a promise to the king and was determined to honor it. And so the village was safe for a long time, the armies afraid to invade. One day the townsfolk wandered up this hill to thank Oisin Quinn for his protection. But when they arrived all they found was this stone, huge and imposing, and shaped very much like the crouching giant of a man that Oisin once was. But Oisin was nowhere to be found. Some thought he'd been killed long ago. Some believed he'd wandered off. But as his friends examined the rock that had never been there before, they realized the rock was Oisin. He'd been magically transformed so that he might guard Ballykirk for centuries to come, never to grow feeble and weak, never to fall to an enemy sword. And though the rock has been worn by the wind and the rain, if you look carefully you can still see the face of Oisin Quinn."

"Do you believe it?"

Fiona reached out and took Riley from her son's arms. "It was the first story your father ever told me. I was just a little girl, but even as a boy, he could weave a fantastic tale. I never doubted him for a instant." She pressed her lips to the top of Riley's head.

"Are you happy you came, Ma?"

"I am. Keely and Rafe were right. We needed to come back." Keely's husband, Rafe Kendrick, had arranged all the details of the trip and paid for the tickets and accommodations. Fiona couldn't imagine the cost of bringing sixteen adults and two children across the Atlantic, much less putting them up in a fancy hotel for a week. But she was glad she'd finally agreed to make the trip.

"Nana."

Fiona nuzzled her grandson's cheek. "And what do you think of Ireland, Riley Quinn?"

"Up, up," he said, reaching out to Oisin's Rock. "Go up."

She chuckled and hugged the two-year-old tightly in her arms as she stared out at the landscape. "I thought it would all seem so unfamiliar. But the moment I breathed in the air and felt the grass beneath my feet, it came back. It's as if I just left yesterday. Where have all the years gone?" She shook her head. "I haven't been able to bring myself to visit the cemetery yet. Money was so scarce that I couldn't afford to come back for the funerals. My mother and father were buried while I was miles and miles away. And my grandmother, too. I've carried that with me for so many years. It's time to say goodbye."

"I've heard so much about the Mighty Quinns. Tell me about your family," Conor said. "I just barely remember my grandparents. Did I ever know my great-grandparents?"

Fiona shook her head. "I didn't know your great-grandfather. His name was Aidan McLain and he was a doctor. My father barely remembered him, but my grandmother, Maura, used to talk about him all the time. She said he was a sensitive man. I took it to mean that he was troubled because there were always whispers when it came to a discussion of his life and death. He was killed in a car accident when my father was just a little boy."

"I do remember Nana McLain," Conor said.

"Maura Sullivan. She came from a very prominent family in Dublin. Her father was also a doctor."

"And what about Da's grandparents?"

"Ah, now, there was a story of a true Mighty Quinn.

Jack Quinn fought for freedom in Ireland, just like Oisin Quinn did hundreds of years before. He was wounded in the civil war and your grandfather Aidan saved his life."

Conor took Riley from Fiona's arms and swung the little boy up onto his shoulders. Then he took Fiona's hand and tucked it into the crook of his arm. As they hiked back down the hill to Ballykirk, Fiona recalled what she knew of Jack Quinn and Aidan McLain, of the history that had brought their two families together, intertwining their destinies for three generations.

But as they walked and talked, she could only wonder at the details of lives lived so long ago, details that she and her children and their own children would never know. How many promises had been made and then broken, how many dreams imagined, then shattered? These hills, this land and this sea, this sun and this wind, had watched it all.

And only Ireland knew what was legend and what was fact.

...NOT THE END...

Watch for THE PROMISE coming February 2005 from Signature Select™ &

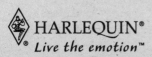 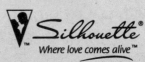

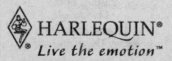

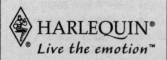